W9-AHA-906

JUPITER

TOR BOOKS BY BEN BOVA

As on a Darkling Plain
The Astral Mirror
Battle Station
The Best of the Nebulas (ed.)
Challenges
Colony
Cyberbooks
Escape Plus
Gremlins Go Home (with Gordon R. Dickson)
Jupiter
The Kinsman Saga
The Multiple Man
Orion
Orion Among the Stars
Orion and the Conqueror
Orion in the Dying Time
Out of the Sun
Peacekeepers
Privateers
Prometheans
Star Peace: Assured Survival
The Starcrossed
Test of Fire
To Fear the Light (with A. J. Austin)
To Save the Sun (with A. J. Austin)
The Trikon Deception (with Bill Pogue)
Triumph
Vengeance of Orion
Venus
Voyagers
Voyagers II: The Alien Within
Voyagers III: Star Brothers
The Winds of Altair

JUPITER

BEN BOVA

A TOM DOHERTY ASSOCIATES BOOK
NEW YORK

This is a work of fiction. All the characters and events portrayed in this novel are either fictitious or are used fictitiously.

JUPITER

This book is printed on acid-free paper.

Edited by Patrick Nielsen Hayden

A Tor Book
Published by Tom Doherty Associates, LLC
175 Fifth Avenue
New York, NY 10010

www.tor.com

Library of Congress Cataloging-in-Publication Data

Bova, Ben.
Jupiter / Ben Bova.—1st ed.
p. cm.
"A Tom Doherty Associates book."
ISBN 0-312-87217-8 (acid-free book)
1. Jupiter (Planet)—Fiction. 2. Astrophysicists—Fiction.
3. Space stations—Fiction. I. Title.
PS3552.O84 J86 2001
813'.54—dc21 00-048021

First Edition: January 2001

Printed in the United States of America

0 9 8 7 6 5 4 3 2 1

To Danny and T.J., my favorite "Jovians."

To Thomas Gold, who would rather be wrong than dull.

And to Barbara, always and forever.

ACKNOWLEDGMENTS

My thanks to Mark Chartrand, George W. Ferguson, and Frederic B. Jueneman, who offered invaluable advice and assistance in writing this novel. The technical accuracy of this story is due in large part to their generous assistance; any inaccuracies stem from my stretching the known facts.

Details of the life of Zheng He and the Ming Empire's "treasure fleet" can be found in Louise Levathe's fine book, *When China Ruled the Seas*, published in 1994 by Simon & Schuster.

The rash assertion that "God made man in His own image" is ticking like a time bomb at the foundation of many faiths.

—Arthur C. Clarke

JUPITER

PROLOGUE: ORBITAL STATION *GOLD*

It took six of them to drown him.

Reluctantly, grudgingly, Grant Archer had stripped himself naked, as they had ordered him to do. But once they pushed him to the edge of the big tank, he knew he would not go into it without a fight.

The augmented gorilla grabbed Grant's right arm; she was careful not to snap his bones, but her powerful grip was painful all the same. Two of the human guards held his left arm while a third wrapped him around the middle and still another lifted his bare feet off the deck so he couldn't get any leverage for his wild-eyed struggles.

All this in nearly total silence. Grant didn't scream or roar at them, he didn't plead or curse. The only sounds were the scuffing of the guards' boots on the cold metal deck plates, the hard gasps of their labored breathing, and Grant's own panicked, desperate panting.

The guard captain grimly, efficiently grasped Grant's depilated head in both big meaty hands and pushed his face into the tank of thick, oily liquid.

Grant squeezed his eyes shut and held his breath until his chest felt as if it would burst. He was burning inside, suffocating, drowning. The pain was unbearable. He couldn't breathe. He dared not breathe. No matter what they had told him, he knew down at the deepest level of his being that this was going to kill him.

No air! Can't breathe!

Reflex overpowered his mind. Despite himself, despite his terror, he sucked in a breath. And gagged. He tried to scream, to cry out, to beg for help or mercy. His lungs filled with the icy liquid. His whole body spasmed, shuddered with the last hope of life as they pushed his naked body all the way into the tank with a final pitiless shove and he sank down, deeper and deeper.

He opened his eyes. There were lights down there. He was breathing! Coughing, choking, his body racked with uncontrollable spasms. But he was breathing. The liquid filled his lungs and he could breathe it. Just like regular air, they had told him. A lie, a vicious lie. It was cold and thick, utterly foreign, alien, slimy and horrible.

But he could breathe.

He sank toward the lights. Blinking, squinting in their glare, he saw that there were other naked hairless bodies down there waiting for him.

"Welcome to the team," a sarcastic voice boomed in his ears, deep, slow, reverberating.

Another voice, not as loud but even more basso profundo, said, "Okay, let's get him prepped for the surgery."

BOOK I

My God, my God, why hast Thou forsaken me?
Far from my deliverance are the words of my groaning.

—Psalm 22

GRANT ARMSTRONG ARCHER III

Despite being born into one of the oldest families in Oregon, Grant Archer grew up in an environment that was far from affluent. His earliest memories were of watching his mother rummaging through piles of hand-me-down clothes at the Goodwill shop, looking for sweaters and gym shoes that weren't too shabby to wear to school.

His father was a Methodist minister in the little suburb of Salem where Grant grew up, respected as a man of the cloth but not taken too seriously in the community because he was, in the words of one of the golf club widows, "churchmouse poor."

Poor as far as money was concerned, but Grant's mother always told him that he was rich in the gift of intelligence. It was his mother, who worked in one of the multifarious offices of the New Morality in the state capital, who encouraged Grant's interest in science.

Most of the New Morality officials were suspicious of science and scientists, deeply worried about these "humanists" who so often contradicted the clear word of Scripture. Even Grant's father urged his son to steer clear of biology and any other scientific specialty that would bring the frowning scrutiny of New Morality investigators upon them.

For Grant there was no problem. Since he'd been old enough to look into the night sky with awe and wonder he'd wanted to be an astronomer. In high school, where he was by far the brightest student in his class, he narrowed his interest to the astrophysics of black holes. Although Grant thrilled to the discoveries on Mars and out among the distant moons of Jupiter, it was the death throes of giant stars that truly fascinated him. If he could learn how collapsed stars warped spacetime, he might one day discover a way for humans to use such warps for interstellar journeys.

He longed to work at the Farside Observatory on the Moon, studying collapsed stars far out in the cold and dark of deep interstellar space. Yet

Grant had been warned that even at Farside there were tensions and outright dangers. Despite all the strictures of the New Morality and the stern rules laid down by the observatory's directors, some astronomers still tried to sneak time on the big telescopes to search for signs of extraterrestrial intelligence. When such prohibited activities were discovered, those responsible were inevitably sent back to Earth in disgrace, their careers blighted.

That did not bother Grant, however. He intended to keep his nose clean, to avoid antagonizing the ever-present agents of the New Morality, and to study the enigmatic and entirely safe black holes. He was careful never to use the dreaded word "evolution" when speaking about the life cycles of stars and their final collapse into black holes. "Evolution" was a dangerous word among the New Morality eavesdroppers.

By the time he was finishing high school, he had grown into a quiet, square-shouldered young man with a thick thatch of sandy-blond hair that often tumbled over his light-brown eyes. He was good-natured and polite; the high school girls considered him a "delta" in their merciless rating system: okay as a friend, especially when it came to help with schoolwork, but too dull to date except in an emergency. A shade under six feet tall and whipcord lean, Grant played on the school's baseball and track teams, no outstanding star but the kind of reliable performer who made his coaches sleep better at night.

As his senior year approached, Grant was offered a full scholarship in return for a four-year commitment to Public Service. The service was inescapable: Every high school graduate was required to do at least two years and then another two at age fifty. The New Morality advisor in his high school told Grant that by accepting a four-year term now, he could get a full scholarship to the university of his choice, with the understanding that his Public Service would be in the field for which he was trained: astrophysics.

Grant accepted the scholarship and the commitment, his eyes still on Farside. He went to Harvard and, much to his delighted surprise, fell in love with a raven-haired biochemist named Marjorie Gold. She made him feel important, for the first time in his life. When he was with her, the quiet, steady, sandy-haired young astronomy student felt he could conquer the universe.

They married during their senior year even though he knew he'd be off to the Farside Observatory for four years while Marjorie would be doing her Public Service with the International Peacekeeping Force, tracking down clandestine biological warfare factories in the jungles of southeast Asia and Latin America.

But they were young and their love could not wait. So they married, despite their parents' misgivings.

"I'll come down from Farside at least every few months," Grant told her as they lay together in bed, contemplating the next four years.

"I'll get leave when you're here," Marjorie agreed.

"By the time I'm finished my four years I'll have my doctorate," he said.

"Then you can get on a tenure track at any university you like."

"And after the four years is over we can apply to have a child," Grant said.

"A boy," said Marjorie.

"Don't you want a daughter?"

"Afterward. After I learn how to be a mother. Then we can have a daughter."

He smiled in the darkness of their bedroom and kissed her and they made love. It was a safe time of Marjorie's cycle.

They both graduated with high honors; Grant was actually first in his class. Marjorie received her Public Service commission with the Peacekeepers, as expected. Grant, though, was shocked when his orders sent him not to the Farside Observatory on the Moon but to Research Station *Thomas Gold*, in orbit around Jupiter, more than seven hundred million kilometers from Marjorie at its closest approach to Earth.

". . . WHICH SIDE YOU'RE ON"

Grant's father counseled patience.

"If that's where they want to send you, they must have their reasons. You'll simply have to accept it, son."

Grant found that he could not accept it. There was no patience in him, despite earnest prayers. His father had been a meek and accepting man all his life, and what had it gotten him? Obscurity, genteel poverty, and condescending smiles behind his back. That's not for me, Grant told himself.

Despite his father's conciliatory advice, Grant fought his assignment all the way up to the regional director of the New Morality's Northeast office.

"I can't spend four years at Jupiter," he insisted. "I'm a married man! I can't be that far away for four years! Besides, I'm an astrophysicist, and there's no need for my specialty at Jupiter. I'll be wasting four years! How can I work on my doctorate when there's no astrophysics being done there?"

The regional director sat behind a massive oak desk strewn with papers, tensely upright in his high-backed chair, his lean, long-fingered hands steepled before him as Grant babbled on. His name was Ellis Beech. He was a serious-looking African American with dark skin the color of sooty smoke. His face was thin, long with a pointed chin; his eyes were tawny, somber, focused intently on Grant without wavering all through his urgent, pleading tirade.

At last Grant ran out of words. He didn't know what more he could say. He had tried to control his anger, but he was certain he'd raised his voice unconscionably and betrayed the resentment and aggravation he felt. Never show anger, his father had counseled him. Be calm, be reasonable. Anger begets anger; you want to sway him to your point of view, not antagonize him.

Grant slumped back in his chair, waiting for some reaction from the regional director. The man didn't look antagonized. To Grant's eyes, he looked as if he hadn't heard half of what Grant had said. Beech's desk was cluttered with paper, from flimsy single sheets to thick volumes bound in red covers; his computer screen flickered annoyingly; he was obviously a very important and very busy person, yet his phone had not beeped once since Grant had been ushered into the warmly paneled, carpeted office.

"I was supposed to go to Farside," Grant muttered, trying to get some response out of the brooding man behind the desk.

"I'm fully aware of that," Beech said at last. Then he added, "But unfortunately you are needed at Jupiter."

"How could I be needed—"

"Let me explain the situation to you, young man."

Grant nodded.

"The scientists have had their research station in Jupiter orbit for nearly twenty years," Beech said, stressing the word "scientists" ever so slightly. "They have been poking around with the life-forms that exist on two of the planet's moons."

"Three," Grant corrected without thinking. "Plus they've found life-forms in Jupiter's atmosphere, as well."

Beech continued, unfazed. "The work these scientists do is enormously expensive. They are spending money that could be much better used to help the poor and disadvantaged here on Earth."

Before Grant could respond, Beech raised a silencing hand. "Yet we of the New Morality do not object to their work. Even though many of those scientists are doing everything they can to try to disprove the truth of Scripture, we allow them to continue their godless pursuits."

Grant didn't think that studying the highly adapted algae and microbes living in the ice-covered seas of the Jovian moons was a godless pursuit. How could *any* attempt to understand the fullness of God's creation be considered godless?

"Why do we not object to this enormously expensive waste of funds and effort?" Beech asked rhetorically. "Because we of the New Morality and similar God-fearing organizations in other nations have seen fit to establish a compromise with the International Astronautical Authority—and the global financial power structure, as well, I might add."

"Compromise?" Grant wondered aloud.

"Fusion," said Beech. "Thermonuclear fusion. The world's economic well-being depends on fusion power plants. Without the energy from fusion, our world would sink back into the poverty and chaos and corruption that spawned wars and terrorism in earlier years. With fusion, we are lifting the standards of living for even the poorest of the poor, bringing hope and salvation to the darkest corners of the Earth."

Grant thought he understood. "And the fuels for fusion—the isotopes of hydrogen and helium—they come from Jupiter."

"That is correct," Beech said, nodding gravely. "The first fusion power plants ran on isotopes dug up on the Moon, but that was too expensive. Jupiter's atmosphere is thick with fusion fuels. Automated scoopships bring us these isotopes by the ton."

Grant asked, "But what's that got to do with the scientific research being done at Jupiter?"

Beech spread his hands in a don't-blame-me gesture. "When we of the New Morality pointed out that the money spent on those scientists could be better spent here on Earth, the humanists of the IAA and the major money brokers of our global economy demanded that the research be allowed to continue. They absolutely refused to shut down their research activities."

Good, thought Grant.

"So the compromise was struck: The scientists could continue their work, as long as it was paid for out of the profits from the scoopship operations."

"The fusion fuels pay for the research operations," Grant said.

"Yes, that's the way it's been for the past ten years."

"But what does all this have to do with me? Why are you sending me to Jupiter?"

"We know what the scientists are doing on the moons of Jupiter. But last year they sent a probe into the planet itself."

"They send lots of probes to Jupiter," Grant pointed out.

"This one was manned," said Beech.

Grant gasped with surprise. "A manned probe? Are you certain? I never heard anything about that."

"Neither did we. They did it in secret."

"No! How could—"

"That is why you are being sent to Jupiter. To find out what those godless humanists are trying to achieve," Beech said flatly.

"Me? You want me to spy on them?"

"We need to know what they are doing—and why they are not reporting their activities, not even to the IAA."

"But I'm no spy. I'm a scientist myself!"

Beech's solemn expression deepened into a scowl. "Mr. Archer, I'm sure that you assume that you can be a scientist and a Believer, both at the same time."

"Yes! There's no fundamental conflict between science and faith."

"Perhaps. But out there at the research station in Jupiter orbit, scientists are doing *something* that they don't want us to know about. And we must find out what they're up to!"

"But . . . why me?"

"God works in mysterious ways, my boy. You have been chosen. Accept that fact."

"It's going to ruin my life," Grant argued. "Four years away from my wife, four years wasted out there doing God knows what. I'll never get my doctorate!"

Beech nodded again. "It's a sacrifice, I realize that. But it's a sacrifice you should be glad to offer up to heaven."

"That's easy for you to say. I'm the one whose life is being turned upside-down."

"Let me explain something to you," Beech said, tapping the paper-strewn desk with a fingertip. "Do you have any idea of what the world was like before the New Morality and similar organizations gained political power across most of the world?"

Grant squirmed slightly in his chair. "There were lots of problems . . ."

Beech spat out a single, sharp "Hah!" His eyes were the color of a lion's, Grant realized. He was staring at Grant the way a lion watches a gazelle.

"I mean, economically, socially—"

"The world was a cesspool!" Beech snapped. "Corruption everywhere. No moral leadership at all. The politicians gave in to every whim that any pressure group expressed. They took polls and strove for popularity, while the people's real problems festered."

"The gap between the rich and poor got wider," Grant recited, recalling his high school lessons.

"And that led to terrorism, wars, crime," Beech agreed, his voice rising slightly. "Civil wars all over the world. Terrorists with biological weapons."

"The Calcutta Disaster," said Grant.

"Three million people killed."

"And São Paolo."

"Another two million."

Grant had seen the videos in school: piles of dead bodies in the streets, emergency workers in space suits to protect them from the lethal biological agents in the air.

"Governments were paralyzed, unable to act," Beech said firmly. "Until the spirit of God was returned to the corridors of power."

"It was something of a miracle, wasn't it?" Grant muttered.

Beech shook his head. "No miracle. Hard work by honest, God-fearing people. We took control of governments all around the world, the New Morality, the Light of Allah, the Holy Disciples in Europe."

"The New Dao movement in Asia," Grant added.

"Yes, yes," said Beech. "And why were we successful in bringing moral strength and wisdom into the political arena? Because religion is a *digital* system."

"Digital?"

"Digital. Religious precepts are based on moral principles. There is right and there is wrong. Nothing in between. Nothing! No wiggle room for the politicians to sneak through. Right or wrong, black or white, on or off. Digital."

"That's why the New Morality succeeded where other reform movements failed," Grant said, with new understanding.

"Exactly. That's why we were able to clean up the crime-ridden streets of our cities. That's why we were able to put an end to all these self-styled civil rights groups that actually wanted nothing less than a license to commit any sinful acts they wanted to. That's why we could bring order and stability to the nation—and to the whole world."

Grant had to admit that from what he'd learned of history, the world was far better off with God-fearing, morally straight governments in power than it had been in the old, corrupt, licentious days.

"We are doing God's work," Beech went on, sitting even straighter than before, his hands splayed on the desktop, his eyes burning. "We are feeding the poor, bringing education and enlightenment to all, even in the worst parts of Asia and Africa and South America. We have stabilized world population growth without murdering the unborn. We are raising the standard of living for the poorest of the poor."

His mind spinning, Grant heard himself ask, "But what does this have to do with Jupiter . . . and me?"

Beech eyed him sternly. "Young man, there comes a point in everyone's life when he must make the choice between good and evil. You've got to decide which side you're on: God or Mammon."

"I don't understand."

"The scientists out at Jupiter are up to something, something that they want to keep secret. We *must* find out what they are doing and why they are trying to hide their actions from us."

"Shouldn't that be a task for the IAA?" Grant asked. "I mean, they're the organization that directs the scientific research."

"We have representatives on the International Astronomical Authority."

"Then shouldn't you leave it to the IAA?"

With an almost pitying expression, Beech said, "The price of great power is great responsibility. In order to maintain stability, to make certain that no one—no scientist or revolutionary or terrorist madman—can threaten all that we've worked so hard to achieve, we must *control* everyone, everywhere."

"Control everyone?"

"Yes. Those scientists at Jupiter think they are beyond our control. We must teach them otherwise. You are our chosen agent to begin this process. You will help us to learn what they are doing and why they are doing it."

Grant was too confused to reply. He realized that the decision had already been made. He was going to Jupiter. They expected him to find out what the scientists were doing there. He could not avoid this duty.

He sat before Beech's desk, his mind awhirl, torn between the duty that he knew he could not avoid and resentment at having absolutely no voice in the decision that would determine the next four years of his life.

Like it or not, he was going to Jupiter.

Then Beech added with a slow, unexpected smile, "Of course, if you find out what they're up to quickly enough, perhaps we can arrange to transfer you to another research facility—such as the Farside Observatory."

"Farside?" Grant clutched at the straw.

Nodding solemnly, Beech said, "It might be arranged, in return for satisfactory performance."

Grant's sudden burst of hope faded. Carrot and stick, he realized. Farside is the carrot that's supposed to encourage me to do what they want.

"You will act alone at the Jupiter station, of course," Beech went on. "No one will know your true reason for being there, and you will tell no one about this."

Grant said nothing.

"But you will not *be* alone, Mr. Archer. You will be watched constantly."

"Watched?"

Smiling thinly, Beech said, "God sees you, Mr. Archer. God will be watching your every move, every breath you take, every thought that crosses your mind."

THE ENDLESS SEA

It is a boundless ocean, more than ten times wider than the entire planet Earth. Beneath the swirling clouds that cover Jupiter from pole to pole, the ocean has never seen sunlight, nor has it ever felt the rough confining contours of land. Its waves have never crashed against a craggy shore, never thundered upon a sloping beach, for there is no land anywhere across Jupiter's enormous girth: not even an island or a reef. The ocean's billows sweep across the deeps without hindrance, eternally.

Heated from below by the planet's seething core, swirled into a frenzy by Jupiter's hyperkinetic spin rate, ferocious currents race through this endless sea, jet streams howling madly, long powerful waves surging uninterrupted all the way around the world, circling the globe over and again. Gigantic storms rack the ocean, too, typhoons bigger than whole planets, hurricanes that have roared their fury for century after century. It is the widest, deepest, most powerful, most dynamic and fearsome ocean in the entire solar system.

Jupiter is the largest of all the solar system's planets, more than ten times bigger and three hundred times as massive as Earth. Jupiter is so immense it could swallow all the other planets easily. Its Great Red Spot, a storm that has raged for centuries, is itself wider than Earth. And the Spot is merely one feature visible among the innumerable vortexes and streams of Jupiter's frenetically racing cloud tops.

Yet Jupiter is composed mainly of the lightest elements, hydrogen and helium, more like a star than a planet. All that size and mass, yet Jupiter spins on its axis in less than ten hours, so fast that the planet is clearly not spherical: Its poles are noticeably flattened. Jupiter looks like a big, colorfully striped beach ball that's squashed down as if some invisible child were sitting on it.

Spinning that fast, Jupiter's deep, deep atmosphere is swirled into bands and ribbons of multihued clouds: pale yellow, saffron orange, white, tawny yellow-brown, dark brown, bluish, pink and red. Titanic winds push the clouds across the face of Jupiter at hundreds of kilometers per hour. What gives those clouds their colors? What lies beneath them? For more than a century astronomers had cautiously sent probes into the Jovian atmosphere. They barely penetrated the cloud tops before being crushed by overwhelming pressure.

But the inquisitive scientists from Earth persisted and gradually learned that some fifty thousand kilometers—nearly four times Earth's diameter—beneath those clouds lies that boundless ocean of water, an ocean almost eleven times wider than the entire Earth and some five thousand kilometers deep. Heavily laced with ammonia and sulfur compounds, highly acidic, it is still an ocean of water, and everywhere else in the solar system where there is water, life exists.

Is there life in Jupiter's vast, deep ocean?

FREIGHTER *ORAL ROBERTS*

"You mean your wife's maiden name is Gold, too?" asked Raoul Tavalera.

Grant nodded. "That's right."

"Same as the research station?"

Tavalera had a long, horsy face with teeth that seemed a couple of sizes too big and watery eyes that bulged slightly beneath heavy black brows. It all combined to give him a sorrowful, morose look. His thick curly hair was pulled back into a long ponytail, at the unbending insistence of the freighter's dour captain.

"It's just a coincidence," Grant said. "There's no relation. The station is named after Thomas Gold; he was a twentieth-century astronomer. British, I think."

"Prob'ly a Jew," said Tavalera.

Grant felt his brows hike up.

"They always change their names, y'know, so nobody can catch they're Jews. He was prob'ly Goldberg or Goldstein, something like that."

Grant started to reply but held back. He and Tavalera were sitting at the only table in the dingy, cramped galley of the freighter. Tavalera was a newly graduated student, too, an engineer who was going to work out his two-year Public Service commitment with the scoopship operations at Jupiter. Except for the two of them the galley was empty; the crew were all at their workstations. The food and drink dispensers were cold and empty at this hour; the metal bulkheads and flooring all looked scuffed, worn, old and hard used.

Grant had gone to the galley to take a brief break from his ongoing studies of the giant planet. He spent most of his time on the tedious journey out to Research Station *Gold* learning about Jupiter and its retinue of moons, catching up on what the researchers out there were discovering.

Tavalera had wandered into the galley a few moments after Grant came in, apparently with nothing better to do than strike up a conversation.

Is he implying that Marjorie is Jewish? Grant asked himself. Grant had thought it was a pleasant coincidence that the research station they were heading for bore the same name as his wife. He knew there was no relation, yet he thought the coincidence was a good omen, nevertheless. Not that he believed in omens. That would be superstition, practically sinful. But he needed something to buoy him up during this long, slow, utterly boring journey out to the Jupiter system.

Grant had thought that he'd be whisked to Jupiter aboard one of the new fusion torch ships, accelerating most of the way so that the journey took only a few weeks. Not so. Grad students traveled by the cheapest means available, which meant that he and Tavalera were stuck in this clunker of a freighter for the better part of a year. What really stunned Grant was the realization that the transit time did not count toward his Public Service.

"Public Service," said the peevish pinch-faced New Morality clerk when he registered for the journey, "means just what the words say: service to the public. Riding in a spacecraft is not service time, it's leisure time."

Grant argued the point all the way up to the national office, and all he got for his efforts was a reputation as a sorehead. Not even prayer helped. Travel was leisure time, according to the regulations.

Some leisure, Grant thought. *Roberts* was old and slow, dreary and dismal. Its habitation unit rotated on a long tether around its massive cargo module, so that the crew and passengers had a simulated gravity about half that of Earth's. Grant's and Tavalera's quarters consisted of a single spare compartment the dimensions of a coffin, with their two bunks shoehorned in one atop the other, with barely ten centimeters between Grant's nose and Tavalera's sagging mattress.

The depressing, decrepit ore boat didn't even have a niche anywhere aboard it to serve as a chapel. Grant had to do his sabbath worship in the scuffed, cheerless galley, using videos of his father's services and hoping that neither Tavalera nor any of the crew would break in on his observances.

The grumpy gray-haired captain snapped at Grant whenever they met. "Just keep out of the way, brightboy!" were the kindest words Grant had heard out of her. The rest of the crew—three men and three women—ignored their passengers entirely. All of them used language that would have brought them up before the local decency committee back home.

So Grant composed long, lonely video messages back to Marjorie, wherever she was in Uganda or Brazil or the ruins of Cambodia. Real-time videophoning was impossible: The distance between them as *Roberts* cruised out toward Jupiter created an ever-lengthening time lag that defeated any attempt at true conversation. She sent messages back to him, not as often as he did, but of course she was much busier. She always appeared cheerful, hopeful. She ended each message by mentioning the number of hours until Grant would return to Earth.

"It's thirty-two thousand, one hundred, and seventeen hours until we're together again, darling," she would say. "And every second brings you closer to me."

Every time he thought about the number, Grant wanted to break down and cry.

He plunged into his studies of Jupiter, sitting for hours on end in the freighter's cramped little wardroom, nothing more really than a metal-walled compartment barely big enough to accommodate a bolted-down table and four of the most uncomfortable plastic chairs in the solar system. With his handheld computer linked to the display screen on the metal bulkhead, Grant spent most of his time in the dingy wardroom, leaving the claustrophobic sleeping compartment to Tavalera except when he became too stupefyingly exhausted to keep his eyes open.

Crew members would come in from time to time, but for the most part they left Grant to his studies without a word. Only the captain interrupted him, now and then, grumbling about being forced to carry free-loading student "brightboys." To her, Grant was excess baggage, using up ship's air and food for no good purpose. She tolerated Tavalera better; at least he was an engineer, he was going to do something worthwhile out in the Jupiter system. As far as she was concerned, Grant was nothing more than a would-be scientist, a brightboy who was going to play around in a research station instead of doing real work.

Grant ignored the captain's hostility as much as he could and pushed doggedly ahead with his studies. He wanted to know all there was to know about Jupiter by the time he arrived at Station *Gold.* If he had to spend four years there, he intended to make them a productive four years, and not merely as a New Morality snoop, either.

Tavalera had a quizzical expression on his usually gloomy face; his lips were pulled back in a rare, toothy grin.

"Glom to it, man, you married a Jew."

Grant suppressed a flare of annoyance. "She's not Jewish, and even if she were, what difference would that make?"

Leaning across the narrow galley table so close that Grant could smell his noxious breath, Tavalera answered in a half whisper, "Th' scoop is, they don't believe in sex after marriage."

He lifted his head and broke into a loud, barking laugh. Grant stared at him. Is that what this conversation was all about? Grant asked himself. He simply wanted to set me up for a creaky old joke?

Still laughing, Tavalera pointed at Grant. "You oughtta see the expression on your face, brightboy! Priceless!"

Grant made himself smile. "I guess I walked into that one, didn't I?"

"You sure did."

They talked for a few minutes more, but as soon as he decently could, Grant excused himself and headed back to the wardroom and his studies. As he walked along the short passageway that ran through the heart of the habitation module, he wondered about Tavalera. Is there more to the engineer than just crude jokes? Was the discussion about Jews a test of some sort? The New Morality had agents everywhere, constantly on the alert for seditious ideas and troublemakers. Are they watching me, wondering if I'll be a reliable spy for them? Beech said they'd be watching me. Is Tavalera reporting to some NM supervisor?

Most likely he was no more than he appeared to be, a newly graduated engineer with a sophomoric sense of humor. But Grant thought that Tavalera was the kind who would report deviant behavior to the nearest NM agent. It would look good on his dossier.

APPROACH

For more than a week Grant spent hours each day watching the flattened globe of Jupiter wax bigger and fatter as tired old *Roberts* slowly approached the giant planet.

Grant had missed seeing Mars close up; the red planet was on the other side of the Sun when they'd crossed its orbit. *Roberts* had sailed through the Asteroid Belt as if it weren't there, nothing but a vast silent emptiness, not a rock, not a pebble in sight. The ship's radar had picked up a few distant blips, but nothing big enough even to reflect a glint of sunlight.

Jupiter was something else, though. King of the solar system's planets, big enough to swallow more than a thousand Earths, Jupiter presented a spectacular display to Grant's eager eyes. Like a true king, Jupiter was accompanied by a retinue. Grant watched, day by day, as the four largest Jovian satellites danced around their master. He felt like old Galileo himself, seeing this quartet of new worlds orbiting the massive colorfully striped globe of Jupiter.

Without realizing it, Grant made a ritual of his daily observations. He went to the ship's wardroom immediately after breakfast in the galley, always alone. He had no desire for company, especially Tavalera's. Once in the wardroom, he would boot up his palmcomp and access the ship's cameras. He began each day by putting a real-time view of Jupiter on the bulkhead screen, unmagnified. He wanted to see the approaching planet just as he would if he were outside looking at it with his unaided eyes. Only afterward would he call up the magnification program and begin to inspect the planet more closely.

Each day Jupiter grew larger. Grant began to see some of the other, smaller moons as they hurtled around the planet's massive bulk. Tiny specks, even in the cameras' best magnification. Captured asteroids, undoubtedly; minor worldlets that had been seized by the king and forced to circle his majesty until one day they approached too close and were ground into dust by Jupiter's enormous gravitational power.

There were some disappointments. The bands of clouds were not as brilliant and gaudy as he had expected. Their hues were muted, softer than the garish tones he had seen earlier. Grant realized that the videos he had been studying were false-color images, where the tints of the clouds had been enhanced to show their swirls and eddies more clearly. Nor could Grant see the slim dark rings that encircled Jupiter's middle, no matter how hard he strove to find them. The ship's cameras just did not have the power to resolve them.

"Take a look at Io, brightboy."

Startled, Grant looked up to see the captain standing in the open hatchway of the wardroom. She was a blocky, dour-faced woman with graying blond hair she wore in a no-nonsense military buzz cut that accentuated her chunky, dough-skinned face. Her faded olive-green coveralls looked rumpled, frayed, shapeless. She clutched an empty plastic cup in one thick-fingered hand.

"Prometheus is erupting," she said.

It was the first time in the whole long trip that she'd spoken to Grant in anything less than a snarl. He was too surprised to answer. He sat at the wardroom table, frozen into immobility.

With an annoyed scowl, the captain came to the table, leaned over Grant's shoulder, and snapped commands into his palmcomp. The bulkhead screen blinked and then showed the mottled orange-red globe of Io, the innermost of the four big Galilean moons.

"The pizza-pie world," she muttered.

Grant saw that Io indeed looked like a pizza, covered with hot sulfur, though, not cheese; splotched and spotted with craters and volcanoes instead of mushrooms or sausage slices.

The captain gave another command, and the view zoomed in on one section of Io's limb so fast that Grant almost felt dizzy. The curve of the moon's limb showed bright sulfurous orange against the black of space, and Grant could see a dirty yellowish plume spurting up into the darkness.

"Prometheus is jacking off again," the captain said, chuckling.

Ignoring her crudity, Grant found his voice at last. "Thank you."

"Wait," she said. "Don't be in such a hurry to run away." She gave the computer another command, leaning so close to Grant that he could smell her faintly sweaty, acrid odor, feel the heat of her body.

"Be patient," she said, straightening up as the view of Io zoomed out again.

Grant kept his eyes on the screen. "What should I be looking for?"

"You'll see."

The splotchy red-yellow disk of Io suddenly winked out. It took half a heartbeat for Grant to realize it had entered Jupiter's broad, deep shadow.

"Give it a moment," the captain whispered from behind him.

Grant saw a faint greenish glow appear, a ghostly pale luminescence, sickly, like the dying light from some weird deep sea creature. He was too surprised to speak.

"Energetic particles from Jupiter's magnetosphere make Io's atmosphere glow. Too faint to see unless Io is in shadow."

Right, Grant thought. He remembered reading about it somewhere. Oxygen and sulfur atoms excited by collisions with magnetosphere particles. Like the auroras on Earth, same physical mechanism. But seeing it was still a surprise, a gift of wonder.

"Thank you," he said again, turning from the screen to look up at her.

The captain shrugged her hefty shoulders. "I wanted to be a scientist when I was your age. Explore the solar system. Seek out new life, make new discoveries." She sighed heavily. "Instead I pilot this bucket."

"It's an important job," Grant said.

"Oh, yes, certainly important." She spoke with an accent Grant could not quite place. Russian? Polish? "So important that the computer runs the ship most of the time and I have nothing to do but make certain the crew doesn't muck things up."

Grant didn't know how to answer that.

"Well, at least I get to carry handsome young brightboys now and then," said the captain, breaking into an unexpected smile.

Suddenly Grant felt trapped in the wardroom, alone with her.

"I, uh . . ." He started to push himself up from his chair. "I still have a lot of studying to do. And I need to send a videogram to my wife. I send her a 'gram every day, and—"

The captain burst into a peal of hearty laughter. "Yes, of course," she said. "I understand, handsome young brightboy. Not to worry."

She laughed and headed for the coffeemaker. "As long as the VR system works, you are perfectly safe, pretty one."

Grant sank back into his chair as she filled her mug, still laughing, and went back to the hatch.

Then she stopped and turned back toward him. "By the way, there's an observation blister just off the bridge. If you want to see Jupiter with your naked eyes, you have my permission to use it."

Grant blinked with surprise. "Um . . . thank you," he said. "Thank you very much. I'm sorry if I—"

But the captain had already turned and started down the passageway toward the bridge, still chuckling to herself.

For long moments Grant sat there alone, wondering if he'd misunderstood the captain and made a fool of himself. But she'd mentioned a virtual reality system. Grant had heard about using VR simulations for sex. That's what she'd meant, he was certain.

He shook his head, trying to dismiss the encounter from his mind. Me, with her? He shuddered at the thought. But immediately he started composing another video message for Marjorie, mentioning nothing about the captain, of course. And, despite himself, wondering what VR sex might be like.

ARRIVAL

Peering through the transparent glassteel of the observation bubble, Grant could see that Jupiter was not merely immense, it was *alive*.

They were in orbit around the planet now, and its giant curving bulk loomed so huge that he could see nothing else, nothing but the bands and swirls of clouds that raced fiercely across Jupiter's face. The clouds shifted and flowed before his eyes, spun into eddies the size of Asia, moved and throbbed and pulsed like living creatures. Lightning flashed down there, sudden explosions of light that flickered back and forth across the clouds, like signaling lamps.

There was life beneath those clouds, Grant knew. Huge balloonlike creatures called Clarke's Medusas that drifted in the hurricane-force winds surging across the planet. Birds that have never seen land, living out their entire lives aloft. Gossamer spider-kites that trapped microscopic spores. Particles of long-chain carbon molecules that form in the clouds and sift downward, toward the global ocean below.

Unbidden, the words of a psalm sang in his mind.

> *The heavens proclaim the glory of God;*
> *And the firmament declareth the work of his hands . . .*

And there was the Red Spot, a gigantic swirling storm that had been raging for more than four hundred years, bigger than the whole planet Earth. Lightning rippled endlessly around its perimeter; to Grant it looked like the thrashing cilia of some titanic bacterium, flailing its way across the face of the giant planet.

Somewhere in a closer equatorial orbit around the planet was Research Station *Gold*, Grant's destination, the largest man-made object in the solar system outside of the space cities orbiting between Earth and its

Moon. But *Gold* was an invisible speck against the enormous, overwhelming expanse of Jupiter.

It's like watching an abstract painting, Grant thought as he stared at the hurtling clouds of delicate pale yellow, russet brown, white and pink and powder blue. But it's a dynamic painting, moving, shifting, flecked with lightning—alive.

Mars was a dead world, cold and silent despite its lichen and ancient cliffside ruins. Venus was an oven: sluggish, suffocating, useless. Europa, Callisto, and Ganymede, nearby moons of Jupiter almost the size of the planet Mercury, bore fragile ecologies of microscopic creatures beneath their perpetual mantles of ice.

But to Grant's awestruck eyes, Jupiter looked vibrant, powerful, teeming with energy.

For the past four days the captain had been gradually increasing the ship's spin, so that now it was revolving around its empty cargo bay fast enough to produce almost a full terrestrial gravity force in the habitation module. After almost a year at one-half g, the increased sense of weight made Grant feel tired, aching, dispirited.

Except when he was in the observation bubble. Sitting there in its lone padded chair, staring out at the immensity of Jupiter, Grant's mind raced as fast as the swirling multihued clouds. He had no idea of what his assignment would be once they made rendezvous with *Gold.* Certainly the International Astronautical Authority had not paid for his transportation all the way out to Jupiter to have Grant study pulsars and black holes, as he would have preferred to do.

No, he thought, still staring in fascination at Jupiter, the IAA's main thrust out here in the Jovian system was with the microscopic life-forms on frozen Europa and Callisto and the creatures living in Jupiter's atmosphere. They should be bringing biologists and geologists for that kind of work, not a frustrated astrophysicist.

Yet the New Morality claimed that the scientists had sent a manned craft into Jupiter's swirling clouds. In secret. Was it true? What did they find? Why would they keep such work a secret? Scientists don't behave that way, Grant told himself. Somebody in the New Morality is paranoid, and I've got to spend four years of my life paying for his stupid suspicions.

With growing despair, he realized that the scientists would probably put him to work running an ice-drilling rig on the surface of a Jovian moon. Or worse, he'd be sent down under the ice into the frigid ocean below. That thought frightened him: sent under the ice, into an alien ocean, a world of darkness with no air to breathe except what the tanks on his back carried. Scary. Terrifying.

"Rendezvous maneuver begins in three minutes," the captain's voice said from the speaker grille set into the bulkhead, sounding slightly scratchy and flat. "All nonessential personnel will confine themselves to their quarters or the galley."

"Nonessential personnel," Grant muttered, hauling himself up from the padded chair. "That means me." And Tavalera, he added silently. His body felt heavy, sluggish, in the full Earthly gravity.

For a long moment he stood in the cramped little blister of the observation bubble, ignoring the ache in his legs, still staring at Jupiter. It was hard to pull his eyes away from its splendor. The research station was still nowhere in sight; or, if it was, it was too small against Jupiter's massive bulk for Grant to notice it. With enormous reluctance, he turned and ducked through the low hatch and stepped out into the passageway that led to the galley.

Tavalera was in the galley, sure enough, sitting at the table with a steaming mug in front of him and an embarrassed expression on his horsy face. He was wiping his chin with a recyclable napkin. Grant saw that the front of his coveralls was stained and wet.

"Be careful drinking," Tavalera warned. "Liquid pours a lot faster now we're in a full gee."

Grant thought he didn't need the warning. His aching legs told him all he needed to know about the gravity. He thumped heavily into a chair on the opposite side of the table from Tavalera.

"Guess this is our last day together," the young engineer said.

Grant nodded silently.

"Got my assignment this morning," Tavalera said, looking somewhere between worried and hopeful. "It's a scoopship, all right: the *Glen P. Wilson.*"

Grant still said nothing. There had been no assignment for him in the morning's communications bulletin. As far as he knew, he was to report aboard the research station and get his assignment there.

"She's an old ship, cranky and creaky, from what I hear. But a good ship. Reliable. High performance rating."

He sounded to Grant as if he were trying to convince himself of something he didn't actually believe.

"Two years," Tavalera went on, "and then I go home, free and clear."

"That's good."

"You'll be out here four years, won'tcha?"

"That's right."

Tavalera shook his head like a man possessed of superior wisdom. "They really suckered you in, didn't they? Four years."

"I won't have to do another two when I'm fifty," Grant pointed out. Then he added, with just a little malice, "But you will."

If Tavalera caught Grant's irritation, he gave no notice of it. He merely waggled one long-fingered hand in the air and said, "Maybe I will and maybe I won't. By the time I'm fifty, I could be too flickin' important for the New Morality to screw with me."

Again Grant found himself wondering if Tavalera was probing his loyalty. Is this conversation being monitored? he asked himself.

Raising his voice a notch, he replied, "I've always felt that Public Service is something you should be glad to do. Give something back to the community. It's important, don't you think?"

Tavalera leaned back in his chair and gave Grant a crafty look. "Yeah, sure. But there's important and really important. Know what I mean?"

The ship quivered. Just a slight tremor, but it was so out of place that both Grant and Tavalera immediately looked up. Grant felt a sharp pang in his gut. Tavalera's eyes flicked wide for an instant.

"Rendezvous maneuver," Tavalera said, after a moment's startled silence.

"Yes, of course," said Grant, trying to make it sound nonchalant.

Pushing himself up from his chair, Tavalera suggested, "Come on, let's go down to the observation bubble and watch."

"But the captain said—"

Laughing, Tavalera headed for the hatch. "C'mon, you don't have to stay in your cage every second of every day. What's she gonna do if she catches us, throw us off the ship?"

The communications chime on the bulkhead screen sounded. "Incoming message for Grant Archer," announced the comm system's synthesized voice.

Grateful for the interruption, Grant said, "Put it on-screen, please."

The screen remained blank. "This is a private communication," the computer warned.

A message from Marjorie, Grant thought. Tavalera will leave me to see it alone; if he doesn't, I can ask him to leave.

"On-screen, please," he repeated.

To his surprise, the screen showed the twin seals of the International Astronautical Authority and the New Morality Censorship Board. Before Grant could react, it flicked off, to be replaced by a lengthy document headed with the words SECRECY AGREEMENT.

Grant saw that Tavalera's eyes were bulging.

"I'd better go to my bunk and read this on my personal handheld," Grant said.

"I guess you better," Tavalera said in a small voice.

As Grant brushed past him to step out into the passageway, Tavalera said, "I never figured you for an NM agent."

"I'm not," Grant blurted, wishing it were true.

"Yeah. Sure."

Grant headed for the claustrophobic compartment he shared with Tavalera, while the young engineer went the other way, toward the observation blister. Once alone in his cramped bunk, Grant read the secrecy agreement very carefully. Twice. Three times. He was being ordered to sign it. The document did not leave him any choice. If he failed to sign, the New Morality could cancel his Public Service contract and have him returned to Earth "at the convenience of the IAA personnel on-station." That meant all the time in transit to Jupiter would have been totally wasted. And all the time spent waiting for transport back to Earth, and the transit time itself, would also be wasted.

Worse yet, Grant got the distinct feeling that once back home he would be assigned the lowliest, meanest, dirtiest Public Service job that the authorities could find for him. They dealt harshly with dissenters and objectors.

So he signed the secrecy agreement. In essence, it was a simple document. It stated that any and all information, data, knowledge, and facts that he acquired while serving his Public Service obligation were classified Secret and were not to be divulged to any person, agency, or computer network. Under punishment of law.

Grant felt whipsawed. The New Morality wanted him to report on what the scientists were doing; the IAA wanted to swear him to secrecy. Then a new understanding dawned within him: They don't trust each other! The IAA and the New Morality may share the responsibility for running station *Gold,* but they don't trust each other. They don't even like each other. And they've put me in the middle. Whatever I do, I'm going to be in trouble, he realized.

Wishing both sides would just leave him alone, wondering exactly what was going on among the researchers at *Gold* that had to be kept so secret, Grant signed the document and—as directed by the automated legal program—held his palm-size computer to first his right eye and then his left, so that whoever was registering his agreement recorded both his retinal prints.

All these precautions left Grant feeling baffled, worried, and more than a little angry. They had one good effect, however. Once *Roberts* established its co-orbital rendezvous with the space station and Grant toted his one travelbag down to the airlock hatch, Tavalera said good-bye to him with newfound respect in his eyes.

It's almost funny, Grant thought. For most of the trip out here I was halfway convinced that Raoul was a New Morality informer. Now he's certain that I'm one.

He almost laughed as he shook Tavalera's hand in a final good-bye.

Almost. Then he realized that he actually *was* a New Morality informer. At least, that's what the NM expected him to be.

"WELCOME TO THE GULAG"

Grant at last got a look at the orbiting research station, a glimpse, nothing more, as he ducked through the transfer tube that had been set up to connect the station's docking hub with *Roberts*'s airlock.

That brief glimpse disturbed him even more.

He was silently offering a prayer of thanksgiving at his safe arrival and a supplication to "make me worthy, O Lord, of the task You have given me."

As he looked up through the transfer tube's overhead window, the curving surface of the station looked huge, mammoth, a gigantic looming structure that filled the observation port like a colossal arch of gray metal, dulled and pitted from long years of exposure to radiation and infalling cosmic dust.

A childhood memory flashed through Grant's mind: the time his parents had taken him to San Francisco and they had somehow gotten themselves lost in a seedy, dangerous part of the city near the enormous dirt-encrusted supporting buttresses of the Bay Bridge. Grant's breath had caught in his throat; for a moment he had imagined the entire weight of that immense bridge crashing down on him, crushing him and his parents in their flimsy open-topped automobile in a thundering tangle of steel girders and ponderous blocks of stone.

As he made his solitary way through the slightly flexible transfer tube, he got that same sudden feeling: This enormous thick wheel of a station was going to come crashing down upon him any moment now. Again his breath caught and for just a heartbeat of an instant he felt very small, very vulnerable, very close to death.

The instant passed. Grant finished his prayer as he strode on alone through the tube; he was the only person transferring from the freighter to the research station. The flooring felt soft and spongy beneath his boots, especially after so many months of the freighter's steel decks. Everything's fine, he told himself. He remembered that the instant he stepped through the hatch at the far end of the tube he was officially engaged in his Public Service duty; every second would count toward his four-year commitment. Every second would bring him closer to Marjorie, to home, to the life he wanted.

But he had seen something in that brief glimpse of the station, something that should not have been. Grant had memorized the station's layout after months of studying it during the long trip out to Jupiter. Research Station *Gold* was a massive fat doughnut of a structure, more than five kilometers in diameter. It rotated once every two minutes to give its interior a spin-induced artificial gravity of almost exactly one g, so that its inhabitants would feel a comfortable Earthly gravity inside the station.

Grant had seen an additional structure sticking out from the doughnut shape, a metallic lenticular section, round and flattened like a discus, connected to the station by a single slender tube, literally poking out from the main body like a sore thumb. It should not have been there. Grant knew the schematics of Station *Gold* by heart; he had pored over its design details and operations manuals for months. There was no extra section hanging out on one side of the doughnut. There couldn't be. It would unbalance the station's spin and inevitably destabilize it so badly that it would shake the structure apart.

It could not be there, Grant knew. Yet he had seen it. He was certain of that.

He felt puzzled, almost worried, as he took the few steps that brought him to the end of the transfer tunnel. Grant had to duck slightly to get through the hatch that connected with the station itself. As he stepped through, he found himself in a small bare chamber. Its metal walls were scuffed, dull; its flooring was metal gridwork. Once it had been painted, Grant saw, but there was nothing left of the paint except a few grayish chips clinging here and there.

A tall, slim man in light-gray casual slacks and soft blue velour shirt was standing there, waiting for him with a listless, bored expression on his angular, ascetic face. Grant had never seen such a pallid complexion; the man looked almost ghostly. His hair was very light, almost white, thin and straight and hanging down to his shoulders. Despite the silvery hair, Grant guessed that the man was only slightly older than himself.

"Grant Archer?" the man asked needlessly, extending his right hand.

Grant nodded as he shifted his travelbag and took the offered hand.

"I'm Egon Karlstad," the man said. His grip seemed measured: not too strong, not too soft.

"Good to meet you," said Grant. He heard the hatch behind him slide shut, then a quick series of clicks and thumps as the transfer tube disconnected.

Karlstad grinned sardonically. "Welcome to Research Station *Gold*," he said. "Welcome to the gulag."

Puzzled, Grant asked, "What's a gulag?"

"You'll find out," Karlstad said resignedly as he turned to lead Grant through a second hatch and into a long, wide passageway.

Gold seemed even bigger inside than it had looked from the outside. The passageway that they trudged along was spacious and even carpeted, although the carpeting seemed threadbare, badly worn. Still, after all those months of tatty old *Roberts*, Grant reveled in the feeling of openness and freedom. Men and women passed them, nodding their greetings or saying hello to Karlstad. He did not introduce any of them, but kept up a constant chatter about what was behind each of the doors set into either side of the corridor: fluid dynamics lab, cryogenic facility, electronics maintenance shop, other titles Grant did not understand.

Grant thought of it as a corridor, not a passageway. He was not on a ship any longer. This was a research station. Even though he knew he was walking inside a big wheel shaped hoop, it looked and felt to Grant as if the corridor were perfectly flat and straight, that's how big the station was. It was only off in the far distance that the corridor appeared to slope upward.

Well, he thought, at least I'll be in reasonably comfortable surroundings. And working with real scientists.

After what seemed like a half hour, Karlstad stopped at an unmarked doorway. "This is your compartment, Mr. Archer."

"Grant," said Grant. "Please call me Grant."

Karlstad made a polite little bow. "Good. And I'm Egon. My quarters are just down the passageway, two doors." He pointed.

Grant nodded as Karlstad tapped the security pad built into the door jamb. "You can set your own code, of course," he said. "Just let the security office know what it is."

The door slid open. Grant's compartment was roomy, with a real bed instead of a bunk, a desk, table, chairs, shelves, even a compact kitchenette with its own sink and microwave unit. It was all strictly utilitarian, like a college dormitory room, not fancy or luxurious in the least. Certainly nothing in the compartment looked new or bright. Everything smelled faintly of disinfectant, even the thin gray carpeting.

"Two of the walls are smartscreens, of course," Karlstad was saying. "That door on the right is your lavatory, the other one's a closet."

Grant stepped in and tossed his travelbag onto the bed. This is fine, he told himself. This is perfectly fine. I can be comfortable here.

Karlstad shut the door and left him alone in his new quarters before Grant could ask him about the strange structure jutting out from the station's perimeter. But as he bounced on the bed to test its springiness, Grant told himself to forget about it. The people running this station wouldn't build anything that would jeopardize their own safety, he thought. That would be crazy.

It didn't take long for Grant to unpack his meager belongings. His clothes hardly filled a tenth of the ample closet space and bureau drawers. He sat at the desk and linked his palmcomp with the wallscreen. The first thing he did was to compose a long, upbeat message to Marjorie, telling her that he had arrived safely at the station and showing her—by swiveling in his desk chair while holding the palm-size computer with its built-in video camera in his hand—how spacious and comfortable his new quarters were. Then he sent an almost duplicate message to his parents, back in Oregon.

But even as he did so, the memory of that odd appendage sticking out from the station's rim kept nagging at him. A flattened circular shape, like a fat discus. It was big, too: several hundred meters in diameter, at least. It bothered him. After sending off the message to his parents, Grant called up the station's schematics, as he had done countless times on the long journey to Jupiter. Nothing. No reference to such a structure anywhere in his palmcomp's files.

"Did I imagine seeing it?" Grant whispered to himself. Then he shook his head. He had seen it, he was certain of that.

He jacked into the station's own files and pulled up the schematics.

Nothing there, either. Frowning with puzzled frustration, he scrolled through the station's files. Many of them were marked ACCESS LIMITED TO AUTHORIZED PERSONNEL. At last he found what he wanted: realtime views of the station from other satellites in orbit around Jupiter.

At first he was mesmerized by the satellite views of Jupiter itself, the ever-changing kaleidoscope of swirling, racing colors, endlessly fascinating. It took a real effort of will to concentrate on finding views of the station.

And there it was, the thick torus of dulled, pitted metal, looking small and fragile against the overwhelming background of Jupiter's gaudy, hurtling clouds. And there was that saucer-shaped thing hanging out from one side of the station's wheel, connected only by an impossibly slim tube.

Grant froze the image and framed the extension on the wallscreen, then asked, "Computer, pull up the schematic for the indicated image."

No response from the computer. His palmcomp merely hummed to itself; the picture on the screen did not change. Feeling nettled, Grant pulled out the keyboard that was built into the desk and connected it to his palmcomp, then typed out his command.

The screen went blank for a moment and Grant started to smile with a sense of victory. But then ACCESS DENIED appeared briefly and the screen went dead.

"Damn!" Grant snapped, immediately regretting his lack of self-control.

Grant rebooted his palmcomp and tried again. He lost track of time, but he was determined to get the better of the stupid computer system. No matter how he tried, though, every attempt ended in the same ACCESS DENIED message and automatic shutoff.

A knocking on his door finally pulled his attention away from his quest. With a disgusted grunt, Grant got up from his desk chair. He was surprised at how stiff he felt; he must have been hunched over the computer for hours.

Egon Karlstad stood at Grant's door, a quizzical little hint of a smile on his pale face.

"You must be somebody special," Karlstad said, standing out in the corridor. "Dr. Wo wants to see you."

"Dr. Wo?" Grant asked.

"As in woe unto thee, rash mortal," said Karlstad. "He's the director of the station. El supremo."

"He wants to see me? Why?"

Karlstad brushed a hand through his silvery hair. "Beats me. He doesn't take me into his confidences very often. But when he rings the bell, you'd better salivate."

Grant stepped out into the corridor and closed his door behind him. "Salivate?"

"Pavlov's dogs," said Karlstad, starting down the hallway. "Conditioned reflex and all that."

"Oh, I remember . . . in biology class, back in high school."

"I'm a biophysicist, you know."

"Really? What're you doing here? Aren't all the biology people at the Galilean moons?"

Karlstad waved hello to a couple of women coming toward them before he replied, "All the work on the moons is headquartered here. People can't stay out there for more than a few weeks at a time: radiation buildup, you know."

"We're shielded here?" Grant asked.

"Hell, yes. Superconducting magnets, just like the storm cellars aboard spacecraft, only bigger. And we're orbiting close enough to Jupiter so that we're inside the van Allen belts, below the heaviest radiation fields."

"That's good."

"Understatement of the year!"

They walked along the corridor for what seemed like kilometers. Karlstad appeared almost to glide along, pale and slim and seemingly weightless, just about. Like a ghost, Grant thought. A pallid, insubstantial phantom. Most of the doors they passed were closed, although they went through an open area that was obviously a galley or cafeteria. People were lining up and getting trays, piling food on them, moving to tables and sitting down. Hearty aromas of hot food and spices wafted through the area, making Grant truly salivate.

"Is it lunchtime?" Grant asked.

"Dinner," Karlstad answered. "Your clock is off by seven or eight hours."

Grant hadn't realized that the old *Roberts* ran on a different clock. He had assumed that all space vehicles kept the same time.

They passed through more open areas, workshops and exercise gyms, then a long span with doors spaced close together. The carpeting here seemed newer, thicker, even though it was the same bland gray as elsewhere. "Executive territory," Karlstad murmured. Each door bore a nameplate.

At last they stopped at a door that said:

L. ZHANG WO
STATION DIRECTOR

"Here you are," said Karlstad.

"You're not going in with me?" Grant asked.

Karlstad raised his hands in mock horror. "He wants to see you, not me. I'm just the delivery boy. Besides"—he hesitated a heartbeat—"the less I see of the Old Man, the better."

LI ZHANG WO

Karlstad walked away, leaving Grant standing alone before the closed door of the director's office. Feeling a little nervous, Grant balled his fist to knock on the door, then hesitated.

There's nothing to be afraid of, he told himself. You haven't done anything wrong. Besides, this is a chance to talk to the top man; you can tell him you're an astrophysicist and bringing you here was a mistake, maybe get him to send you back to Earth or at least to the Moon.

Summoning up his courage, he tapped lightly on the door.

No response.

He glanced up and down the corridor. No one in sight. Karlstad had melted away. It was as if no one wanted to be anywhere near here.

Taking a deep breath, Grant rapped on the door again, harder.

Again no response. He wondered what to do. Then a muffled voice from inside the office said, "Enter."

Grant slid the door open and stepped in. The room was overly warm, sticky with humidity, like a hothouse. Grant felt perspiration break out on his upper lip, yet the director wore a high-collared tunic buttoned all the way up to the throat as he sat behind his desk.

Director Wo's office was austere rather than imposing. The room was about the same size as his own quarters, Grant guessed, furnished with a large curved desk of gleaming metal, its surface completely clear except for a small computer screen and an incongruous vase of delicate red and white chrysanthemums. There was a chair of tubular stainless steel padded with fawn-colored cushions in front of the desk and a small oval conference table with four stiff plastic chairs in the far corner. The wallscreen behind the desk showed a stark desert: empty sand stretching to the horizon beneath a blazing sun. It made Grant feel even more uncomfortably hot. The other walls were utterly bare; the only decoration in the room was that paradoxical vase of flowers on the director's desk.

They can't be real, Grant thought. Nobody would waste the time and resources to grow flowers on this station. Yet they looked real enough. And the vase was a graceful Oriental work of art, like something from a museum.

Without looking up from his desktop screen, Dr. Wo gestured bruskly to the padded chair in front of his desk. Grant obediently sat in it, thinking that the director was playing an old power-trip game: pretending to be so busy that he can't even say hello. Grant had run into this type before, at school and among the bureaucrats of the New Morality.

All right, he thought. As soon as he does look up I'll tell him that I'm an astrophysicist and I should be at Farside. Enough of this spying and secrecy agreements.

Feeling sweat dampening his scalp, Grant studied Dr. Wo's face as he sat waiting for the director to take notice of him. It was a fleshy, broad-cheeked face, solid and heavy-featured, with small coal-black eyes set deeply beneath brows so slight that they were practically nonexistent. Skin the color of old parchment. The man had a small mustache, little more than wisps on his upper lip. His hair was cropped so close to his scalp that it was difficult to tell its true color: light gray, Grant thought. His hairline was receding noticeably. His head looked big, blocky, too heavy even for the powerful shoulders that strained the fabric of his tunic.

At last Director Wo looked up from the screen and fixed his eyes on Grant. They glowered like the embers of a smoldering fire.

"I heard you knock the first time," he said. His voice was hoarse, strained, as if he were suffering from a throat infection.

Grant blinked with surprise. "When no one answered I thought—"

"You are an impatient man," Wo accused. "That is not good for someone who wants to become a scientist."

"I . . . I didn't think you'd heard me," Grant stammered.

"You are also too curious for your own good." Wo jabbed a finger at the desktop screen, like a prosecuting attorney making a point. "The extension to this station is off-limits to unauthorized personnel, yet the first thing you do when you arrive here is poke your brightboy nose into it. Why?"

"Uh, well . . . it seemed odd to me, sir, having an extension hanging on one side of the wheel and nothing to balance it."

"Oh, so you are a design engineer, are you?" The man's voice made Grant want to wince. It seemed so harsh that it had to be painful to speak that way.

"Nosir, but it does make me wonder."

Wo huffed impatiently. "Better men than you have designed that extension, brightboy. And when you get an access-denied message on your screen you should take your curiosity elsewhere. Understand me?"

"Yessir. If I may, though, I want to—"

"You set off all kinds of alarms, trying to pry into sensitive information."

"I didn't realize there was anything that sensitive being done here," Grant said. Even as he said it, Grant realized it was a lie. He'd been sent here *because* of the scientists' secrecy.

"You didn't realize . . .? Didn't you sign a secrecy agreement?"

"Yes, but I thought—"

"You thought it was just a bit of paperwork, did you?" Wo hunched forward, both hands balled into fists atop the desk. His hands looked powerful, thick wrists and heavy forearms that bulged in his tunic sleeves. "Another pointless piece of red tape from the bureaucrats running this station."

"Nosir. But about my assignment here—"

"You have been assigned to this station. Under my direction. You will follow the terms of the secrecy agreement you signed. That is mandatory. No exceptions."

"I . . ." Grant swallowed hard. "I didn't associate the secrecy agreement with the access-denied message on my screen. As you said, sir, my curiosity got the better of me."

Wo stared coldly at Grant for several long moments. At last he said, "Very well. I will take you at your word. But my security people are buzzed up about you."

Grant knew when to behave meekly. "I'm sorry if I've caused any trouble, but, you see, I'm actually an astrophysicist and I don't understand why I'm here."

"The trouble is on your shoulders, brightboy. Report to the security chief immediately for an extended briefing on proper handling of sensitive materials."

"But I—"

"Immediately, I said! Don't just sit there! Get to the security chief's office. Understand me?"

Grant scrambled to his feet and headed for the door.

"You've gotten off on the wrong foot, Archer," the director called from his desk.

Turning, Grant saw that he had swung his chair away from the desk slightly. It was a powered wheelchair. Beneath his full-length tunic the director was wearing ridiculous-looking green plaid shorts, and Grant could see that Wo's legs were pitifully thin, emaciated, scarred and twisted, dangling uselessly from his chair. He looked like a gnome or a troll from childhood tales.

If Dr. Wo was bothered by Grant's shocked stare, he gave no hint of it.

"Get on the right track and stay on it," he snapped. "Or else."

"Yessir," Grant said. "I will, sir."

Once outside in the blessed cool of the corridor again, Grant realized that Wo gave him no chance to ask for a reassignment to Farside. Or anywhere else, for that matter. Feeling wretched, he wondered where the cursed security office might be. He knew it had to be along the corridor somewhere, there was only this one main passageway that went through the entire wheel-shaped station, if he remembered the schematics correctly. But the station was so big, Grant realized he could be walking for an hour or more.

The corridor was still empty and silent; no one in sight to ask for directions. Then he spotted a videophone on the wall up ahead. He used it to pull up the station layout and found the office of the security chief, someone named Lane O'Hara.

The office was actually only a few dozen meters up the corridor. Grant hustled to it and rapped on the door, which bore O'Hara's name.

"Come in."

It was a much smaller room than the director's. Grant saw that it must be an anteroom; nothing but a small desk and a single straightbacked chair in front of it. A pert young woman sat at the desk. An assistant, no doubt. There was an unmarked door on the far wall. That must be O'Hara's office, he said to himself.

"I'm Grant Archer. The director sent me here to see Mr. O'Hara."

"Miss O'Hara," she corrected. "That's me." Rising from her chair, she extended her hand over the desk. She was at least two centimeters taller than Grant.

Surprised, Grant shook her hand as he blurted, "You're the security chief?"

"Lane O'Hara . . . Elaine, if you look up my baptismal record."

"Oh," said Grant.

Lane O'Hara was no more than Grant's own age, slim as a willow, her boyish figure clad in a loose slate-gray turtleneck pullover and odd-looking shiny black leather leggings lined with rows of dull gray metal studs along the outside seams. Her face was elfin, with high cheekbones, a tilted nose, a slightly sharpish chin, and delicate lips that were curved into a pleasant smile. Her eyes were bright green, and they were smiling, too. She wore her chestnut hair tied into a tight bun at the back of her head.

"What were you expecting?" she asked. "Some great brute of a policeman, maybe?" There was a lilt in her voice that Grant had never heard before: charming, musical.

"I guess I was," he said, smiling back at her as he followed her gesture and took the chair in front of her desk.

"Oh, we have them, too," she said as she sat back in her little swivel chair. "On a station this size you need a few thumpers here and there, now and then."

Grant pictured some of the stern-faced beefy security guards he'd seen at school.

"Now then," O'Hara said lightly, "the director's all fussed about your prying into the station schematics, looking to find out what he's got in the annex."

"I was curious . . ."

"Of course you were. Everybody is. But the director is just a wee bit paranoid about the annex. It's his special project, you know."

"I didn't know," Grant said.

"How could you, seeing that you just arrived an hour or so ago?" She shrugged her slim shoulders. "Well, I'm required to put you through the standard security briefing and there's nothing to it. I'll try to run through it quickly enough so we can get finished with it before the cafeteria closes for the night."

Grant asked, "What time is it here?"

O'Hara shook her head sorrowfully. "They didn't even give you a chance to adjust your clock, did they?"

Grant realized he liked this security chief. In fact, he thought he was going to enjoy the briefing.

"OUR INTELLECTUAL COUSINS"

He didn't. Once she got started on the station's security regulations, O'Hara became strictly business. She called up on her wallscreen a bewildering set of rules and restrictions, then quizzed Grant about them mercilessly for what seemed like hours.

At last, with a reluctant, "I suppose that will have to do." She dismissed Grant—but only after telling him that the cafeteria would stop serving dinner in fifteen minutes.

"I don't know where the cafeteria is," Grant bleated.

"Turn right outside my door and follow your nose," O'Hara said.

Grant got up from the chair, aching slightly from having sat in it for so long.

"Better dash," O'Hara said.

"What about you? Aren't you going to eat?"

She sighed heavily. "I hope so. But I've got a bit of work to finish first. Scamper, now!"

Grant headed straight for the cafeteria, stopping only to use one of the wall phones to find its exact location.

He could have followed his ears, he realized as he approached the busy, crowded, clanging, clattering noisy cafeteria. For the first time since he'd left Earth, Grant found himself in a familiar environment. The odors of food, real cooked food instead of the microwaved packaged meals he'd had aboard *Roberts*, almost brought tears of joy to his eyes.

The cafeteria was a wide, busy open area on both sides of the station's main corridor. Against the curving bulkheads on either side stood steam tables and automated dispensing machines, apparently the same on both sides. A few other latecomers were lined up there with trays in their hands, making their dinner selections. Tables were scattered across the carpeted floor, except for the cleared area of the corridor. People walked back and forth, picking tables, finding friends.

Grant realized that he didn't know anyone in this crowd. Even though half the tables were empty, there must have been more than a hundred men and women there, chatting, eating, laughing noisily—and all of them were strangers to him.

Then he spotted Egon Karlstad sitting at a table with two women and a muscular-looking black man. But there were no empty chairs at that table. So Grant went through the line glumly, expecting to eat alone, or with strangers. His mood quickly changed, though, once he saw the quality and variety of the food available. The meats were undoubtedly soy derivatives or other synthetics, but the vegetables looked crisp and fresh, and the fruits seemed straight out of the Garden of Eden: luscious and tempting.

Those flowers on Wo's desk are real, Grant told himself. They must have tremendous hydroponics farms here.

He loaded his tray, even taking the largest-sized cup of soymilk the machines offered, then wandered through the maze of tables, looking for a place to sit.

"Archer!" someone shouted. "Grant! Over here."

He turned to see Karlstad standing and waving at him. Feeling immensely grateful, Grant headed toward his table.

"I don't want to interrupt . . ." he said lamely as he reached the table. All four seats were still occupied.

"Nonsense," Karlstad snapped as he pulled a chair from the next table, startling the couple who were hunched toward each other deep in intense conversation.

Grant carefully laid his tray on the table and sank into the proffered seat. "Thank you," he said.

He took his plates and cup off the tray, then—as he had seen others do—slid the tray under his chair. He started to say a swift, silent grace over his food, but Karlstad interrupted.

"Ursula van Neumann," Karlstad said, pointing to the petulant-looking blond Valkyrie sitting on Grant's left. She smiled as if it hurt her face. "Ursa's one of our best computer docs. You have a problem with a simulation or an analysis, go see Ursula."

She nodded somberly. "He tells that to so many that I am always swamped with work."

Before Grant could reply, Karlstad turned to the other woman, a petite Oriental with a face as round and flat as a saucepan. "Tamiko Hideshi, physical chemist."

"You come to see me," Hideshi said, with a sparkle in her dark eyes, "if you have a problem understanding the chemistry going on in Europa's ocean."

Everyone at the table laughed, except Grant.

"I'm afraid I don't get the joke," he admitted.

Hideshi touched Grant's arm gently. "The joke is that *no one* understands the chemistry going on under that damned ice. They've been splashing around in it for more than ten years now, with thirty years of automated probes before that, and the complexity is still beyond us."

"Oh," said Grant. "I see."

"I wish I did," Hideshi answered ruefully.

"This big bruiser here," Karlstad said, jabbing a thumb toward the black man, "is Zareb Muzorawa. Fluid dynamics."

"My friends call me Zeb," said Muzorawa, in a slow, deliberate tone.

From the looks of him—muscular build, shaved scalp, a trim beard tracing his jawline, red-rimmed eyes of deepest brown—Grant expected his voice to be a powerful leonine rumble. Instead it came out soft, almost amiable, despite his grave attitude. Then he smiled and all the fierceness of his bearded face vanished in a warm friendliness.

Muzorawa was wearing a comfortably soft turtleneck pullover. Grant could see that his trousers were black, metal-studded leggings, the same as Lane O'Hara had worn. Van Neumann wore a sleeveless chemise, cut low enough to show how amply she was built. Hideshi was in frayed olive-drab coveralls.

Grant said, "I'm very happy to meet all of you." He started to put his fork into the salad he'd selected, but Hideshi interrupted with:

"What's your discipline?"

"I'm an astrophysicist."

"Astrophysicist?"

With a nod, Grant added, "My special field of study is stellar collapse. You know, supernovas, pulsars, black holes . . . stuff like that."

"What in the name of sanity are you doing here?" van Neumann asked.

"Why did Dr. Wo pick you?" Karlstad added.

Grant could only shrug. "I'm doing my Public Service duty. I don't think Dr. Wo asked for me in particular; I'm just the brightboy that the personnel board sent here."

Karlstad nodded knowingly. "Just a warm body to fill an open slot."

But Muzorawa countered, "I'm not so sure of that. The director is always very careful about his personnel selections. Very exact. No one comes to this station unless he wants that precise individual."

Grant knew that was wrong. He'd been sent to this station to spy on Dr. Wo and the other scientists. Maybe Wo knows that, he thought suddenly. That's why he's so ticked at me.

Van Neumann's brows knit into a worried frown. "Well, there's no astrophysics work for you to do here, that's for certain."

Grant looked at each of his four companions: biophysics, computer engineering, physical chemistry, and fluid dynamics. What did it add up to? he wondered.

Aloud, he asked, "Just what *is* the work you're doing here?"

Hideshi quickly answered, "Ursula and I are supporting the teams investigating the Galilean moons."

Turning to Muzorawa, "And you?"

Muzorawa glanced at the ceiling, then replied guardedly, "I'm part of a different team, studying Jupiter."

"The planet itself, not its moons?"

"That's right."

"Fluid dynamics," Grant mused aloud. "Then you must be studying Jupiter's atmosphere. The clouds—"

"And the life-forms," Karlstad interrupted.

"Those big floating balloons," said Grant. "Why are they called Clarke's Medusas? They don't look anything like medusas on Earth."

"They're about a thousand times larger," van Neumann said.

"And they drift through the Jovian atmosphere," added Hideshi. "Not the ocean."

Muzorawa said, "There's a fascinating ecology in the atmosphere. Soarbirds that nest on the Medusa balloons, for example. They live their entire life cycles aloft, never touching the surface of the ocean."

"It's a mutilated ecology," Karlstad said. "It's just starting to come back from the disaster of Shoemaker-Levy."

Grant felt briefly confused, then remembered from high school that the comet Shoemaker-Levy 9 had struck Jupiter with the force of thousands of hydrogen bombs.

"That was almost a century ago," he said. "Its effects are still being felt?"

Karlstad nodded, tight-lipped. "It must have wiped out god only knows how many species."

"But it didn't affect the manna," said Hideshi.

"Manna?"

"The organic compounds that form in the clouds," Karlstad explained. "Carbon-chain molecules that drift down into the sea below."

"Have you found any life-forms in the ocean?" Grant asked.

The four of them looked at one another. Then Karlstad answered, "Officially—no."

Grant forgot his untouched dinner sitting in front of him. "But unofficially?" he asked.

Before he could answer, a short, bustling, red-haired man with a thick brick-red mustache stepped up to the table and grabbed Karlstad roughly by the shoulder. "How's it goin', mate? This th' new bloke, is it?"

Karlstad grinned and nodded. "Grant Archer," he said. "Grant, this is one of the most important men in the station: Rodney Devlin."

"Better known as the Red Devil," van Neumann added dryly.

"Pleased to meetcha, Grant," said Devlin, sticking out his hand. "Just call me Red."

From the food-stained white jacket Devlin was wearing, Grant guessed that he was a cook or some sort of cafeteria employee. He had one of those perpetually youthful faces, lean and lantern-jawed, with a big toothy grin beneath the bushy mustache.

"Red is the chef here," Karlstad explained.

"An exaggerated job description, if I ever heard one," jabbed Hideshi.

"More than that," Karlstad went on, unperturbed, "Red is the man to see if you want anything—from toilet paper to sex VRs. Red actually runs this station, in reality."

Muzorawa smiled pleasantly. "Dr. Wo doesn't know that, of course."

"Don't be too sure o' that, Zeb," Devlin said jovially. "Grant, old sock, anything you need, you come see me. I'll take good care o' you. Right?"

The others all nodded or murmured agreement. Devlin banged Grant on the back, then made his way to the next table.

Grant turned back to his tablemates. "Is he really that important around here?"

Van Neumann muttered, "You'd better believe it."

"He runs *everything*?"

"Unofficially," Muzorawa said. "Red is a kind of expeditor."

"A facilitator," Karlstad added.

"Every organization has one," Muzorawa went on. "Every organization needs one: a person who can get around the red tape, operate in between the formal lines of the organization chart."

"A procurer," van Neumann said flatly.

"Facilitator," Karlstad insisted. "That's a better word."

Van Neumann shrugged as if it didn't matter to her. She plainly did not like Devlin, Grant could see.

Then he remembered their interrupted conversation. "Let's get back to where we were . . . you said there's life in Jupiter's ocean?"

"Not so loud, please!" Muzorawa hissed.

Karlstad leaned across the table toward Grant. "The only thing we can tell you is that some of the deep probes have recorded things moving around down there," he whispered.

"Things? Living things?"

"We don't know," said Muzorawa, his voice also low. With a glance at Karlstad he added, "And we are not permitted to talk about it unless you've been specially cleared for sensitive information."

Grant slumped back in his chair. "All right," he said. "I understand. I don't want to get you into any trouble."

"Or yourself," said van Neumann.

"Hey, that's right," Karlstad said, brightening. "How'd your session with the Woeful Wo turn out?"

Grant jabbed at his salad. "He wasn't very happy with me."

"Why not?" Hideshi asked.

The others had all finished their dinners. Grant tried to eat as he talked.

"I was curious about that extension hanging off to one side of the station. Tried to look up its schematic in the computer system."

"Uh-oh," said van Neumann.

"You tripped an alarm," Muzorawa said.

Grant nodded as he swallowed a mouthful of greens.

"So what did Old Woeful say?" Karlstad asked, grinning.

Before Grant could answer, Muzorawa nudged Karlstad in the ribs. "You should be more careful about the way you talk," he said in a near whisper.

Karlstad's grin faded. "He can't have the whole cafeteria bugged."

"You hope," said the black man.

Turning back to Grant, Karlstad asked in a quieter, more guarded tone, "So what did the director say to you?"

"He told me to keep my nose out of sensitive areas and sent me to see the security chief."

"No flogging?" van Neumann joked.

"Who's on the security desk this week?" Hideshi wondered.

"O'Hara," said Muzorawa.

"So you saw our little Lainie," Karlstad said.

"She's not so little," Grant replied. "I mean, she's taller than I am, a bit."

His grin widening, Karlstad asked, "Was she cruel to you?"

Grant was startled by his question. Before he could think of what to answer, Hideshi piped up: "Egon has an illicit sweat over Lainie. Fantasizes about her."

"It's more than a fantasy," Karlstad said, his grin getting toothy.

"In your dreams," van Neumann retorted.

"Wait," said Grant. "You said she's on the security desk this week? Does that mean that she's not always the security officer?"

Muzorawa nodded soberly. "All the scooters take turns at it."

"Scooters?"

"Scientists," Hideshi explained. "Anyone on the scientific staff is called a scooter."

Grant wondered where the term came from, but before he could ask, Karlstad chimed in. "Old Woeful doesn't trust any one of us enough to appoint a permanent security chief, so he rotates the assignment among us."

"Why does he need a security chief at all?" Grant asked. "What's going on here that's so sensitive?"

Again they hesitated, glancing at one another.

"Why should possible life-forms in Jupiter's ocean be regarded as sensitive information?" Grant persisted.

At last Muzorawa said quietly, "That's Dr. Wo's decision. You'll have to ask him about it."

With a glum shake of his head, Grant said, "No thanks."

"So you met Lainie, eh?" Karlstad asked, grinning again as he deftly returned to his subject.

Grant nodded as he dug into his dinner.

"She's a marine biologist, you know."

"Oh?"

"Makes me wish I was a marine," Karlstad said with a leer.

The others laughed. Then van Neumann said, "Why don't you take Grant down to the fish tanks?"

"Yeah," Hideshi added, teasing. "You might bump into Lainie there, Egon."

"Not a bad idea," said Karlstad.

While Grant mopped up his dessert of fresh melon and soymilk ice cream, a mountain-sized young man in coveralls that seemed about to burst grabbed an empty chair, flipped it around in one hand, and swung a heavy leg over it, resting his beefy arms on the chair back. His dark, drooping mustache made him look like a bandit in Grant's eyes.

Karlstad said, "Grant Archer, this is Ignacio Quintero."

"Nacho," said the newcomer, in a surprisingly sweet tenor voice.

"Macho Nacho, he's known as," Karlstad said.

Quintero looked like a football lineman: big in every direction. He was smiling pleasantly, though, and his brown eyes looked friendly.

He stuck out a big hand. "Good to meet you, amigo. Bienvenido and all that."

Grant shook hands with Quintero.

"Nacho works with us," Karlstad explained. "He's a structural engineer, but his main talent is entertainment."

"Entertainment?" Grant asked.

Quintero shrugged massively. "I try to keep people amused. It gets too dull around here. Too solemn."

"Once he sprinkled black pepper in the air circulation system, and when people started sneezing their heads off he spread a rumor about a mysterious virus causing a plague."

Quintero made a hushing gesture with both hands. "Hey, not so loud, amigo. The medics still don't know it was me who did it."

"And then there was the incident of the pornographic data dump . . ."

"You can't blame me for that one," Quintero said, shaking a finger at Karlstad. "I had plenty of help."

"Sure you did."

"So what do you do, Grant?"

Grant explained that he was an astrophysicist and hadn't yet received his work assignment.

"Astrophysicist?" Quintero scratched his head. Grant noticed that his dark hair was tightly curled, almost kinky. "You're in the wrong part of the universe for that."

Before Grant could reply, Karlstad said, "I'm taking Grant down to the aquarium. Want to come?"

Something flashed across Quintero's face, an expression that came and went so quickly Grant could not tell what it was.

"No can do, amigo. Got too much work to catch up with. Wo's got us on double shifts now."

"Double shifts?" Grant asked. "What are you working on?"

Quintero glanced at Karlstad, then hauled himself to his feet. "Got to run. Nice to meet you, Grant. Adios, muchachos!"

He practically ran out of the cafeteria.

Once Grant finished his dessert, Karlstad led him out into the corridor.

"We could do this tomorrow," Grant said. "I mean, if it's your time to retire for the night—"

"No, no," Karlstad said quickly. "Sometimes I stay up even past ten o'clock."

Grant didn't know if that was supposed to be a joke or not, so he stayed silent. Karlstad seemed impatient to get to the fish tanks, whatever they were. Grant couldn't believe the station had an aquarium built into it, but then why was there a marine biologist on the staff?

Karlstad set a brisk pace as they walked through the corridor. He glided along, wraithlike, but the expression on his wan face seemed eager. The corridor was deserted, empty of people, all the doors closed for the night.

Up ahead, though, the corridor seemed to end in a metal wall with a single small door set into it. No, not a door, Grant saw as they got nearer. It was a pressure hatch, much like the kind of hatch he'd seen on airlocks, with a security keypad set into the bulkhead alongside it.

Letters in fading, flaking red paint above the hatch proclaimed AUTHORIZED PERSONNEL ONLY. Someone had scrawled beneath it *No fishing allowed.* The metal of the bulkhead seemed to be covered with freshly scrubbed areas and patches of new-looking paint. Apparently other graffiti had been written or scratched into the bulkhead and then erased or painted over.

"Wo tries to stay ahead of the graffiti artists," Karlstad explained. "If he catches you at it, you spend the next week of your off-duty time with Sheena, scrubbing and painting."

Pointing to the official notice above the hatch, Grant asked, "Are we authorized personnel?"

Karlstad shrugged his slim shoulders. "We are if we know the entry code."

He tapped on the keypad with quick, nervous fingers. The red light atop the keys turned green and the hatch popped open with a thin puff of chill, dank air from the other side of the bulkhead.

Karlstad pulled the hatch open, grunting. "Lainie gave me the combination," he said. "She likes to play in here. She likes an audience."

Completely puzzled, Grant stepped over the coaming of the hatch. This section of the station felt cooler, chilly, and clammy with humidity. The corridor was much narrower here, and dimly lit, but Grant could see a glow along the wall.

Then his breath caught in his throat. It was an aquarium! The glow was from a thick, long window. On its other side swam a dizzying assortment of fish, big ones, little ones, some nuzzling the gravelly bottom, others weaving through swaying fronds of plants. They were every color of the rainbow: bright stripes, bold patterns of spots, gleaming silvery squid slithered through the water, tentacles waving.

"Aquaculture," said Karlstad. "That's how it started. The first settlers on the Moon found that they could grow more protein in less space from fish farming than from meat animals."

With a pang, Grant remembered that he should be at Farside, on the Moon, or at least in Selene or one of the other lunar communities. Instead . . .

"Come on," Karlstad beckoned, heading along the narrow passageway. "You've got to see this."

They passed more tanks filled with fish. The pale glow from the underwater lights made Karlstad look more ghostly than ever, with his silvery hair and pallid complexion.

He stopped and jabbed a thumb at the next window. "This is where Lainie likes to do it," he said with a malicious grin.

Grant stared into the tank. A pair of dolphins were swimming there, sleek and huge, bigger than horses, gliding effortlessly, playfully, through the water.

"Their tank is almost a kilometer long," Karlstad said. "At feeding time it's opened to the other tanks."

Grant gaped, slack-jawed. He heard himself ask, in an awed, faint voice, "Why in the world did you bring dolphins all the way from Earth?"

Karlstad made a derisive grunt. "It's Wo's idea. Our 'intellectual cousins,' he calls them. Old Woeful thinks the dolphins can help us to explore Jupiter's ocean."

"Our intellectual cousins," Grant repeated slowly, still staring at the graceful dolphins. They seemed to be smiling at him as they swam past, then turned to stare back at him.

"There's something else you should see," Karlstad said, motioning Grant farther along the passageway.

"What is it?" Grant asked, following the biophysicist as they walked past the end of the dolphins' tank. The lighting was dimmer here, the walls on both sides of the narrow corridor blank metal.

"Quiet now," Karlstad whispered, a finger to his lips.

Slowly, softly the two men walked down the dimly lit way. Karlstad stopped and motioned Grant to move ahead of him. "It's on the right," he whispered.

Grant tiptoed through the shadows until he saw an opening in the wall on his right. He glanced back at Karlstad, who motioned him to go through it.

Puzzled, Grant stepped into the wide entryway and found himself in some sort of darkened chamber. There was something in the far corner, a large heap of—

A full-grown gorilla opened its eyes not more than three meters in front of Grant. He realized it had been slumped down on its haunches, asleep. There were no bars between Grant and the gorilla, no partition at all.

Before Grant could move or think or even yowl with terror the gorilla shambled to its feet, huge, fierce, leaning on its knuckles, fangs bared. Grant could feel the heat of the animal's body, smell its breath and its hideous, hairy stench.

He stood there petrified as the gorilla raised a powerful, hairy arm, thick as Grant's torso, its massive paw nearly brushing his face.

"No!" it said in a rasping voice. Its open hand was bigger than Grant's head. "You go! Now!"

SHEENA

Grant stood transfixed, too frightened to move, unable to breathe, almost, as the angry gorilla took a shambling step toward him, fangs bared, eyes glaring.

And she talked! "Go!" she repeated. "You go!"

He heard Karlstad making a strange, strangled noise behind him. Turning his head ever so slightly, Grant saw the biophysicist nearly choking with barely suppressed laughter. The gorilla blinked, put down her raised arm.

Karlstad stepped up beside Grant and said lightly, "Now, Sheena, it's all right. You know me." He was grinning broadly, barely able to contain his merriment.

The gorilla hunkered down on her knuckles. Grant saw her red-rimmed eyes shift from Karlstad's face to his own and then back again.

"Ee-ghon," the gorilla said. Her voice was a raspy, painful whisper. It reminded Grant of Director Wo's hoarse, strained voice.

"Good girl, Sheena!" Karlstad said brightly, as if speaking to a two-year-old. "You're right, I'm Egon. And this is Grant," he added, pointing.

He's talking to a three-hundred-kilo gorilla, Grant said to himself. And the gorilla's talking back!

"Grant is a friend," Karlstad said amiably.

"Grant," the gorilla whispered.

"That's right." Turning slightly toward him, Karlstad said, "Grant, this is Sheena. She works with us."

It took Grant two hard swallows to find his voice. "H-hello, Sheena."

Sheena blinked at him, then slowly, solemnly, extended her massive right hand toward Grant.

"Just put your hand on her palm," Karlstad told him, sotto voce. "Gently."

His heart thumping wildly, Grant stretched out his right arm and let his fingertips touch Sheena's leathery palm. His hand looked minuscule in the gorilla's huge paw; Grant got a vision of her closing her fist and crushing his hand to a bloody pulp. But the gorilla merely let it rest on her palm for a few moments. She stared at Grant, then at his hand. Slowly she bent her head forward slightly and sniffed noisily at Grant's hand.

Then she said, "Grant," as if to fix his name in her memory.

She pulled her hand away, and Grant let his arm drop to his side with a gusting sigh of relief.

"We're going now, Sheena," Karlstad said, still in the tone that a man would use with a small child.

Sheena thought that over for a few seconds. "Yes," she said at last. "You go."

"Say good night to her," Karlstad told Grant.

"Uh . . . good night, Sheena."

"Grant," the gorilla answered. "Grant."

Karlstad turned slowly and walked out of the gorilla's compartment, with Grant so close behind him they might have been Siamese twins. They headed back along the glowing fish tanks toward the hatch where they had entered the aquarium. Grant could hear the gorilla's heavy breathing and knew the beast was shuffling along behind them, not more than a step or two away. The dolphins seemed to be grinning at them, as if they were enjoying the show.

"This is the tricky part," Karlstad said softly as they walked slowly away from the gorilla. "Females don't usually attack, but when they do it's when your back is to them."

Grant felt his knees go rubbery.

"Don't look back!" Karlstad cautioned. "If she decides to rush us there's not a damned thing we can do about it."

His voice shaky, Grant heard himself ask, "Has she ever attacked anyone before?"

Karlstad did not answer for several heartbeats. Then: "Not really attack. But she's so pissing strong she's broken people's ribs by accident."

"What . . . how is she able to talk?"

"That's Wo's brilliant idea. Built a voicebox for her. Injected her brain with neuronal stem cells to see how much he could boost her intelligence."

"Our intellectual cousins," Grant remembered.

They had reached the hatch. Karlstad pushed it open and they stepped through. Grant helped to push it closed. He saw Sheena standing on all fours, so big that her shoulders brushed either wall of the narrow corridor. He felt a lot safer once the hatch clicked shut.

"Sheena's a long way from being an intellectual cousin," Karlstad said, his voice louder now, firmer, as they started walking briskly back toward their quarters.

"But she talks," Grant said. "She can obviously think."

"To a degree. Like a two-year-old, that's all. There isn't enough room in her cranium to grow a human-equivalent brain."

"I see."

Karlstad laughed grimly. "Wo wanted to open up her skull, enlarge it so there'd be more room for cerebral growth."

"What happened?"

"Sheena was smart enough to recognize what was going on. As soon as she entered the surgical theater she tore loose and ran away. That's when she broke ribs. Arms, too."

"She understood what was going to happen?"

"You bet! She ran back to her own quarters and no one could coax her out. Wo wanted to sedate her and go ahead with the surgery but the medical staff was so banged up that it was impossible."

"And he didn't try again?"

"Not yet," said Karlstad. "But he will. Wily Old Woeful doesn't give up. Not him."

The corridor was down to its nighttime lighting, Grant realized. Most of the research station's personnel were in their quarters or already asleep. No one in sight, except a middle-aged couple strolling hand in hand through the twilight dimness toward them.

"So we have a gorilla roaming around loose back there?" Grant asked.

Karlstad did not reply until the approaching couple passed them. Then, his voice lowered, he answered, "Sheena works as a guard for the aquarium."

"Why does the aquarium need a guard?"

"It doesn't. It's all Wo's brilliant idea," Karlstad said, still in a near whisper. "He carted the animal all the way out here when she was an infant, so he's got to show some practical reason for the expense."

Grant shook his head in wonder.

"At least there's one advantage to Sheena's limited brainpower."

"What's that?"

"She can clean out her own cage," Karlstad said. "And she's toilet trained." He laughed. "You should've seen the mess she made the first time she squatted on a regular toilet. We had to build a specially reinforced bowl for her."

"I guess so," Grant said, not wanting to visualize the scene.

When he got to his own room and slid the door shut, Grant considered sending a message back to Ellis Beech's office on Earth. Dolphins and gorillas. Our intellectual cousins. Then he thought that the New Morality must know about that already. Wo couldn't smuggle a gorilla into the station in total secrecy, even a baby gorilla. And dolphins!

Besides, he thought tiredly, what does it all add up to? Why did Dr. Wo bring these animals here? What's he up to? That's what I've got to find out. That's my ticket out of here, my ticket back to Marjorie and Farside.

It wasn't until he was in bed and drifting toward sleep that he realized Karlstad had tricked him. Meeting Sheena must be one of the initiation rites around here, he thought. I wonder how many guys have fainted from sheer fright. Or wet themselves.

Thinking about it, Grant thought he'd acquitted himself pretty well. Not much for Karlstad to tell the others about, he thought. There's an advantage in being so scared you can't move, he realized.

When Grant finally dozed off, his first night on Research Station *Gold*, he slept fitfully, dreaming of gorillas chasing him while Dr. Wo growled and glared angrily. Marjorie appeared in his dreams briefly, but somehow she changed into tall, slim Lainie smiling at him beckoningly. He tried to move away from her, but Sheena blocked his path. Grant felt trapped and alone, beyond help.

A buzzing noise blurred his dreams, insistent, demanding. He pried his gummy eyelids open and for a moment had no idea of where he was. Then it came into focus: his quarters on *Gold*. His bedsheets were tangled and soaked with his perspiration. With a lurch in the pit of his stomach, Grant realized he had made a nocturnal emission.

It's all right, he told himself, while that stubborn buzzing noise kept rasping in his ears. Wet dreams are natural, beyond your conscious control. There's nothing sinful about them as long as you don't take pleasure from the memory.

The buzzing would not stop. Grant slowly realized it was the phone. He could see its yellow light on the bedside console blinking at him in rhythm with the angry buzzing.

"Phone," he called out, "audio response only."

The screen on the opposite wall lit up to show Zareb Muzorawa's dark, somber face.

"Have I awakened you?" Muzorawa asked.

"Uh, yes," Grant replied. "I guess I've overslept."

"That's natural, your first morning here. Ask the pharmacy for the timelag hormone mix. It will set your internal clock for you."

"Oh . . . really? Okay, I will."

"I've been assigned to your orientation," Muzorawa said, his voice more businesslike. "How quickly can you get to conference room C as in Charlie?"

Still blinking sleep from his eyes, Grant said, "Fifteen minutes?"

Muzorawa smiled, showing gleaming white teeth. "I will give you half an hour. Get to the pharmacy first, then meet me there."

"Yessir," said Grant.

Grant spent the entire morning in a small conference room with Muzorawa, his head spinning with details. The day was a blur of orientation videos, schematics of the station's layout, organization charts of the staff personnel, lists of duties that the various departments were responsible for. Grant had thought he'd known the station's layout and organization from his months of study on the trip out, but apparently most of his information had been terribly out of date.

"Let's break for lunch," Muzorawa said, pushing his chair back from the small oval conference table. The wallscreen went blank and the stuffy little room's overhead lights came on.

"Fine," said Grant, getting to his feet.

As they headed for the cafeteria, Grant noticed that Muzorawa seemed to be lurching as he walked; not staggering, exactly, but the man walked with a hesitant, slightly uncertain gait, as if afraid that he were about to bump into some unseen obstacle or stumble drunkenly into a wall. He was clad in another turtleneck pullover shirt that hung loosely over the same bulky-looking black leather leggings, with metal studs running down their outer seams. His feet were shod in what appeared to be soft moccasins.

Most of the station's other scientific personnel wore casual shirts and slacks, as Grant himself did. The engineers and technicians usually wore coveralls that were color-coded to denote the wearer's specialty.

Once they had filled their trays and found a table, Grant asked, "I'm still not clear about what you actually do here."

Moving his lunch dishes from his tray to the table, Muzorawa asked, "Do you mean me personally, or the station in general?"

"Both, I guess," said Grant, sliding his emptied tray under his chair.

"This station is the headquarters for the ongoing studies of Jupiter's moons," Muzorawa said, as if reciting from a manual. "Almost everyone here on the station is support staff for those studies."

Grant shook his head, unsatisfied. "Okay, I know there are teams studying the life-forms under the ice on Europa and Callisto—"

"And the volcanoes on Io."

"And the dynamics of the ring system."

"And Ganymede and the smaller moons, too."

"But you're not involved in any of that, are you?"

Muzorawa hesitated a moment, then replied, "No. Not me."

"Neither are Egon or Lainie."

"She prefers to be called Lane."

"But none of you is studying the moons, right?"

Reluctantly, Grant thought, Muzorawa replied, "No, we are part of a small group that is studying the planet itself, not the moons or the ring system."

"And Dr. Wo?"

An even longer hesitation, then, "Dr. Wo's official title is station director. He runs the entire operation here. He reports directly to the IAA, back on Earth."

Grant saw that Muzorawa looked distinctly uneasy when Wo's name was mentioned. And no wonder. The director must have the power of life and death over all of us, just about, Grant reasoned.

Lowering his voice to a near whisper, Muzorawa said, "Wo is more interested in Jupiter itself than its moons. That's why he's split us away from the rest of the staff and set us up to study the Jovian atmosphere."

"And the ocean," Grant prompted.

Again Muzorawa hesitated. Grant got the impression that the man was arguing with himself, debating inwardly about how much he should tell this curious newcomer.

"Wo has assigned a small team to study the ocean," he said at last.

"There are only ten of us—plus Dr. Wo himself. And the medical and technical support staffs, of course."

"Why do you need a medical support staff?" Grant wondered.

"The ocean is Wo's obsession," Muzorawa added, actually whispering now. "He is determined to find out what's going on down there."

"So what do you actually work on?"

"Me? The fluid dynamics of the Jovian atmosphere and ocean."

Grant said nothing, waiting for more.

"The atmosphere/ocean system is like nothing we've seen before," Muzorawa said, his tone at last brightening, losing its guarded edge, taking on some enthusiasm. "For one thing, there's no clear demarkation between the gas phase and the liquid, no sharp boundary where the atmosphere ends and the ocean begins."

"There's no real surface to the ocean," Grant said, wanting to show the older man that he wasn't totally ignorant.

"No, not like on Earth. Jupiter's atmosphere gradually thickens, gets denser and denser, until it's not a gas anymore but a liquid. It's . . . well, it's something else, let me tell you."

Before Grant could respond, Muzorawa hunched closer in his chair and went on, "It's heated from below, you see. The planet's internal heat is stronger than the solar influx on the tops of the clouds. The pressure gradient is *really* steep: Jupiter's gravity field is the strongest in the solar system."

"Two point five four gees," Grant recited.

"That's merely at the top of the cloud deck," Muzorawa said, waggling one hand in the air. "It gets stronger as you go down into the atmosphere. Do you have any idea of what the pressures are down there?"

Grant shrugged. "Thousands of times normal atmospheric pressure."

"Thousands of times the pressure at the bottom of the deepest ocean on Earth," Muzorawa corrected. A smile was growing on his face, the happy, contented smile of a scientist talking about his special field of study.

"So the pressure squeezes the atmosphere and turns the gases into liquids."

"Certainly! There's an ocean down there, an ocean ten times bigger than the whole Earth. Liquid water, at least five thousand kilometers deep, perhaps more; we haven't been able to probe that far down yet."

"And things swimming in the water?" Grant guessed.

Muzorawa's smile vanished. He glanced over his shoulder. Then, leaning closer to Grant, he lowered his voice to answer, "The unofficial word is, the deepest probes have detected indications of objects moving in the Jovian ocean."

"Objects?"

"Objects."

"Are they living creatures?"

Muzorawa looked up toward the ceiling, then hunched still closer to Grant, close enough so that Grant could smell a trace of clove or something pungent and exotic on his breath.

"We don't know. Not yet. But Wo intends to find out."

Grant felt a stir of excitement. "How? When?"

Actually whispering again, Muzorawa said, "A deep mission. *Really* deep. And crewed."

"Crude?"

"Crewed. Not robotic. A team of six people."

Grant's jaw fell open. "Down into the ocean?"

Muzorawa made a hushing motion with both his hands and turned to glance guiltily over his shoulder. "Not so loud!" he whispered. "This is all supposed to be top secret."

"But why? Why should it be secret? Who's he keeping it a secret from?"

Muzorawa drew back from Grant. With a shake of his head he said only, "You'll find out. Perhaps."

LEVIATHAN

Leviathan followed an upwelling current through the endless sea, smoothly grazing on the food that spiraled down from the abyss above. Far from the Kin now, away from the others of its own kind, Leviathan reveled in its freedom from the herd and their plodding cycle of feeding, dismemberment, and rejoining.

To human senses the boundless ocean would be impenetrably dark, devastatingly hot, crushingly dense. Yet Leviathan moved through the surging deeps with ease, the flagella members of its assemblage stroking steadily as its mouth parts slowly opened and closed, opened and closed, in the ancient rhythm of ingestion.

To human senses Leviathan would be staggeringly huge, dwarfing all the whales of Earth, larger than whole pods of whales, larger even than a good-size city. Yet in the vast depths of the Jovian sea Leviathan was merely one of many, slightly larger than some, considerably smaller than the eldest of its kind.

There were dangers in that dark, hot, deep sea. Glide too high on the soaring currents, toward the source of the bountiful food, and the waters grew too thin and cold; Leviathan's members would involuntarily disassemble, shed their cohesion, never to reunite again. Get trapped in a treacherous downsurge and the heat welling up from the abyss below would kill the members before they could break away and scatter.

Best to cruise here in the abundant world provided by the Symmetry, between the abyss above and the abyss below, where the food drifted down constantly from the cold wilderness on high and the warmth from the depths below made life tolerable.

Predators swarmed through Leviathan's ocean: swift voracious Darters that struck at Leviathan's kind and devoured their outer members. There were even cases where the predators had penetrated to the core of their prey, rupturing the central organs and forever destroying the poor creature's unity. The Elders had warned Leviathan that the Darters attacked solitary members of the Kin when they had broken away from their group for budding in solitude. Still Leviathan swam on alone, intent on exploring new areas of the measureless sea.

Leviathan remembered when the abyss above had erupted in giant flares of killing heat. Many of Leviathan's kind had disassembled in the sudden violence of those concussions. Even the everlasting rain of food had been disrupted, and Leviathan had known hunger for the first time in its existence. But the explosions dissipated swiftly and life eventually returned to normal again.

Leviathan had been warned of another kind of creature in the sea: a phantasm, a strange picture drawn by others of the Kin, like nothing Leviathan had ever sensed for itself, small and sluggish and cold, lacking flagella members or any trace of community. It was pictured to have appeared once in the sea and once only, then vanished upward into the abyss above.

None of the others had paid much attention to it. It was so tiny that it could barely be sensed it at all, yet for some reason the vision of its singular presence in the eternal ocean sent a chilling note of uneasiness through Leviathan's entire assemblage. It was an unnatural thing, alien, troubling.

SLAVE LABOR

Grant finished his lunch with Muzorawa in guarded silence, his mind spinning with the idea of sending a crewed mission into the vast ocean beneath Jupiter's hurtling clouds.

And it's not the first one, Grant told himself. *Beech knew there'd already been at least one human mission to the planet.*

Once they left the cafeteria, Muzorawa said brightly, "Very well, newcomer, you have received the official orientation."

"And then some," said Grant.

Muzorawa shook his head. "None of that, now! What I told you was strictly in confidence, between the two of us. Besides, most of it was conjecture."

Grant nodded, but his mind was still racing. *What's he afraid of? Why all this secrecy? If there are life-forms in the Jovian ocean, why doesn't Wo announce it like any other scientific discovery? And why is the New Morality so torqued up over this?*

He thought he knew the answer to that last question. Finding any kind of alien life was seen as a threat to belief in God. Every time scientists discovered a new life-form anywhere, some people gave up their faith. Atheists crowed that the Bible was nonsense, a pack of scribbling by ancient narrow-minded men steeped in superstition and primitive ignorance.

Even when biblical scholars and scientists who were also true Believers pointed out that no scientific discovery could disprove the existence of God, the fanatical atheists howled with glee with each new discovery, especially when the cliffside ruins on Mars showed that an intelligent race had lived there millions of years ago.

He hardly heard Muzorawa telling him, "Now you are to go to the personnel office, where you will receive your work assignment."

"What assignment could they possibly have for an astrophysicist?" Grant complained.

Muzorawa grinned at him. "I'm sure Dr. Wo has something in mind for you."

That sounded ominous to Grant.

The personnel office was little more than a closet-sized compartment in the station's executive area. It was only a few doors from the director's more spacious and imposing office.

To his surprise, when he slid open the door marked PERSONNEL, Egon Karlstad was sitting behind the tiny metal desk.

"You're the personnel officer?" Grant blurted.

"This week," Karlstad replied smoothly. "I told you that Wo likes to rotate us through the administrative jobs."

"No, you said—"

"It lets him keep the beancounters down to a minimum, so he can bring more scooters out here," Karlstad continued. "Of course, that means we scooters have to pull double duty all the time, but that doesn't bother our peerless leader. Not at all."

Karlstad seemed too large for the desk. His knees poked up and it looked as if he could touch the opposite walls of the compartment merely by stretching out his arms. The desk itself was scuffed and battered from long use; someone had even kicked a dent into its side.

"Have a seat," Karlstad said.

Grant took the only other chair: It was molded plastic, solid yet comfortably yielding.

"Okay," Karlstad said, turning to the screen built into the desktop. "Archer, Grant A."

Grant could see the glow from the screen reflected on Karlstad's pale features. It made him look even more ethereal than usual.

Without looking up from the screen, Karlstad said, "Grant Armstrong Archer the Third, eh? Illustrious family, I imagine."

"Hardly," Grant replied, feeling a bit annoyed.

"First in your class at Harvard?" Karlstad whistled. "No wonder Wo wanted you here."

"I don't think he picked me personally," Grant said.

"Don't be so sure, Grant A. the Third. Zeb might be right; our wily Dr. Wo can stretch out his tentacles and— Hey! You're married?"

He's got my complete file there, Grant realized. My whole life is on that screen.

Karlstad turned his pallid, watery eyes to Grant. "Did you think being married would get you out of Public Service?"

"Of course not!" Grant snapped. "I love my wife!"

"Really?"

"Besides, Public Service isn't something to be avoided. It's a responsibility. A privilege that goes with adulthood and citizenship, like voting."

"Really?" Karlstad repeated, dripping acid.

"Aren't you doing your Public Service?" Grant demanded.

Karlstad made a derisive snort. "I'm serving out a prison sentence," he said.

"I mean really—"

"It's the truth," Karlstad insisted. "Ask anybody. I'm serving my time here instead of languishing in jail. The Powers That Be decided they'd spent too much money on my education to have me rot in prison for five years."

"Five years!" Grant was shocked. "What did you do?"

"I helped a young married couple to obtain fertility treatments. They had been denied treatment by the government. Population restrictions, you know. I was in the biology department at the University of Copenhagen and I knew a lot of the physicians at the research hospital. So they came to me and begged me to help them."

"But it was illegal?"

"According to the laws of the European Union, which take precedence over the laws of Denmark."

"And the authorities found out about it?"

Karlstad's face twitched into a bitter scowl. "The two little bastards worked for the Holy Disciples—our version of your New Morality."

"It was a sting," Grant realized.

"I was stung, all right. Sentenced to five years. When they offered me a post here, doing research instead of jail, I leaped at it."

"I guess so."

Karlstad huffed. "One should always look before one leaps."

Grant nodded sympathetically. "Even so . . . this is better than jail, isn't it?"

"Marginally," Karlstad conceded.

"I never realized . . ." Grant let the idea go unexpressed.

"Realized what?"

"Oh . . . that the New Morality, or whatever you call it in Europe, I never realized they would entrap people and sentence them to jail."

"They don't like scientists," Karlstad said, his voice going sharp as steel. "They're afraid of new ideas, new discoveries."

"They're trying to maintain social balance," Grant argued. "There's more than ten billion people on Earth now. We've got to have stability! We've got to control population growth. Otherwise we won't be able to feed all those people, or educate them."

"Educate them?" Karlstad's thin eyebrows rose. "They're not being educated. They're being trained to obey."

"I—" Grant saw the pain in the man's pale eyes and clamped his mouth shut. No sense arguing with him about this. One of the first lessons his father had taught him was never to argue over religion. Or politics. And this was both.

Karlstad apparently felt the same way. He forced a smile and said, "So now you know my life story and I know yours."

Grant conceded the point with a nod.

"Let's get on with it."

"Okay."

Turning back to the desktop screen, Karlstad called out, "Computer, display work assignment for Archer, Grant A."

Immediately the synthesized voice responded, "Grant A. Archer is assigned as assistant laboratory technician for the biology department."

Grant jumped out of his chair. "Biology department? That can't be right! I'm not a biologist!"

Karlstad waved him gently back into his seat. "The details are on my screen, Grant. The assignment is correct."

"But I'm not a biologist," Grant repeated.

"I'm afraid that's got nothing to do with it. The operative term is 'assistant laboratory technician.' It doesn't matter which lab you're assigned to; they just need a warm body to do the scutwork."

"But—"

"You're a grad student, brightboy. Slave labor. Cheaper than a robot and a lot easier to train."

"But I don't know anything about biology."

"You don't have to. You can push a broom and clean a fish tank; that's what you're needed for."

"I'm an astrophysicist!"

Karlstad shook his head sadly. "Look, Grant, maybe someday you'll be an astrophysicist. But right now you're just a graduate student. Slave labor, just like the rest of us."

"But how can I work toward my degree cleaning fish tanks?"

With a wry grin, Karlstad replied, "Why do you think nobody's developed real robots? You know, a real mechanical man with a computer for a brain?"

"Too expensive?"

"That's right. Too expensive—when compared to human labor. Grad students are cheap labor, Grant. I've always thought that if anybody does invent a practical robot, it'll be a grad student who does it. They're the only ones with the real motivation for it."

"The biology department." Grant groaned.

"Cheer up," said Karlstad. "Biology department includes the aquarium. You'll get to work with Lainie. Maybe she'll show you how to do it like dolphins."

SOLACE

Grant stumbled back to his quarters, stunned and hurt and angry. Assistant lab technician, he grumbled to himself. Slave labor. I might as well be in jail. This is ruining my life.

He tried praying in the privacy of his quarters, but it was like speaking to a statue, cold, unhearing, unmoved. He remembered that when he'd been a child, back home, he could always bring his tearful problems to his father. It wasn't so much that Dad was a minister of the Lord; he was a wise and gentle father who loved his son and always tried to make things right for him. Later, in school, Grant found that even the most pious spiritual advisor didn't have the warmth and understanding of his father. How could they?

Yet, alone and miserable on this research station half a billion kilometers from home—so distant that he couldn't really talk with his father or wife or anyone else who loved him—Grant sought counsel.

Research Station *Gold* had a chapel, Grant knew from his studies of the station's schematics. A chapel meant there must be a chaplain. Sure enough, Grant found half a dozen names in the phone computer's listing for chaplains. To his surprise, Zareb Muzorawa was one of them, listed under Islam.

There were three Protestant ministers listed: a Baptist, a Presbyterian, and a Methodist. He tried the Methodist first, but was told that the Reverend Stanton was on a tour of duty on Europa.

In Grant's phone screen the Presbyterian minister, the Reverend Arnold Caldwell, looked like a jolly, red-cheeked character from a Dickens novel. Grant's heart sank; Caldwell did not appear to be the kind of strong spiritual guide he needed. But he was available.

"I'll be finished my shift here in the life-support center in less than thirty minutes," he said cheerfully. "Why don't you meet me in the chapel a few minutes after the hour."

Grant agreed, fidgeted in his room for half an hour, then walked briskly to the chapel.

It was an austere compartment, about the size of three living quarters put together. A bare altar stood on a two-step-high platform. There were no decorations of any kind on the walls, not even a crucifix. Two files of empty benches could hold perhaps fifty people, at most, Grant thought.

"Ah, there you are."

Grant turned to see the Reverend Caldwell striding up the central aisle toward him. Round in face and portly in stature, his shoulder-length hair was graying, but his eyes were bright sapphire blue and his ruddy lips were curled into a smile. He looked like a clean-shaven Santa Claus, wearing a technician's olive-green coveralls.

"Reverend Caldwell?" Grant asked, knowing it was an inane question.

"Yes," said Caldwell. "And you must be the young man who phoned me a bit ago."

"Grant Archer."

As they shook hands, Grant said, "You're on the technical staff?"

Caldwell bobbed his head up and down enthusiastically. "Yes indeed. Station policy. There's no room here for full-time clergy, so we all have to work at some secular job and do our ministering on our own time."

"I see," said Grant, thinking that explained Zeb's listing as the Moslem minister.

"I'm with the life-support group, actually. Rather a neat combination, don't you think? By day I worry about people's bodies, by night I care for their souls."

He laughed at his own joke. Grant forced a smile.

Still chuckling, Caldwell murmured, "It seems rather cold in here, doesn't it." Before Grant could answer, Caldwell skipped up the dais to the altar and clicked open a small door built into its side.

The chapel suddenly bloomed into a minicathedral, with stained glass windows lining the walls, a crucifixion scene from the high Renaissance behind the altar, and rows of candles burning. Grant even thought he smelled incense.

"Oh dear, wrong key," Caldwell muttered. "That's the Catholic scheme."

He tried again and the elaborate decorations faded, replaced by slim windows along the side walls streaming sunlight and a gorgeous rosette of deep blues and reds on the rear wall above the entry.

"Ah, that's better."

"Holograms," Grant realized. "They're holograms."

"Yes, of course," said Caldwell. "Many faiths share this chamber, and no two of them agree on the proper kind of interior decoration. The Moslems allow no icons whatsoever, while the Buddhists want to see their revered one. And so on."

Grant nodded his understanding. Caldwell gestured to the first row of benches and they sat side by side. Fearing that a worshipper might come in and interrupt him, Grant spilled out his story as quickly as he could, leaving out only the fact that the New Morality wanted him to spy on Dr. Wo. The Reverend Caldwell listened sympathetically, nodding, his trace of a smile ebbing slowly.

At last Grant finished with, "They're taking four years of my life. Four years away from home, away from my wife. At least I thought I could accomplish something, earn my doctorate, but now . . ." He ran out of words.

"I see," said Caldwell. "I understand."

"What can I do?" Grant asked.

Caldwell was silent for several moments. He seemed lost in thought. His smile had faded away completely.

He heaved a mighty sigh, then said, "My son, the Lord chooses our paths for us. He has obviously sent you here for a reason."

"But—"

"Neither you nor I can see the Lord's purpose in all of this, but I assure you He has a design for you."

"To be an assistant lab technician?"

"Whatever it is, you must accept it with all humility. We are all in God's hands."

"But my life is being ruined!"

"It may seem that way to you, but who can fathom the purposes of the Lord?"

"You're telling me I should accept this assignment and let it go at that? I should be content to be a virtual slave?"

"You should pray for guidance, my son. And accept what cannot be altered."

Grant shot to his feet. "That's no help at all, Reverend."

"I'm sorry, my son," Caldwell said, pushing his rotund bulk up from the bench. "It's the best advice I can offer you."

It took an effort to bite back the angry reply that Grant wanted to make. He held his breath for a moment, then said between gritted teeth, "Well . . . thanks for your time, Reverend."

Caldwell nodded, and his little smile returned. "Come to services Sunday. We have the ten o'clock hour. You'll meet others of the faithful."

"Yes," Grant temporized. "Of course."

"Perhaps if you meet others of your own age it will help you to adjust to your new life."

"Perhaps," Grant said.

He shook hands with the minister and turned to walk up the aisle and out of the chapel, thinking, *The Lord helps those who help themselves. But what can I do to help myself? What can I do when Dr. Wo is against me?*

EXPERIMENTAL ANIMALS

For weeks Grant toiled away in menial drudgery, cleaning glassware in the bio labs, looking up references for the biologists, running their tedious and often incomprehensible reports through computer spellcheck and editing programs, and even scrubbing out the fish tanks in the station's extensive aquarium.

He quickly found that his major function was repairing old and faulty equipment. From laboratory centrifuges to a wallscreen that had developed a maddening flicker, Grant's most intellectual pursuit was reading instruction manuals and trying to make sense of them. One whole afternoon he spent trying to free up a stubbornly stuck drawer in a biochemistry department file cabinet. He finally got the drawer open, but his fingers were battered and the knuckles of both his hands were raw and bleeding.

It was mindless work, sheer dumb labor that a trained chimpanzee could have done. Grant realized that much of the station's equipment was outmoded and long due for replacement. Like the furniture in the living quarters, like the cafeteria and the threadbare carpeting along the main corridor, the laboratory equipment was shabby.

His schedule seemed to be at odds with those of the few friends he had made. Only rarely did he see Karlstad or Muzorawa or any of the others he knew, and when they did manage to sit together in the cafeteria, they discussed their work, the scientific problems they were struggling with. All Grant could talk about was his hours of sweatshop labor.

Muzorawa introduced him to two more members of the small team focused on Jupiter itself: Patricia Buono was a medical doctor, short, plump, with curly honey-blond hair so thick and heavy that Grant wondered how she could keep her head up under the load. Kayla Ukara was from Tanzania, her skin even darker than Zeb's, her eyes seething with a fierce emotion that Grant could not fathom; she seemed perpetually on guard, always ready to snap or snarl.

Karlstad grinned when Grant told him he had met the two women. "Patti and Kayla," he said, with a knowing air. "The butterball and the panther."

"Panther," Grant mused. Yes, it suited Ukara, he thought. A prowling black cat, sleek and powerful and dangerous.

"Know what Patti's name translates to?" Karlstad asked, still grinning.

"What?"

"Patti Buono . . . it means 'pat well.'"

Grant shook his head. Dr. Buono seemed more motherly than sexy. "She's not my type," he said.

"Mine, neither. I like 'em long and lean, like Lainie."

Grant attended chapel services most Sundays, but the people he met there seemed totally indifferent to him. A newcomer, he was not part of their social life. And he didn't know how to break into their cliques and make friends with them.

Then, one Sunday, he saw Tamiko Hideshi at the worship service. Delighted to see a familiar, friendly face, Grant slipped out of his pew to sit next to her.

"I didn't know you were a Presbyterian," Grant said as they left the chapel together.

"I'm not," she said with a toothy grin. "But they don't have any Shinto services, so I rotate among the services that are available. Today is my Presbyter Sunday."

"You go to all the services?"

"Only one per week," she said. "It's like being a spy, sort of: checking on the competition."

Grant's breath caught when she said *spy*, but Tami's cheerful expression showed she had no inkling of his own situation.

He bumped into Lane O'Hara now and then, mostly in the aquarium, but she was strictly business, a staff scooter telling a grad student which chore had to be done next. Now and then he saw her swimming in the tank with the dolphins, a sleek white wetsuit covering her completely yet revealing every curve of her lean, lithe body. She swam among them happily, playfully, as if she were at home with the dolphins, glad to be with them in their element, much friendlier to them than she was to Grant.

Every night Grant prayed for release from his slavery. How am I going to get a doctorate when I'm stuck washing glassware and fixing broken-down equipment?

He felt so depressed, so ashamed of how low he had fallen, that he couldn't bring himself to talk about it in his messages to Marjorie. Guardedly, he told his parents about the situation. His mother was nearly in tears when she replied; his father counseled patience.

"They're just testing you, I'm certain. Do your best and soon enough they'll see that you're too talented to remain a lab helper. This is a test, you'll see."

Grant hoped his father was right but didn't believe a word of it. He begged his parents not to reveal his problem to Marjorie.

He tried to be upbeat and smiling when he spoke to his wife, avoiding any mention of the work he was doing. Worst of all, he realized he was not accomplishing one iota of progress toward his doctorate in astrophysics. There wasn't even another astrophysicist in the station to serve as his mentor—assuming he had time to continue his studies.

Marjorie's messages to him became rarer, as well. She was obviously busy and immersed in her work. She still seemed cheerful and energetic, smiling into the camera for him even when she looked tired and sheened with perspiration. Often she appeared to be in a tent or in some clearing in a tropical forest. Once he saw a raging fire behind her, hot flames licking angrily through the trees and thick oily black smoke billowing skyward, while heavily armed troops in the sky-blue helmets of the International Peacekeeping Force prowled past. Yet she always seemed chipper, enthusiastic, telling Grant excitedly of their success in tracking down hidden drug factories or caches of biological weapons.

Yet Grant saw something in Marjorie's bright, joyful face that puzzled him. For weeks he tried to determine what it was. And then it hit him. She was pleased with herself! She was delighted with the work she was doing, excited to be helping to make the world better, safer—while all Grant was doing was janitorial work in a remote station hundreds of millions of kilometers from home.

And he realized one other thing, as well. Marjorie no longer ended her messages with a count of the hours until they would be reunited.

I've lost her, Grant told himself. By the time I get back to Earth we'll be strangers to each other.

Still he could not bring himself to mention his fears to Marjorie. He could not tell her of his loneliness, his weariness, his growing desperation. He tried to be cheerful and smiling when he spoke to her, knowing that she was doing the same in her messages to him. Is she trying to keep my spirits up? Grant asked himself. Or is she just being kind to me? Does she still love me?

Then he wondered if he still loved her, and was shocked to realize that he did not know whether he did or not.

He saw Sheena often enough, shambling through the narrow corridor of the aquarium or sitting quietly in her glassteel pen, munching on mountains of celery and melons. The gorilla was like a two-year-old child: Her repertoire of behaviors was quickly exhausted and her conversation was limited to a dozen simple declarations. In the back of his mind Grant marveled at the fact that he could accept a talking gorilla as commonplace.

On the other hand, Sheena was so massive and strong that she frightened Grant, even though she showed no indication of violence. But every time he looked into the gorilla's deep brown eyes he saw *something* there, some spark of intelligence that was chained inside her hugely powerful body. Grant had nightmares of Sheena suddenly turning into a roaring, smashing, murderous beast who grabbed him in her enormous hands and began to tear him apart.

The only touch of gratification in Grant's life was the dolphins. Sleekly streamlined, they glided effortlessly through the big aquarium tanks, permanent grins on their faces, clicking and squeaking to one another like a group of chattering schoolkids.

There were six of them, plus a nursing pup that grew noticeably larger every day. They seemed to watch Grant as he stood outside their tanks and looked at them. He thought he could see their eyes focus on him. Grant would wave to them and get a burst of clicking from them.

"They're saying hello to you."

Startled, Grant whirled around to see Lane O'Hara standing a few paces away. Her turtleneck shirt was a warm sunshine yellow, a good complement to her light-brown hair.

"Wave to them again," she said.

Grant did, and got another burst of chatter from the dolphins.

"Did you hear? The same response, don't you know."

"All I heard was a bunch of clicks," Grant said.

"Aye, but it was the *same* bunch of clicks. They have their own language, you know."

"I know they seem to communicate with each other."

"And we're trying to communicate with them."

Grant said, "I've read about attempts to speak with dolphins. They go back more than a hundred years."

"They do," she said.

"With no success," Grant added.

"No success, d'you say? Are you certain about that?"

Thrown on the defensive, Grant replied, "I haven't heard of any."

"Well, then, listen to this." Lane walked to a phone built into a metal partition between transparent glassteel sections of the tanks.

With a knowing look toward Grant, she pressed the phone's ON button and said into its speaker, "Top o' the morning, Lancelot. And to you, Guinevere."

Two of the dolphins swam toward O'Hara, bobbing up and down in the water as they emitted a series of rapid clicks and a squealing whistle.

"And how is little Galahad this morning?"

More chatter from the dolphins. The pup came up toward the window, followed by another adult. Grant stood and watched, trying to suppress a growing feeling of annoyance. Either she's joking with me or she's fooling herself, he thought.

O'Hara said, "I've got to be going now. And it'll be your feeding time in a few minutes. I'll be seeing you all again later."

She jabbed the phone's OFF key and turned away from the window. The dolphins chatted for a few moments, then swam away.

O'Hara was smiling impishly, as if she'd won a major debate. "You see?" she said.

Grant tried to be noncommittal. "Well, you spoke and they chattered, but I don't think you can call that communication."

"Can't you now? Then come with me to the lab."

She started off down the corridor. There was barely room for the two of them to walk side by side in the narrow corridor of the aquarium. As Grant followed her, he noticed that she was limping slightly.

"Did you hurt your leg?" he asked, coming up beside her.

"Hurt it, yes," O'Hara replied. "You might say that."

"How?" he asked. "When?"

"It's not important."

That shut off the conversation. Grant trudged along beside her, noticing that she was still wearing the studded black leggings that Muzorawa and a few others always seemed to wear. He wanted to ask about it, but O'Hara's abrupt cutoff of his questions kept him from speaking.

They ducked through the hatch at the end of the aquarium section and went down the broader main corridor of the station, right past all the biology labs. Grant began to wonder where she was leading him when she stopped and slid open a door marked COMMUNICATIONS LAB—AUTHORIZED PERSONNEL ONLY.

Grant followed her into a compartment that looked like the back room of an electronics shop. Computers lined the walls, most of them blank and unattended, but a few technicians were sitting at desks, earphones clamped over their heads and pin microphones almost touching their lips.

O'Hara directed Grant to an unoccupied computer and told him to sit down and boot it up. Once he'd done that, she leaned over his shoulder and picked up the headset resting on the desktop. She was wearing some kind of scent, Grant realized: something herbal that smelled of flowers from a faraway world.

"Well, put it on," she said, thrusting the headset into his hands.

Grant slipped the set on; the padded earphones blotted out the hum of the machines and the drone of the other subdued voices. As he swung the pin mike close to his mouth, O'Hara doggedly pecked at the keyboard with one extended finger. Her nails were polished a delicate rose pink, he saw.

Then she lifted one of his earphones slightly and said, "There's no visual. You'll just be getting the audio recording."

Grant nodded as she let the earphone snap itself back in place. The computer screen showed the day's date and a time; Grant realized it was just a few minutes ago. This must be a recording of her talking to the dolphins, he thought.

Sure enough, he heard O'Hara's voice: "Top o' the morning, Lancelot. And to you, Guinevere."

Then he heard the clicks and whistles of the dolphins. The computer screen printed: **GREETINGS O'HARA.**

"And how is little Galahad this morning?"

BABY IS GROWING.

O'Hara said, "I've got to be going now. And it'll be your feeding time in a few minutes. I'll be seeing you all again later."

GOOD-BYE O'HARA. GOOD FEEDING.

The screen went blank.

Grant pulled off the headset and looked up at O'Hara. She had an expectant grin on her face. He noticed for the first time that her mouth had just a trace of an overbite; it looked strangely sensuous.

"Well now," O'Hara said. "What do you think of that?"

Grant knew he should be diplomatic, but he heard himself say, "I think the computer could have printed out those responses no matter what kinds of noises the dolphins made."

Her eyes flashed for a moment, but then she nodded thoughtfully. "All right, then. You'll make a fine scientist someday. Skeptical. That's good."

"I mean—"

"Oh, I know what you mean, Mr. Archer. And you'd be right, except for the fact that the computer has stored thousands of the dolphins' responses and categorized them and cross-indexed them very thoroughly."

"That still doesn't mean it's translating what those noises actually mean to the dolphins."

"Doesn't it now? Then how do you explain the fact that every time I say 'good morning' to them they respond with exactly the same expression?"

"How do you know their expression means that they understood what you said and returned your greeting?"

"The phone translates my words into their language, of course."

"Still . . ."

She seemed delighted with Grant's disbelief. Eagerly O'Hara snatched a headset from the computer next to the one Grant was using, slipped it over her chestnut hair, and said into the microphone, "Language demonstration one seventeen, please."

Grant didn't realize he was staring at her until she unceremoniously took him by the chin and pointed his face back to the display screen.

A QUESTION OF INTELLIGENCE

It wasn't a demonstration so much as a tutorial. By Dr. Wo, no less.

Grant sat and watched and listened. And learned. Building on nearly a century of researchers' attempts to communicate meaningfully with dolphins, Wo and a handful of the station's biologists—including Lane O'Hara—had created a dictionary of dolphin phrases.

"If the same phrase is used in the same situation every time," Wo's voice was saying over a video scene of three dolphins swimming in lazy circles, "then one may conclude that the phrase represents an actual word, constructed from actual phonemes—deliberate sounds intended to convey a meaning."

As Grant watched, two human figures clad in black wetsuits entered the tank, trailing sets of bubbles from the transparent helmets that encased their heads. Grant could not make out their faces, but one of them had the supple, slim figure of O'Hara.

The human swimmers bore oblong boxes of metal or plastic strapped to their chests. Dolphinlike clicks and whistles came from them, and the dolphins responded with chatter of their own.

"One may conclude," said Wo's off-camera voice, "that the dolphins have developed a true language. We have been able to transliterate a few of their phrases into human speech sounds, and vice versa."

There was something strange about Wo's voice, Grant thought. It seemed richer, deeper than he remembered it from his one stressful meeting with the director. Then Wo's voice had seemed harsh, strained, labored. Listening to the director on this video presentation, though, his voice came through relaxed and smooth. Maybe it's just me, Grant thought. Maybe he sounded worse to me than he actually was. Still, the difference nagged at him.

" . . . conclusive evidence that the dolphins truly use language can be seen in this demonstration," Wo was saying.

Another human voice—O'Hara's, it sounded like—asked, "Can you blow a ring for me?"

One of the dolphins swam toward her and expelled a set of bubbles from its blowhole that formed a wobbly but recognizable ring. As the circle of bubbles expanded and drifted toward the tank's surface, the dolphin nosed upward and swam through it, squeaking and clicking rapidly.

"Observe," said Wo's voice, "that no reward has been offered for this performance. The only exchange between the human experimenter and the dolphin subject was an audible communication."

At the end of the video Wo appeared in his office, sitting at his desk, peering intently into the camera.

"While much of the dolphins' language remains beyond our grasp, for reasons that are undoubtedly due to the wide gap in environment and socialization between our two species, we have succeeded in creating a primitive dictionary of dolphin speech. That is, we can accurately and repeatedly transliterate human speech sounds into dolphin phonemes, and vice versa. While this is limited to a dozen or so phrases, the work continues and the dictionary will grow."

Wo got up to his feet and walked slowly around his desk. "Our aim, as stated at the outset of this demonstration, is to understand the intellectual workings of an alien intelligence. Thank you for your attention."

The screen went dark, but Grant continued staring at it for several moments more. In the video, Dr. Wo could stand and walk. Yet when Grant had seen him, his legs had been terribly wasted, useless; the man had to stay in a powered wheelchair. But in this video his legs were strong, normal.

As Grant pulled the headset off, O'Hara asked smilingly, "Well, are you convinced now, Mr. Skeptic?"

"What happened to Dr. Wo?"

Her smile winked off. "Ah, yes. That video was made before the accident."

"What accident?"

Her lips tightened, almost as if she were biting them. With a shake of her head, O'Hara replied, "That's best left unsaid, Mr. Archer. Sensitive information, don't you know."

Grant leaned back in the wheeled typist's chair to look up into her brilliant green eyes. "What can be so all-hallowed sensitive? Who am I going to tell? I'm locked up in this station, the only people I see already know all about all this dratted sensitive stuff!"

O'Hara started to reply, then apparently thought better of it. She took a breath, then said, "Those are Dr. Wo's orders. Information is sensitive if he says it is. He's the director and we do what he tells us . . . or else."

"Or else what?" Grant snapped, feeling more irked by the second. "What can he do to us? We're stuck out here already. What's he going to do, send us home with a bad report card?"

She gave him a pitying look. "You don't really want to know what he can do to you, believe me, Mr. Archer."

"Grant," he said automatically. It came out surly, almost a growl.

"Grant," she agreed. "And my friends call me Lane."

He knew she was trying to mollify him, trying to get his mind off the issue of sensitive information and Dr. Wo's powers as director of the station.

But there's something going on here that Wo is keeping secret. He's not even letting the IAA know what he's doing. Is that because the New Morality has its own representatives on the IAA's council?

With a glance at her wrist, O'Hara said, "It's almost past time for lunch. Come on, let's get to the cafeteria before they close it."

Grant followed her through the humming, quietly intense communications laboratory and out into the main corridor. It was bustling with people going back and forth.

Walking alongside Lane, Grant again noticed her limp. *But if I ask her about it she'll tell me to mind my own business,* he thought. *Maybe that's sensitive information, too.*

Instead he asked, "You said your friends call you Lane?"

"That's right." She nodded.

"I heard someone refer to you as Lainie."

Her eyes flicked toward him for just an instant. "And who might that be?" she asked coolly.

Grant hesitated a moment, thinking. "Egon, if I remember correctly."

"Dear old Egon," she murmured.

"Is Lainie a special name? I mean, well . . ."

"It's not a name I prefer. Call me Lane, if you please."

Grant nodded as they continued walking toward the cafeteria. They seemed to be swimming upstream; a tide of people were heading in the opposite direction, coming out of the cafeteria.

"What else did Egon say about me?" O'Hara asked.

An image of her swimming naked with Karlstad amid the dolphins flashed through Grant's mind. But he said, "Um, nothing much."

"Egon has a way of talking about his fantasies as if they were real, don't you know."

"Oh, sure."

She stopped and pulled Grant over to one side of the corridor, practically pinning him against the wall. He felt the strength of her grip against his biceps, the intensity of the glare in her eyes.

"He's said things about me before, you know. Things that are utterly untrue."

Grant looked up into those green eyes and saw smoldering anger.

"What did he tell you?" she demanded.

Shaking his head, Grant said, "I . . . uh, I don't really remember. It was my first day here. Maybe it wasn't him who said it, there were several others around the table."

"And he mouthed off to all of them."

"I don't recall," Grant lied.

"As bad as that, is it?"

Grant had no idea of what to say. He certainly had no intention of repeating what Karlstad had said—boasted about, now that he thought of it.

O'Hara stomped off toward the cafeteria, hurrying through the crowd despite her limp. Grant headed after her.

Sure enough, Karlstad was sitting at a big table, with Patti Buono, Nacho, and several others. Quintero was regaling them with some story that had them all laughing hard. O'Hara seemed to ignore them; she went to the steam table and began filling her tray with a bowl of soup, a sandwich, fruit cup, and soda.

Feeling somewhat relieved but still cautious, Grant slid his tray toward her, grabbing a sandwich and a salad. As he was filling a mug with fruit juice, O'Hara carried her tray toward Karlstad's table.

Grant followed her as O'Hara headed to their table. Karlstad and the others looked up as she approached. Their laughter died away. Grant thought they looked kind of guilty, although that might have been just his overworked imagination.

Karlstad smiled up at O'Hara as she put her tray on the table next to him. Then she picked up her bowl of soup and emptied it onto his head.

Everything stopped. The cafeteria went completely silent, except for

Karlstad's shocked sputtering. He sat there with soup dripping from his ears, his nose, his chin; soggy noodles festooned his thin silver hair.

O'Hara said absolutely nothing. She merely smiled, nodded as if she were satisfied with her work, then picked up her tray and limped off to a different table.

Quintero burst into roaring laughter. Karlstad scowled at him, but the others started to laugh, too.

Grant left his tray and headed out of the cafeteria. He had no desire to be caught in any crossfire.

SUMMONED

For several days Grant steered clear of both Karlstad and O'Hara. He became something of a recluse, avoiding everyone, taking his meals in his quarters, coming out only for his hours of work. But it was impossible to escape the gossip flickering all through the station.

It was a lovers' spat, some said. Other maintained that O'Hara had somehow been wronged by Karlstad and the soup dumping had been her revenge. No, still others insisted: He had rejected her, and she'd humiliated him because he had humiliated her.

He saw O'Hara now and then, despite his best efforts not to. She was constantly working with the dolphins, swimming with them, talking with them. Grant tried to head the other way whenever he saw her, but there was no way to avoid all contact. She seemed cheerful and friendly, though, as if nothing had happened. For that matter, so did Karlstad, when Grant saw him—usually at a distance, in the cafeteria or in passing along the main corridor.

One night, when he couldn't sleep despite watching Marjorie's two latest messages and reading from the Book of Job for what seemed like hours, Grant pulled on a pair of slacks, stuffed a shirt into its waistband, and padded barefoot out to the empty, darkened cafeteria.

He punched the automated dispenser for a cup of hot cocoa. The machine seemed to take longer now to make the brew than it did during the busy hours of the day.

"Can't sleep, hey?"

Startled, Grant spun around to see Red Devlin standing beside him. The Red Devil's bristling hair and mustache stood out even in the shadows of the dimly lit cafeteria. His white jacket was limp, sweaty, unbuttoned all the way down, revealing Devlin's olive-drab undershirt.

"You're up pretty late yourself," Grant replied.

"It's a lot o' work, runnin' this joint."

"I guess it is." The dispenser beeped at last. Grant slid up the plastic guard and reached for his steaming cup of cocoa.

"Need somethin' to put in it?" Devlin asked.

Grant shook his head. "It's got enough sugar already, I'm sure."

"I meant somethin' stronger."

Grant blinked at him.

"I know you're a straight arrow an' all that," Devlin said, "but a man can't go without *some* stimulation now an' then, can he?"

"I don't drink," Grant said.

"I know." Devlin patted Grant's shoulder. "An' you don't even take sleepin' pills, do ya?"

"I've never needed them."

"Until now, huh?"

"I don't want any. Thanks."

"Maybe some entertainment?"

"Entertainment?"

"VR, y'know. I could fix you up with some very good stuff. Just like the real thing. Make a new man o' you."

"No thanks!"

"Now wait, don't get all huffy on me. You're a married man, aren't you?"

"What's that got to do with it?"

"I can work up a VR sim for you, special. Just gimme some videos of your wife and I'll put together a sim that'll be just like she was with you, just about."

Grant's jaw dropped open.

"Sure, I can do it!" Devlin encouraged, mistaking Grant's shocked silence. "I did it for 'Gon, y'know. Fixed him up with Lainie . . . in virtual reality."

My God in heaven, Grant thought. So Egon's fantasies about Lane aren't just wet dreams, after all. He's got a VR session with her in it. Maybe more than one.

"How about it, Grant?" Devlin urged.

But Grant was thinking, If Lane knew about this she'd kill the two of them.

"Well?"

"No thanks," Grant said firmly. "Not for me."

He turned and strode away, splashing hot cocoa from the mug onto his hand, thinking that he'd never let that filthy devil get his paws on videos of Marjorie. Never.

Days later, Grant was in the biochemistry lab, checking the delicate glassware he was taking out of the dishwasher, to make certain nothing had been broken or chipped. The glass tubes and retorts were still warm in his hands. He'd been thinking that it would be much more efficient if they made the lab apparatus out of lunar glassteel, which was unbreakable, but then figured it would cost too much. Cheaper to gather up the broken bits and recast them. Just as graduate students were an economic advantage over robots, old-fashioned chippable lab glassware was used instead of glassteel.

"I haven't seen you for a while."

The voice startled Grant so badly he nearly dropped the hand-blown tubing he was holding.

Looking up, he saw it was Zareb Muzorawa.

"Oh . . . I've been around," said Grant. "I've . . . uh, been pretty busy, you know."

Muzorawa hiked one leg on a lab stool and perched casually on it. Still in those metal-studded leggings, Grant saw.

Very seriously he said, "What happened between Lane and Egon was not your fault, my friend."

"Yeah, sure. I know that." Grant turned back to emptying the dishwasher.

"Lane told me about your conversation with her."

Grant said nothing, kept busy unloading the glassware.

"You can't hide all the time, Grant," Muzorawa said. "The station isn't that big."

Straightening and facing the man, Grant said, "I guess I'm embarrassed, pretty much. I feel really rotten about it."

"It was not your fault. No one is angry at you. Lane and Egon aren't even angry at each other, not anymore."

"I don't see how that could be."

Muzorawa laughed gently. "They had a peace conference. He agreed to stop telling tales about her and she agreed not to decorate him with food anymore."

"Really?"

"Really."

Grant felt better than he had in days. "And they're not boiled at me?"

"Why should they be?"

Before Grant could think of a reply, Muzorawa abruptly changed the subject. "Are you enjoying your work?"

Grant's heart sank again. "That's not a joking matter."

"I was not joking."

Unloading the dishwasher and putting the gleaming glassware in their proper cabinets as he spoke, Grant confessed, "I don't mind the labor; it's the *time* I'm losing that hurts."

"Ah, yes," said Muzorawa, shifting slightly on the stool, stretching his legs as if they pained him.

"I'm supposed to be working toward my doctorate in astrophysics," Grant went on, growing angrier with each word. "How in the name of the Living God can I do that when there isn't even another blast-dratted astrophysicist on the station?"

Muzorawa nodded solemnly. "Yes, I see. I understand."

"I could spend my entire four years here without making a nanometer of progress toward my doctorate."

"That would be a shame."

"A shame? It's a tragedy! This is wrecking my whole life!"

"I put in many hours of dog work," Muzorawa said, "back when I was a grad student in Cairo."

"You're Egyptian?" Grant assumed Egyptians were tobacco-hued Arabs, not deeply black Africans.

Muzorawa shook his head. "I am Sudanese. Sudan is south of Egypt, the land that was called Nubia in ancient times."

"Oh."

"I received my degrees at the University of Cairo."

"I see."

"It's easier for a black man there than at most European universities."

"We have laws against racial prejudice in the States."

Muzorawa grunted. "Yes, I know of your laws. And the realities behind them."

"The New Morality sees to it that there's no racial bias in the schools," Grant said.

"I'm sure."

"They do!"

With a shrug of his broad shoulders, Muzorawa asked, "Tell me, did you take any undergraduate courses in fluid dynamics?"

Caught off-guard again by another sudden change of subject, Grant answered hesitantly, "Uh, one. You need to know some fluid dynamics to understand how stellar interiors work."

"Condensed matter."

Grant nodded. "And degenerate matter."

Muzorawa nodded back and the two of them quickly slipped into a discussion of fluid dynamics, safe and clean, a subject where mathematics reigned instead of messy, painful human relationships.

Within a few minutes Muzorawa was using one of the chem lab's computers to show Grant the problems of the planet-girdling Jovian ocean he was working on. Grant understood the basics, and listened avidly as the Sudanese fluid dynamicist explained the details. In the back of his mind he felt warmly grateful that Muzorawa was taking the time to bring some spark of interesting ideas into his dull routine of drudgery.

It ended all too soon. Glancing at the clock display in the lower corner of the computer's screen, Muzorawa said, "I'm afraid I must go. Wo has called a big meeting with the department heads. Budget proposals."

Nodding, Grant said, "Thanks for dropping in."

Muzorawa flashed a dazzling smile. "It was nothing. And stop being a hermit! Join us at dinner."

"Us?"

"Egon, Tamiko, Ursula . . ."

"Lane?"

He cocked his head slightly to one side. "Yes, maybe even her. But we'll keep her on the opposite side of the table from Egon!"

Grant laughed.

"We'll sit her next to you."

He was as good as his word.

Apprehensive, uncertain, Grant entered the cafeteria with the first surge of people coming in for dinner. As he slowly made his way along the serving line, pushing his tray and making his selections absentmindedly, he looked around for Muzorawa or Karlstad or any of the others. None of them in sight.

Then he saw O'Hara getting into the line, with Muzorawa's bearded face a few heads behind her. By the time he had finished loading his tray, Karlstad, Kayla Ukara, and Tamiko Hideshi were also in line.

Feeling awkward, Grant hesitated a moment, then decided that it was foolish to just stand there dithering. Most of the tables were unoccupied as yet, so he picked an empty one big enough for six and sat down facing the line.

Sure enough, O'Hara came straight to him, still limping slightly. Then Muzorawa and the others. They all sat at Grant's table and said hello as if nothing had happened. Finally Karlstad picked his way deftly through the line and joined them. Muzorawa had saved a seat for him on the opposite side of the table from O'Hara, who had placed herself next to Grant.

Just as Karlstad sat down, the light panels in the ceiling flickered once, twice. They all looked up.

"Uh-oh," said Hideshi.

"Wait," Muzorawa replied softly. "I think it's stabilized . . ."

The lights suddenly went out altogether, plunging the crowded cafeteria into complete darkness. Grant heard the throng of diners moan, an instinctive collective sob of fear and tension that quickly dissolved into grumbling and muttering. He felt his heart thumping beneath his ribs.

"It's stabilized, all right," Karlstad sneered.

"What is it?" Grant asked, breatheless with anxiety. "What's going on?"

Dim emergency lighting winked on, throwing the cafeteria into pools of faint light and deep shadow.

"Power outage," Ukara said, almost hissing the words.

"It happens every now and then," Muzorawa said, calm and reassuring.

We need electrical power to keep the air pumps going, Grant realized, sitting wire-tense in his chair.

"It might be Io's flux tube expanding," Karlstad suggested.

"More likely a plasma circuit between Io and the planet," said Ukara.

"Yes," Muzorawa agreed. "We probably passed through a plasma cloud and it overloaded our generators."

"I don't like this," Hideshi admitted, her voice trembling.

Grant asked, "Plasma clouds jump from the cloud tops to Io?" His own voice sounded high and shaky.

"Not often," Muzorawa replied. "But it has been observed from time to time."

Karlstad muttered, "And we're just lucky enough to be in the middle of it."

"How long—"

The lights came back on. Everyone sighed gratefully. The cafeteria echoed with a hundred chattered, relieved conversations.

It took a while for Grant to feel at ease again. Losing electrical power could be fatal. There are backup generators, he reassured himself. And superconducting batteries that can run the life-support systems for days on end. Still, he treasured the bright, glareless light from the ceiling panels.

Everyone seemed to relax.

"Hell, I was looking forward to a candlelight dinner," someone shouted. People laughed: too loudly, Grant thought.

They're forcing themselves to forget the blackout, he realized. To bury it, pretend it never happened, or at least pretend it'll never happen again.

Karlstad started making cynical jokes about someone in the biology department whom Grant actually knew, a fussy little neurophysiologist who was counting the days until his time was up and he could head back to Earth. O'Hara added to the moment with a story of how she had slipped data from the neurophysiologist's own brain scan into the file for Sheena.

"That was after the gorilla's brain-boost?" Hideshi asked.

"It was," said O'Hara, grinning broadly. "Just a few days after he'd injected Sheena with the neuronal growth hormones."

"But he was looking at data from his own brain?" asked Karlstad.

"That he was. He took one look at the neuronal activity and thought he was going to get the Nobel Prize!"

They all roared with laughter.

"Didn't Sheena break his arm later on?"

"No, that was Ferguson."

"Oh, right. The surgeon."

Abruptly the overhead speakers blared, "GRANT ARCHER, REPORT TO THE DIRECTOR'S OFFICE."

Suddenly fearful, Grant look up toward the ceiling. "What does he want me for?"

"It won't be good news," Karlstad muttered. "It never is when he calls you to his office."

"You'd better get going," Muzorawa said.

"Now? In the middle of dinner?"

Karlstad pointed a finger at him. "When our peerless leader calls, you answer. Without hesitation."

"And without dessert," O'Hara added.

Grant pushed his chair back and got to his feet. "Doesn't he care at all about us?"

Karlstad shook his head. "To tell you the truth, I don't think he cares about anything anymore. Since the accident he's been   "

Muzorawa laid a heavy hand on his wrist and Karlstad snapped his mouth shut with an audible click of his teeth.

"You'd better get to the director's office," the fluid dynamicist said softly. "Dr. Wo doesn't like to be kept waiting."

Grant nodded and headed out of the cafeteria.

There was a dinner tray on Dr. Wo's desk, but Grant saw that the director had hardly picked at his food. The office was uncomfortably warm, as before. Is it part of his dominance technique? Grant wondered. Does he enjoy watching me sweat?

Finally he looked up at Grant, scowling. "You have been in this station long enough to know your way from the cafeteria to this office," Wo rasped as Grant sat before his desk.

"Yessir, I do."

"Then why did it take you so long to get here?" Wo demanded in his grating voice. "Did you go the long way around?"

Grant felt like getting up and storming out of the office, but he held his temper and said nothing.

After a long, silent moment, the director announced grudgingly, "Your duties as a lab assistant are finished. You will report to Dr. Muzorawa tomorrow morning to begin training with the fluid dynamics group."

Grant felt an electric current of surprise race through him.

"That is all. You may go."

"I'll be working with Dr. Muzorawa?" he heard himself say, his voice high with wonder and disbelief.

"That is what I told you, isn't it? Now stop wasting my time. The working day begins at eight hundred hours. Sharp! Understand me?"

"Yessir," Grant said, scrambling to his feet, trying to keep his face impassive and hide the ecstatic grin that wanted to break out. "Thank you, sir."

Wo waved one hand as if brushing away an annoyance.

Grant stepped out into the corridor, slid Dr. Wo's door shut, and leaned against it, his legs rubbery. I'll be doing real work! he rejoiced. Not astrophysics, but real, actual scientific research!

Then his surge of joy drained out of him. I'll be learning more about what they're doing, he thought. I'll be finding out things I should report to the New Morality.

BOOK II

Make me know Thy ways, O Lord;
Teach me Thy paths.

—Psalm 25

COMING-OUT PARTY

When Grant got back to the cafeteria and broke the news of his promotion to his friends, Muzorawa smiled as if he'd known it all along. Grant realized that this was so; the Sudanese must have asked Wo to allow Grant to join his team.

"Zeb, you did this for me!" he gushed. "I don't know how to thank you!"

Muzorawa said, "I did it for *me*, my friend. I need as much help as I can get Wo to give me. Just do a good job, that's all the thanks you need to give."

"This calls for a celebration," said Karlstad. "It's not every day that a grad student is elevated to the ranks of we scooters."

"I'm a scooter now!" Grant realized.

They all nodded, laughing. Ukara actually thumped him on the back.

"What kind of celebration, 'Gon?" asked O'Hara.

"We could go to the staff lounge, I suppose," Muzorawa suggested.

"And drink fruit juice while Wo records every word we say?" Karlstad sneered.

"The lounge is dull," Ukara agreed.

"And bugged," added O'Hara.

Gesturing to the remains of their dinners, littered across the round table, Karlstad replied, "Back in my quarters I've got something a little more celebratory than this glorified pond scum."

"Soymeat isn't pond scum," Hideshi said, feigning indignation. "It's a staple for half the world's population."

"He's talking about the algal salad," Ukara said, almost growling. "And I agree with him."

"Come on," said Karlstad, getting up from the table. "You're all invited to Grant's coming-out party."

"Coming out?"

"Out of slavery," Karlstad said. "Out of the bondage of lab assistantship—"

"And into the indentured servitude of scooterdom," O'Hara finished for him.

As they went down the hall, Grant asked, "Where did that term 'scooter' come from?"

"It means scientist," Ukara answered. "It's a derogatory term invented by the administrators."

"You mean the beancounters," Hideshi said.

"But why 'scooters'?" Grant persisted. "How'd that word get chosen to mean 'scientist'?"

"It's likely a corruption of the word 'scholar,' I should think," said O'Hara.

"Which was in and of itself a derogatory term created by the beancounters," Karlstad added.

"The only time they ever showed any creativity whatsoever," Ukara said, her tone bitter with contempt.

"Maybe it's a corruption of the word 'scoter,'" Hideshi suggested.

Karlstad asked, "Scoter? Isn't that some kind of duck?"

"That's right. An appropriate name for a scientist, don't you think?"

"Queer ducks, that's what we are, for certain," O'Hara agreed.

"Quack, quack," Ukara added, a rare burst of humor for her.

"You mean quark, quark," said Karlstad.

"Only if you're a physicist," O'Hara said. "And a theoretical physicist, at that."

Karlstad's quarters were almost identical to Grant's, as far as their dimensions and layouts were concerned. But Karlstad had decorated his room with long hydroponic trays of plants, and as soon as they entered the room the wall screens lit up with views of beautiful Earth forests and meadows. Soft music began to play, too. Grant could not recognize it, but it sounded symphonic, melodious, relaxing.

"Welcome to my humble abode," Karlstad said grandly as they entered and looked around.

Most of the floor was covered with a colorful carpet. Where did he get that? Grant wondered.

"You said something about celebratory ingestants?" Ukara asked.

"Indeed I did," Karlstad replied, heading for the closet.

Grant felt a pang of worry. He must have alcoholic spirits, he thought. Then, realizing that Karlstad was a biophysicist and his room thick with green plants, Grant wondered, Is he growing something illegal in here? Stimulants? Narcotics?

Instead, Karlstad pulled several plump cushions from the closet and tossed them onto the floor. As the others settled themselves on the cushions, Karlstad led Grant to the one upholstered chair in the room.

"You get the seat of honor tonight," he said grandly.

Grant saw that Muzorawa had hunkered down next to him, leaning his back against the wall. Karlstad went to the small refrigerator in his kitchenette area.

"Wine," he announced, pulling out a dark-colored flask and holding it over his head. "The finest rocket juice, fresh from the rock rats in the Belt. Guaranteed never to have seen an Earthly grape."

"One hundred percent totally artificial, is that it?" huffed Ukara.

"The finest product of the prospectors out among the asteroids," Karlstad said.

Grant took in a breath. He had drunk wine before. It was all right.

But Muzorawa bent close to him and said in a near whisper, "If you're not accustomed to alcoholic drinks, be careful of that stuff. It's quite potent."

"I don't have enough glasses," Karlstad told them. "You'll just have to pass the flask around."

"How unsanitary," Hideshi said, grinning. She grabbed the flask out of Karlstad's hand and took a swallow. She gagged, coughed, then croaked out, "Smoooooth," and handed the flask to Ukara.

"Hey, wait," Karlstad snapped. "The guest of honor should go first." He recaptured the flask and handed it to Grant.

Cautiously, Grant barely let the liquor touch his lips. It burned the tip of his tongue and went on burning all the way as he let the minuscule sip trickle down his throat. Feeling his eyes tear, he handed the flask to Muzorawa.

Who solemnly passed it on to Kayla Ukara without touching it. Moslem, Grant realized. Alcohol is forbidden to them.

Standing in the middle of the room as the five others passed the flask around, Karlstad said, "I also have some chemical concoctions for those who don't care for asteroidal wine."

Muzorawa said pleasantly, "Some hash would be welcome."

Grant felt totally shocked.

Heading for his fridge again, Karlstad said, "Devlin says he's run out of stock—"

"The Red Devil, out of stock?" O'Hara looked totally shocked at the idea.

"He's probably just trying to run up the price," Ukara grumbled.

"Whatever," Karlstad said as he handed Muzorawa a pair of pinkish gelatin capsules. "Doesn't matter. I've got a couple of bright kids in the biochem lab who swear this stuff is an almost exact analog of one of the tetrahydrocannabinols."

Seeing Grant's horrified expression, Muzorawa smiled. "It's perfectly all right, my friend. This concoction is quite similar to one used medicinally to alleviate stress . . . even by members of the New Morality."

"It is?"

Holding the capsules in the palm of his hand, Muzorawa said, "It's a tranquilizer. Nothing more. I believe in the States it's marketed under a trade name: De-Tense, I believe."

"Oh."

"Although this is a rather higher concentration of its active ingredients, I should think." With that, Muzorawa popped the capsules into his mouth and swallowed them dry.

Grant wished he had some fruit juice, but he felt too intimidated to ask Karlstad for some. Instead, he pretended to sip at the asteroidal wine when the flask passed his way again and sat watching as the real drinkers got louder and happier.

After several rounds the flask was empty. Karlstad pointed to the refrigerator. "Help yourselves to whatever you can find," he said, slightly slurring the words. "Mi fridge es tu fridge." He knitted his brows in puzzlement for a moment. "Or is it esta?"

That started a boisterous discussion about the Spanish language, which quickly evolved into an argument about the charms of Barcelona versus the attractions of Paris. Then someone brought up Rome.

"Cairo," Muzorawa murmured dreamily. "None of you have been to Cairo, have you?"

"That pesthole?" Hideshi said. "It's overcrowded and filthy."

Resting his head against the wall, Muzorawa smilingly replied, "That overcrowded and filthy pesthole has the grandest monuments in the world sitting just across the river."

"The pyramids," said O'Hara.

"And the Sphinx. And farther upriver the Valley of the Kings."

"And Hatshepsut's tomb. One of the most beautiful buildings of all antiquity."

"You've seen it?" Muzorawa asked.

O'Hara shook her head. "Only in virtual reality tours. But it's truly grand and impressive."

Without Grant's seeing her do it, O'Hara had unpinned her hair. Now it flowed like a long chestnut cascade over one shoulder and down almost to her hip.

But she was deep in conversation with Muzorawa now. The others were all talking among themselves, as well. Karlstad and the two other women were head to head off by his bed in an intense three-way discussion of something or other. Grant was completely out of it. Some guest of honor, he thought. His mouth felt dry, so he got up from the chair and went to the refrigerator. Its shelves were bare, except for a small plastic case that held three more capsules and what looked like the last few slices of a loaf of bread, green with mold.

Grant suddenly felt tired. And bored. He thought parties should be more fun than this. I'll go back to my quarters and send a message to Marjorie, he thought.

He crossed the room and reached the door without anyone paying any attention to him.

Clearing his throat loudly, he said to them, "Uh, thanks for the party. It was great."

"You're leaving?" Karlstad looked shocked.

Grant forced a smile. "I've got to start work with the fluid dynamics group tomorrow morning, bright and early. Director's orders."

Muzorawa gave him a wobbly wave. "Good man. See you at eight sharp."

Grant nodded, opened the door, and stepped out into the corridor. No one said another word to him. Karlstad barely looked up. As he shut the door, Grant recognized that he wasn't the central focus of the party, he was merely the excuse for having it.

DESSERT

Grant was surprised to see so many people still roaming along the corridor. His wristwatch read 21:14. It's early, he saw. For several moments he simply stood there as people passed by, staring at the quickly flicking numerals counting out the seconds. How many seconds until I can get back to Earth, back to Marjorie—if she still wants me? He didn't dare try to calculate the number.

It was only a few meters to his own door. Better get to sleep, he told himself, and start tomorrow fresh and alert. But just as he started to tap out his security code, he felt a hand on his shoulder.

It was O'Hara. Tall and lithe, with her hair still tumbling down past one shoulder. She smiled at him.

"You never had dessert," she said.

Grant had to think a moment. "That's right," he said. "I never did."

"Come on." She tugged gently at his arm. "I've got a cache of ice cream in my place. And some real Belgian chocolate."

Grant allowed her to lead him to her quarters, only a few paces farther along the corridor.

"Has the party broken up already?" he asked.

"No, but it was going downhill, don't you think? Egon and the colleens were getting pretty frisky with each other. I don't like group scenes."

"What about Zeb?"

"He's retreated into his own private little mirage. Lord knows what he dreams about, but it's not fun watching him staring off into space."

They had reached her door. She pecked out the security code and they stepped in.

O'Hara's room was the same size and shape as the other quarters, but it was completely different from anything Grant had seen in the station. The wallscreens displayed underwater scenes from Earth's oceans: myriads of colorful fish, octopi pulsing and waving their suction-cupped tentacles, sharks gliding past menacingly. The floor began to glow, too. Before Grant's eyes a coral reef swarming with more fish took shape and fell steeply off into an endless, bottomless abyss. Grant flattened himself against the closed door, suddenly giddy with vertigo.

O'Hara noticed his near panic. "Now don't be alarmed. The floor's quite solid." She tapped on it with one moccasined foot. "See? I forget that people are thrown off by the effect. I don't have visitors in here very often."

Taking a breath, Grant stepped out onto the floor. It felt firm enough, but it seemed he could stare down into the teeming crystal-clear sea for thousands of meters.

"Look up, why don't you," O'Hara suggested.

The stars! Instead of a ceiling, Grant saw the infinite bowl of black night, spangled with thousands of stars. The underwater scenes on the walls vanished, replaced by more stars. It was like being far out at sea on a clear moonless night.

"That's what we'd see if we were outside the station," she explained. "Minus Jupiter, of course. I could put Jupiter into the display but it would overpower the grand view of it all, don't you think?"

He nodded dumbly, staring at the stars. They looked back at him, solemn, unblinking.

"That one's Earth," O'Hara said, standing close enough to touch shoulders and pointing to one bright bluish dot of light among the hosts of stars.

Earth, Grant thought. It looked awfully far away.

"It's a regular planetarium," he heard himself say in a hushed voice.

"My father ran the planetarium in Dublin," O'Hara said. "He sent me the program."

"But . . . where's the projector? How do you get all those stars on the ceiling . . . and make it look, well, almost three-dimensional?"

"Microlasers," she said, moving away from him. "I sprayed the ceiling and floor with 'em."

"There must be thousands of them," Grant conjectured.

"Oh, yes," O'Hara replied, halfway across the room. "And more on the floor, of course."

"How did you do it? Where did you get them?"

"Built them in the optics shop." She popped open the door of the small refrigerator; its light spilling into the room broke the illusion of being out in the middle of the sea.

"I promised you ice cream and chocolate and that's what you're going to have," O'Hara said, as if there had been some question about it.

But Grant's mind was on more practical matters. Walking through the starlit darkness, across the softly glowing floor, he asked, "You built thousands of microlasers? All by yourself?"

"They're only wee crystals, a hundredth of a cubic centimeter or so." She was rummaging in a drawer by the light of the still-open fridge.

"And you built thousands of them?"

"I had some help."

"Oh."

She handed Grant a small plate with a scoop of vanilla ice cream in it, topped by a small dark piece of chocolate.

"I used nanomachines," she said.

"Nanomachines?"

"Of course. How else?"

"But that's against the law!"

"On Earth."

"The law applies here, too. Everywhere."

"It doesn't apply at Selene or the other Moon cities," O'Hara pointed out.

"But it should. Nanomachines can be dangerous."

"Perhaps," she said, slamming the refrigerator door shut with a nudge from her hip.

"I mean it," Grant said. "On a small station like this, if the machines get loose they could kill everybody."

Holding her own plate of ice cream in one hand, O'Hara took Grant by the sleeve and guided him to a low couch beneath the stars. He sat awkwardly and sank into the couch's yielding softness.

Sitting beside him, she said, "Eat your ice cream before it melts."

He was determined not to be deterred. "Lane, seriously, nanomachines are like playing with fire. And what if Dr. Wo found out?"

She laughed. "Wo started using nanotechnology here more than a year ago."

Grant felt stunned.

"It's all right, Grant," said O'Hara. "We're not terrorists. We're not going to develop nanobugs that eat proteins. We're not going to cause a plague."

"But how can you be sure?"

"They're *machines*, by all the saints! They don't mutate. They have no will of their own. They're nothing but tiny wee machines that do what they're designed to do."

Grant shook his head. "They're outlawed for good reason."

"Certainly," she agreed. "On Earth, with all its billions of people, nanotechnology could easily fall into the hands of terrorist fanatics, or lunatics, or just plain thrill-seekers. But it's different here, just as it's different in the lunar cities."

"They claim they need nanotechnology to survive on the Moon," Grant muttered.

"Of course they do. And we need it here, too."

Looking up at the stars, Grant sneered. "For interior decoration?"

In the darkness, he heard her take in a sharp breath. Then she answered, "For that. And other things."

"Such as?"

She hesitated again. "Maybe you'd better ask the director about that."

"Sure," Grant said. "Wo is going to unburden his soul to me. All I have to do is ask."

She laughed gently. "You're right. Wo's just allowed you to step up a notch. This wouldn't be the time to ask him sensitive questions."

"There's that word again."

"Which word?"

"Sensitive. Every time I ask just about anything, somebody tells me it's sensitive information."

"Ah, yes."

"What's going on, Lane? What on earth is so blasted sensitive about studying Jupiter?"

For long moments she was silent. Then, in the starlit shadows, she reached up and removed the long cascade of hair that had draped down her back. Grant saw that her scalp was completely bald.

Even in the dimmed lighting she saw his shocked expression. "It's the depilation treatments, don't you know. We've got to be completely hairless, all over."

"Hairless? Why?"

"For the immersion," Lane said. "Once we're in the ship."

"What ship?"

"The submersible that's being repaired for the deep mission."

Grant felt an electric jolt of alarm flash through him. Then he asked, very deliberately, "What in the name of the Living God are you talking about?"

O'Hara took a deep breath. "It's just not fair to keep you totally in the dark. Now that you're a scooter, you'd think Dr. Wo would tell you about it."

"Why don't you tell me?"

"I will. I am. But don't let anyone know I told you. Not a word to anyone! Promise?"

Grant nodded. "I promise."

She drew in another breath. Then, in a hushed voice, a faint whisper, as if she were afraid of being overheard, she began, "There was a mission below the clouds, into the ocean, but we had an accident. A scooter was killed. Poor Dr. Wo and his second-in-command were both terribly injured."

"You too?" And Zeb?"

"All of us were battered. We asked Selene for medical help—nanomachines to inject into the injured bodies and repair the damage."

"But what about tissue regeneration? You don't need nano—"

"The damage was too severe."

"Too severe even for stem cell regeneration?"

She nodded in the dim light of the stars. "As I said, a man was killed. They had to put poor Dr. Wo's legs in frozen stasis until the experts from Selene arrived. By the time they came, most of his injuries were beyond repair. The spinal cord neurons had degenerated too far even for the nanomachines to rebuild them properly."

Grant sank back into the couch's cushiony softness. "So that's why he's in a powerchair."

"Yes. And they had to send Dr. Krebs back to Selene for microsurgery."

"Who's Dr. Krebs?"

"She was second-in-command of the mission."

"And this all happened more than a year ago?" Grant asked.

"It did."

Grant thought a moment, then asked, "So what's that got to do with that saucer thing stuck on the far side of the station?"

"That's the ship they were in."

"Oh, for the love of God."

"They had entered Jupiter's ocean. That's when the accident happened."

"In the Jovian ocean," Grant muttered. "And Wo wants to go back."

"They're rebuilding the submersible."

"But Wo's in no physical condition to go."

He heard the clink of her spoon on the dish she was holding. "It's melting," she said.

"Wo can't go on the next mission into the ocean. Zeb told me it's supposed to be a deep probe."

"He told you that?"

"Yes."

"You're right, I suppose. Although I don't really know. Wo is a very determined man. He's taking all kinds of nanotherapies and stem cell injections. He still thinks he can rebuild his body, regenerate the spinal cord neurons or replace them with biochip circuitry."

"He's crazy!"

"Of course," she said calmly. "Aren't we all? But he's in charge here, and he's determined to find out what those things in the ocean are."

Grant's head was starting to spin. He dipped his spoon into the ice cream. It was soupy.

"Zeb and I are going to start training for the next mission," O'Hara said. "That's why Zeb needs you to take over some of his load in the fluid dynamics program."

"You're going?"

"Oh, yes," she said in a flat, resigned tone. "All the survivors of the first mission have been assigned to the new one."

"Is that why you wear those leggings?"

"That's for the implants. They wired our legs with biochips. It's the first step in the mission adaptation."

"Wired . . . ?"

With a struggle, O'Hara pushed herself up from the couch. Grant heard her spoon clatter to the floor.

"Oh, dear. I've spilled the ice cream."

Grant said, "I'll help you clean it up." But it wasn't easy to get out of the couch. He put his plate on the floor, yet it still took two tries before he could stand up.

"I'm afraid some of it got onto your slacks," she said, heading for the kitchenette.

"That's all right. It'll wash out."

"Here's a washcloth," she said, coming back toward him and handing him the damp cloth.

Grant couldn't see very well in the starlight. The glow from the floor simply threw most of his slacks into a soft shadow. He dabbed at the stain.

"I'm terribly sorry to be so clumsy," O'Hara said, sounding genuinely upset about it.

"It's all right. Accidents ha—" He didn't finish the thought, remembering what she'd just told him about Wo's disastrous mission into the Jovian ocean.

"It's my legs, you see," she went on. "I haven't been able to work them right since they implanted the biochips. They tell us not to worry, that legs are pretty useless anyway when you're floating around in the ship, but that doesn't make it any easier here and now, not at all."

"Don't worry about it." Grant thought it sounded inane, but he didn't know what else to say.

They were standing together in the starlit dimness, so close that he could feel her breath on his cheek. Grant wanted to hold her, clasp her close and kiss her and lift her off her feet and carry her back to the couch. He could feel the electricity crackling between them.

Lane stood before him, silent now, unmoving, as if waiting for him to do something, make a move, speak a word.

"I'd better be going now," he heard himself say, his voice shaky.

"I suppose so," she responded.

"Thanks for telling me," he said. Then, trying to lighten the moment, he added, "And for the ice cream."

She smiled sadly. "You're wearing it on your slacks, I'm afraid."

He made a shrug. "Not a problem."

They walked to the door together and she slid it open. On impulse, he kissed her swiftly, lightly on the lips.

She rested one hand on his shoulder but whispered, "It doesn't work that way, Grant. Not anymore. It's the biochips, you see . . . it's like being neutered."

Grant stumbled back from her, shocked.

"Maybe after the mission," O'Hara said, sounding bleak and hopeless as an orphaned child. "Maybe then, when they remove the biochips . . ."

Not knowing what to say, not knowing if there was anything he *could* say, Grant stepped out into the corridor and strode quickly away.

Neutered! The word echoed in his mind. Wo did this to her. To Zeb and everyone else who's assigned to the mission. No wonder she got so boiled at Egon; he knows damned well she wouldn't . . . she can't . . .

His mind spun. But then, as he walked aimlessly past his own door and continued blindly along the corridor, he realized that Lane had said she'd be interested in him after the mission, after the neurosurgeons had restored her to normal.

She knows I'm married, Grant said to himself. And I kissed her. I wanted her! I would've broken my marriage vows. He knew he should feel ashamed, desolated. Infidelity in the mind was almost as bad as actual adultery, he knew.

Yet, instead, he felt strangely excited, almost pleased with himself. That's wrong, he raged silently. You're committing a sin.

Three uniformed guards were walking up the corridor toward him, two women and the guard captain, a tall, burly Albanian with a large patrician nose and a graying buzz cut. He had the physique of a weight lifter: muscles bulged beneath his skintight shirt.

"Working late, are you?" asked the captain in an easy, friendly tone. Still, Grant felt a slight hint of menace beneath the words.

"I'm just heading for my quarters," Grant said.

The three of them glanced at the wet stain on Grant's slacks. Both women grinned.

Grant felt his cheeks burn. It must look like I've wet myself. Or—he reddened even more. My god, what am I going to do? How can I survive here?

DYNAMICS

Grant buried himself in his new job in Muzorawa's lab. To his happy surprise he found himself becoming truly fascinated by the fluid dynamics of Jupiter's ocean.

Muzorawa had constructed a computer model of the planet-girdling ocean, based on data from the probes they had sent below the clouds. It was at best a set of rough approximations. Grant was determined to refine them and generate a true picture of how that vast ammonia-laced sea actually behaved.

They worked together in the fluid dynamics lab. Grant thought it was slightly ridiculous to call the cramped little compartment a laboratory. There was no real experimental work going on. The only equipment there was a desktop-size hypersonic wind tunnel, a small shock tube—which looked like nothing more than a narrow length of stainless steel pipe—and a two-meter-tall transparent tank that served as a cloud simulator. There was nothing in the lab that could simulate the pressures and temperatures of the Jovian ocean. Actually, there was no laboratory apparatus in the solar system that could come close to simulating Jovian conditions. So they worked with computer simulations, instead: electronic approximations to reality, programs that accepted what little they knew and played it back to them.

GIGO, Grant thought. Garbage in, garbage out. On outdated computers, at that. Equations were no substitute for real data.

"This research would make a good doctoral thesis," Muzorawa told him one day as they sat side by side at the computer desk.

"Doctoral thesis?" Grant echoed.

The Sudanese cocked his head slightly, as if thinking about the matter. At last he replied, "Yes, if you don't mind switching your subject to planetary astrophysics instead of stellar."

Grant mulled the idea. I could put my time here to good use, he thought. Instead of wasting the four years I could come out of this with a doctorate . . . and then go on to what I want to do after I get a university post.

"You would have to do all the course work, naturally," Muzorawa went on in his deliberate, considered manner. "We can get the necessary materials sent from my department at Cairo. I can provide the supervision for it and—"

Grant's eyes widened. "You're on the faculty at Cairo?"

"In the physics department," Muzorawa answered matter-of-factly. "Professor of fluid dynamics."

"That's the oldest university in the world," Grant marveled.

Muzorawa smiled slowly. "Yes, true. Al-Azhar was founded in the tenth century by the Ismali Fatimids. It was co-opted into the University of Cairo somewhat later." His smile broadened. "The physics department is a comparatively new addition."

"But what are you doing here if you've got a full professorship at Cairo?"

Muzorawa seemed almost surprised by Grant's question. "I am here to study Jupiter's interior. It's the greatest problem in fluid dynamics that is accessible to direct observation."

"You're here voluntarily?"

The black man nodded gravely. "I intend to remain here as long as I can. Jupiter's ocean is the kind of problem that can take a lifetime and more."

Grant could only shake his head in awe. This is my mentor, he thought with pride. He's going to be my thesis advisor. It didn't occur to Grant to wonder about the sanity of a man who willingly chose to live in an orbiting station that never got closer to Earth than six hundred million kilometers.

That night, for the first time in months, Grant sent genuinely happy messages to Marjorie and his parents. He hadn't heard from his wife in more than a week, but he knew she was busy. She'd looked tired in her last message, weary and apprehensive. Is she ill? He wondered. Is she hiding something from me? Does she still love me?

He wondered about that. How can you stay in love with someone when you're separated for six years, millions of kilometers apart? He was struggling to keep thoughts of Lane O'Hara out of his conscious mind, out of his dreams, even. Marjorie was surrounded by handsome young military officers and university graduates on their Public Service tours of duty: dozens of them, hundreds of them.

Still, he had good news to tell her for the first time since he'd shipped off Earth, and he kept smiling all through his message to her. It wasn't until the computer was off for the night and all the lights in his room were turned down and he was alone in bed in the darkness that his fears about Marjorie warped his face into a pained mask of misery. He tried to pray, but the words felt empty, useless.

As the weeks passed, Muzorawa spent more and more of his time training for the coming crewed mission, less and less on the fluid dynamics problem.

"I'm afraid it's going to be mostly on your shoulders," Muzorawa told Grant.

"I can handle it."

"I'm sorry to lay all this work on you," Muzorawa went on, staring at the graph Grant had put on the wall screen.

"You can't be in two places at one time," Grant said.

"Still . . . I wanted to get this work in better shape before handing it off to you."

"You've done the lion's share," Grant assured him. "Setting up the basic equations and all."

Muzorawa nodded, but his face showed that he was not satisfied with the situation.

Grant was. For the first time since leaving Earth he had some real work to do. A challenge. It wasn't stellar astrophysics, but it was almost as good. Nobody understood how Jupiter's interior worked. Nobody! It was unexplored territory and Grant had the opportunity to blaze a trail through the unknown. He intended to make the best of it.

He'd been surprised, at first, when he found that Muzorawa's fluid dynamics "group" consisted of the Sudanese alone.

"I thought Tamiko worked with you," Grant had said.

"She did, studying the clouds, mainly," Muzorawa replied. "But she was reassigned to the problem of Europa's ocean."

There had been two other fluid dynamicists, Muzorawa told him.

"Lucy Denova was a fine scientist," he recalled, "with a first-rate mind. But the instant her tour of duty here ended she fled back to Selene.

She's teaching at the university there now. She still checks in with me now and then." He chuckled wryly. "But she wants no part of this station. Not at all. She prefers her home on the Moon."

Grant couldn't blame her, especially if she had a position on a tenure track at Lunar U.

"And who was your other assistant?" he asked.

"Not an assistant, my friend. He was Dr. Wo himself."

"He's a fluid dynamicist?"

"He was, before he was elevated to the directorship. Even so, we worked together quite a lot—until . . ." Muzorawa hesitated.

"The accident," Grant finished for him.

"You know about that."

"A little."

"A little knowledge can be a dangerous thing," Muzorawa misquoted.

"Then I ought to get more knowledge," said Grant.

Muzorawa didn't argue the point. Neither did he add to Grant's knowledge of the accident.

The fluid dynamics problem he faced, Grant quickly learned, was that they were trying to study conditions that had never been experienced before. With meager data, at that. Hundred of automated probes had been sent into the unmeasured deeps of the Jovian ocean, but the data they returned were nothing more than a series of pinpricks in a sea of ignorance ten times wider than the whole Earth.

Squeezed relentlessly by Jupiter's massive gravity, the thick, turbulent Jovian atmosphere is compressed into liquid some seventy thousand kilometers below the visible cloud tops: a strange and unknown ocean, water heavily laced with ammonia and sulfur compounds. Yet the ocean's temperature is far below the Earth-normal freezing point; under Jupiter's merciless pressure, the water liquefies despite its frigid temperature. With increasing depth, though, the sea becomes increasingly warmer, heated by the energy flow from the planet's seething interior.

That ocean is at least five thousand kilometers deep, Grant saw. More than five hundred times deeper than the deepest trench in any ocean on Earth.

And that was barely scratching the surface of gigantic Jupiter. For the first time, Grant began to understand how truly immense the planet was.

The numbers didn't even begin to tell the story; they couldn't. Jupiter was just too mind-numbingly *big* for mere numbers.

An ocean more than ten times wider than Earth and five hundred times deeper, yet it is nothing more than a thin onion-skin layer on the planet's titanic bulk. Below that ocean lies another sea, an immense brain-boggling sea of liquefied molecular hydrogen almost sixty thousand kilometers deep. Nearly eight times deeper than the whole Earth's diameter!

And below *that* the pressure builds more and more, millions of times normal atmospheric pressure, compressing the hydrogen into solid metal, sending the temperature soaring to tens of thousands of degrees. There might be another ocean deep below those thousands of kilometers of metallic hydrogen, an ocean of liquid helium. On Earth, helium liquefies only a few degrees above absolute zero. Yet deep within Jupiter's interior, helium becomes liquefied despite the ferocious temperatures at the planet's core because all that incredible pressure squeezing down from above doesn't give its atoms room enough to go into the gaseous state.

At the planet's very heart lies a solid rocky core, at least five times larger than Earth, seething with the appalling heat generated by the inexorable contraction of the stupendous mass of material pressing down to its center. For more than four billion years Jupiter's immense gravitational power has been squeezing the planet slowly, relentlessly, steadily, converting gravitational energy into heat, raising the temperature of that rocky core to thirty thousand degrees, spawning the heat flow that warms the planet from within. That hot, rocky core is the original protoplanet seed from the solar system's primeval time, the nucleus around which those awesome layers of hydrogen and helium and ammonia, methane, sulfur compounds—and water—have wrapped themselves.

Jupiter's core was far beyond any physical probe. Grant had to be satisfied with equations that estimated what it must be like. But that onion-skin ocean of water, that was his domain now. He was determined to learn its secrets, to probe its depths, to resolve its mysteries.

Grant's task was to learn as much as he could about that huge ocean. The first crewed mission had failed disastrously because they had been unprepared for the conditions to be found down there. Grant drove himself fiercely to make certain that the next human mission into Jupiter's ocean would not end the same way.

There were currents in that sea, swift vicious currents that tore through the planet-girdling ocean, ferocious jet streams racing endlessly. With the heat flowing from deep below, the Jovian ocean pulsed and throbbed in constant turbulent motion. Storms raced across its surface and roiled the sea with the energy of a million hurricanes.

Muzorawa spent very little time in the lab now; almost his every waking hour was taken by his training for the probe mission. The Sudanese physicist dropped in to the fluid dynamics lab now and then, but for the most part Grant worked alone, struggling with the attempt to map out the major global jet-stream patterns. At first Grant had been upset by his mentor's increasingly long absences, but as the weeks ground past, Grant realized that Zeb trusted him to do the necessary work. I'm freeing him for the deep mission, Grant told himself. If I weren't here to do this job, he wouldn't be able to prepare for the mission.

Late one afternoon Muzorawa stepped into the lab and sagged tiredly into the empty chair next to Grant.

"How goes the struggle, my friend?"

"You'd think that someone would have solved the equations of motion for turbulent flow," Grant complained, looking up from his work.

"Ah, yes, turbulent flow." Muzorawa flashed a gleaming smile despite his evident weariness. "In all the centuries that physicists and mathematicians have studied turbulent flow, it still remains unresolvable."

"It's chaotic," Grant grumbled. "You can't predict its behavior from one blink of the eyes to the next."

"Is that a new unit of measurement you've invented, the eyeblink?" Muzorawa chided gently.

Grant saw the weariness in Zeb's red-rimmed eyes. "No," he joked back, "I think Galileo invented it."

"If you could solve the equations of turbulent flow you could predict the weather on Earth months in advance," Muzorawa said, stroking his bearded chin. "That would win you a Nobel Prize, at least."

"At least," Grant agreed.

"Until then, you must do the best you can. We need to know as much as possible about the currents and how they change with depth."

"I'm working on it," Grant said, without feeling much confidence. "But the data points are few and far between, and the mathematics isn't much help."

"Situation normal," said Muzorawa. "All fucked up."

Grant flushed with shock. He'd never heard Muzorawa use indecent language before.

"I've got to get some sleep," Zeb said. "Dr. Wo's been driving us all very hard." He struggled to his feet, then added, almost as an afterthought, "And the Old Man is pushing himself harder than any of us."

Grant got out of his chair. "Wo's driving himself? Why?"

With a weary smile, Muzorawa explained, "He intends to lead the mission. Didn't you know?"

"You mean he's going to go with you?"

"That is his intention."

"But he can't walk! He can't even get out of his chair."

"Yes, he can. The therapies are beginning to help him, at last. He can stand up by himself now—with braces on his legs."

"He can't lead a mission into the ocean in that condition."

Muzorawa started for the lab door, and Grant saw that he himself was not walking very well. With a shake of his head, the Sudanese replied, "He claims it doesn't matter. We really don't need our legs inside the craft."

"You don't?"

"We'll all be immersed in pressurized PFCL. It's the only way to survive the gravity pull and the pressure of a deep dive."

"What's PFCL?" Grant asked.

"Perfluorocarbon liquid. It carries oxygen to the lungs and removes carbon dioxide. We'll be breathing in a pressurized liquid."

"You'll be floating, then," Grant said.

"Correct. It's something like zero gee. That's why we're training for the mission in the dolphin tank."

"I didn't know."

Muzorawa placed a finger over his lips, the sign for silence. "Now you do, my friend."

SIMULATIONS

Grant wanted to ask Lane about the dolphin tank, but he had forced himself to stay clear of her since the evening he'd spent in her quarters. Avoid temptation, he kept telling himself sternly. He spent his evenings sending long, rambling messages back to Marjorie and rereading hers to him.

Somewhat to his surprise, there had been no repercussions over his stained trousers. Either the guards who'd seen him that night hadn't thought enough of the incident to repeat it to anyone else, or the station's gossip-mongers didn't consider it worth their notice. Whenever he bumped into O'Hara she was cordial and polite, businesslike but friendly at the same time. No mention of the brief kiss that bothered Grant so much. No personal emotions at all that he could discern.

You're making a mountain out of a molehill, Grant told himself time and again. But he dreamed about O'Hara, despite his strenuous efforts not to. How do you *not* think about something? he demanded of himself. Take no pleasure in it, he heard the advice of his moral counselor from his teen years. If you rigorously reject any thought that's pleasurable, then there's no sin to it.

He prayed for strength to resist temptation. Yet the more he prayed, the more he thought about Lane. Neutered, she had said. The electronic biochips somehow block out the sex drive. Is that a side effect, an accident? Or did Wo make it that way on purpose?

Each message he got from Marjorie he read over and over again, like a rare treasure, like a drowning man clutching at a lifebuoy. Until . . .

Marjorie was sitting at a desk in some sort of office, or perhaps it was a hospital. Grant couldn't see enough of the background to tell. Besides, his attention was focused on Marjorie, on her soulful brown eyes and beautiful dark hair. She'd clipped her hair short; it framed her face in thick, luxuriant curls.

"I guess that's all the news from here in Bolivia," she said cheerfully. "They're sending me back home for a month's R&R. I'll take a trip to see your parents."

Before Grant could even think about that, she added, "Oh, and Mr. Beech called to say he hasn't heard from you. He'd like you to send him a call when you get a chance."

Ellis Beech.

"That's all for now, darling. I'll send you a 'gram when I'm at your folks' house. Bye! I love you!"

The display screen went blank as Grant sagged back in his chair. Beech wanted to hear from him. I'll bet he does, Grant thought. But I don't have anything to tell him.

So far, the New Morality had exerted no pressure at all on Grant; they hadn't even tried to communicate with him, until now. And all Grant could report to them is that one crewed probe into the ocean failed disastrously and Dr. Wo was readying another mission. They already know that, Grant said to himself. I've been here for months now and I don't know more than *they* knew when they sent me here.

In a way, though, he felt almost glad of that. He resented being ordered to spy on the scientists, resented being shipped out to Jupiter to suit the prying whims of a man like Beech and his unseen but powerful superiors. You've got to decide which side you're on, Grant remembered Beech telling him. Why do there have to be opposing sides? Why can't we study Jupiter without the New Morality poking their noses into it?

Confused, miserable, Grant sat up for hours watching and rewatching all of Marjorie's messages to him. He found that he couldn't picture her face if he didn't study her videos.

Sleep just would not come. He was too upset, too resentful. His mind kept spinning the same thoughts over and over again. At last he pulled on a pair of coveralls and trudged barefoot down to the cafeteria for some hot chocolate. The place was empty, the overhead lights turned down to a dim nighttime setting.

As he stood before the dispensing machine, wondering if a cup of tea wouldn't be better for him, he noticed Red Devlin making his way through the empty, shadowed tables.

"Up late, eh?" Devlin said cheerfully as he approached.

Grant nodded. "I can't seem to get to sleep tonight."

Devlin cocked his head to one side, like a red-crested woodpecker.

Jabbing a finger toward the dispensing machine, he said, "Nothing in there will help much, y'know."

Grant replied, "Maybe some hot chocolate . . ."

Devlin shook his head. "I've got just what you need. A couple pops o' these"—he pulled a palmful of pills out of his trousers pocket— "and you'll sleep like a baby."

"Drugs?" Grant yelped.

With a laugh and a shake of his head, Devlin countered, "And whattaya think chocolate is? Or caffeine?"

"They're not narcotics."

Devlin put the pills back in his pocket. "Against your religion, eh?"

Nodding, Grant bit back the reply he wanted to make. A man who sells narcotics is evil personified, he knew. Yet Devlin seemed only to be trying to help—in his own benighted way.

"Maybe what you really need is some stimulation," the Red Devil mused. "A VR program. I've got some real hot ones: fireballs, y'know."

Before Grant could answer Devlin laughed and said, "But that'd be against your religion, too, wouldn't it?"

"Yes, it would," Grant said stiffly.

"Well, I'm afraid there's not much I can do for you, then," Devlin said good-naturedly. "But if you ever need me, you know where to find me." He strolled off down the shadowy corridor, whistling a tune that Grant didn't recognize.

Dr. Wo shouldn't let him stay on this station, Grant told himself. What he sells is wrong, sinful. Still, he found himself wondering what virtual reality sex might be like. Would it really be a sin? Maybe if he could imagine himself with Marjorie . . .

Grant spent almost all his waking hours in the fluid dynamics lab, doggedly working out a point-by-point map of the turbulent currents in the Jovian ocean based on the scant data returned by the automated probes. The course work sent by the University of Cairo remained in his computer, untouched, ignored.

Late one afternoon Karlstad mosied into the lab, a knowing, superior grin on his pallid face. Grant was alone among the humming computers and silent experimental equipment.

"You do tend to make a hermit out of yourself, don't you?" he asked, pulling up the wheeled chair next to Grant's.

Looking up from the graphs displayed on his screen, Grant muttered, "The work doesn't do itself, Egon."

"It's a shame you're not into biology, then," Karlstad said easily. "Like, right now I'm helping the bio team from Callisto to culture some of their subzero foraminifera."

"Are you?" Grant turned back to his screen.

"Damned right," said Karlstad, leaning back in the chair and clasping his hands behind his head. "Helpful little creatures. The forams are multiplying all by themselves in the rig I built for them. It simulates the ice-covered sea on Callisto very nicely. The fora do all the work and I roam around the station—"

"Interrupting people who're trying to get their work done," Grant finished for him.

Karlstad pretended to be wounded. "Is that any way to treat a fellow scooter?"

Grant admitted, "No, I suppose it wasn't polite."

"I'm not here to interrupt you. I'm here to offer you a learning experience."

"What?"

Karlstad leaned closer. "Zeb and Lainie are going into the tank together."

Grant felt his jaw drop open. "What do you mean?"

Laughing, Karlstad said, "Relax. Put your eyes back in your head."

His face reddening, Grant tried to erase his mental image of O'Hara and Muzorawa together in the dolphin tank. They can't do anything! He told himself. They're both implanted with biochips. Still he saw her sleek and naked, gliding through the water.

"They're going into the simulation tank," Karlsad said, obviously enjoying Grant's unmistakable consternation.

Before Grant could reply, he added, "And Old Woeful is going to join them."

"The simulation tank," Grant said dully.

Nodding, Karlstad said, "The test is supposed to be strictly off-limits to everybody except the technicians running the sim."

The way he said that convinced Grant that Karlstad had an ace up his sleeve. Sure enough, Karlstad went on, "But I have a direct pipeline to the cameras recording the test."

"You do? How?"

Raising one hand in a gesture of patience, the biophysicist said, "I cannot reveal my sources. But if you'll allow me . . ."

He turned to the computer console next to Grant's and pulled out the keyboard. Blowing dust from the keys, he booted up the machine manually and then tapped in a long, complex string of alphanumerics. Grant watched, fascinated despite himself, as the desktop display screen flickered and glowed.

And there was O'Hara standing in the narrow corridor outside one of the dolphin tanks in a sleek white skintight suit that glistened as if it were already wet. They seemed to be looking down at her from above. Grant realized they were watching the view from a camera set into the ceiling panels in the corridor.

"Shall we put it on the wallscreen?" Karlstad asked.

"What if someone walks in?"

He shrugged. "I'll wipe the screen before they have a chance to figure out what we're watching."

"All right," Grand said, nodding.

The wallscreen image was life size but a little grainy. He must be using a microcamera, Grant thought, with a fiber-optic link. O'Hara's slick white wetsuit clung to her like her own skin. She doesn't have that much of a figure, Grant told himself. Slim, almost boyish. Almost.

Muzorawa stepped into view. His suit was bright green but left his powerful looking legs bare. They were studded with implants, his skin thick with them, like a leper's sores. No wonder they wear long trousers all the time, Grant thought, recoiling inwardly at the ugliness of it.

Half a dozen technicians in gray coveralls milled around. Karlstad clicked at the keyboard and the view abruptly shifted. Now they were looking into the dolphin tank, over Muzorawa's shoulder. But there were no dolphins in sight. Instead, the tank contained what looked like a mockup of a control panel, a broad curving expanse of display screens and rows of lights and buttons.

Grant said, "I hope Sheena doesn't burst in on them."

"No, no," Karlstad assured him. "Little Sheena's safe in her pen, sedated up to her bony brow ridges. She's sleeping like a three-hundred-kilo baby."

Two technicians in dark-gray wetsuits clambered up the ladder built into the partition between tanks and cannonballed into the water with huge splashes, one after the other.

Grant watched them settle down to the bottom of the tank, trailing bubbles from their face masks.

"Can't you fugheads get into the tank without sloshing half the water outta it?" groused a scornful nasal voice caustically. The test controller, Grant thought, monitoring everything from some central location.

The pair of techs waved cheerfully as they sat on the bottom of the tank.

"Okay," came the voice of the controller, slightly scratchy from static. "Let's get this sim percolating."

O'Hara nodded and pulled the hood of her suit over her bald scalp, then slipped on a transparent visor that covered her entire face. Two of the technicians helped her work her arms through the shoulder straps of what appeared to be an air tank, then connected a slim hose from the top of the tank to her face mask. They slid a belt of weights around her slender hips. O'Hara clicked its clasp shut.

Two other techs were doing the same for Muzorawa. Finally they checked that the air was getting through properly.

"I'm okay," O'Hara said, her voice muffled by the mask.

Muzorawa asked for a slightly stronger air flow, and a tech adjusted a knob on the back of his tank. Then he nodded and made a circle with his right thumb and forefinger.

O'Hara turned and scampered lithely up the ladder to the top of the tank. Grant saw that her feet were bare.

"Radio check," said a disembodied voice.

"O'Hara on freak one," she said. It sounded somewhat fuzzy to Grant. He realized there must be a small radio built into the full-face mask.

But the controller's voice said, "In the green. Go ahead and dunk."

O'Hara swung her long legs over the edge of the tank and slipped into the water with hardly a ripple.

"Now that's the way you get into the pool." The controller's voice was admiring.

The two techs already in the tank made exaggerated motions of applause.

Muzorawa climbed the ladder, considerably slower and more ponderous than O'Hara. It seemed to Grant that Zeb had some trouble getting his legs to work right. But he made it to the top, swinging both legs together almost as if they were inert lengths of lumber, and dropped gracelessly into the water.

"Now comes the boring part," Karlstad murmured.

"What's that?"

With a smirk, Karlstad answered, "The work, of course."

O'Hara and Muzorawa, with the two technicians hovering behind them, glided to the control panel and slid their bare feet into loops set into the floor.

"Sim one-a," the controller's voice announced. "Separation and systems checkout. Manual procedure."

The panel was chest high, Grant realized. The two scooters stood at it, anchored by the floor loops, and began working their way through a long countdown, punctuated by the controller's check-off of each action they took. It was boring, Grant agreed. Repetitious and dull.

"You said Dr. Wo was going to be part of this," Grant said to Karlstad.

"He'll show up."

"When?"

"When the dull routine stuff is finished Old Woeful will make his dramatic entrance, never fear."

I ought to be working, Grant thought. I ought to be inserting the data points from last month's probes into the equations to see how they affect the flow maps. But instead he watched O'Hara and Muzorawa as they patiently, methodically, went through the simulation.

"This is the separation procedure," Karlstad said. "This is what they'll have to do to disconnect the saucer from the station."

"It takes so long?" Grant wondered aloud.

Karlstad grunted. "You don't want to fire your jets and find that there's still an umbilical linking you to the station proper. Could ruin your whole afternoon."

"But still, can't these procedures be automated? I mean, launch crews have automated—"

"Hold it!" Karlstad snapped. "Here he comes."

All that Grant could see was the technicians outside the tank turning to look down the corridor at something beyond the camera's view. He heard Karlstad clicking on the computer keys again, and the view shifted to show Dr. Wo rolling toward the test tank in his powered chair. He was wearing a bright red wetsuit, with shining metal braces over the lower half of his pitifully thin, weak legs.

Wo rolled up to the tank and the technicians made a reverential half circle around his chair.

"Dr. Wo," said the controller's disembodied voice. "We've completed the separation procedure. Ready to start ignition and entry simulation."

"Good," said Wo. "I will join the crew now."

No one said a word. No one moved. Wo pushed himself to his feet and stood unsteadily on his steel-braced legs for a long, breathless moment. Then he took a step toward the ladder. Another step. My god, Grant thought, he's clunking along like Frankenstein's monster. He'll never make it up that ladder without their help.

As if he could read Grant's thoughts, Karlstad said, "The deal our woeful master made with the test controller is that if he could get up the ladder unassisted, he could go into the tank and participate in the sim. Otherwise, no."

"As if the simulation controller could say no to him," Grant sneered.

"During the sim, the controller is god almighty. If he says no, it's no. Doesn't matter who he's talking to. He's the absolute boss during the simulation."

"And afterward?"

Karlstad shrugged.

Wo stood uncertainly at the base of the ladder and took a deep breath. Grant felt almost sorry for the man. It had taken all his energy to make the few steps from his chair to the ladder. Surely he won't be able—

Wo suddenly seized the rungs of the ladder and pulled himself up, hand over hand, his legs dangling uselessly. Grant could see sweat break out on the man's face, see his snarling, teeth-gritted determination. He made it to the top of the ladder and swung his legs over the edge, letting his feet dangle in the water.

Two of the technicians swarmed up the ladder behind him, carrying his face mask, air tank, and weights. In minutes they had Wo properly rigged. He pushed himself off the edge of the tank and splashed awkwardly into the water. One of the technicians started to applaud, but when he saw he was alone he froze in midclap, a mortified look on his face.

Wo sank to the bottom of the pool and swam easily to the control panel, taking his station between O'Hara and Muzorawa.

"You've got to admit that he's got guts," Karlstad said reluctantly.

Grant agreed with a nod.

"You'll never see me getting into that fish tank," Karlstad went on.

"But aren't you part of the mission?"

"Me? Don't be ridiculous!"

"But I thought . . ."

"Wo put me on the team, yes," Karlstad admitted. "I'll be one of the monitors in the control center when they go. But that's all! They couldn't get me into that death trap unless they put a gun to my head. Maybe not even then."

THE WRATH OF WO

It was boring and fascinating at the same time, watching the three of them going through the simulation. Grant kept telling himself that he should get back to his work, he shouldn't be wasting his time this way, but he could not take his eyes from the wallscreen.

Wo was clearly in charge, and enjoying it. Instead of remaining anchored at the instrument panel as O'Hara and Muzorawa did, he pulled his feet free of the floor loops and floated easily, almost lazily in the big tank. Hovering over the other two, drifting slightly from one side to the other, Wo gave orders and did all the talking with the test controller.

"He's enjoying himself, isn't he?" Grant asked rhetorically.

Karlstad hmmphed. "First time he's been able to get around without his chair since the accident."

"No wonder he likes it."

"He also likes the feeling of power, don't forget that."

"He gets that all the time," Grant countered. "He's got more power around here than God . . . just about."

"There are different kinds of power, Grant. Right now, in that tank, he feels *physically* strong. I'll bet he's thinking in the back of his mind that he could grab Lainie and pop her and she'd welcome the thrill."

Grant felt his face flush again and Karlstad snickered at him. "Hit a nerve, did I?"

"You can be pretty crude sometimes."

With a tilt of his head, Karlstad replied, "Why not? Sticks and stones, you know. Words can't hurt you."

"I thought the biochips short-circuited the sex drive," Grant said.

"Who told you that?"

"Lane."

Karlstad's knowing grin turned into a smirk. "The chips don't do anything about the drive: That's in the head, in the brain."

"But—"

"They apparently shut down all the sensory nerves in the groin, though," Karlstad went on. "That must've been Wo's brilliant idea."

"Why would he do that?" Grant wondered.

"The crew on the deep mission will be cooped up in that saucer for weeks. Wo doesn't want any of them distracted by human frailties."

Grant nodded, thinking, He's taken away the sensations but left the desire. That must be as close to hell as a man can get.

"I've got to get back to my work," Grant said, surprised to hear his own words.

"You don't want to watch the rest of this?"

"It's not all that interesting."

"Watching luscious Lainie in that skintight suit? That's not interesting?"

Grant turned back to his desktop and commanded the computer to bring up its active screen again. The screen saver's fractal pattern disappeared, replaced by the same graph Grant had been working on when Karlstad had interrupted him.

"Or maybe," Karlstad said with a wolfish grin, "watching Lainie is *too* interesting for you. Is that it?"

Grant snapped, "I have too much work to do to sit around watching—"

"Hold one!" the simulation controller's voice called out. "Medical hold."

The three people in the tank looked up reflexively, bubbles rising from their masks.

"Dr. Wo," said the controller, "we're getting a sharp rise in your blood pressure readings. Your pulse is starting to spike, as well."

"It's temporary. Monitor and—"

"Test procedures call for a halt when a subject exceeds the preset medical parameters, sir," the controller said, his tone respectful but firm.

"It's temporary, I say!"

O'Hara and Muzorawa had stopped their work at the instrument panel. Glaring red lights were blinking along the panel, casting shimmering highlights in the water.

Even more reasonably, the controller said, "Dr. Wo, I have no choice but to shut down the simulation."

"Not necessary!" Wo snapped, flailing his arms.

"But the safety protocols—"

"This is the medical officer," a woman's voice broke in. "This simulation is terminated."

Karlstad, still sitting beside Grant, broke into a low chuckle.

"What's funny?" Grant asked.

"Several things. First, seeing Wo's macho act collapse around his tiny little ears."

Wo was still arguing with both the controller and the medical officer. But now all the lights on the panel were a steady glowering red.

"Second, knowing that his blood pressure is going up even higher because he can't get his way."

Grant didn't think it was funny.

"But the funniest thing of all is the medic," Karlstad went on. "Old Woeful can't muscle her."

"The medical officer can't be overruled?"

"Not this one. She's due to ship out on the next supply craft. And she's got a full residence at the university hospital in Basel. Wo can't do a thing to her."

"She's shut down the sim."

"She certainly has. And I imagine she's shut down Wo's plan to head up the deep mission, as well."

The next few weeks were quickly dubbed "the Wrath of Wo."

Frustrated in his desire to command the upcoming deep mission, the station director turned his fury on everyone and anyone who crossed his path. Dozens of scooters were summarily banished from the station, sent out to the frozen wastes of Europa and the other Jovian moons, exposed to Jupiter's intense radiation bombardment, forced to live for weeks on end inside armored pressure suits while grappling on the ice with drilling equipment like common oil-field roughnecks.

All the technicians who worked the ill-starred simulation were relocated. Several were sent packing back to Earth, with the worst possible job ratings that Wo could write. The simulation controller was shipped off to Selene, with a stinging evaluation inserted into his dossier. Even so, they were all glad to get away with their skin still intact.

"He can't do anything about Lainie and Zeb," Karlstad said confidently to Grant in the midst of the weeks-long rampage. But he whispered now, and spoke of the director only when the two of them were alone. "He needs them for the mission."

"Who's going to command the mission?" Grant whispered back.

"Zeb will, if Wo's got any shred of common sense left in him. Zeb's the most capable person on the team."

Grant wondered. He stayed as far away from Dr. Wo as he could, working steadily in the fluid dynamics lab, keeping his nose clean—and on the grindstone. He even tried to avoid being seen with O'Hara and Muzorawa, on the theory that although Wo could not directly punish them for witnessing his humiliation, he might very well punish their friends.

"He can't let the mission drift into limbo," Karlstad said, still whispering even though they were alone in his quarters, well after the cafeteria had closed for the night. "He's got to appoint a new commander and realign the crew assignments."

"There's a vacancy on the crew," said Grant. "Doesn't that mean that one of the backups will be put on the active list?"

Karlstad's eyes went round. "There's only three backups."

"And you're one of them."

"He won't pick me," Karlstad said, shaking his head as if to get rid of the very idea of it. "Irene and Frankovich are much better qualified."

Grant had barely met the other two; Irene Pascal was a medical specialist in neurophysiology, Bernard Frankovich was a biochemist.

"But you're one of the available backups," Grant said, surprised at how much he was enjoying the look of sheer terror in Karlstad's normally ice-calm eyes.

"He won't pick me," Karlstad muttered again. "He won't. He can't!"

Several days later all of the Jovian team were called into a meeting by Dr. Wo. To his surprise, Grant was included in the summons. Why me? he asked himself. But he made certain to show up at the conference room next to the director's office several minutes ahead of the appointed time.

Nine men and women crowded into the small, austere conference room, four of them in the black studded leggings that marked them as crew or backup. They milled around for several minutes, talking in guarded whispers until the moment for the meeting arrived.

Precisely at that second, the door from Dr. Wo's office slid open.

Everyone froze in place as the director wheeled himself to the head of the conference table, the faint hum of his chair's electric motor the only sound in the room. Suddenly they all scrambled for seats at the far end of the table, away from the director. It was like a brief, intense game of musical chairs. Faster than most of the others, Grant grabbed one toward the end of the table and sat down, flanked by O'Hara on his right and Pascal, the neurophysiologist. Karlstad sat exactly opposite him.

Without preamble Wo began, "The medical people have scrubbed me from the mission."

He paused. Everyone around the conference table made sympathetic noises.

"Therefore," the director went on, "it is necessary to appoint a new mission commander."

He looked toward the open door to his office, and a woman stepped hesitantly through, limping noticeably. A sigh of recognition wafted through the room, almost a moan, Grant thought. The woman was a stranger to him, but obviously most of the others knew her. Grant glanced across the table at Karlstad; his long, pallid face looked aghast.

"Most of you already know Dr. Krebs," said Wo. "She will be commander of the next mission and deputy director of the station, with the specific duty of preparing for the crewed flight."

Grant got an eerie feeling, a strange tingling at the base of his neck. The aura around the table was tense, almost terrified. If most of the people here know Dr. Krebs, he thought, they certainly don't like her.

Krebs was short and stocky, barely taller than the seated Dr. Wo, her arms thick and heavy. Her legs were already encased in the studded leggings that told Grant she'd been implanted with biochips. Her face was square, blocky, her deeply black hair obviously a wig cut in a short Dutch boy style with bangs that came down to where her eyebrows should be. The complexion of her face was a pasty gray, as if she hadn't seen sunlight or a UV lamp in many years. The expression on that face was granite-hard: square jaw thrust out pugnaciously, pale-blue eyes surveying all the faces turned toward her, peering at each individual in the room for a few seconds and then turning to the next. She seemed to be saying, I know you don't like me; the feeling is thoroughly mutual.

Those accusing eyes focused on Grant for a moment, freezing him even though he wanted to turn away.

At last she turned her attention to the next person. Grant felt as if he'd just been freed from a police interrogation.

"You," she said, pointing at Karlstad.

"Me?" he asked, his voice squeaking slightly.

"Karlstad," she said.

"Yes."

"You will join the crew. Prepare for the surgery immediately."

Grant stared across the table at Karlstad. He looked like a man who had just seen his own death.

KREBS

"Christel Krebs," Frankovich said, hunching forward gloomily over the cafeteria table. "She's Wo's ultimate revenge on us."

Muzorawa nodded glumly. Even O'Hara looked worried. The four of them unconsciously leaned their heads together and whispered like conspirators. The cafeteria was only half filled, yet echoing with the noise and clatter of other dinner conversations. Still, they whispered to one another.

Frankovich was a short, roundish, balding man. Grant had seen the biochemist often enough in his days as a lab technician, but the man had hardly spoken six words to him before this.

"What are they doing to Egon?" Grant asked. "What's the surgery that Krebs spoke of?"

"Wiring the biochips into his legs," Muzorawa said.

"And teaching him to breathe underwater," added Frankovich, with a shudder.

Grant knew that the crew would be immersed in a thick perfluorocarbon liquid during the mission. It was the only way they could withstand the enormous pressures of the Jovian ocean. They would be living in their own high-pressure liquid environment, breathing oxygen from the perfluorocarbon, hoping that the pressure inside the cells of their bodies could be raised high enough to balance the pressure outside their ship. It worked in theory. It worked in tests. During the first mission into Jupiter's ocean, though, one crew member had been killed and the others injured. Wo had never recovered from his mangling; Grant wondered if Krebs was fully recuperated.

"Poor Egon," O'Hara said. "He was terrified of having this happen to him."

"Couldn't he refuse?" Grant asked. "I mean, we've still got our legal rights."

With a shake of his head, Muzorawa replied, "Egon doesn't. Technically, he's a convicted felon, serving out his sentence here."

"That's why Krebs picked him. He can't refuse."

"I'm just glad it wasn't me," Frankovich said fervently.

"It's not that bad," said O'Hara. "Once you get over the surgery, once you're connected to the ship."

"Connected?" Grant wondered aloud.

"The biochips link you to the ship's systems," Muzorawa explained. "Instead of using keypads or voice commands, your nervous system and the ship's systems are directly linked."

Grant felt his eyebrows hike up.

"It's . . . different," O'Hara said. "Sort of a feeling of power, you know. You *feel* the ship's machinery. You and the ship become one."

Muzorawa nodded. "I've never experienced anything like it. It's . . ." He groped for a word.

"Intimate," said O'Hara.

"Yes. A sort of out-of-body experience, yet it's happening within your own skull."

"Almost like sex," O'Hara said.

"Better," said Muzorawa.

"Better, is it?" she challenged.

Muzorawa smiled knowingly. "It lasts longer."

Grant changed the subject. "But what about Krebs? Who is she? Where did she come from?"

"She was on the first mission," Zeb answered. "She was Wo's second-in-command."

"She actually piloted the mission craft," said O'Hara, "and she got pretty badly smashed up in the accident."

"Some people claim she *caused* the accident," said Frankovich. "And now Wo's put her in command."

"I thought she was at Selene," Grant said.

"She was," O'Hara replied. "Recuperating from the accident, don't you know."

"She must be fully recovered," Muzorawa offered.

Frankovich shook his head. "Physically, perhaps. But did you get a look at her eyes? Like a homicidal maniac."

Neither Muzorawa nor O'Hara replied.

Another question rose in Grant's mind. "If you were linked with the submersible's systems when the accident happened, what did it feel like? Did you feel pain? What?"

Muzorawa closed his eyes briefly. "Lane and I were off duty when it happened."

"Thank the saints in heaven," O'Hara whispered.

"Jorge Lavestra was killed. Krebs and Dr. Wo were badly injured."

Frankovich hunched forward in his chair and clasped his hands on the tabletop. "From what I hear, Lavestra had just plugged into the ship's systems. He wasn't physically injured. He died of a cerebral hemorrhage."

"A stroke?"

"Yes, that's true," said O'Hara. "Being linked to the ship at the wrong time can be fatal."

NEW ASSIGNMENTS

Grant woke up the next morning soaked in a cold sweat, his bedsheet twisted and tangled around his legs. Vaguely he remembered a dream, a nightmare, about strangers pinning him down and slicing away his flesh with sharp scalpels while he struggled and screamed for mercy.

It was early, he saw. He phoned Karlstad, but there was no answer. Recovering from his surgery, Grant guessed as he showered, then pulled on his slacks and shirt and headed for the cafeteria. It was nearly empty at this hour, although Red Devlin was laughing and chatting with a few of the early birds. He must sleep behind the counters, Grant thought.

It wasn't until the next evening, at dinner, that he saw Karlstad again. Egon entered the cafeteria, walking uncertainly, his legs sheathed in the same kind of studded black leggings, wearing the same kind of turtleneck pullover that O'Hara and Muzorawa always wore, his head completely hairless.

Grant left his half-finished dinner and rushed to Karlstad.

Egon smiled halfheartedly as Grant came up to him.

"Well," he said shakily, "I survived the surgery, at least."

"Are you all right?"

Instead of answering, Karlstad pulled down the collar of his turtleneck pullover. "Meet Frankenstein's monster," he said.

There were circular plastic gadgets inserted into either side of his neck. The skin around the things looked red, inflamed.

"What're those?"

"Feeding ports. When we're in the soup we can't eat regular food. We get fed intravenously."

"For how long?"

Letting the turtleneck collar slide back into place, Karlstad answered grimly, "For as long as we're on the mission."

"My God," Grant muttered.

"I'll live through it—I think."

Grant stayed with him as Karlstad selected a meager salad and a mug of fruit juice. The man tottered slightly as he walked back to Grant's table.

"Where's Lainie and Zeb and the others?" Karlstad said as he slowly, carefully, sat down.

"Not here yet."

"Um." Karlstad picked at his salad.

Grant tried to finish his dinner, but he'd lost interest in eating.

"You want to know what it's like, don't you?" Karlstad said, his voice flat, dead.

"I don't want to pry."

"Pry away, I don't mind. The worst is over. They sliced me up and put their damned chips into me. But first they drowned me."

"Drowned . . . ?"

"It's all done underwater. Or in that fucking perfluorocarbon gunk. It's like trying to breathe soup. Freezing cold soup, at that. Easier to prevent infection while they slice away at you, they claim."

Karlstad spent the next quarter hour describing in horrendous detail everything they had done to him. Listening to him, Grant lost his last shred of appetite.

"So now all I have to do is learn to walk again," he finished bitterly.

"You seem to be doing fine," Grant said.

"For an outpatient, yes, I imagine so."

Desperately trying to lighten his friend's mood, Grant asked, "What I don't understand is why they put the biochips in the legs. Wouldn't it make more sense to put them in the brain?"

Karlstad gave him a pitying look. "Not enough room inside the skull. They'd have to break through the bone, the way they want to do with Sheena."

"Oh."

"The chips are connected to the brain, though. I've got fibers running up my spine right into my cerebral cortex. Whatever those electrodes in my legs pick up is transmitted to my brain. Very efficient."

"There he is!"

Grant looked up and saw O'Hara rushing across the cafeteria toward them. Muzorawa was a few steps behind her. Neither of them had taken a tray. Both of them limped noticeably.

"How do you feel?" O'Hara asked, pulling up the chair next to Karlstad's.

"Terrible, thanks."

"Welcome to the club," said Muzorawa, sitting down beside Grant.

"Shipmates," Karlstad said sourly.

"Don't take it so hard," said O'Hara, with an impish smile. She rubbed Karlstad's bald pate. "I think you look better this way."

"Without eyebrows?" Karlstad said scornfully.

"Once you're connected to the ship you'll feel differently."

"Powerful," Muzorawa agreed. "It's like nothing you've ever experienced."

"Better than sex," O'Hara teased.

For the first time since Krebs had pointed her finger at him, Karlstad smiled.

That Sunday Tamiko Hideshi showed up at the Reverend Caldwell's services again. Grant edged through the sparse congregation to sit with her. Afterward, they headed for the cafeteria.

"The Catholics go for doughnuts after mass," she informed Grant as they got into the food line. "The Moslems take coffee and fruit."

"What about the Protestants?" Grant asked, laughing.

"Brunch," Tamiko answered, grinning back at him.

Grant selected a fruit salad and soymilk; Hideshi filled her tray with cereal, smoked fish, hot tea, and four slices of toast.

"How do you stay so thin when you eat so much?" Grant asked as they sat at a table.

She shook her head. "I'm not so thin. My body's like a block of cement."

"You're not fat."

"I guess I burn off the calories at work."

That started them talking about her studies of the ice-covered ocean on Europa.

"We're making sense of it, little by little," Hideshi said. "How's your job going?"

Grant nodded as he chewed down a slice of melon. "About the same: making sense of it, little by little."

"Making sense of the Jovian ocean?" Her eyes seemed to go wider.

"Little by little," Grant repeated.

"Maybe we can help each other," she suggested. "I mean, we're both working on fluid dynamics, after all. Maybe we should compare notes."

Grant hesitated, then said, "I'd love to, Tami, but we're into sensitive areas. I can't—"

She waved a disapproving hand. "Oh, Dr. Wo and his silly security rules. There aren't any secrets in physics."

"Maybe not," Grant admitted, "but I'm not allowed to discuss my work with anybody outside the group."

She put on a hurt expression. "Not even with me?"

Grant thought about it. It might make some sense, at that. After all, we're both trying to figure out the dynamics of alien oceans.

But he heard himself say to her, "I can't, Tami. Wo would flay me alive."

She sighed and shook her head. "How can you do science when you're afraid to communicate with other scientists?"

Grant brightened. "I could ask Dr. Wo for permission to collaborate with you. If he okays it—"

"No!" Hideshi snapped. "No, I don't think that would work. Wo's so paranoid he'd send the two of us off to god knows where."

"But maybe he'd see the sense of our cooperating," Grant said.

Hideshi shook her head. "Don't breathe a word to Wo. He's crazy enough as it is."

With a shrug, Grant admitted, "Maybe you're right."

"I know I am," said Hideshi.

It surprised Grant when he realized that he'd been aboard Research Station *Gold* for six months. He awoke one morning to see that his phone light was blinking. When he answered, still yawning and scratching his jaw, Dr. Wo's grim face appeared on the phone's tiny screen.

Grant automatically sat up straighter on the bed and tried to pat down his sleep-tousled hair. But the message was a recording.

"Be prepared for your six-month review tomorrow at eleven hundred hours in my office," Wo said bluntly. Then the screen went dark.

Grant took a deep breath. Six-month review, he thought. Great. That means there's only three and a half years left to this prison sentence.

He almost smiled. Until he remembered that sessions in Dr. Wo's office were never pleasant.

The next day, precisely at eleven hundred hours, Grant rapped sharply on the director's door. No response. He stood in the corridor, resisting the urge to bang on the door again, as people walked by. Wo's little power trip, Grant knew. He wasn't going to fall for it again, as he did the first time he'd been summoned to the director's office.

At last he heard, "Enter." He slid the door back and stepped into Wo's office.

The office was overheated, as usual. Even the bloodred tulips in the delicate vase looked wilted, sagging. The director, however, was brusque, all business. It seemed to Grant that Wo was seething with anger and barely managing to control his fury. He reviewed Grant's first assignment as a lab assistant and his more recent work with Muzorawa in the fluid dynamics lab. Grant sat rigidly on the chair in front of Wo's desk, keeping his face as calm and impassive as he could.

"All in all," Wo concluded, looking up from the desktop screen that displayed Grant's dossier, "a moderately acceptable six months. At least you haven't made any major mistakes."

Grant wondered what minor mistakes the director saw in his record.

"Now then, some changes are in order," said the director.

"Changes, sir?" Grant asked apprehensively.

"First, Dr. Muzorawa will be fully engaged in training for the upcoming deep mission and will be unable to serve as your thesis advisor until the mission is completed."

Grant's heart sank.

"Therefore I will take his place as your advisor. You will continue as a distanced student of the University of Cairo. I have been granted a visiting professorship by the university's administration."

"*You're* going to be my thesis advisor?" Grant asked, his voice an octave higher than normal.

"Do you have any objections to such an arrangement?"

"Oh, no, sir. None at all," Grant lied. The thought of having Wo over him in still another capacity brought something close to despair to Grant's soul, but he knew there was no way around it.

"Good," said Wo.

"In fact, sir, I'm flattered," Grant heard himself say, trying to make the best of a situation he could not control.

Wo nodded, although his dour expression did not change by a hair. Then he went on, "The second change may be less pleasant for you. I need someone to work with Sheena."

"With the gorilla?"

"Yes. Her intelligence level has plateaued. Any increase in her intelligence will require cranial surgery."

"Oh," Grant said. "That would be difficult, wouldn't it?"

"Not at all. The animal can be sedated and the surgery performed in perfect safety. It is the recuperation phase that may present problems."

Grant got a mental picture of three-hundred-kilo Sheena with a bandaged skull and a nasty headache. It was not a happy thought.

"We will need someone to handle Sheena after the surgery, someone whom she will not connect to the medical personnel. A friend, so to speak."

"Me?"

"You. You will spend at least two hours each day with Sheena. You will bring her fruits and new toys. The toys will be learning games and devices, of course; there is an extensive supply of such in storage."

"But my studies—"

"This duty will be in addition to your fluid dynamics work, of course. It will take two hours per day from your personal time, no more."

I don't have any personal time, Grant grumbled to himself. I spend all my waking hours working on the drat-damned ocean's dynamics. But he kept his mouth tightly shut.

"Remember, your task is to befriend the gorilla so that she will be able to deal with you as a trusted companion after the brain surgery."

Wonderful, Grant said to himself. I'm going to get my neck broken by a postoperative gorilla.

If the director sensed Grant's dejection or fear, he gave no outward sign of it. "Are there any questions?" Wo asked sourly.

Grant steepled his fingers unconsciously, then quickly put his hands down on his lap once he realized it looked as if he were begging—or praying.

"Yes, sir, I do have a question."

Wo nodded once.

"Sheena . . . the dolphins . . . why are we studying their intelligence? I mean, we're supposed to be investigating the planet Jupiter. Why are we spending time and energy on the intelligence of these animals?"

Wo's face took on the implacable expression of a teacher who is resolved to make his dull-witted student solve his own problems.

"That is a question that you should meditate upon while you are entertaining Sheena." The slightest trace of a smile moved the corners of his mouth a bare millimeter.

LEVIATHAN

Cruising through the eternal sea, Leviathan's sensory members warned of the storm ahead. Its eye parts could not see the storm, it was much too far away for visual contact, but the pressure-sensing members along Leviathan's immense bulk felt the tug of currents that wanted to draw the whole world ocean into the storm's voracious maw.

It was a huge vortex, its powerful spiral generating currents that grew stronger and stronger until even creatures as powerful as Leviathan and its kind could no longer resist and would be sucked into a whirling, shattering dismemberment.

Leviathan felt no anxiety about the distant storm, no dread of its insatiable lure. At this distance the storm was too weak to be dangerous, and Leviathan had no intention of approaching it any closer. Yet it felt a tendril of curiosity. No member of the Kin had ever gone close enough to the storm to actually see it. What would that experience be like?

The food that sifted down from the cold abyss above seemed to be concentrated more thickly the closer Leviathan cruised to the storm's vicinity. The inward-pulling currents generated by the storm's powerful spinning vortex were sucking in the drifting particles until they became veritable streams, thick torrents of food flooding into the storm's maelstrom, impossible to ignore and difficult to resist. The Elders should be shown this, Leviathan thought.

Far, far off on the horizon Leviathan's eye parts detected a faint flickering, nothing more than the slightest rippling of light, barely discernible. Yet it alerted Leviathan to the fact that it was getting close enough to the storm to actually see it. Leviathan felt a strange thrill, a mixture of excitement and apprehension.

Darters! the sensory members warned.

Leviathan's eye parts focused on them, the Darters were that close.

Swift, streamlined shapes, lean and efficient, heading straight toward Leviathan. There were dozens of them, spreading out in a globe to surround Leviathan, intent on pressing their attack home. They would not be content with a quick nip at its outer hide; an armada of this size meant to kill and feast on all of Leviathan's members.

Escape lay in retreat, but retreat was in the direction of the storm. The Darters had hatched a clever hunting strategy, knowing that if they pursued Leviathan close enough to the swirling storm front, its members would instinctively disassemble and become easy prey for the voracious hunters.

Leviathan estimated the distance to the storm's towering ringwall of turbulence, tested the pull of the currents plunging into the storm, and planned a strategy of its own. It commanded its flagella members to row as fast as they could toward the ceaseless streaks of lightning that showed where the storm raged. No questions, no doubts came back from the flagella; they were blindly obedient, always.

Now it was a race, and a test of strength. The Darters chased after the fleeing Leviathan, eager to chew through its thick outer armor and puncture the vital organ-members deep within. Leviathan felt the storm's currents tugging, pulling it closer and closer to the cloud wall. Lightning stroked the clouds, and Leviathan's sensor members cringed at the storm's mindless, endless roar. Members sent signals of alarm to Leviathan's central brain: Soon they would automatically begin to disintegrate; they had no control over their hard-wired instincts.

Darters were close enough now to nip at the thickened dead tissue of Leviathan's outer hide. Leviathan swatted at them, turning the faithful mindless flagella into brutal clubs that could rupture flesh, crush bone.

Driven to frenzy by the scent of torn flesh, the Darters redoubled their attack. Leviathan felt their teeth tearing into its hide; all its members flashed signals of pain and fear as the ever-growing pull of the storm's mighty currents dragged Leviathan closer to involuntary dissociation.

Now! Leviathan suddenly shifted course, moving to parallel the spinning currents of the storm, battering its way through the net of Darters surrounding it. The Darters were too close to the lightning-racked storm to be able to resist the inward-pulling currents. Like helpless specks of food they were sucked into the vortex, one after another, struggling futilely against the storm's overwhelming power, shrieking their death howls as they spun into the raging clouds.

Leviathan struggled, too, straining mightily to slide around the face of the lightning-streaked cloud wall, gradually spiraling away from the storm.

When at last it was free of danger, Leviathan felt drained, exhausted—and hungry. But there was no food here; on this side of the storm the sea was empty, barren. Only gradually did it realize that it had been swept far from its usual haunts, into a region of the all-encompassing ocean that it had never seen before.

Leviathan flashed out a call to the others of its kind. There was no response. Alone, weak and bleeding, Leviathan began to search for food, desperately hoping to build enough strength to swim far from the storm, wondering how it could find its way back to the familiar haunts of the Kin.

SHEENA'S GENTLEMAN VISITOR

Grant considered hiding his new assignment from his friends, but he knew that would be impossible. The station was too small to keep such secrets. Only the mighty Wo, with the inscrutability of the East and the powers of the director, could hold secrets from the staff.

So he wasn't surprised when Karlstad began ragging him at dinner the very first night after Wo's announcement of his new duties.

"I hear Sheena has a gentleman visitor," the biophysicist said archly as he spooned up soup from the bowl before him. He seemed fully recovered from his surgery, back to his old sarcastic ways.

Ursula van Neumann glanced at Grant, then replied, "Oh, really?"

"Who might that be?" asked Irene Pascal, falling into the game. The neurophysiologist was a petite brunette who always wore miniskirted sleeveless flowered frocks over her black leggings. Normally she was quiet and introspective, but now her hazel eyes twinkled mischievously.

"It's me," Grant admitted, wishing that Muzorawa or O'Hara were at the table. They'd put an end to this nonsense of Egon's, he thought.

"That's what I'd heard," Karlstad said, grinning broadly. "I understand you brought her flowers and candy last night."

"It's all Dr. Wo's idea," Grant protested.

"Flowers and candy?" asked Pascal.

"Have you kissed her yet?" van Neumann teased.

"It's a good thing Grant's not Roman Catholic," said Karlstad, quite seriously.

Pascal played straight man. "Why do you say that?"

Spreading his hands in a gesture of explanation, Karlstad said, "If Grant was Catholic, then any offspring they produce would have to be raised in the Church."

The two women sputtered laughter as Karlstad guffawed at his own joke. Grant took it in good-humored silence, forcing a smile at his own expense, thinking that he hadn't encountered such doltishness since he'd said good-bye to Raoul Tavalera on the old *Roberts*.

They joked about dating behavior and made sexual innuendos all through dinner. At last the subject seemed to wind down. By the time they were digging into the fruit cups and soymilk ice cream of their desserts, Grant thought they were finished with it.

Then Pascal asked, quite seriously, "Do you think you could get Sheena to undergo a brain scan?"

Grant blinked with surprise. "You mean an NMR scan of her brain?"

"More detailed," said Pascal. "I have the equipment in my lab, but Sheena put up a fight the last time we tried to get her in there." Her voice was a warm contralto, caramel rich, heavy with concern.

Grant thought a moment. "Is the equipment portable?"

Pascal made a Gallic shrug. "Like a desk-sized console. Or a small refrigerator."

"I guess you'd have to sedate her, then."

She shook her head. "But I want her conscious. I need to see how her brain functions when she's active."

"Can't you do it remotely?" Karlstad suggested. "I mean, you have neural net headgear, don't you?"

Van Neumann agreed, "Yes, I've worn those damned fishnets myself, for days on end."

With a sardonic smile, Pascal said, "And if you found it uncomfortable, Ursula, how long do you think Sheena would wear one?"

"How long do you need?" Grant asked.

"As long as I can get, of course."

Nodding, Grant amended, "I mean, what's the minimum time you'd settle for?"

She thought a moment. "Ten minutes. Fifteen. Half an hour would be excellent."

"Would you need any special equipment in her pen while she was wearing the headgear?"

Again the shrug. "Oh, the recording receiver needn't be in the pen with the beast. It can be outside in the corridor."

"How far away?" Grant asked.

"Ten meters . . . fifteen."

"Okay," Grant said. "Bring the console into the area tomorrow. Just leave it in the corridor without plugging it in."

"But it's useless unless Sheena wears the net on her head."

"I understand. The first step, though, is to get her to accept the recording equipment and not see it as a threat."

"Oh-ho," Karlstad said. "Our gorilla-dating scooter is turning into a primate psychologist."

Grant smiled at him. "Play your cards right, Egon, and I'll get you a date with Sheena."

Karlstad held up his hands in mock terror. "No, no! I can do without that!"

Van Neumann smirked at him. "Come on, Egon, this might be your only chance to get laid for months to come."

Grant and the others laughed. Karlstad frowned unhappily.

Every evening Grant brought "presents" to Sheena: a simple wooden jigsaw puzzle of four pieces big enough for the gorilla's thick fingers to handle; a spongy Nerf ball and a Velcro target that Grant glued to the wall of her pen so she could practice throwing; flash cards showing numbers up to ten and the letters of the English alphabet.

And with every new toy he brought, Grant also carried a few fruits or hard candies that Sheena immediately crunched in her powerful jaws and slurped down, licking her lips noisily and asking for more.

Sheena had the run of the aquarium section, which was sealed off with pressure hatches from the rest of the station. Usually Grant found the gorilla prowling the narrow corridor of the aquarium area or sitting quietly on her haunches, staring with endless fascination at the fish and dolphins.

After only a few nights of visiting, Grant found the gorilla waiting eagerly for him at the hatch he always came through. He soon found himself throwing an arm around Sheena's thick neck and hugging her, hoping that she would restrain herself and not crack his ribs as she hugged him back, desperately praying that neither Karlstad nor any of his other human friends saw him being affectionate with her.

The thought startled him. I said it, he realized. I said "human friends." For the love of the Living God, I'm thinking of this animal as a friend.

He was sitting on the floor of the corridor, tossing the Nerf ball back and forth to Sheena. The gorilla sat ponderously a few meters away, letting the ball bounce off her chest before she smothered it in her huge hands and then threw it—left-handed, Grant noticed—back to him.

"Good throw, Sheena!" Grant called as he caught the ball. "You're getting better every night."

"Good throw," the gorilla said back to him in her labored, rasping voice.

She is a friend, Grant told himself. Like a child, a little niece or some kid who lives up the street from you. They tossed the ball back and forth until the overhead lights dimmed to their nighttime setting.

"Time for bed, Sheena," Grant said, clambering slowly to his feet.

The gorilla got up on all fours and turned ponderously toward her pen, walking slowly on her knuckles. She was so big that Grant had to follow her; there was no room in the narrow corridor to walk beside her.

She never argues about bedtime, he thought. With an inward smile he realized that Sheena was better behaved than most of the human children he'd known back on Earth.

Pascal and her assistants had finally moved the recording equipment into the corridor a few meters from Sheena's pen, Grant saw. Awfully close to her pen, he thought. Maybe too close for comfort. The gorilla stopped at the open doorway of her pen, stared hard at the squarish gray metal console, then turned back toward Grant.

"It's all right, Sheena," he said. "Just some equipment from the neuro lab. It won't hurt you. Nothing to worry about."

He knew she couldn't understand all his words but hoped that his tone would reassure her.

Sheena shuffled up to the inert machine, sniffed at the blocky metal console suspiciously, patted it with both hands, then abruptly slapped it hard enough to rock it slightly off its locked wheels.

"No, no!" Grant exclaimed, rushing up to her, wondering how much punishment the solid-state electronics could take.

Sheena turned to him again. It was impossible to read an expression on her face, but Grant thought he saw something in her eyes—puzzlement? worry? fear?

"It's all right, Sheena," he repeated. "Nothing to worry about."

"Bad," Sheena rasped. "Bad." And she pushed at the console.

"No, it's not bad. Don't be frightened of it. It won't hurt you."

She sat down heavily and turned her head from Grant to the silent electronic equipment and back to Grant again.

"Why?" she asked.

Grant forced a smile. "We need to see how your brain works, Sheena. That's all."

"No," the gorilla said firmly. "Bad thing."

Grant instinctively reached out and rubbed Sheena's thickly boned head. "I won't let anybody hurt you, Sheena. I just won't let them."

"Grant friend."

"Yes," he said, nodding. "I'm your friend. I won't let them hurt you. Not ever."

The gorilla seemed to think this over for a few moments. Then she asked, "Why you?"

"I'm your friend, Sheena," Grant said again.

"Not me."

Grant didn't understand what she meant.

"Grant not me," Sheena rasped.

"I'm Grant, yes. And you're Sheena."

"Grant not me."

What is she trying to tell me? he wondered.

"Lane not me."

It struck Grant like a thunderclap. She realizes that the humans are different from her!

"Fish not me," Sheena added, pointing a long powerful arm toward the aquarium tanks.

"You're . . ." Grant hesitated. How do I answer her? He took a deep breath, then said, "You are Sheena. Sheena is big. Sheena is strong."

"No like me."

"That's right, Sheena, nobody else is like you. You're the only gorilla within half a billion kilometers."

"Why no like me?"

"I wish I could explain it to you, Sheena," Grant said, his eyes misting. "I really wish I could."

INTELLIGENCE

It's official," Muzorawa said. "We go in thirty days."

He had dropped into the fluid dynamics lab, he'd said, to check on Grant's progress with the ocean-mapping work. Grant was glad to see him. Muzorawa had been spending almost all his time training for the deep mission, and Grant found he'd missed the Sudanese dynamicist's strong, calm companionship.

"Thirty days," he said.

Muzorawa nodded solemnly. "I don't suppose I'll see much of you between now and then. Wo is putting us in quarantine."

"Quarantine?"

"For security, he says. None of the crew will be allowed to take meals in the cafeteria. They're setting up one of the conference rooms to serve as a wardroom for us."

"I won't see you at all, then," Grant said.

Muzorawa flashed his warm smile. "I'll drop in on you now and then, but I won't be able to work with you very much."

"You'll be busy, I know."

"This mapping work you've done, it will be a big help. A very big help."

"I hope so."

Grant was sitting at a computer desk that the technicians had rigged with a holographic screen so that he could view the ocean currents in three dimensions. The imagery was in garish false colors, electric blues and fire-engine reds, to make it easier to visualize the swirling turbulent flows streaming through the ocean. Still, Grant found that he had to sit at precisely the right spot and hold his head at just the proper angle to get the three-dimensional effect.

From the seat beside him, Muzorawa asked, "So . . . do you have anything new to show me?"

"I think maybe." Grant picked up the headset he'd left on the desktop and called for his latest graph. The holographic view winked out, replaced by a flat diagram of undulating curves sprinkled with a hail of red data points.

"Buckshot pattern," Muzorawa muttered.

"Not exactly," said Grant. Tracing one of the curves with an extended finger, he explained, "If you integrate all the data points by time, you get what looks like a periodicity."

Muzorawa sat up straighter. "Periodicity?"

"The thunderstorms carry energy from below into the upper atmosphere, right?"

Guardedly, Muzorawa conceded, "Right."

Jabbing a finger at the screen, Grant said, "The thunderstorms come in cycles. Both their frequency and intensity shifts every few days. Earth days, that is."

"How could they shift like that?"

Smiling now, Grant said, "I think it's a tidal effect."

"Tidal?"

"It seems to correlate with the positions of the four big moons. Look . . ." He pointed to the curves again. "When all four of them are on the same side of the planet, storm activity peaks—on that side of the planet."

Muzorawa squinted at the screen for long, silent moments. At last he asked, "How reliable is this data?"

"Some of it goes back a quarter century," Grant admitted. "I even have points from the earliest remote missions, before this station was built."

"Tidal effects." Muzorawa shook his head. "Hard to believe."

"But there they are," Grant insisted. "Small but definitely there."

"How in the name of the Prophet could tidal effects influence the thunderstorms?"

With a small wave of one hand, Grant replied, "There might be electromagnetic forces involved as well as gravitic."

"Electromagnetic?" Wide-eyed incredulity was plain on his normally somber face.

"Io's flux tube," Grant suggested, waving his hands. "The other Galilean moons cut Jupiter's magnetic field lines, too, don't they?"

Muzorawa settled back in his chair, deep in thought. Without thinking consciously about it, Grant punched up a real-time view of Jupiter on the big wallscreen above the desks. The planet loomed over them, huge and awesome, clouds racing and swirling, flashes of lightning flickering like fireflies along the terminator and into the night side of the planet's immense bulk. Fireflies, Grant thought. More like hydrogen bombs; each lightning bolt released megatons of energy.

With growing enthusiasm, Muzorawa said, "This is very interesting, Grant. Extremely interesting. I'll have to check the records as far back as we can go . . . all the way back to the *Galileo* probe, if necessary."

"I'll check the records," Grant said. "You have enough to do over the next few weeks."

With a reluctant nod, Muzorawa agreed. Then he asked, "Have you seen any tidal effect in the Red Spot?"

Grant was surprised by the question. "You're not planning to go into the Spot, are you?"

"God forbid!" Muzorawa raised both hands. "I only wondered if the Spot changes in any predictable way."

"There's just not enough data from inside the Spot," Grant said. "I've got a scattering of data from more than five years ago, but even then the probes didn't last long enough to send back much."

"They stopped sending probes into the Spot when Wo took over the station," Muzorawa explained. "He said it was a waste of time and effort."

"He's right. That's an awfully powerful cyclone down there."

"Yes, that's true enough. Still . . ."

"You're not going near the Spot, are you?" Grant asked again, staring at the view of the giant planet.

"No, of course not. We'll be on the opposite side of the planet."

"How deep do you plan to go?"

"Deep enough to find whatever those things are that we saw swimming on the first mission."

"Do you really think they're alive?" Grant asked.

Muzorawa turned from the wallscreen to look at Grant. "How high is up?" he asked.

Grant understood. Don't ask useless questions. The first mission had detected objects in the ocean. This new mission would try to determine what those objects might be. Until they got more data, questions about the nature of the objects could not be answered.

But then Muzorawa nodded, ever so slightly. Barely a dip of his chin.

"I believe they are alive, yes. But that is only a belief, a matter of faith—or perhaps it would be better to say a matter of hope. Until we obtain hard evidence, that is all we have to go on: our individual faith, our hopes, our fears."

"Fears?"

"Oh, yes. Fears." Muzorawa pointed to the big wallscreen. "There are many people who fear what we might discover underneath those clouds."

Grant blinked with surprise. "Who? Nobody here on the station, is there?"

"Probably not," Muzorawa replied. "Wo has screened all the personnel here rather thoroughly." He hesitated, thinking over his next words, then said, "He was afraid of you at first, you know."

"*He* was afraid of *me*?"

Smiling, "Certainly. He feared you were an agent from the Zealots, come to spy on his work."

"The Zealots?"

"The ultraconservatives. They are always among us, those who fear new knowledge. Nearly a thousand years ago they destroyed a great Persian astronomer and mathematician: Omar Khayyám."

"Omar . . . I thought he was a poet."

Muzorawa shook his head slowly. "His quatrains were a hobby. He was a scientist. He understood that Earth goes around the Sun three centuries before Copernicus. For that the mullahs destroyed him. To this day no one knows where he lies buried."

"Ultraconservatives," Grant muttered. "Zealots."

"In my part of the world they call themselves the Sword of Islam. You have them among your New Morality, don't you?"

"But I'm not one of *them*!"

"Dr. Wo wasn't sure of you. That was why he gave us orders to keep sensitive information from you."

"But why would the New Morality, or the Zealots, or whatever, want to spy on him?" Grant hated himself for saying it, for lying to his friend and mentor. But I'm not a Zealot, he told himself. I'm not working for fanatics. I'm not!

Muzorawa gripped Grant by the shoulder. "My friend, there are powerful forces among the Zealots who fear new knowledge. They do not appreciate our studies of extraterrestrial life-forms."

"I know some of the more conservative Believers are uncomfortable with the idea of alien life," Grant admitted. "But—"

"If they are uncomfortable with alien bacteria and lichen," Muzorawa interrupted, "how do you think they feel about meeting *intelligent* aliens?"

"Intelligent?"

"The possibility exists."

Grant's inside felt suddenly hollow. "Intelligent creatures? You mean, here, on Jupiter?"

"The possibility exists," Muzorawa repeated.

"But there's no evidence . . ."

"You haven't seen any evidence. Dr. Wo still does not trust you as fully as that."

"The things you saw in the ocean?"

"He believes," Muzorawa said.

"Intelligent?"

"There isn't enough data even to confirm that they are living organisms. But the director believes they may be not only living but intelligent."

Understanding flooded into Grant's mind. "That's why he brought in the dolphins. And Sheena!"

"To study nonhuman intelligence. Yes. To help us in the effort to communicate with the Jovians."

"All this . . . based on his *belief*? On his hunch? His guess?"

"Belief is a very powerful force, my friend. More powerful than you can imagine. Copernicus believed the Earth revolves around the Sun. Maxwell believed light is a form of electromagnetic radiation, based on nothing more than the coincidence of numbers in his equations."

"And the Zealots believe that God created us in His image. Extraterrestrial life threatens that belief."

"And *intelligent* extraterrestrial life demolishes it."

Grant countered, "But we've known about the Martians for decades now."

"They are extinct," Muzorawa said. "And they can be explained away by the faithful."

With a nod Grant conceded the point. His own father firmly believed that the long-vanished Martians had actually come to Earth and that Mars had been the original Garden of Eden. All the archeological evidence showed that such an idea was nonsense, it was impossible, but that is what the faithful believed. What they *wanted* to believe, Grant knew.

"Intelligent extraterrestrial life," Muzorawa went on, "that in no way looks like us, is a frightening idea for many people, in many religions."

"God created man in His image," Grant muttered.

"If we find intelligent life that does not resemble us . . ."

"It disproves Scripture," Grant concluded.

"That is why the conservatives everywhere have opposed space exploration. That is why they opposed using telescopes to search for signals from extraterrestrial civilizations."

"And Wo thought I might be one of them, just because I'm faithful to my religion."

"I think he trusts you now."

Grant nodded uncertainly. "Maybe."

"He has taken you under his wing, hasn't he? He's working with you on your thesis."

Grant nodded again, but he thought, A man like Wo is smart enough, devious enough, to keep me under his wing so that he can keep a close watch on me. Maybe he knows about Beech. Maybe he knows I'm supposed to be spying on him.

Beech. Grant saw in his mind's eye the solemn, intense, tawny-eyed face of Ellis Beech. Him, a fanatic? Grant wondered. It couldn't be. Ellis Beech was just a functionary, a bureaucrat, a man who sat behind a desk all day and shuffled papers. He couldn't be a Zealot. He just couldn't be!

Precisely at that moment, the overhead speaker of the station's intercom system blared, "GRANT ARCHER, REPORT TO THE DIRECTOR'S OFFICE IMMEDIATELY."

Startled, Grant thought, By the Living God, the man can read my mind!

COUNTDOWN

If Dr. Wo really could see what Grant was thinking, he gave no sign of it. His perpetual scowl seemed a bit less fierce than usual as he gruffly waved Grant to the chair in front of his desk. As always, the desk was bare, except for the vase of flowers—thickly lush peonies, this time—the only touch of color in the starkly functional office. Despite the almost stifling warmth of the room, Wo's high-collared tunic was buttoned up to his throat, as usual.

"Dr. Muzorawa has told you that the mission is scheduled for launch in thirty days." It was a statement, not a question.

"Yes, sir," Grant replied, thinking, He must have every lab and compartment in the station bugged.

"I have been reviewing your work on the ocean dynamics," Wo said in his labored harsh whisper. "Tidal variations. Very interesting. That bears further study."

"Yessir, I agree."

"And how is Sheena reacting to the idea of wearing the neural headgear?"

Grant had worn the spiderweb of electrodes draped over his own head the previous night, to get Sheena accustomed to the idea of the net. The gorilla might have been amused; she was unable to laugh, of course, but she referred several times to "Grant hat."

"I think she'll be okay with it, in a week or so. She's not spooked by the console any longer. It just takes her a little time to get comfortable with new things—especially things that have the smell of a laboratory about them."

Wo drummed his stubby fingers on the desk. "She has a long memory."

"She doesn't forget something that frightened her, or gave her pain."

"The neural net will not hurt her in any way."

"But it could frighten her, unless she sees it as a toy or a game."

"Yes," Wo conceded. "Very clever."

"It doesn't take much to outsmart a two-year-old," Grant heard himself say, with some bitterness. "Only time and patience."

Wo gave him a sardonic smile. "I am pleased that you are learning patience."

"Sheena's a good teacher, in that regard."

The director's thin smile widened. "You are becoming almost Confucian in your growing wisdom, Mr. Grant."

Not knowing what else to say, Grant replied, "Thank you, sir."

"I am afraid, however, that I have still another duty to place upon your shoulders."

"Another?"

"I have appointed you to join the deep mission team. You will report to the mission control center tomorrow for intensive training. You must be capable of assisting the mission controllers by the time the mission is launched."

"Intensive training?" Grant echoed. "But . . . when? How can I . . . there aren't enough hours in the day for everything that's on my plate."

Curtly Wo replied, "Then I shall remove some items from your plate. Your duties in the fluid dynamics lab will be suspended until the mission is completed."

"But my thesis!"

"It can wait for a few weeks."

"The ocean mapping . . . you'll need that for the mission."

"The mapping is sufficiently detailed for the purposes of the mission. Further refinement is not necessary."

Shaking his head vehemently, Grant argued, "How can you say that? How can you tell how much information is enough? The more data I generate—"

Wo cut him short with an angry slash of one hand. "It is *my* responsibility to say how much is enough."

"You're making an arbitrary decision."

"Yes. Of course I am." Wo looked away from Grant for a moment, as if trying to control his anger, then said in a more reasonable tone, "As a scientist, I agree with you. Wholeheartedly. The more data the better. Keep probing, keep learning."

"So then—"

"But I am not merely a scooter. I am director of this station and chief of this deep mission. I must make hard decisions. I must decide how to use the personnel I have at my disposal, and I have decided that the best use for you is to assist in the control center during the mission."

"There are several dozen technicians on this station who can do that job, and do it better than I could."

"Perhaps," Wo conceded, "but I do not choose to bring additional personnel into this mission."

"Why not? Wouldn't it be smarter to—"

"Enough!" Wo snapped. "I have made my decision and you will carry out my orders. End of discussion."

Grant fell silent for a moment. The two of them glared at each other across the director's gleaming desk.

"This is a security matter, isn't it?" Grant asked in a much softer voice. "You don't want to bring additional people into the mission for fear of a security leak."

Wo did not reply for several heartbeats. Grant felt perspiration trickling down his ribs. Why does he keep this office so hellishly hot? he wondered silently.

At last Wo said, "Dr. Muzorawa has told you about the Zealots."

Grant conceded it with a nod. Lord Almighty, he really *does* listen in on all our conversations.

"I fear them," Wo said, so low that Grant barely heard the words.

"But surely, here on this station, we're millions of kilometers away from them."

"Are we? Who among those dozens of technicians you spoke of might be a Zealot? Who among the scooters working on Europa or studying Io?"

"Not a scientist," Grant protested.

"Why not? You are a Believer, are you not?"

"Yes, but I'm not a fanatic."

Wo's eyes bored into Grant's, as if trying to pierce to his soul. "No," he said at last, "I trust that you are not."

It was that word "trust" that hit Grant. He heard himself say, "When I was assigned to come to this station, the New Morality asked me to report back to them on what you are doing."

Wo said nothing; his expression did not alter one millimeter.

"They asked me to spy on you," Grant admitted.

"And have you?"

"I haven't told them a thing. I haven't learned anything that they didn't already know. But if you're going to make me a part of this deep mission . . ."

Dr. Wo closed his eyes and nodded. "I see. Your loyalties are divided."

"No, they're not," Grant snapped. "I'm a Believer, and I'm a scientist, also. But my loyalties are clear. I'm not a spy, and whatever the New Morality people back on Earth want to know has nothing to do with faith in God. What they've asked me to do is politics, not religion."

Again Wo lapsed into silence. Grant waited for several moments, then said, "You can trust me, sir. I'm not a spy. I never wanted to spy on you. They never gave me a choice."

"I want to trust you, Archer. There are very few people aboard this station whom I can trust. That is why my team for the deep mission is so pitifully small."

"That's why you put the team in quarantine," Grant said.

Wo's chin sunk to his chest. In a voice trembling with inner rage he added, "It would take only one of them, you must understand. One Zealot. This station is a very fragile place. One fanatic could destroy us all."

"A terrorist?"

"A man—or a woman—who is convinced that our search for intelligent alien life is sinful. One person who is willing to die in order to kill all of us."

"Don't the psych profiles screen out such fanatics?"

Wo glowered at his naïveté. Then his anger seemed to fade. "I should never have allowed nanomachines in this station," he whispered, so low Grant could barely hear him. "That was a mistake. A personal frailty." He shook his head disconsolately.

Grant had no response for that. The idea was too foreign to his thinking, alien to everything he believed.

"If this station is destroyed, it will never be replaced," Wo continued, his anger palpable. "Never. It is difficult enough to get the funds for maintenance and repair. They would never allow a new station to be built."

"No, that can't be true. The work that we're doing here—"

"They *despise* the work we do! If it weren't for the profits that the scoopships make, they would have stopped all our funding and shut down this station."

"They wouldn't do that! They couldn't!"

"You think not?" Wo almost sneered at him. "At this moment there is a group of IAA officials in a fusion torch ship on a high-acceleration burn, racing to get here."

"IAA people?"

"An 'inspection and evaluation team'," Wo said, his voice burning with acid. "How many of them are New Morality members? How many belong to the Holy Disciples or to the Sword of Islam? One of them is a Jesuit, that much I know. An astronomer, no less."

"And they're coming here?"

"'To review our work. That's why I believe that you have not made an effective spy for them; they would close us down outright if they knew what we are doing."

Grant shook his head. "You think they're coming here to close down the station?"

"Why else? 'Inspection and evaluation' indeed!"

"Not necessarily," Grant said. "The IAA isn't controlled by the New Morality."

"Pah!"

"All right, I admit there are ultraconservatives in the New Morality and other groups who want most scientific research stopped. But they're only a small minority of the movement. A noisy, vocal minority, but still only one small segment of the whole. The people in power, the ones in high office, they understand the importance of exploring the universe."

"Such as the ones who asked you to spy on us?"

Grant had no reply for that. He realized that Dr. Wo was probably right. The IAA depended on national governments for its funding, and most of those governments were thoroughly under the influence of movements such as the New Morality.

Wo broke the growing silence. "Why is nanotechnology forbidden?"

"Nanotechnology?" Grant asked, wondering what this had to do with the IAA or the New Morality. "They use it on the Moon."

"Only under very strict controls. The luniks had to fight an outright war against the United Nations to keep their right to use nanomachines. And people who have nanomachines in their bodies aren't allowed on Earth at all."

"Nanomachines can be turned into weapons," Grant pointed out. "That's why they're banned."

Wo snorted disdainfully. "Pah! Why do you think you are using computer systems that are at least ten years old? Why don't you have an artificial intelligence system to assist you in your work?"

Confused by another sudden shift in subject, Grant replied, "No one's been able to make an AI system that performs reliably."

"Not so," the director snapped. "Twenty years ago research on AI systems was stopped. Why? Because the researchers had produced a prototype that *did* work. Quite reliably."

"How could they stop all research—"

"Because they feared where AI research was heading. They feared the creation of machines with the intelligence of humans. With higher intelligence, inevitably."

Grant just sat there, trying to digest this flood of accusations.

"If they knew where our exploration of Jupiter is heading, if they understood what we might uncover . . ." Wo left the thought unfinished.

"They'd be afraid that we might find intelligent life in the ocean," Grant heard himself whisper.

"Exactly. That is why I keep our security so tight. That is why I refuse to bring in more people. One of them might turn out to be a Zealot fanatic."

Grant tried to sort it all out in his mind. "But there's no evidence for intelligent life down there. We don't even know if there's any form of life at all in the ocean."

"Don't we?" Wo jabbed a stubby finger at the keyboard built into his desktop. One of the walls dissolved into a murky, grainy featureless scene.

"This video was salvaged from the first mission into the ocean," Wo explained, his rasping voice labored, tired.

Lightning flickered in the distance. Lightning? Grant asked himself. Underwater?

As he stared at the wallscreen, Grant realized that what he was seeing was not lightning. The flashes of light were red, yellow, deep orange.

Slowly, before his fascinated eyes, the lights took shape. They were *things* in the water, a dozen or more of them, coasting through the ocean together, lights flickering back and forth.

Living creatures! Grant realized. And they're *signaling* to one another!

Grant watched, fascinated. The lights winked back and forth, back and forth. There was a pattern to them, it seemed. First one, then all the others lit up in the same colors. He couldn't tell if the lights formed any particular shape or form; the creatures were too far away for him to make out anything except a bright momentary glow against the vast darkness of the sea. Maddening. If only he could get closer, get better detail—

The scene winked off. The screen became a metal bulkhead once again. Grant felt like a child who'd just had a Christmas present yanked out of his hands.

He turned back to Dr. Wo. "They're alive," Grant whispered.

"I believe so. But the evidence is hardly conclusive."

"And they were signaling back and forth!"

"Perhaps."

"Is that the closest you got to them?"

"We were slightly less than fifteen hundred kilometers' slant range when the accident ended our mission. They were considerably deeper in the ocean than we were."

"Fifteen hundred . . ." Grant blinked with disbelief. "Then the creatures must be huge, to see them at that distance."

"On the order of five to fifteen kilometers in diameter," Wo said flatly.

"That's *enormous*!"

Wo nodded slowly. "That is the dimension that our computer analysis shows. It may be wrong, of course."

"But . . . how . . . why . . . ? Grant's thoughts were swirling.

"Organic particles form in the clouds," Wo said. "That we have seen; we have even sampled them. They rain downward, into the ocean. Like manna from heaven, *food* drops down from the clouds into the ocean."

"But they must be destroyed by the chemistry in the ocean," Grant mused.

"Or they could be eaten by those creatures you just saw."

"Living Jovians."

Wo counted off on his stubby fingers. "There is an energy flow from the planet's core. There is an ocean of liquid water—"

"Heavily laced with ammonia and God knows what else. An acid ocean, really."

Ignoring that, Wo continued, "There is a constant food source raining down into that ocean. Energy, water, food: Wherever those factors have been found, life exists. Those are living Jovians swimming in that ocean."

"But intelligent . . . ?"

"Why not? They appear to signal to each other. In that immense ocean, over billions of years of time, why should not intelligence evolve?

On Earth, dolphins and whales show considerable intelligence. Why not the same on Jupiter? Or even better?"

"Better?"

"Why not?" Wo repeated.

Then Grant remembered, "But if the IAA team is really coming here to shut down the station—"

"That is why I am pushing to get the deep mission off as soon as possible."

"When are they scheduled to arrive here?"

Wo did not need to look at a calendar. "In thirty-nine days. The deep mission will be in the ocean by then," he gloated. "There will be no way for them to call it back." The director broke into a rare smile.

"In the meantime," Grant muttered, "if the Zealots find out about this, they'll try to destroy the station."

Wo's enthusiasm drained away. He sighed. "One suicidal fanatic, that is all it would take."

"But . . . suppose you do confirm that there are intelligent Jovians down in the ocean. What then?"

Wo leaned back in his chair and gazed at the metal mesh of the ceiling. "Then we beam the information back to Earth. To the headquarters of the International Astronautical Authority, to the scientific offices of the United Nations, to all the news networks, to every university. Simultaneously. We make our announcement so loud, so wide, that it cannot possibly be overlooked or suppressed."

"It would certainly shock a lot of people," Grant admitted.

Wo nodded slowly. "Yes. That discovery will shake the foundations of everything. They will be *forced* to continue our work, even to expand it. The people of the world will demand it."

"Maybe," Grant said, wondering if that were true. What would the people of the world think if we found intelligent creatures here on Jupiter? Living intelligent aliens! How would the people of the world react to that?

"Or maybe," he added, "the Zealots or some other gang of crazies will try to kill us all, out of fear and hatred."

Wo snorted disdainfully. "What of it? Once the discovery is announced, no one can erase the information."

"But they'll kill us!"

"Yes, they might," the director admitted easily. "That does not matter. It will be worth our lives to have made such a discovery."

CONTROL CENTER

Grant told no one of his conversation with the director. He's a fanatic, Grant realized. He's just as crazy in his own way as the Zealots or any other radical extremist. I wonder if any of the others know how he really thinks.

Yet he spoke of it to no one. Not even Lane or Zeb or the others who must already know about it. Grant agreed with the director in one respect: The fewer people who know what's really going on, the better.

Wo's concept of a quarantine was very loose, Grant found. He and the other members of the mission team took their meals in a conference room and worked together, but they still slept in their own quarters and were able to mingle with the rest of the station's personnel. It was more a matter of attitude, of a sense of responsibility, that kept them from talking about the mission with the "outsiders."

Krebs reinforced the attitude in her own grim style. The first evening that Grant had dinner with the team, she showed up in the conference room, glaring at everyone.

"You will discuss our work with no one," she said, out of a clear sky. "That is vital! Maximally vital! Each of you has signed a security agreement. Violate that agreement and you will suffer the full penalties of the law. Nothing less."

Then she sat down to eat. No one sat within three chairs of her.

Grant forgot about his thesis work, his research on the Jovian ocean's dynamics. If those things really are living creatures, if they're intelligent . . . we're sitting on top of the biggest discovery in history! Maybe what the cameras saw are really submarines, giant mobile underwater habitats. Maybe the Jovians have a technology equal to our own. Or better.

Then a voice in his mind warned, You're sitting on top of the biggest powder keg in history. Watch your steps carefully. You could get yourself killed over this.

The control center, he found, was an unremarkable chamber crowded with six computer-topped desks and communications gear that looked to Grant as if it had been shoehorned into a compartment several sizes too small to accommodate it all. There was barely enough room to squeeze into the little wheeled desk chairs. Director Wo had a separate desk all to himself, though, smack in the middle of the room, with an aisle from the corridor door straight to it—the only open space in the compartment.

The wallscreens were connected to the simulations chamber down at the aquarium, so Grant got to see Muzorawa and O'Hara and the others every shift, at least on-screen. And Karlstad, too, looking tense and almost frightened as he stood at his underwater post, anchored to the deck by plastic loops set into the flooring.

Dr. Wo placed Grant at the console that monitored the submersible's electrical power systems. Frankovich, at the life-support console alongside him, was assigned to teaching Grant what he had to know.

"So he sucked you into this, too," Karlstad said through his face-mask radio when Grant first showed up in the control center and said hello to the crew in the tank.

"We're just one tight little family," Grant replied.

"Never think that," Karlstad muttered. "We're prisoners. Puppets on his strings. He wiggles his fingers and we do the dancing for him."

Krebs splashed into the simulator tank and Karlstad went silent.

Grant turned to Frankovich, sitting at the console beside his. "You'd better start showing me what I'm supposed to do here," Grant said, sliding awkwardly into the tight little chair.

"Trying to get on Wo's good side?" Frankovich asked lightly. "That's a dubious procedure. I'm not certain our revered leader has a good side."

Evenings Grant spent with Sheena, no matter how tired he was from the long hours in the control center. He understood Wo's interest in the gorilla and the dolphins now. How do we communicate with another species? How do we make ourselves understood to creatures that have nothing whatsoever in common with us?

Often Grant took his dinner down to the aquarium and ate with the gorilla. Karlstad twitted him about it, of course, but Grant wanted Sheena to accept the neural net headgear with as little commotion as possible. After several nights of feeling silly with the wires draped over his head, Grant brought an extra set and offered it to the gorilla.

Sheena seemed torn between curiosity and fear. At first she merely looked at the headgear, one set draped over Grant's sandy hair, the other lying casually on the floor beside him.

Grant was sharing his fruit cup dessert with Sheena when she picked up the net from the floor with her syrup-sticky fingers. She held it in front of her face, studying it, the electrode-studded wires hanging in her massive hand like some arcane set of jewelry.

Tapping his own net, Grant smiled and said, "Funny hat, Sheena."

"Funny hat," she echoed in her painful whisper.

"I brought it for you."

The gorilla's deep-brown eyes shifted from the dangling net to Grant's face and then back again.

Grant said nothing.

Sheena slowly lifted the net higher and then clumsily plopped it on her head. It slid to the floor with a metallic clicking noise.

"Let me help you," Grant said, reaching for the wires.

"No." Sheena pushed Grant back, just a brush of her hand, but it was almost enough to bowl him over. He'd forgotten how strong the gorilla was. I'm taking her for granted, he thought. That's a mistake.

Sheena fumbled with the net, using both hands this time, and draped it over her head once more. It was lopsided and came down over one eye, but it stayed put.

Grant wanted to laugh at the ludicrous sight, but he held himself to a broad grin. "Good girl, Sheena!" he approved.

"Funny hat," said the gorilla.

"Funny hat," Grant agreed, patting his own head.

In a week or so we can connect the net and start taking readings of her brain patterns, he thought. Let her get accustomed to it first. And I'll get Pascal to show me how to work the console. No sense bringing strangers in here. It would just upset Sheena.

His ribs twinged when he took a deep breath. No, Grant told himself, I certainly don't want to upset Sheena.

BOOK III

For he sees that even wise men die . . .
But man in his pomp will not endure;
He is like the beasts that perish.

—Psalm 49

FINAL REHEARSAL

The month flashed past like a single brief day. Grant worked double shifts in the mission control center, squeezed in beside Frankovich, watching as the wallscreens showed Lane, Karlstad, Irene Pascal, and Muzorawa working in the aquarium on the simulators under Dr. Krebs's baleful eyes.

At first they used only the manual controls in the simulator tank, but after a few days they began to link through the biochip electrodes with the ship systems.

Wo sat at the central console in the control chamber during each simulation run, but to Grant's eyes the director often looked distracted, unresponsive to what was going on in the aquarium tank. He's worrying about that IAA inspection team on its way here, Grant thought. They're due to reach the station exactly seven days after the mission is launched.

Each evening they ate in the conference room and hashed over the day's work. Krebs rarely had dinner with them, and when she did she was almost completely shunned by the others, eating alone at the head of the table, glowering. The only words she had for the team were warnings about security and complaints that their work in the simulator was sloppy or downright poor.

Most evenings Grant stole away early to spend some time with Sheena; the others were so intent on the mission that they barely mentioned Grant's "dates" with the gorilla. Even Karlstad had found a new topic for dinner-table discussion.

"My God," he said at dinner one evening, "being plugged in like that really is better than sex—almost."

"When you get really adept at it," Muzorawa explained, "you can even link with each other. It's almost like telepathy."

"Really?" Karlstad turned toward O'Hara, leering.

"Get your mind above your beltline, Egon," she said. "It's all mental, not physical."

"The brain is the most important sex organ in the body," he countered.

She shook her head, frowning.

Muzorawa explained for Grant that the electrode implants also contain microminiaturized semiconductor lasers linked through the fiber-optic lines to connect with the ship's systems.

"Photo-optics can carry loads more information than electronics," said O'Hara.

"But the human nervous system is electrical, isn't it?" Grant asked.

"Electrochemical," Karlstad corrected.

"Then if all this photo-optical data is pumped into your nervous system—"

"It produces an overload," Muzorawa said.

"And the wildest sensations you've ever experienced," O'Hara added.

Karlstad sighed mightily.

After dinner Grant went as usual to Sheena. He was trying to get the gorilla accustomed to the neural net. She still could not fit it over her head properly, but gradually Grant got her to accept his help in placing the spiderweb of electrodes properly over her skull.

"If only we could shave her head," Pascal said yearningly over a late-night snack in the conference room.

Pascal was pulling double duty, too: watching Grant with Sheena each evening through the surveillance cameras and working in the fish tank on the mission simulator. She looked as exhausted as Grant felt.

"She wouldn't like being shaved," Grant pointed out.

"We could sedate her."

"It wouldn't work," Grant said as he picked at his open sandwich of simulated roast beef. "By the time she got accustomed to the fact that she'd been shaved, her hair would've grown back again."

Pascal sighed. "Yes, I suppose you're right."

"If she'd let me fasten the net under her chin, then you'd get a decent contact."

"If she'd let you." Pascal put down her fork, frowning. "Do you realize that the laboratory animal is running this experiment? It's infuriating."

It surprised Grant to hear Sheena referred to as a laboratory animal.

And it surprised him even more when he realized that he thought of the gorilla as a person.

Trying to soothe the neurophysiologist, Grant said, "I'll get Sheena to wear the net and make good contact with the electrodes. Give me a few more days."

"We'll be launching in six days."

"Sheena can't be put on a schedule, I'm afraid."

"Yes, yes, I understand," Pascal said. "Still, it's very frustrating. Maddening."

"I can run the console for you," Grant said. "I'll collect the data and have it ready for you when you come back from the mission."

Pascal gave him a dubious look but said nothing.

The door to the corridor slid open and Red Devlin stepped into the conference room as casually as he might stroll along a city boulevard.

"Irene, luv, how are you?"

"What are you doing in here?" Grant demanded. "You're not supposed—"

"Now, now," Devlin chided. "Don't get your shorts in a twist, Grant. Who d'you think brings your food and goodies in here, eh? Somebody's gotta check on your coffee supply, mate."

"It's all right," Pascal said softly. "He's just doing his job."

"Right you are, Irene luv. And you, Grant, how's Sheena treatin' you these days?"

"Fine," Grant said, weary of jokes about him and Sheena.

Devlin pulled a plastic vial from his pocket and handed it to Pascal. "You sure you need these?" he asked, sounding genuinely concerned. "Looks to me like you need somethin' to help you sleep, not keep you awake."

"I sleep very well," Pascal replied. "I need to be alert during the day."

"In the simulator, eh?" Devlin asked.

Pascal nodded.

"How's it goin'? When do you push off?"

Before Pascal could answer, Grant said, "Dr. Wo doesn't want us to discuss the mission with anyone who isn't on the team."

Devlin stiffened into a lampoon of a soldier's coming to attention, clicked his heels, and snapped off a salute. "Aye, aye, sir!"

Grant laughed despite himself.

Pascal said, "Grant is correct. We are not supposed to discuss the mission with you."

"I understand," Devlin said, relaxing. "No worries."

"But in three days you will not see me for a while," she added.

Grant felt a surge of dismay. He knew it was silly, but rules are meant to be followed, not broken. Krebs and Dr. Wo might be paranoid, but Grant thought it was better to be paranoid than the victim of some terrorist's fiery zeal.

As Devlin headed for the coffee urn, Grant leaned toward Pascal and whispered, "Irene, you told him three days. But the mission doesn't launch until six days from now."

"Yes," she agreed, nodding. "But in three days the crew goes into immersion. We do not come out once we are immersed."

"I didn't realize—"

"Once we begin breathing that awful liquid, we do not come into the air again until the mission is completed," she said.

Grant thought she looked grim, like a prisoner about to be swallowed up by an inescapable jail. And she looked more than a little frightened, too.

He walked with Irene back to their quarters. Pascal's compartment was a few dozen meters up the corridor from Grant's. The corridor was dim, shadowy in its nighttime lighting. They saw no one else along the way except a solitary security guard pacing sleepily along his rounds; it was too late at night for casual strollers.

So it surprised Grant to see Kayla Ukara sitting on the floor next to Pascal's door, her back propped against the wall, her head resting on her knees as if asleep.

"Oh," Irene said in a small voice.

Ukara's head snapped up, her eyes fully alert. Instead of her usual fierce, pantherlike expression, she actually smiled up at Irene.

As Ukara scrambled to her feet, Pascal turned to Grant, red-cheeked with embarrassment. "Thank you for walking me home," she said in a quick, low voice.

Grant nodded, puzzled. "It's okay. My place is just down the corridor."

But Pascal was not paying any attention to him. Her eyes were on Ukara and no one else.

Grant muttered a good night to them both and continued down the corridor. He glanced once over his shoulder at them. Pascal was tapping out the security code on her door lock; Kayla had a long, slim arm around Irene's waist.

They're lovers! Grant felt shocked. He knew he shouldn't, knew it was none of his business, that the two women were adults and had the right to their own personal lives. Yet deep in the core of his being he felt that what they were doing was wrong, deeply wrong.

It's none of your business, Grant told himself. Forget about it.

Still, it bothered him.

The next night Grant tied the neural net he was wearing under his chin.

"See?" he said to Sheena. "It looks better."

Sheena eyed him suspiciously.

They were sitting on the plastic-tiled floor of Sheena's spacious pen, Grant facing the gorilla. Her bulk loomed over him like a hairy mountain.

"And it won't fall off." Grant shook his head vigorously. The net stayed snug around his skull.

Sheena waggled her head ponderously and her net slid clattering to the floor.

She huffed and stared at the net at her feet. Then she picked it up and draped it over her head again. Grant expected her to try to tie its loose ends, but instead she simply looked down at her open hands.

"No," she said, and Grant thought it sounded discouraged, disheartened.

She looked at Grant. "Hands . . . no . . . Sheena can't do."

Grant felt a wave of sadness wash over him. She knows her hands aren't dexterous enough to tie the ends. She knows how limited she is.

"Grant do," said Sheena.

"Sure, Sheena," he said, scrambling toward her. "I'll be happy to help you."

"Grant help Sheena."

"Yes, I will." He knelt before her powerful body, feeling the heat of her, knowing that those arms of hers could crush his ribs, and carefully tied the neural net under her chin.

"There," he said, sitting back on the floor again. "Now we're the same."

"No." Sheena swung her heavy head from side to side slowly. "Not same. Sheena not Grant. Grant not Sheena."

He gulped once, wondering what he could say. When he found his voice, he replied, "I'm your friend, Sheena. You and I are friends."

"Friends." Sheena seemed to think that over for a while. Then she said again, "Grant help Sheena."

"Yes," he said. "I'll help you all I can."

When the overhead lights went down to their nighttime level and Sheena lumbered into the corner of her pen where the plastic padding had been wadded up into a sleeping nest, Grant climbed wearily to his feet and stepped out into the narrow corridor.

"Good night, Sheena," he called.

She must have already fallen asleep, because she did not reply. Grant tiptoed to the electronic console sitting a few meters up the corridor. Gingerly he flicked on the power and activated the scanners.

Four small display screens along the top of the console lit up. Green worms of lines crawled across them. Squinting in the dim lighting, Grant checked to make certain that the equipment was recording Sheena's brain waves. He nodded, satisfied, hoping that the data would cheer Pascal before she left on the deep mission. Maybe we'll catch her dreaming, he hoped.

The next morning he located Pascal in the lockers where the mission crew changed into their wetsuits. No one else was in the locker area. The others had already gone to the aquarium for the day's simulation tasks.

Pascal was pleased that they were getting data at last, but Grant could see that her mind was obviously focused on the mission.

"By the time you get back," he said, trying to sound cheerful, "you'll have enough data to write a book."

"*If* we get back," Pascal muttered.

"If?"

She zippered up the front of the suit, then reached for the plastic full-face mask on the shelf above the empty suit rack. Grant realized that her legs were bare. Glittery electrodes lined the outside of both legs from her hips to halfway down her calves. They looked like the ends of silver bullets embedded in her flesh. It took a conscious effort for Grant not to stare at them.

"The closer we get to launch, the more fearful I become," Pascal confessed.

"That's natural, I suppose," said Grant. "Nerves."

"Yes," she said bitterly. "Entirely natural. But not pleasant to experience."

Pascal headed for the doorway, her bare feet padding softly on the plastic tiles. Grant saw that she had forgotten her air tank. He picked it up from the floor of her locker, surprised at how heavy it was, and started after her.

Christel Krebs appeared at the doorway, her bulky form effectively blocking it. Pascal stopped, holding her transparent mask in both hands in front of herself, as if for protection.

Krebs stepped awkwardly toward her. Her thick legs were studded with electrodes, too, Grant saw.

She seemed to peer at Pascal quizzically.

"I'm sorry I'm running late, Dr. Krebs," Pascal began. "You see—"

"Dr. Pascal," said Krebs, as if recognizing her for the first time. She blinked, then went on, "The others are all waiting for you. We have no time to waste."

"Yes, I understand," said Pascal.

"Irene," Grant called. He held out the air tank. "You'll need this, won't you?"

Pascal hesitated, then put her mask down on the floor, and allowed Grant to help her slip the tank's straps over her shoulders.

"Archer, isn't it?" Krebs said.

"Yes, ma'am."

"You should be at the control center, not here."

"That's right, ma'am," Grant replied. "But I wanted Dr. Pascal to know about last night's work with Sheena."

"That is of no relevance to this mission," Krebs snapped, her voice sharp as a whipstroke. "Get to your post immediately."

"Yes'm."

It was tense in the control center. Even Dr. Wo, sitting in the center of the crowded, overheated chamber, looked coiled tight with tension.

This is the last simulation, Grant knew. If there are no slip-ups today, tomorrow they practice in the sub itself.

Krebs floated above the four crew members, snapping commands, hovering over their shoulders as they stood at their positions, held down to the deck by foot loops, and went through the procedures for separating the ship from the station and launching it into an independent orbit around Jupiter.

O'Hara, Pascal, Karlstad, and Muzorawa worked together like a smooth, well-oiled machine. They barely had to touch the manual controls. Even Krebs's snarls toned down almost to a purring satisfaction with their performance.

Grant watched, fascinated, as the simulator's equipment responded to their control, untouched. It's like magic, he said to himself, awed even though he knew the biochips were transmitting control signals to receiving electrodes in the ship systems.

Out of the corner of his eye, Grant could see Dr. Wo studying the displays on his console. He wasn't watching the wallscreens at all, so intent was he on the readouts that showed the simulated ship's systems and the medical monitors of the five people in the aquarium tank.

Grant concentrated on his own display screens. He was responsible for the propulsion and electrical power systems, which were running just a shade below design optimum. He could goose either one for more power if necessary, but the simulation did not require it unless there was an emergency.

Which Dr. Wo suddenly provided.

In the simulation, the crew had successfully separated the submersible from the station. They were on their own now, as far as the sim was concerned, running on the ship's internal power.

Wo tapped a single button on the console keyboard before him and abruptly half of the lights on Grant's console turned a baleful red.

"Power outage!" Grant yelled, just as Muzorawa said exactly the same words—but in a much calmer tone.

"Switch to auxiliary power," Krebs called out.

Grant knew that he was supposed to keep his hands off the controls in front of him and let the crew work out the problem. But the temptation to cancel the outage and return the simulator to full power made him twitch with anticipation.

"Auxiliary power," Muzorawa announced.

Glancing up at the wallscreen, Grant saw that the simulator was now dimly lit, and red lights glared across half the consoles in there.

"Life support decaying," O'Hara said, her voice tight, pained. "The circulation pumps need more power."

"Return to the station," Krebs commanded. It was standard operating procedure. This soon after separation, the safest thing to do was to return and hook up with the station's power supply. If they lost power later in the mission they would have to solve the problem on their own, Grant knew.

His fingers still itching to correct the damage that Dr. Wo had deliberately inflicted, Grant watched passively as the crew simulated their return and remating to the station's docking module. It was all done with smooth efficiency. They hardly had to touch a keypad or a switch. *It's only a simulation,* Grant reminded himself, but he still found that he was soaked in perspiration by the time Krebs announced their successful redocking.

"Very well," Wo said into his microphone. "Take a break. But do not leave the simulator. Next we will see what you do when you have an emergency after you have entered the clouds."

All of the crew members groaned. All except Krebs, Grant noticed. She actually smiled.

He turned to Frankovich, crammed in at the next console with barely enough room for his legs.

"Captain Krebs is enjoying herself," Frankovich said. Then, leaning closer to Grant, he whispered, "But Dr. Wo takes this all very seriously."

Grant glanced over at Wo. The director's face looked grim, baleful. With an inward nod, Grant said to himself, *Yes, Dr. Wo takes all this very seriously indeed.*

BREAKDOWN

Bone weary from the long day's simulator runs, Grant picked up his dinner in the conference room, stopped by the cafeteria for a bowl of fruits for Sheena, then trudged alone down to the aquarium with two sets of neural nets stuffed into his trouser pockets.

He passed the rows of fish tanks, their underwater lights glimmering against the solid bulkhead on his left. The dolphins were swimming lazily in their big tank, sleek and silent. Grant stopped for a moment at the tank that held the simulator. It was empty now. Technicians would start dismantling the hardware after the ship actually left on its mission. Grant wondered if they would store it in anticipation of future missions. Most likely so, he guessed.

He felt slightly uneasy that Sheena was not out in the corridor to meet him. Usually she was prowling along the fish tanks, waiting for him with the eagerness of a two-year-old child. On the other hand, it gave him the opportunity to power up the monitoring console in the corridor outside her pen. Grant saw that it was working properly and receiving a steady flat signal from the net in his left pocket. The one in his right was deactivated, a dummy whose only purpose was to deceive Sheena into thinking that he was wearing the same "hat" that she was.

When he came to Sheena's pen he saw that the gorilla was sitting on her haunches, bent over a large wooden jigsaw puzzle. She had filled in eight of the ten big pieces.

She looked up as Grant stepped in.

"Food!" she said in her rasping voice, and scrambled up onto all fours. Grant knew she couldn't smile, but he thought she was glad to see him—and the bowl he had brought for her.

"Fruit," he said, placing the tray on the floor.

"Fruit," echoed Sheena. "And Grant food."

He nodded. "I've got a soyburger and salad and ice cream for dessert."

Sheena picked up the bowl of fruit but stared hard at the ice cream. Then she looked up at Grant. "Grant ice cream?"

"Would you like some ice cream, Sheena?"

"Yes," came the immediate answer.

"Okay." Grant handed the small dish to her. Tucking the fruit bowl under one arm, Sheena grabbed for the ice cream with her free hand.

Grant laughed at her unabashed greed. "Save some ice cream for me."

"Yes," Sheena replied. But within less than a minute the ice cream was gone, except for a few smears around her muzzle. Then she started in on the fruit.

Grant wolfed down his burger, surprised at how hungry he suddenly felt. He offered Sheena a few leaves of his salad, but she sniffed at the dressing and refused them.

Once the fruit was gone Sheena asked, "Grant bring hat?"

He pulled the neural nets from his pockets. "Here they are, Sheena. One for you and one for me."

She leaned toward him and allowed him to place the net over her head and tie it under her chin. Then he did the same for his own.

"Let's finish the puzzle," Grant said, once he had both nets in place.

"Grant do."

"No, no, Sheena. You've put most of the pieces together. There are only two left. You do them."

"Grant do first."

He nodded understanding. "You want me to do one piece?"

Sheena said, "Yes." And brought one big hand up to her skull.

"No, no!" Grant blurted. "Don't rub your head! You'll mess up your hat."

"Hurts," Sheena said.

Grant forced a smile for her. "No, it doesn't hurt, Sheena. My hat doesn't hurt. Your hat doesn't hurt."

She had knocked the net slightly askew. Grant got to his knees and straightened it out for her.

"Hurts," Sheena repeated.

"It can't hurt you," Grant said. "Here, let's finish the puzzle."

He picked up one of the two remaining pieces and put it in place. Sheena stared at the puzzle for a moment, then reached for the last piece.

Suddenly she flung it away. "Hurts!" she growled, and reached up to yank at the neural net.

Grant saw a tendril of smoke rising from one of the electrodes. My God, it's burning her!

Sheena ripped the net off her head and smashed it to the floor. She roared with pain and lurched up onto her hind legs.

She's going to kill me! Grant thought.

The gorilla balled one mighty fist and smashed it against the steel wall of her pen. The metal buckled.

Grant scrambled to his feet. Sheena towered over him, immense, fangs bared.

"Grant hurt Sheena!" she rasped.

"No, I didn't mean to—"

"Grant no friend!"

He started to back away from her, toward the entrance to her pen. There was an emergency control outside that could slide a thickly barred gate across the entry.

Sheena dropped down to all fours, and Grant could see a burned spot on her skull. She glowered at him as he backed away. Don't turn your back to her! Grant remembered. Gorillas seldom attack a man who's facing them. *Seldom* echoed in Grant's mind.

It all seemed to be happening in slow motion, as if in a nightmare. Grant edged toward the pen's entrance, Sheena growled and glared at him, then took a knuckle-walking step toward him.

Grant bolted through the doorway and banged the emergency gate control. The bars slid swiftly across the entrance and clanged shut. Sheena grasped one of the bars in a big, hairy hand. Grant thought she could have bent it if she'd wanted to.

"I'm sorry, Sheena," he babbled. "I didn't mean to hurt you. One of the electrodes must've been defective. I didn't mean to hurt you."

"Grant no friend," the gorilla rasped again. Then she turned her back to him and shambled to the far corner of her pen.

Grant stood there, heartbroken. You're right, he admitted silently to the gorilla. I'm not your friend. I never was, even though I wanted to be.

IMMERSION

The following night the departing crew held a glum little farewell party for themselves in O'Hara's quarters. Lane herself invited Grant to attend. Still miserable about Sheena, and afraid to get near the gorilla again, Grant accepted.

He was the last one to arrive. O'Hara's room was in its planetarium mode again as she admitted him and then slid the door shut behind him. Even the floor was speckled with stars. For a dizzying moment Grant felt as if the others were sitting in empty space, floating in the middle of the universe. The faint, ethereal music of a single keyboard floated through the shadows.

"No stimulants, I'm afraid," Lane said in a hushed voice. "The mission, you know."

Grant nodded his understanding, then padded across the starry floor to sit between Muzorawa and Pascal. Zeb's beard was gone, Karlstad was totally bald. Pascal's wig was slightly askew; not nearly as natural-looking as Lane's. All the crew members have been depilated, Grant realized. Because of the immersion; it's more sanitary.

"I thought you would be with Sheena," said Pascal.

Grant felt his jaws clench. With an effort, he told her, "I had a problem with her last night."

"Oh?"

He described the fiasco with the burned-out electrode.

Instead of disappointment, Pascal immediately asked, "Did you get data?"

He blinked at her. "I don't know. I didn't check. Everything was so—"

"The other electrodes should have worked," Pascal said. "You should have some data, at least. Anger. Pain. Such data is priceless!

Betrayal, Grant thought. What kind of brain waves will show feelings of betrayal?

"Do you blame yourself for what happened?" Muzorawa asked gently.

Grant shrugged. "Who else was there?"

"Sometimes experiments blow up on you," he said. "Equipment can fail."

"That's great to hear on the eve of our dunking," Karlstad grumbled. He'd been sitting on Muzorawa's other side.

"Do you think Sheena will stay angry with you?" O'Hara asked.

"I don't know," Grant said. "Right now, I'm kind of scared to go back and see her again."

"Lovers' quarrel," Karlstad said.

Grant was in no mood for his quips. "Speaking of lovers, isn't Dr. Krebs coming to this party?"

Karlstad threw up his hands. "God forbid!"

Muzorawa chuckled. "That's right, Egon. She did specifically tap you for the mission. She must have a special place in her heart for you."

"That means she hates me, then," Frankovich chimed in. "Thank goodness!"

O'Hara said, "I didn't think inviting Krebs here would be such a lovely idea."

"Why not?" Karlstad snapped. "Maybe she'd perk up this party. We could certainly use something to liven up the proceedings."

"D'you notice how she seems to stare at you when she talks to you?" O'Hara asked no one in particular. "It's positively spooky, don't you think?"

"Yes," Pascal said. "She never did that before the accident."

"It's the evil eye," said Karlstad. "She's learned witchcraft."

"Whatever it is, it makes my blood run cold," O'Hara said.

"You think it runs cold when she gives you the fish-eye," Karlstad said, almost smirking, "wait until you're immersed in that PFCL gunk. That'll chill your blood down to the marrow."

For a long moment no one spoke a word. Grant knew what they were facing and shuddered inwardly.

"There's an IAA inspection team on its way here," Frankovich muttered.

"I'd heard that," said O'Hara. "It's really true, then?"

Karlstad grumbled, "That's why our woeful leader wants to get this mission off so fast. He's afraid the IAA officials will stop it, once they find out about it."

"Why would they stop it?"

"Risking human lives."

"Finding things they don't want to find," Grant heard himself say. The others all turned to him.

"They'll be here in ten days," Grant added. "You should be safely on your way by then."

"Safely?" Karlstad sneered. "I wish."

Muzorawa said, "Let us remember one thing: We will be exploring a region where no human has gone before. We will be searching for life on a world that is utterly alien to us. We will be seeking intelligent life, if it exists down in that sea. Those are good things to do, no matter how much discomfort we must endure."

For a moment Grant thought that Zeb would say they're doing God's work. But the Moslem scientist stopped short of that.

Sitting at his console in the mission control center, Grant was almost quivering with anticipation. This morning the consoles no longer connected to the simulator in the aquarium. Now, as he looked up at the big wallscreen, Grant saw the interior of the submersible itself.

It was empty, as yet. No, not really empty, Grant told himself. It's filled with that PFCL gunk instead of air. The crew will be breathing that soup, immersed in it, living in it for days on end, weeks.

"Ready for immersion procedure," Dr. Wo said from his position at the central console, lapsing unconsciously into the clipped speaking style of the controllers.

The image on the wallscreen changed to show the airlock in the docking module. Krebs and the other crew members stood in a small huddle by the outer hatch. They each wore snug-fitting bodysuits, more for modesty than need, Grant understood. The tights left their legs bare, and he could see the studs of electrodes lining their flesh, like obscene metal leeches attached to their skin.

"We are ready," Krebs said, peering directly into the monitoring camera. She had an odd way of staring, as if she were focusing only one eye on you.

"Proceed," said Dr. Wo.

Starting with Muzorawa, the crew entered the airlock one by one. Surveillance cameras watched as the hatch sealed tight and the lock slowly filled with the thick liquid perfluorocarbon, rather than air. It looked to Grant as if each of them were being deliberately drowned. Each one floated upward as the chamber filled, instinctively lifting their heads to suck in their last lungful of air. When the liquid finally filled the airlock, each of them spasmed with inborn reflex, eyes popping wide, mouths gaping and gasping, arms and legs flailing.

Grant had to force himself to sit still, to say nothing, as he watched his friends' desperate convulsions. This must be what it's like to watch an execution, he thought, his fists clenched, his own pulse racing hard.

Then, after what seemed like hours of struggle, each member of the crew began to breathe almost normally and opened the inner hatch of the airlock to swim into the sub's interior. Grant blinked with disbelief when he checked his console clock and saw that Muzorawa's reflexive struggles had lasted less than thirty seconds. The others did almost as well.

Krebs was the last to enter the airlock. She hardly struggled at all. In fact, Grant thought he saw a smile cross her heavy, gray-skinned face as the liquid closed over her head.

SEPARATION

For most of the day the crew simply accustomed themselves to the submersible. Grant was surprised, as he watched the wallscreen display, at how cramped the interior was. Despite the outer size of the ship, the bridge was no bigger than the simulator in the aquarium had been. The galley was nothing more than a shoulder-tall console built into one of the bulkheads.

Of course, Grant realized. They won't be eating normally; they'll get their nutrition intravenously, through the ports in their necks.

Krebs had assigned each of them a privacy berth, where they could sleep and get away from the others for a while. They reminded Grant of the coffin-sized quarters he'd shared with Tavalera aboard *Roberts*.

Their voices were different: deeper, slower, as if someone were playing a recording at lower than normal speed.

No one left the control center for more than a few minutes. When noon came, Dr. Wo told Grant to go to the cafeteria and bring back enough sandwiches and drinks for all five of them.

"Big appetite, mate," Red Devlin wisecracked as Grant loaded his tray.

Grant merely nodded.

"What's goin' on, eh? Big doin's?"

"You might say that," Grant replied as he hefted the tray.

"You need help with that?" Devlin called after him as Grant made his way past the incoming people and started down the main corridor.

"No thanks," he yelled over his shoulder, nearly bumping into a technician coming up the corridor.

Feeling like a lackey instead of a scientist, Grant juggled the heavily laden tray all the way back to the control center. This is why they call us scooters, he guessed.

As he slid back into his console chair, munching a sandwich, he saw on the wallscreen that Krebs was starting to organize the crew for linking electronically with the ship's systems.

Muzorawa had taken up his station at the control panel, with O'Hara and Karlstad flanking him. Pascal was nowhere in sight. Grant thought that Lane looked tense, perhaps worried. It was harder to read Zeb's expression; he seemed totally focused on the controls.

Four hairless humans, naked except for their skintight bodysuits, electrodes studding their legs. Hair-thin fiber-optic wires led from the implants to sets of plugs in the consoles. The wires seemed to float gently in the liquid-filled chamber.

Krebs hovered behind and slightly above the crew, like a levitating sack of cement, watching everything they did. Wires trailed from her stocky legs to a panel set into the ceiling above her.

"Remember," she said, her voice oddly booming, "that once we are linked, the manual controls will be used only as a backup."

The four crew members nodded. Grant found himself folding his hands in his lap, to keep them off the controls on his console. This is for real now, he told himself. This isn't a simulation anymore.

Dr. Wo said, "Proceed with systems linkup."

It was eerie. Grant watched as, one by one, the crew members activated their implanted chips. Nothing seemed to happen. There were no sparks, no lights, no changes of expression on any of their faces. Maybe they stiffened a little, when the linkage first came through their nervous systems. He thought he saw a slight tic in Karlstad's cheek. But nothing more.

He forced himself to look down at his console. All the telltales were green: all systems functioning within their design parameters.

"Begin systems checkout," Wo said. His voice seemed weak, breathless, as if he were excited.

"Systems checkout," Krebs repeated.

It went very smoothly; flawlessly, Grant thought, except that Quintero, monitoring the sensor array, reported that coolant on one of the infrared telescopes was low. Karlstad was assigned to check it out after separation.

"It might be a leak," Krebs warned.

"More likely it merely was not filled properly to begin with," said Wo.

Karlstad said, "I'll attend to it. It's not vital, in any case. The backup is functioning in the green."

Grant thought that Egon was showing some real professionalism. He hates being on the mission, but as long as he's in, he's going to conduct himself like a pro. Good for Egon!

The crew finished its checkouts and retired to their privacy compartments for the night. Dr. Wo stayed at his console in the mission control center but allowed the other four controllers to leave for the night. Grant got up and left the cramped chamber, feeling tired and sweaty.

He argued with his conscience about going down to see Sheena. No, he decided. She'll still be flared up over the burned-out electrode. Still associating me with pain and betrayal. The image of her rearing up in fury, fangs bared, made Grant's stomach twist. Better to let her cool off for a while, he convinced himself. I'll see her tomorrow night—or maybe after the ship's gone.

The entire next day was spent slowly ratcheting up the pressure inside the sub. Free to inspect the ship's schematics from his console in the control center, Grant saw that it was built of four separate hulls, nested inside one another, with high-pressure liquid between each of the hulls.

That's why it looks so small inside, he realized. The section where the crew worked and lived was only a tiny part of the submersible's total volume.

The reason for immersing the crew was to allow them to withstand the immense pressure of the Jovian ocean. The higher the pressure that the crew could take, the deeper the submersible could go into the Jovian ocean. So, under Wo's watchful eyes, the pressure of the perfluorocarbon mixture in the crew's space was gradually increased.

With all his lights green, Grant spent the time watching the crew on the wallscreen display. Lane looked a little apprehensive, he thought, although that might have been merely a projection of his own tension. Zeb was checking out the computer programs that digested the sensors' inputs. He looked as calm and at ease as always, methodical, capable. The only difference that Grant could see was that Muzorawa's trim beard was gone.

Patti Buono, at the medical console, peered fixedly at her readouts. "Any discomfort?" she called out again and again. Karlstad complained of a headache. Pascal said she felt a tightness in her chest.

"Psychosomatic," Buono proclaimed. "The monitors show blood

pressure, heart rate, all your physical readings are well within normal range."

Pascal, looking strangely gnomish without a wig covering her bald dome, turned to look into the camera. "And just what is normal range under immersion?" she asked, her voice a deep baritone.

Krebs snapped, "Stop this bickering."

Pascal shook her head but said nothing.

When the pressure reached 90 percent of the design goal, Krebs said, "Hold it there for one hour. Give them a chance to adjust."

Wo agreed, "We will hold at ninety percent for one hour."

The next morning Buono asked each crew member how they had slept. The worst impact of the full pressurization, apparently, was that O'Hara suffered a slight nose bleed and Muzorawa—of all people—reported he had experienced a nightmare.

Buono had no interest in Zeb's dream; she concerned herself only with the crew's physical condition. After a careful check of her medical sensors, she pronounced the crew fully fit for duty.

"In that case," Krebs announced, "we are ready to begin separation sequence."

"Wait," said Dr. Wo, raising one hand, palm out, fingers splayed. "This is the proper moment to name the ship."

"Name it?" Krebs stared into the camera. Grant could not tell from her frowning expression whether she was perplexed or irritated.

"Yes," Wo replied, perfectly serious. "On the first mission the ship had no proper name. That was unfortunate. The ship should have a name of its own, a name that will be propitious."

Krebs's frown soured. Grant could see that she was annoyed with the director's sudden burst of Chinese superstition.

Unperturbed, Dr. Wo announced, "The name of this vessel will be *Zheng He*."

No one said a word. They're all puzzled, Grant thought. What in the world does "Zheng He" mean?

At last Krebs said, "Very well. *Zheng He* is ready for the separation sequence."

"Proceed," said Wo.

Grant felt a tightening in his chest. The ship's disconnecting from the station, going out on its own. They'll be heading down into Jupiter's clouds and then deeper, into the ocean. If they get into trouble we won't be able to help them. They'll be on their own.

The separation sequence was automated. Grant could not hear the latches releasing or the connectors unsealing themselves. He watched the wallscreen, with quick glances at his console board to make certain all the propulsion and power systems were functioning properly. *Zheng He* disconnected from the access tube and used the station's magnetic shield to push it free of the great toroidal mass of Research Station *Gold*.

Grant almost smiled. That magnetic screen was intended to repel energetic subatomic particles that the Jovian magnetosphere sometimes spat out during a magnetic storm. Now it was pushing a somewhat larger "particle," *Zheng He*, away from the station's hull.

The submersible and the station remained side by side, separated by a mere kilometer, for two orbits of Jupiter, slightly more than six hours. Grant watched the wallscreen that showed the sub, a tiny metallic lenticular shape against the gigantic, overwhelming background of Jupiter's tumultuous, turbulent cloud deck. The crew rechecked all the ship's systems. Then Krebs reported they were ready for entry into the Jovian atmosphere.

"Insertion burn," Krebs ordered.

Grant saw a tiny flicker of light at one side of the saucer. For a heart-stopping moment he thought the insertion rockets had failed. *Zheng He* seemed to remain alongside them, hovering helplessly. But within a few eyeblinks he could see that it was indeed moving away, faster now, allowing Jupiter's powerful gravity to pull them along, down into those swirling clouds.

Dr. Wo said something aloud, in Chinese.

"Good luck," said Frankovich, his voice slightly husky.

"Safe journey," Kayla Ukara called to the departing crew.

Grant licked his lips. His throat was suddenly dry. Then he found his voice and said, "Godspeed."

REVELATION

All five of the controllers watched *Zheng He* disappear into the clouds of Jupiter. For several minutes Grant simply stared at the wallscreen showing the planet's colorful cloud deck. The ship had gone. It was as if it had never existed.

But my friends are in that submersible, Grant said to himself. They're going down through those clouds right now, while I sit here with nothing to do but watch over this dumb console. If anything happens to them, I'll be powerless to help them.

"Status reports," Dr. Wo called out, his rasping voice sharper than usual. "Life support?"

"Functioning within nominal limits," replied Frankovich.

"Structural integrity?"

Nacho Quintero answered, "No problems."

The medical monitors and sensor systems were all showing completely normal performance. Even the troublesome infrared telescope's coolant level was back to normal. When Wo asked for the power systems, Grant swiftly scanned his monitor.

"Power all green," he reported.

Wo swiveled his gaze across the cramped, stuffy compartment, from one controller to another, and then looked up at the wallscreen. It still showed nothing but Jupiter's endless clouds.

"Should we call them?" Patti Buono wondered aloud. "Make voice contact?"

"They are due to report in three minutes," Wo pointed out, gesturing to the mission schedule timeline displayed on his main console screen.

The time ticked by so slowly that Grant thought his console clock might have stopped. Not a word was spoken in the control center. No sound at all except the electrical hum of the monitors and the distant whisper of the air circulation fans. Wo seemed to turn into a block of wood, a statue, unmoving, unblinking. Grant wondered if the man was even breathing. Sweat beaded his own upper lip and brow; he felt it trickling along his ribs.

"Control, this is *Zheng He.*" Krebs's voice shattered the silence.

"I hear you," Wo said, as calmly as if she were sitting next to him.

"All systems functioning normally. No problems."

"Good," said Wo, with a satisfied nod of his head.

"We are preparing for the descent. Communications blackout will prevent further"—she seemed to search for a word—"further communications."

"I understand," Wo replied. "We will track your beacon as long as possible."

The sub actually carried two beacons, Grant knew: a long-wave radio transmitter and an infrared communications laser. Both would be absorbed by Jupiter's deep, turbulent atmosphere, swallowed up in the raging storms and lightning strokes that awaited *Zheng He*'s crew. By plotting the signal strength and dispersion of the beacons, though, Grant and the other scooters aboard the station could learn more about the dynamics of the Jovian atmosphere.

Even if it kills the crew, Grant heard a sardonic voice in his head whisper.

The submersible also carried half a dozen "torpedoes": small, self-propelled automated capsules that could be fired from the sub to pop up to the top of the cloud deck and broadcast a prerecorded message.

None of the controllers left their consoles as long as the submersible maintained communications contact. But after six more hours, even the radio beacon was drowned out by the constant flicker of Jovian lightning. They would hear nothing more from *Zheng He* unless and until the crew popped a message-bearing capsule.

Wo pushed his wheelchair back from his console. "There is nothing more to do here," he said, sounding tired, weak. "They are on their own now."

He wheeled himself out of the control center. The plan was to have one person at the central console—Wo's usual post—throughout the mission. Quintero had drawn the first four-hour shift; Grant was last.

"Let me make a quick run to the toilet," Quintero said, squeezing his bulk past Grant's console.

"I'll sit in until you get back," Grant said to Nacho's rapidly disappearing back.

"Even Macho Nacho has to pee sometime," Patti Buono said, trying to lighten the tension that had smothered them all.

"Don't you?" asked Ukara, heading for the corridor right behind Quintero.

"Now that you mention it . . ." Buono got up and followed her.

Grant didn't bother bringing a chair to the central console, he simply stood in front of its darkened lights and stared up at the wallscreen. Might as well turn it off, he told himself. The radio speaker built into Wo's console hissed static that crackled every few seconds from a lightning bolt.

Quintero came back and hauled his own chair over to the central console. "Thanks, amigo. I'm okay now."

"Good," said Grant, suddenly realizing that his own bladder needed relief.

The nearest rest room was a dozen meters down the corridor. Grant headed for it, but saw that Dr. Wo was sitting in his powerchair near its door.

"Uh . . . do you need help, sir?" Grant asked.

Wo looked up at him disdainfully. "What I need—" he began in a snarl, then stopped himself. For a moment Grant didn't know what to expect. Then, much more softly, Wo said, "Come with me, Mr. Archer."

He followed Dr. Wo to the director's office. As always it was overheated, uncomfortably warm. But Grant saw that the vase atop Wo's desk was empty.

Wheeling himself behind the desk, Wo gestured Grant to sit, then said, "I understand you have run into a setback with the gorilla."

Nodding, Grant admitted, "I'm afraid I've thrown away several weeks' work."

"Patience, Mr. Archer. Patience."

"Checking the neural net before I put it on her would have saved me this setback," Grant muttered.

Wo nodded. "So you must start over."

"I suppose so."

"Just as the crew is doing in *Zheng He*. We failed in our first attempt to explore the ocean, and now they are trying again."

"Before the IAA inspectors can stop them," Grant said.

Wo exhaled a sigh and nodded once.

"May I ask a question, sir?"

"You may ask," said Wo.

"What does 'Zheng He' mean? Is it the name of a person, or what?"

The director actually smiled. "A good question. An excellent question!"

Grant waited for more.

"Zheng He was a great explorer. Commander of the Ming emperor's navy in the fifteenth century. Fifty years before Columbus and his pitiful little boats crossed the Atlantic, Zheng He's treasure fleets sailed all across the Indian Ocean, to Africa, Arabia, the islands of the East Indies, even to Australia."

"I never heard about that," Grant said.

"Great ships, ten times bigger than the Spanish caravels," Wo continued. "Hundreds of ships! Thousands of sailors! Half the world was in China's sway while the Europeans still believed the world was flat!"

"Then why—"

"But the emperor Zhu Di died, and his successor had the great ships burned. They destroyed the fleet! They forbade exploration and commerce! China turned inward and decayed. By the time the Europeans reached China's shores, the Empire of Heaven was weak, poor, divided, easily conquered."

He fell silent. Grant thought over what Wo had just told him, then said, "It could have been the other way around, then, couldn't it? If they had allowed Zheng He to continue, China could have conquered Europe."

"Easily."

"Why did they stop?"

Wo took a deep breath and ran a weary hand over his eyes. "Zheng He was a eunuch."

Grant felt shocked. "You mean he'd been castrated?"

"Many were, in those days. In Europe, also. Boys with sweet singing voices were castrated well into the nineteenth century, I believe."

"Zheng He was a eunuch," Grant repeated in a whisper.

"Most of the palace officials who promoted his fleet were eunuchs. The Confucian bureaucrats who ran the rest of the government opposed the eunuch's position of power with the emperor."

"Palace politics."

"Yes," said Wo. "Palace politics. And the losers were often executed."

"The Confucians won?"

"Eventually. When the emperor Zhu Di died, the Confucians tightened their grip on his successor. The great treasure fleet of Zheng He was destroyed."

"And China crumbled."

"It took China more than five hundred years to recover. Even today China is not as rich or powerful as it could have been."

"It was lucky for the Europeans, then."

"Yes, very fortunate for them," Wo grumbled.

Grant tried to lighten the mood. "But today we're beyond all that. Asians and Europeans and Africans—we're all working together."

"Are we?"

"Aren't we?"

"If your Zealots had their way, this station would be closed . . . destroyed just the way Zheng He's fleet was destroyed."

"They're not *my* Zealots," Grant retorted, as firmly as he could manage.

"I feel very close to the spirit of Zheng He," Wo said, closing his eyes. "His spirit touches my own."

Grant said nothing.

"In a way, I am also a eunuch. My manhood was destroyed in the accident."

"I didn't know," Grant blurted.

"So I sit here, weak and helpless, while others sail into the unknown sea."

"You're not helpless."

"They blame Krebs for the accident. It was really my fault. I panicked."

"I never heard that," said Grant.

"Krebs is too loyal to reveal it. She has taken the blame so that I could remain as director."

"What happened?"

Wo waved a hand. "What does it matter? Now I sit here and wait for word from them."

"They should be in the ocean by now," Grant mused.

"Yes. And while we struggle to explore, the Confucians, the bureaucrats who have the positions of power back on Earth, are on their way here to destroy us. They fear what we are doing here. They despise us."

"They can't stop us. We're doing what we came here to do."

"I should be down there with them."

Grant looked at the older man's tired, dejected face. Lines of fatigue and worry and self-doubt were etched into his flesh.

"If it weren't for you, sir," he said, "they wouldn't be out there exploring the ocean at all. None of us would be here."

And he realized as he said it that he himself would probably be back on Earth, or at Farside, if it weren't for Wo's monomaniacal determination to find intelligent life in Jupiter's vast ocean.

Yet, for the first time, Grant felt that he'd rather be here—even as a lowly grad student—than anywhere else. *Wo's passion has infected me,* he realized.

LEVIATHAN

Weakened by its battle against the Darters, slowly starving in this barren region of the sea, Leviathan allowed the powerful currents surging out of the eternal storm to drive it farther from the towering, roaring wall of seething water and its menacing bolts of lightning.

Its wounded members flared with pain signals. Leviathan needed food, and plenty of it, to heal the flesh torn and shredded by the Darters' teeth. Yet there was no food to be found.

At least there were no Darters in this empty part of the ocean. Leviathan doubted its members would have the strength to fight them. Food. Leviathan had to find food. Which meant it had to circle the immense storm, return to the side where the currents flowed into it and the food streamed thickly.

Riding the circling currents, drifting rather than propelling itself through the ocean, Leviathan wondered if there might be some food—any food—up higher. It was dangerous to rise too high into the cold abyss above, but Leviathan knew it would be death to remain at this depth, where no food at all was available.

Slowly, cautiously, Leviathan made its flotation members expand. The immense creature drifted higher, nearing exhaustion, nearing the moment when its members would instinctively disintegrate and begin their individual buddings, in the last desperate hope of survival by spawning offspring.

The old instincts would be of no avail now, Leviathan knew. The members could separate and reproduce themselves in the hope of uniting into renewed assemblies, but what good would that do where there was not enough food even for one? Even if a few individual members survived temporarily, how could they live without the unity of all the others? Apart they were helpless. What could flagella members do without a brain to guide them? How could a brain member exist without sensor members and digestive members and—

Leviathan halted its pointless musing. There *was* food drifting in the currents above. The sensor members felt its faint echo vibrating through the water. The storm's merciless flow swept the particles into its own mindless vortex before they could sift down to the comfortable level where Leviathan swam.

It would be cold up there, numbingly cold. Leviathan's kind traced tales of foolish youngsters who rose too high in their haughty search to outdo their elders and never returned, disintegrated by the cold and their members devoured by Darters or the eerie creatures that haunted the abyss above.

But remaining at this level meant starvation. Leviathan needed enough food to allow it to circle around the great storm and return to the familiar region where the food rained down without fail.

Upward Leviathan rose, straining against the growing cold, heading toward the meager trickle of food that its sensor members had detected.

It was not food, Leviathan realized. Despite the numbing cold and the continuing pain signals from its wounded members, Leviathan's eye parts showed that the echoes the sensors detected came not from a thin stream of food particles but from one single particle, much larger than any food it had ever known, yet puny compared to Leviathan or even to the Darters.

It was that alien thing that had been seen before. Far, far off in the distance, up so high that Leviathan dared not even try to approach it, a strange circular object was struggling through the abyss above, sending out eerie signals that made no sense whatsoever.

Is this real? Leviathan wondered. Or are we so close to disintegration that our brain is beginning to fail?

The alien continued to flash signals mindlessly into the vast ocean, totally oblivious to Leviathan drifting in the cold empty sea, far out of range of its sensing systems.

EMERGENCY

Grant left Dr. Wo's office feeling strangely upset, conflicted, wondering where his true loyalties lay, what he was truly loyal to.

He threw himself on his bed and immediately fell into an exhausted, dreamless sleep. The next morning he took his shift at the mission control center and spent four hours looking at the silent consoles and dead wallscreen. Nacho Quintero relieved him, laughing about his latest prank: Last night he'd sprayed epoxy on the cafeteria chair next to his own.

"Kayla sat in it and couldn't get out," Quintero wheezed, laughing almost to the point of tears. "She hadda unzip her coveralls and wiggle out of 'em. You oughtta see the underwear she's got!" He waved a big, meaty hand as if to fan himself.

As Nacho got up from his chair Grant said, "I'll bet Kayla really loves you for that."

Quintero's laughter doubled, and tears actually did leak from his squeezed-shut eyes.

"You shoulda seen it! She grabbed one of Red's frypans an' chased me halfway down to the aquarium!"

Grant made an amused face, mumbled the right words, and left Quintero still shaking with laughter. Once outside the control center, he headed for the fluid dynamics lab. It's time to get back to my thesis, he told himself.

He plopped down on one of the lab's little wheeled chairs and called up the three-dimensional map he'd made of the Jovian ocean currents. But he could not concentrate on the work. Wo's confession of guilt, his near-paranoid fears of the Zealots, the others—Zeb, Lane, and all—in the sub, probing the depths of the Jovian ocean.

And here I sit, worrying about my damnable thesis, he told himself.

Then another voice in his mind said, That's not what's bothering you.

I know, Grant admitted.

It was Sheena. Grant felt terrible that he had ruined Irene Pascal's experiment and even worse that he had hurt the gorilla. It's like betraying a child, he thought. Sheena *trusted* me. And now she doesn't. How could she?

With a startled flare of recognition Grant realized that he had come to like Sheena as a friend, a two-year-old friend, perhaps, but the relationship between them had become important to him.

How can I rebuild that trust? How can I become her friend again?

He hauled himself to his feet. You can't do it here, he said to himself. You've got to go down to her pen and face her.

His fists clenched at his sides, his insides fluttering, Grant strode along the main corridor toward the aquarium. He passed dozens of people, scooters and coverall-clad technicians and administrators in their neatly pressed shirts and slacks. All of them working on the studies of Jupiter's moons, all of them intent on their careers, their lives. There's only ten of us involved in the real work, Grant reminded himself. Eleven, counting Wo. None of these others knows what we're doing.

Or do they? he wondered. It's impossible to keep the deep mission totally secret. Certainly Red Devlin knows more about it than he should. Anybody can see that the submersible is gone.

Looking into the faces of the people as he passed them, Grant asked himself, Which one of them is a Zealot? Which one of them would kill us all, just to stop Wo's crazy notion that there's intelligent life down there? God, he's just as fanatical as any of them!

Grant found himself in front of the closed hatch that led into the aquarium. A new graffito had been scrawled in bloodred ink next to the keypad on the bulkhead:

If fish is brain food, why ain't we
smart enough to get home?

With a sigh of understanding, Grant tapped out the entry code. The lock clicked and Grant pushed through. The aquarium was chilly and quiet. No one here. Grant walked slowly, hesitantly, along the big tanks, seeing the gliding, gulping fish only out of the corner of his eye.

She ought to be around here someplace, Grant thought. She wouldn't be in her pen in the middle of the day.

But Sheena was nowhere to be found. With a sudden lurch in the pit of his stomach, Grant bolted from the aquarium and sprinted for the surgical laboratory, down by the station's infirmary.

"Sheena?" The lone nurse on duty at the infirmary glared at him. "I wouldn't let that ape within fifty kilometers of here. Do you have any idea of what she did the last time we tried to work on her?"

Leaving the angry-faced nurse, Grant went to the first wall phone he could find out in the corridor and asked the computer where Sheena was.

"There is no listing under Sheena," said the synthesized voice.

She doesn't have a phone, Grant realized. That was stupid.

Not knowing what else to do, Grant asked the phone for Dr. Wo.

"The director is not to be disturbed, except for emergencies."

"This is an emergency!" Grant snapped.

Wo's face immediately appeared on the phone's tiny screen. "I am unable to take your call. Leave a message."

Grant wanted to pound the wall with frustration. "Dr. Wo, I can't find Sheena! Nobody seems to know where she is."

The screen went blank.

Security, Grant thought. I ought to notify security. If Sheena's loose somewhere in the station . . . He hesitated. Security might panic. They might hurt her.

He made up his mind and strode through the corridor to the administrative area. I wonder who's on security this week. Maybe it's somebody I know.

It was a stranger sitting behind the minuscule desk of the security office. A tall, rangy man with a stubbly beard and dark tousled hair. He wore a zippered set of coveralls. Probably a technician of some sort, Grant thought.

"This may be silly," he started, without introducing himself. "But Sheena seems to be missing and—"

"The gorilla?"

"Yes. She's not in her—"

"This time of day she's usually taking her afternoon exercise in the gym. Did you look there?"

Grant gaped at him. "The gym? No . . . I didn't know . . ."

The security officer punched at his phone keypad. "Hey, Ernie, is the monkey in there with you?"

Grant couldn't see the phone's screen, but he heard the reply. "Sure, she's playing with the— "

"EMERGENCY!" the overhead speaker blared. "ALL MISSION CONTROL PERSONNEL REPORT TO YOUR STATIONS IMMEDIATELY!"

The voice was Dr. Wo's. It sounded frantic.

ACCIDENT

Grant raced to the control center, thudding into Nacho Quintero when the two of them tried to get through the narrow aisle to the consoles at the same time. Ordinarily both of them would have laughed at their clumsiness.

"Watch it, estupido," Quintero snapped.

"Lard ass," Grant snarled silently.

Ukara and Frankovich were already at their consoles. The wall-screens were dark, and Grant saw that all the screens were lifeless, as well. All except Wo's: His console was lit up like a Christmas tree—almost all green lights, although there were several amber and one glaring red.

"Where is Dr. Buono?" Wo demanded, his rasping voice trembling slightly.

"Here," the physician called as she hurried through the doorway to sit at her console.

"We received the following message from Captain Krebs," Wo said, his fingers deftly tapping on his keyboard.

Everyone's console lit up. Grant was grateful that the propulsion and power systems seemed to be in no trouble. Two amber lights, the rest solidly green.

Krebs's face appeared on the wallscreen, five times bigger than life, strained, etched with anxiety. Or maybe fear, Grant thought.

"Dr. Pascal has collapsed," Krebs reported with no preliminaries. "She complained of a chest pain and then lost coordination of her limbs. Within ten minutes she doubled over, vomited bile, and lost consciousness."

Grant glanced at Patti Buono's console. The physician was frowning worriedly as more and more of the lights on her board flared a sullen, glowering red.

"Transmit her complete medical readouts," Buono called out. "The patient may be undergoing cardiac—"

"She can't hear you," Wo snapped. "This is a recording from a data capsule."

"How long ago was the message recorded?"

Wo glanced at his console screen. "One hour and seventeen minutes ago."

"Are they heading back?"

"I don't know," Wo answered, shaking his head slowly. "I would presume so."

"Then there's nothing we can do until we hear from them again."

"You can diagnose Dr. Pascal's condition!"

Buono bit her lips. "The data given here isn't enough for an effective diagnosis. Besides, if we can't communicate with them, what's the use—"

"What has happened to Pascal?" Wo demanded.

The physician's eyes flared angrily. But she turned back to her console lights and said, "It looks like cardiac arrest, but it might be an infarction or something else altogether. I just can't make a definitive diagnosis on this meager data!"

"What has caused her to collapse?" Wo insisted.

"I don't know!"

"Could it be from the high pressure they are exposed to?"

"Yes," Buono said. It sounded almost desperate to Grant. "Or it could have nothing to do with the pressure."

"Pah!" Wo smacked his hands on his emaciated thighs in frustration.

"Life-support systems are all in the green," Frankovich reported, trying to relieve the tension. "At least, they were when Krebs fired off the data capsule."

"What of it?" Wo snapped. "If Pascal is incapacitated, we must learn *why*."

Incapacitated? Grant thought. What a bloodless way of putting it. Irene could be dead, for God's sake.

A yellow light started to blink on Wo's console: the communications indicator. He banged it with a heavy fist.

The wallscreen image immediately changed. It was Krebs again, but the picture was grainy, streaked with interference. But it was a real-time image; the submersible was in contact with the station again.

"We are forced to return to the station," she said. "Please acknowledge."

"Acknowledged," Wo said, almost in a snarl.

"What is Dr. Pascal's condition?" Buono asked.

Krebs blinked at the camera. "She is unconscious. We have placed her in her berth and put a breathing mask on her, to force extra perfluorocarbon into her lungs."

Buono was working her keyboard swiftly, fingers almost a blur. Each of the crew had medical sensors fixed to their skin. Grant saw what he thought was an EKG trace on Buono's console screen, but the green wormline tracing Irene's heartbeat looked weak, irregular, to him.

"Put pressure cuffs on her legs and arms," Buono ordered. "Keep the blood in her torso and head."

There was a slight but noticeable delay in Krebs's answer. Grant realized that *Zheng He* was still deep below the cloud deck.

"There are no pressure cuffs in the medical stores," Krebs said.

Buono muttered something under her breath.

Grant leaned toward Frankovich and asked, "Is Irene going to die?"

Frankovich shrugged elaborately, said nothing.

Grant tried to look past Krebs's dour, grim face to see the rest of the crew, but the camera was set at an angle that did not show them.

"Patti," he called to the physician, "should you check on the monitors for the rest of the crew?"

Buono shot him a venomous glance. "And what good would that do?"

Grant had to admit she was right. There was nothing they could do to help the crew, not until they returned to the station.

"It's all being recorded," Buono added in a softer tone.

"Yeah, okay," Grant said.

After more than six hours of communicating with Krebs, Wo told Grant, Quintero, and Ukara that they could leave the control center.

"But you are to consider yourselves on standby alert," the director added. "Be ready to return to duty instantly."

Slowly, tiredly, Grant slid out of his seat. Quintero sprang up, quick and lithe despite his bulk.

"Do you want me to bring you a tray?" Grant asked Frankovich.

"I'm not hungry," he said.

"You're going to be here for a long time," Grant pointed out. "I'll bring some sandwiches and something to drink."

Frankovich conceded with a nod. “Maybe some fruit, too.”

“Right.” Grant started for the door.

“And remember,” Wo said sharply, “you are to discuss this incident with no one. No one! Understand me?”

The three of them nodded.

Grant headed for the cafeteria. He saw that it was early for dinner, yet a fair number of people were heading the same way he was. The line at the sandwich counter was short, though, and in quick order Grant filled his tray.

“Why so glum, chum?”

It was Tamiko Hideshi, grinning at him. It took Grant a moment to realize that, to all the hundreds of other people in the station, this was a perfectly normal workday. Nothing unusual was happening in their lives. Things were going along as always. They weren’t worried about a friend who might be dying in a ship beneath the clouds of Jupiter.

“Hi, Tami,” he said.

Nodding at his heavily laden tray, Hideshi said, “For a guy who’s stoking up for a picnic, you look awfully unhappy. What’s up with you?”

Grant shook his head. “I’ve got to get back to the control center.”

“The picnic’s in there?”

He stepped past her, offering over his shoulder, “It’s no picnic, believe me.”

RETURN

Even though he had been relieved of duty, Grant stayed in the control center, at his console. Under Krebs's command, *Zheng He* rose through Jupiter's turbulent atmosphere, a saucer-shaped aircraft instead of a submersible. Once above the clouds, Krebs lit the ship's plasma rockets and *Zheng He* established itself in orbit, a spacecraft once again.

Buono never left her console. All the indicators from Pascal's medical sensors showed that her condition was slowly deteriorating. It's a race against time, Grant thought, to get her here where she can get proper medical care before she dies.

It took several orbits around the gigantic planet, many tense hours, before *Zheng He* was in position to start redocking maneuvers. Krebs handled the tricky pas de deux flawlessly, and Grant thought he could feel the thump of the ship's airlock connecting with the station's access tube. It was nonsense and he knew it, but still he thought he caught a hint of a vibration down in his guts, a visceral affirmation that the crew had returned safely.

They loped down the main corridor, all pretense of secrecy forgotten, in their hurry to reach the access tunnel. Wo, in his powered wheelchair, scattered startled people like a bowling ball rolling through sentient pins capable of getting out of its way—just barely.

Despite himself, Grant grinned at the shouted curses and yells of anger that echoed along the corridor as he and the others sprinted after Wo's speeding powerchair.

Wo was yelling into the chair's built-in phone as he careened along the corridor. He was calling someone. Grant could make out the words ". . . security" and ". . . seal off the area . . ." Apparently the director wanted to make certain there were no gawkers at the access tunnel when they brought out the ship's crew.

They skidded to a stop at the tunnel's entry hatch. Sure enough, two burly security guards were standing there. And there were two more at the airlock hatch.

"You two get up to the entry area," Wo commanded. "Clear the entire section of corridor between here and the infirmary."

They hustled up the tunnel, leaving the five controllers and Dr. Wo facing the sealed airlock hatch.

"I've got to get in there," Buono said, pushing herself up beside Wo in his chair. "The sooner—"

"You can't go through," the director said. "They're in high-pressure fluid. You're not equipped to breathe it."

Buono's jaw sagged open. "I'd forgotten . . ."

"They must be depressurized," Wo went on. "The procedure will take several hours."

"How will that affect Irene's condition?" Ukara asked urgently.

Wo shrugged his heavy shoulders. "Who knows?"

"We know one thing," Buono said gloomily. "The longer it takes to get her into the infirmary, the worse her chances will be."

Pascal was the first one out of the hatch. Under Wo's orders, telephoned into the pressurized airlock, Karlstad and Muzorawa placed the unconscious woman in the airlock and slowly pumped out the perfluorocarbon liquid. They followed the preplanned procedure exactly, despite the urgency; it took the better part of an hour for her lungs to drain.

Patti Buono fidgeted nervously every instant of the wait. Grant saw that even Wo looked tense, almost frightened, his eyes darting back and forth like a trapped animal's.

Once Krebs told them that the airlock was down to normal air pressure, Quintero swung the heavy hatch open. Irene Pascal lay limp and still, on her side, her electrode-studded legs folded to fit the cramped area of the airlock floor. Her skinsuited body looked cold and still dripped oily liquid. Grant could not tell if she was breathing.

Ukara leaped past the startled Quintero into the airlock and sank to her knees beside the prostrate body.

"She's not breathing!" Kayla cried.

Patti Buono slapped an oxygen mask over the prostrate woman's face. "Quick, help me carry her to the infirmary. Quickly!"

Quintero reached for Pascal, but Ukara pushed him away. "No!" she snapped. "Let me do it."

She grasped the unconscious Pascal under the shoulders while Grant squeezed into the airlock and picked up her feet. Together they ran past the guards and down the corridor toward the infirmary. The corridor was completely empty except for them and Buono, her moccasins thumping on the thin carpeting as she tried to keep pace. Grant saw another trio of uniformed guards pacing up and down a few meters beyond the infirmary's entrance.

And Sheena was knuckle-walking alongside them. What are they doing with her? Grant wondered as, puffing from the exertion, he helped Ukara carry Pascal's limp body into the infirmary. A quartet of medics was already there. Buono pounded in behind them and immediately began shouting orders. Grant and Kayla were shooed away, back into the corridor, and the infirmary door slid firmly shut.

Wo was wheeling up the corridor, with Frankovich puffing along beside him. The director impatiently yanked open the infirmary door and rolled inside. Grant could see the team of green-gowned medics huddled over Pascal's bed.

Frankovich stopped at the door, chest visibly heaving.

"What about the rest of the crew?" Grant asked.

"They're okay," said Frankovich. "Decompressing and coming through the airlock one at a time."

The guard captain showed up, ducked into the infirmary for a few moments, then came out and shut the door again. He folded his arms across his chest and stood there with a stony expression on his face, the picture of inflexible authority, obviously intending to keep anyone else from entering the infirmary until Dr. Wo gave his permission.

Grant hesitated, not knowing what to do, where to go. He saw Sheena again, farther up the corridor, accompanying the guards. If the gorilla had noticed Grant, she gave no sign of it. She just shambled along on her knuckles, a dozen paces in one direction, then back the other way, like a soldier on guard duty.

Grant asked the taciturn guard captain, "Why is Sheena here?"

Barely moving his lips, the captain said, "We use her now and then for crowd control."

"Crowd control? There isn't any crowd here."

"Ah, you see? It works."

"Sheena shouldn't be exposed to crowds," Grant said.

The ghost of a smile flickered across the captain's stern, hawk-nosed face. "It's the other way around, rather. People are frightened of the ape."

"She wouldn't hurt anyone!"

"They don't know that."

Sheena wouldn't hurt anyone, Grant repeated to himself. Not unless someone hurt her first.

The captain said flatly, "The director wants to keep this section clear. The gorilla discourages people from coming close."

"I see."

"You ought to be leaving now," said the captain.

"I want to wait here," Ukara said.

"All of you, on your way," the captain insisted. "There's nothing more for you to do here."

Ukara snarled, her hands arching into red-tipped claws. For an instant Grant thought she was going to leap at the guard captain, a coiled steel panther attacking a stolid, well-muscled buffalo.

Then Frankovich touched her arm and said, "He's right, Kayla. Let's go help the others."

Ukara visibly shuddered. But she turned away from the captain and followed Frankovich down the corridor, back toward the airlock, in the direction opposite Sheena.

Still unmoved, the guard captain jabbed a finger at Grant's chest. "You, too. On your way."

Grant took a deep breath and walked toward the three uniformed guards patrolling with Sheena. The gorilla stopped her shuffling walk when she saw Grant approaching.

"Hello, Sheena," he said softly. The small burned patch of hair on her skull looked a deliberate brand of shame to Grant.

The gorilla stared at him out of deep-brown, red-rimmed eyes. "Grant," she said.

Grant held out his hand, palm up, as if begging. The guards watched with amused grins.

"Are we still friends, Sheena?"

"Grant hurt Sheena."

"I didn't mean to. It was an accident."

"Hurt."

"I'm sorry."

Sheena looked down at Grant's hand, still outstretched toward her. At last she said, "You go now."

"Sheena, I want to be your friend again," Grant pleaded.

"You go!"

"But, Sheena—"

The gorilla shook her head, a gesture that involved her massive shoulders, as well. "You go!"

Defeated, Grant let his hand drop and turned his back to Sheena. As he walked away, he heard one of the guards stage-whisper, "Would you believe it? A lovers' quarrel with an overgrown monkey!"

One by one, the crew of *Zheng He* came through the airlock. Karlstad and O'Hara were already out in the access tunnel, wrapped in blankets. Lane looked sad, close to tears. Egon was hollow-eyed, all his old snide cockiness wiped from his face.

The hatch sighed open and Muzorawa stepped through, sucking in big chestfuls of air, oily liquid still dripping from the tip of his nose and running in thin rivulets down his neck and arms.

Kayla Ukara threw a blanket around Zeb's shoulders.

"Thanks," he said, shivering visibly. "This is the first time I've felt warm since we went into the soup."

"Are you all right?" Grant asked.

"Yes. I believe so. No injuries. How's Irene?"

"Don't know," Frankovich answered. "We ran her down to the infirmary. Patti's working on her."

"What happened?" Ukara asked.

Zeb shook his head. "I'm not certain. We had entered the ocean . . . at least, the sensors indicated the outside environment was in the liquid state."

"Who was on duty?"

"We all were. Krebs wanted us all connected to the ship's systems until we were cruising at our first depth objective."

"Irene was connected, then?"

"Yes," said Muzorawa. "Everything seemed completely normal, but she suddenly gave a scream and doubled over, almost into a fetal posture."

"Krebs said she'd complained of chest pains," Frankovich pointed out.

"Yes, that's true. She seemed to lose her physical coordination, but that isn't unusual when the pressurization starts to rise. It happens to all of us. It's a temporary thing."

"Then she doubled over?" Grant asked.

"Yes. I think she had a heart attack."

Frankovich scratched his balding pate. "She had a clean bill of health, though. No indicators of cardiovascular problems."

Muzorawa made a helpless little shrug. "It's different down there, my friend. Very different."

They stayed by the airlock, talking, guessing, worrying, until the hatch slid open again and Christel Krebs stepped through, blinking uncertainly, like a burrowing animal exposed to unaccustomed light.

"Where is Pascal?" she asked, her voice sharp, cutting.

"In the infirmary," Grant said.

"Take me there. Immediately." And she extended her hand to Grant like a blind person asking to be led.

"WITH YOUR SHIELD . . . "

Grant got only as far as the security guards stationed at the access tunnel's entrance. One of them took Krebs up the corridor, toward the infirmary, while another told the rest of them to follow him. He walked the group to the small conference room that they had been using as a wardroom.

The guard captain was already there, standing at the head of the oval conference table.

"Dr. Wo wants you to stay here until further orders," he told them.

"What about dinner?" Frankovich bleated. "We haven't had anything to eat all day, just about."

The captain eyed Frankovich disdainfully. "We'll bring in dinner trays for you a bit later on. For now, you remain here. The director's orders. No exceptions."

He left and closed the door firmly.

Karlstad puffed out a breath. "That's the longest speech I've ever heard from old eagle-beak."

"We're prisoners," said Ukara, scowling at the idea.

Grant wanted to try the door, but realized that even if it was not locked, there would be guards posted in the corridor. Maybe even Sheena was out there.

Abruptly the door slid open. Startled, Grant jumped back.

Krebs stepped into the room, stopped, peered at Grant as if she could barely see him. She was fully dressed in a turtleneck sweater and jeans.

"How is Irene?" O'Hara asked. She and the others had not been able to put on fresh clothes. They still held blankets wrapped around themselves.

Krebs turned toward the sound of her voice. "They are still trying to revive her." She limped to the table, leaned both hands on it. "We are to remain here until Dr. Wo can talk with us."

"Well," said Muzorawa, clutching his blanket, "I suppose we should follow the ancient dictum: When handed a lemon, make lemonade."

And he pulled out one of the molded plastic chairs from the table and sat down. The chair creaked slightly.

Krebs made her way to the head of the table as the others took chairs for themselves. Instead of sitting, though, she remained on her feet.

"We should use this time to review what happened," she said, flat and cold. No room for disagreement or even discussion.

"Could we get some decent clothing, d'you think?" O'Hara asked.

"Later," said Krebs.

She used the conference room's smartwalls to display the mission's data records. Grant studied the propulsion and power systems' performance. Nothing out of the ordinary. Everything functioned normally, with smooth efficiency. No one else seemed to find any anomalies in their areas, either.

Even Pascal's medical data showed her to be fine, until suddenly her heart rate, blood pressure, and pulse all spiked at once.

"There's nothing to indicate the chest pain she complained of," Frankovich noted.

Krebs snapped, "Then it was not severe enough to register on the monitoring systems."

"Let's look at her EEG," Muzorawa suggested. "That loss of limb control should show something in the record."

It did not.

O'Hara murmured, "Could it've been psychosomatic, do you think?"

They went through the data for hours. Two guards came in with dinner trays. Krebs ordered them to bring clothes for the three blanket-clad crew members. They ate as they talked, discussed, argued over the data.

"As far as the records are concerned," Kayla Ukara said, frowning angrily, "*nothing* went wrong."

"Not until Irene doubled over," Muzorawa said. He looked troubled, Grant thought.

Karlstad had recovered some of his old flippancy. "Maybe she scared herself to death."

"She's not dead!" Ukara snapped.

"Want to bet?" Karlstad sneered. "If she was okay, Patti or maybe even Old Woeful himself would have come in here and told us."

"They are still working on her, most likely," said Muzorawa.

"If they're still working on her after this many hours, she's a goner," Karlstad said.

"That's a terrible thing to say," O'Hara muttered.

Karlstad shrugged nonchalantly. "It's like the ancient Spartan mothers used to tell their sons, 'Come back with your shield or on it.' Irene came back on hers."

"I still think it's a terrible thing for you to say," O'Hara repeated.

Ukara glowered at him.

"Why? Are you afraid that my saying it will make it come true?"

"I—"

The corridor door slid open and Dr. Wo wheeled his powerchair into the room. He looked exhausted, drained. For the first time, Grant thought of the director as *old*.

"Dr. Pascal died without recovering consciousness," he said, his grating, rough voice desolate, bleak. "All attempts to revive her were useless."

Grant read the emotions on their faces: shock, loss, fear. Kayla looked angry, but beyond her grim expression Grant thought he saw tears in her eyes.

"Mr. Archer," said Dr. Wo, "you will assume Dr. Pascal's place in the crew. You will prepare yourself for the necessary surgery tomorrow."

It hit Grant like a thunderclap. Me? Surgery? Stunned, Grant felt his heart flip in his chest. He looked across the table at Karlstad, smirking at him now.

"With your shield or on it," Karlstad mouthed silently.

SURGERY

With growing nervousness, Grant smeared the depilating cream over every part of his body. They're going to immerse me in that goo, he kept saying to himself. They're going to drown me.

It had been difficult enough to chop the hair off his head and then shave the remainder down to bare skin. The depilating cream worked only on thin body hair or shaved stubble. Trying to reach his calves and buttocks in the cramped confines of his lavatory made him feel clumsy and stupid. He kept banging elbows and stubbing toes as he contorted his limbs. The cream was slick and slimy; when he washed it off it was furred with his hair. He wondered if it would clog the shower drain, then realized that he really didn't give a damn.

No matter how many times he told himself that it was all right, that he'd be able to breathe the liquid PFCL just the way Lane and Zeb and all the others did, Grant felt the fear rising inside him. And resentment, growing into anger. I don't want to do this, he thought, but Wo's given me no choice. He points his finger and I get dunked into the drowning tank. It's just as Egon said: Wo pulls the strings and we puppets dance. No questions, no appeals, no help.

He found himself praying as he washed the antiseptic-smelling cream off his legs, his arms and armpits, his groin. He prayed for understanding, for acceptance, and above all for courage. Don't let me make an ass of myself when it's time to go into the immersion tank, he asked silently. Don't let them see how scared I am.

Well, he told himself, if Egon can go through with it, I can. Still, his hands shook.

The harsh buzz of the phone startled him so badly he dropped the washcloth.

"Answer phone," he called out.

From the lavatory, Grant couldn't make out whose face it was on his desktop phone screen, but he heard the guard captain's coldly insolent voice. "The surgical team is waiting for you. Should I send some of my men to fetch you?"

"I'm almost ready," Grant answered, the heat of anger flushing his face. "I'll get there on my own."

"Ten minutes," said the captain. "Otherwise I'll have to come after you."

Grant finished his washing as best he could, then pulled on a fresh set of coveralls and moccasins. He went to the door, hesitated. You've got to do it, he told himself. You have no option.

Seething with irritation and a growing, helpless apprehension, he yanked the door back and strode up the corridor toward the immersion center. As he stalked along, his anger gave way more and more to outright fear.

The Lord is my shepherd, Grant said silently. I shall not want . . .

By the time he reached the immersion center, he'd repeated the psalm a dozen times.

The captain and half a dozen guards were waiting for him. Sheena was there, too, hunkered down on the floor by the tank, munching on a pile of celery stalks. She hauled herself up onto all fours and knuckle-walked toward Grant.

"Hello, Sheena," he said tightly.

"Grant swim," the gorilla rasped. "Like fish."

He swallowed hard.

The guard captain came up. "We're running late."

"Sorry," Grant muttered, kicking off his moccasins. Then he unzipped his coveralls.

One of the guards whistled as Grant stepped out of his clothes. "Nice legs."

The others snickered.

"Let's get started, then," said the captain.

"Wait a second. I want to— "

They didn't wait. The captain pushed him toward the edge of the big tank.

"No, wait," Grant said, his chest heaving with fright, his eyes wide, darting.

Sheena grabbed Grant's right arm; she was careful not to snap his bones, but her powerful grip was painful all the same. Two of the guards held his left arm while a third wrapped him around the middle and still another lifted his bare feet off the deck so he couldn't get any leverage for his wild-eyed struggles.

None of the guards said a word. Grant could hear his own desperate, panicked gasping, the scuffing of the guards' boots on the cold metal of the floor, the hard grunts of their labored breathing.

The guard captain grimly, efficiently grasped Grant's depilated head in both his big meaty hands and pushed his face into the tank of thick, oily liquid.

Grant squeezed his eyes shut and held his breath until his chest felt as if it would burst. He was burning inside, suffocating, drowning. The pain was unbearable. He couldn't breathe. He dared not breathe. No matter what they had told him, he knew down at the deepest, most primitive level of his being that this was going to kill him.

Reflex overpowered his mind. Despite himself, despite the terror, he sucked in a breath. And gagged. He tried to scream, to cry out, to beg for help or mercy. His lungs filled with the icy liquid. His whole body spasmed, shuddered with the last hope of life as they pushed his naked body all the way into the tank with a final pitiless shove and he sank down, deeper and deeper.

He opened his eyes. There were lights down there. He was breathing! Coughing, choking, his body racked with uncontrollable spasms. But he was breathing. The liquid filled his lungs and he could breathe it. Just like regular air, they had told him. A lie. The perfluorocarbon liquid was cold and thick, utterly foreign, alien, slimy and horrible.

But he could breathe.

He sank toward the lights. Blinking, squinting in their glare, he saw that there were other naked hairless bodies down there waiting for him.

"Welcome to the team," a sarcastic voice boomed in his ears, deep, slow, reverberating.

Another voice, not as loud but even more basso profundo, said, "Okay, let's get him prepped for the surgery."

They strapped him down onto the surgical table.

"Christ," rumbled a disgusted voice, "you were supposed to depilate yourself."

Grant tried to say that he'd done the best he could, but he gagged instead.

"We'll have to shave him, goddammit."

"Get the lawnmower."

Someone put a mask over Grant's face and he quickly, gratefully, slipped into unconsciousness.

When he awoke he was lying on his back in a narrow cubicle enclosed with what looked like flimsy plastic screens. The infirmary, Grant realized. Medical monitors hummed and beeped softly somewhere over his head.

I'm breathing air!

The surgery didn't work, was his first thought. I won't be going on the mission. He wanted to laugh, but disappointment and shame washed out his sense of relief.

His legs ached. Lifting his head took some effort, but when he did he saw that he was wearing a loose-fitting green hospital gown that reached to his mid-thighs—and his legs were studded with metal electrodes. The flesh around them was puckered, red, raw-looking.

With trembling hands Grant reached up to his neck. Plastic ports for the intravenous feeding tubes had been inserted just behind his ears. They were hardly bigger than penny coins, yet they made his skin crawl, feeling those . . . those *things* inserted into his flesh. He knew that beneath his skin the ports were plugged into his jugular veins.

"How do you feel, my friend?"

Turning slightly, Grant saw Muzorawa sitting beside his bed. Zeb was smiling slightly, tentatively, like a man hoping for good news.

"Kind of dizzy," Grant said, letting his head sink back on the pillow.

"That is normal." Pointing toward the monitors lining the wall, Muzorawa said, "Your condition seems fine."

"How long have I been unconscious?"

"About six hours, I believe."

"You've been sitting here all that time?"

Muzorawa chuckled softly. "No, we took turns. I only arrived here a few minutes ago. If you had awakened sooner, it would have been Lane sitting with you."

"Oh."

"The surgery went smoothly," Muzorawa told him. "You were an excellent patient."

"That's good, I guess."

"Better than you know." Then Muzorawa's smile evaporated. "While you were under, we got Irene's autopsy report."

"What did it show?"

"Her blood was loaded with amphetamines."

"What?" Grant snapped to a sitting position despite his dizziness.

Muzorawa spread his hands. "Apparently the stimulants affected the central nervous system more strongly in the high-pressure environment than they do normally."

"That's what caused her heart attack?" Grant couldn't believe it.

Muzorawa nodded.

"But why would she take uppers?" Grant wondered.

"To control her fear, perhaps. Or to heighten her reactions, make her more alert . . ." His voice trailed off.

"You don't believe that, do you?"

The fluid dynamicist shook his head. "No. I have never known Irene to take drugs of any kind. Certainly not a cocaine derivative."

"She took something from Red Devlin," Grant remembered.

"When?"

"Several nights before you went into immersion. Uppers, he called the pills."

Muzorawa frowned. "I will speak with Devlin. But I can't believe Irene would put amphetamines into her system during the mission. She knew better."

"But maybe . . . if she was frightened . . ."

"It would be very unlike her."

"Then how did it get into her blood?" Grant asked.

Muzorawa leaned closer to the bed. "Perhaps the amphetamines were fed to her without her knowledge."

"Somebody slipped them into her food?"

"Or drink."

"But who would do that?"

"A Zealot."

"Devlin?" Grant yelped.

"Perhaps."

"No," Grant blurted. "It's impossible. How would he know how it would affect Irene when she was immersed in the sub? How would anybody know?"

Very gravely, Muzorawa replied, "My friend, you assume that the

Zealots are all ignorant, irrational fools. That is wrong, I think. A man might be quite well educated and still a fanatic."

"It couldn't be Devlin," Grant muttered, more to himself than Muzorawa. "He's . . . he's just a glorified cook."

"He is a very ingenious man," said Muzorawa. "Very capable, in his own way."

"But he's not a Zealot. He couldn't be!"

"Why? Do you think all the Zealots are wild-eyed hysterics? A man may smile and still be a villain, as Shakespeare pointed out."

"But . . . Devlin?" Grant looked into Muzorawa's wary, red-rimmed eyes. "Don't you think it's more likely to be one of us? One of the crew?"

"No, not at all. That would be like committing suicide."

"But a Zealot wouldn't mind dying if it accomplished his goal. Or hers."

"I cannot believe it would be Egon or Lane."

"What about Krebs?"

"Krebs?"

"She's weird, Zeb. I think maybe she's crazy."

Muzorawa blinked slowly several times. Then he said, in a voice hushed with fear, "If it is Krebs then we are all doomed."

TRAINING

The surgeon who implanted the biochips and electrodes in Grant was a baby-faced, sharp-tongued martinet: young, almost Grant's own age, obviously gifted and obviously well aware of his talents, impatient with his meager staff, his enforced Public Service duties, the station facilities, and especially with his patients.

"You can't stay in bed forever," the surgeon snapped as soon as he yanked back the plastic screen on the side of Grant's cubicle. Two other medics stood behind him at a respectful distance, watching. "Wo wants you up and on your feet. Now."

With some trepidation, Grant swung his legs off the bed. They felt like lengths of lumber, as if they didn't belong to him.

"Let go of the bed!" the surgeon demanded. "Stand on your own feet!"

Grant tried it and stood there, swaying slightly, feeling as if he would topple over any second. The surgeon glared at him, fists on his hips. Two other medics watched in silence.

"All right, now walk to me," the surgeon said, holding out his hands.

Grant took a hesitant, clumsy step. His legs hurt; stinging pain stabbed through them.

The surgeon backed away, urging, "Come on, come on."

Grant moved his other foot. It was like dragging a dead weight, but a dead weight that burned with pain.

"Walk, damn you!" the surgeon yelled. The medics behind him retreated, keeping their distance from their chief.

Grant forced himself to take another step, then stumbled. He grabbed for the surgeon, but all he managed to do was clutch the man's sleeve as he crashed painfully to the floor.

"Jesus H. Christ!" the surgeon yowled. "You ripped the sleeve out of my damned shirt!"

He turned his back on Grant and stamped angrily away. His aides scampered after him, leaving Grant alone in a heap on the floor.

"Clumsiest damned idiot yet," he heard the surgeon complaining loudly. "Goddamned clod! Wo's going to have a stroke when he hears about this one."

Reaching for the bed for support, Grant slowly pulled himself back to his feet and propped his rump on the edge of the mattress, panting with exertion. His legs felt as if they were on fire. I'm going to be a cripple, he said to himself. I can't walk!

For what seemed like hours Grant sat on the infirmary bed, his legs aching, his pulse racing with the certainty that his legs had been ruined. I'll be just like Wo, he told himself. I'll be stuck in a powerchair for the rest of my life.

He even thought he could hear the thin humming whine of a powerchair's electric motor. Looking up from his ruined legs, he saw Dr. Wo rolling past the mostly empty infirmary beds toward him.

Grant flinched inwardly. But as Wo approached, he felt a steely anger flow over him. His fists clenched on the bedsheets. He sat up straighter.

He can't scare me, Grant told himself. He can't intimidate me. I don't care what he says . . .

Wo stopped his chair a good five meters from Grant's bed. The director looked Grant up and down, from his completely bald head to his electrode-studded, useless legs.

"I know it is difficult, at first," the older man said calmly, almost gently. "But we have no time to spare. The IAA inspection team will be here in little more than eight days. *Zheng He* must be beneath the clouds before they enter this station."

Grant shook his head sadly. "I know. I understand what you're trying to do, but—"

"Your legs are physically strong. You can walk. It merely takes a bit of practice to reestablish the nerve pathways."

"I can't even stand up," Grant said.

"Yes you can."

"I tried . . ."

"Try again," Wo said softly. "Try with me."

The director grasped the arms of his powerchair and pushed himself to a standing position. There were no braces on his legs, Grant saw. Dr. Wo stood, trembling with the effort.

"If I can do it," he said, perspiration breaking out on his upper lip and brow, "you can, too."

Hardly breathing, his anger forgotten, Grant slid his legs off the bed and stood up. The legs hurt, but he stood erect.

"Good," said Wo. "Excellent. Now walk to me."

Grant took a tottering step. Wo did the same, holding his arms out as if to balance himself. Another step. Grant's legs felt as if they did not belong to him. He had to consciously *tell* them to move. Wo stepped shakily toward him, arms extended. Grant walked, slowly, hesitantly, feeling like Lazarus rising up from death.

"Good," Wo encouraged. "Very good."

The director's legs suddenly buckled. As he sagged Grant reached for him, grabbed him under the arms, and held him up.

"Thank you," Wo gasped. "Your legs are strong enough to support the two of us."

Grant laughed, and the director even allowed a slight chuckle to escape his lips. Grant helped the older man back into his powerchair. Wo sat gratefully, squirming a little to make himself comfortable. Grant stood in front of him, feeling a little shaky but knowing now that he would not be a cripple. Even the pain seemed lessened.

"Very good, Mr. Archer," said Wo, looking up at Grant. "Report for intensive training immediately. *Zheng He* is scheduled for launch in three days."

Wo abruptly spun the chair around and rolled out of the infirmary, leaving Grant standing there, flabbergasted, not knowing whether to be angry or grateful.

For the rest of the day, Lane, Egon, and Muzorawa took turns working with Grant, helping him to learn to walk again.

"You have to reestablish the neural paths," Karlstad told him, as Grant hung onto his shoulder while they walked slowly along the row of beds in the infirmary. Only two of them were occupied. One of the patients was an engineer whose spacesuit had been slightly ruptured while she was out on the surface of Io. She'd breathed a whiff of sulfur dioxide before the team she was with sealed her suit. The other was a station beancounter being treated for alcoholism.

"Get the nerves in your legs that connect with the spinal cord to start talking to each other again," Karlstad coaxed as he helped Grant along. "It takes a day or so."

"We don't have a day or so," Grant muttered, perspiring with the effort of trying to walk normally. "Wo wants to launch in three days."

Karlstad shrugged. "Well, you don't really need to be able to walk once you're immersed in the goo."

Lane helped him, too, although it troubled Grant to cling to her as they walked together. He closed his eyes and tried to picture Marjorie, but Lane's softly subtle perfume kept his wife's image a confused blur.

Muzorawa worked with him all through the night: helpful, nondemanding, patient. He was strong enough to lift Grant and carry him the length of the station's main corridor, Grant knew, yet he offered only as much help as was needed, nothing more.

"It's tough," Grant said as he limped past the row of beds. He was walking on his own now; the pain he felt was almost entirely psychosomatic, the infirmary staff assured him; he was making good progress.

"Of course it's tough," Muzorawa sympathized, pacing slowly beside Grant. "You must learn to walk all over again. We all had to."

"I'm pretty slow, aren't I?"

"You are like the centipede in the old story."

"Centipede?"

"You know, one of the animals in the forest asks the centipede how he can possibly control all those feet. And the centipede replies that it's simple, really. But as he explains how he does it, and he begins thinking about how he controls his one hundred little feet, he becomes so confused that he can't walk at all."

Grant nodded. "Yes, I remember that from kindergarten."

"We all learned to walk so early in life that we take it for granted. When we are forced to learn it all over again, we begin to see how much effort it takes."

Grant stumbled slightly and reached for one of the empty beds for support.

"Four-legged animals don't need to be taught how to walk," Muzorawa said, keeping his hands at his sides as Grant straightened up and resumed pacing. "Human babies crawl on all fours quite naturally. But they must be taught how to walk on their two feet—that's a sign that we evolved from four-legged creatures, I believe."

"You really think so?" Grant asked.

"I am not a biologist, but, yes, I believe that is so."

"You believe in Darwinian evolution."

"Does that offend you?"

"No," Grant answered truthfully. "I suppose I do, myself."

"Suppose?" Muzorawa asked, arching a brow.

Grant swiftly changed the subject. "Wish we were in zero-gee."

"That's the irony of it," said Muzorawa. "On the mission, we will be immersed and floating buoyantly. We won't need our legs for walking. Not at all."

"That's pretty ironic, all right," Grant agreed.

Lifting a hand like an ancient seer about to deliver a prophecy, Muzorawa went on, "But our legs will have a different function, a far more important function, during the mission."

And he smiled, as if remembering something that was beautifully pleasurable.

Grant started to realize what Muzorawa was talking about when he began his hurried training sessions in the simulator.

Driven by Dr. Wo's increasingly anxious prodding, Grant stumbled from the infirmary to the aquarium, donned a wetsuit and full-face mask, and joined Zeb, Lane, and Egon in the converted fish tank—under Krebs's remorseless command.

If she's a Zealot, Grant thought as he fumbled his way through the first day's simulations, *she's hiding it very well. She acts as if this mission is her personal quest.*

Maybe it is, a voice in his head answered. *If she's seeking some sort of next-world reward by destroying us all, what better way than to be in absolute command of the mission?*

Very soon, though, Grant was far too busy to even think about Krebs's true loyalties. She drove them through the simulator session mercilessly, demanding that they go through the entire simulation of disconnecting from the station and entering the Jovian atmosphere without a break.

"Stop whining! You'll get no time for relaxation when we are diving into those clouds," Krebs snarled at them.

They used the manual controls for the first session. When at last it was finished, Wo told them from his post in the control center, "Tomorrow you will be immersed and work in *Zheng He* instead of the simulator."

"Does that mean we performed okay?" Grant asked, from inside his transparent mask.

Muzorawa gave him a grin and a thumbs-up. But Krebs said sourly, "It means that we must stick to the accelerated schedule no matter how poorly you oafs have performed."

Immersion frightened Grant all over again, but at least this time he faced it without the security guards forcing him.

He felt cold as he stood in the access tunnel with the others, clad only in flimsy tights. We might as well be naked, Grant thought. These tights don't conceal anything. He had to force his eyes away from O'Hara's nipples and stare at the curved blank metal wall of the tunnel.

Muzorawa went through the airlock first, then Lane. The butterflies in Grant's stomach felt the size of pelicans. His legs still ached; they probably would forever, if Karlstad and the others were to be believed. Accept it, Grant told himself. It's a cross you'll have to bear. He glanced at Karlstad and saw that Egon looked just as jumpy and frightened as he himself felt.

The airlock hatch sighed open a crack. It was his turn. Grant swung it wide enough to step into the blank, coffin-sized lock. He touched the control stud that shut the hatch and sealed it. Trying to stay calm, he prayed, "The Lord is my refuge and my strength . . ."

The airlock was lit only by a single fluorescent set into the ceiling and the telltale lights on the control panel. The oily liquid began to pour into the airtight chamber, chill as death. Grant gritted his teeth and pressed both palms against the cold metal walls.

"Our Father, which art in heaven . . ."

His feet floated off the airlock floor. His head bumped against its ceiling. Through the thick, slimy liquid he could see the glimmer of the control panel's tiny lights, a faint row of green.

The liquid reached his armpits, his shoulders, his chin. He clamped his lips tight as the cold, clinging perfluorocarbon rose above his mouth. He was trapped in this metal coffin, freezing cold, drowning in the slick clinging alien liquid. His lungs were burning. He had to breathe. It's all right! he raged at himself. Stop fighting it and let it happen.

Squeezing his eyes shut, Grant took a tentative breath. And gagged.

His chest heaved, his entire body convulsed. Pain spasmed through him. I can't breathe! he screamed silently.

Yet he was breathing.

Coughing, sputtering, his whole body racked with reflex spasms, Grant desperately tried to calm his mind. It begins with the mind. You know what's happening to you; you understand the process. Relax! he raged at himself. Accept it. Take a deep breath and embrace whatever God has chosen for you to endure.

The spasms slowed, then stopped altogether. He could breathe without gagging, without coughing. He took a long, deliberate, testing breath. The perfluorocarbon still felt bitterly cold and now it was flooding his lungs, his entire body. But he could breathe it without choking. He still felt discomfort, pain actually, but he no longer felt fear.

"Are you going to stay in there all day?"

Grant hardly recognized Krebs's voice; in his new immersed world her words sounded like the deep, booming thunder of God himself.

"I'm opening the inner hatch now," he answered. His own voice sounded strangely low, slurred.

Grant floated through another long, narrow access tunnel, flicking its curved walls with his fingertips while he kicked his feet gently. I'm swimming, he realized. And Dr. Wo said we don't need our legs when we're buoyant. He was wrong.

Zheng He's bridge seemed bigger than it had looked when Grant had watched the crew from the control center. O'Hara and Muzorawa were already there, floating easily.

"Welcome aboard," said Lane, with a big smile. Even her voice sounded lower, sluggish, like a recording played back at a slow speed.

Grant tried to grin back at her, but he wasn't sure he made much more than a nervous twitch of his lips.

"I believe you Christians have a ceremony of immersion," said Muzorawa, his voice finally deep enough to match his powerful appearance.

"Baptism, yes," said Grant.

"Some of your sects use immersion to symbolize a rebirth, do they not?"

"Born-again Christians," Grant replied.

"I see!" said O'Hara, actually laughing in the frigid soup of the submersible's environment. "We've been born again."

Nodding, Muzorawa added, "Into a new world."

For a moment Grant thought that they were teasing him, making fun of a kind of religion that neither of them believed in. But then he realized that they were at least accurate, if not totally serious. We have been born into a new world, he told himself. We've undergone a ritual of immersion in preparation for this mission.

The politicians want to stop us, he thought. The Zealots want to destroy us. But maybe we're really doing God's work here. Maybe we're *meant* to explore Jupiter and seek out whatever's living beneath those clouds.

The idea hit Grant with the force of a physical blow. Could this be God's will? Part of His plan for us?

"All right, I'm here," Karlstad announced, shattering Grant's train of thought. "We've got a foursome; boot up the computer and let's play bridge."

O'Hara said, "We'll not be playing bridge, Egon. We'll be working on this bridge."

"Too true," Karlstad conceded.

Their bantering ended when Krebs joined them. She quickly had them at their posts, standing side by side along the bridge's consoles, their feet anchored in the floor loops. Grant was assigned to the power and propulsion systems, just as he had been in the control center.

"Today we simulate powering up the ship's systems, disconnecting from the station, and entering Jupiter's cloud bank," Krebs told them, as if they hadn't already gone through the simulation plan themselves. "None of the ship's systems will actually be functioning. This is a simulation only."

Grant nodded his understanding. The station's simulations computer would be running the show. No matter what kind of crazy emergencies Dr. Wo threw at them, it was all make-believe.

But that would change soon enough, he knew.

CONNECTED

Krebs drilled them mercilessly. All four crew members spent the whole day on the bridge, simulating the first stages of their flight into Jupiter's ocean over and over again, until their moves became almost like reflex actions.

Standing at his console with O'Hara on one side of him and Muzorawa on the other, Grant felt that he could power up the ship's generators and propulsion units and go through the procedures of separating from the station and insertion into the cloud bank with his eyes closed. In his sleep, even.

Still Krebs made them go through it again. It was the only part of the mission that could be simulated. No one knew what to expect once they dived through the clouds and entered the vast, turbulent ocean.

Dr. Wo changed the ship's internal pressure time and again, increasing the pressure to its highest design value and then dropping it back again. Grant never thought that his ears could pop underwater, but they did, more than once.

"He's trying to see if the pressure changes bother us," Karlstad told Grant.

"They bother me," Grant admitted. "Changing the pressure back and forth is damned uncomfortable."

The two of them had been given a brief meal break by Krebs. Meals on *Zheng He* consisted of coasting over to the dispenser at the back of the bridge and plugging one of its plastic tubes into one of the intravenous ports in your neck. It made Grant shudder to do it, but it didn't hurt at all, and it had the advantage of pumping a full meal's worth of nutrition into your system in only a few minutes. No chewing, no digestive action; the food was already liquefied and ready to be dispersed through the body by the bloodstream.

"The Woeful One must be trying to see if the pressure changes had anything to do with Irene's heart attack," Karlstad said.

"I thought the amphetamines did it."

"Under normal conditions the dose she took wouldn't have killed her."

"I thought it was a very high dose," Grant said.

"Not that high . . . it wouldn't have been fatal normally."

"It would have disoriented her, wouldn't it? Made her unfit for duty?"

Karlstad started to answer, hesitated, then asked, "Do you think she was trying to get out of—"

The dispenser's signal bell chimed—clunked, really, in the high-pressure fluid they were breathing—and its light turned red.

"Your dinner's finished," Karlstad said needlessly. "Want some dessert?"

Wincing, Grant pulled the slim plastic tube from the socket in his neck. "Dessert's included," he said, trying to sound breezy. "No extra charge."

"Stop your jabbering and get back to your stations," Krebs snarled at them.

When the long, grueling simulation was at last finished, Krebs relieved only O'Hara and Karlstad. Grant and Muzorawa stayed at their posts on the bridge while the other two went to their berths. Krebs herself remained on the bridge.

Doesn't she ever sleep? Grant asked himself.

Soon he began to wonder if Krebs was ever going to allow him to sleep. The simulations were finished, as far as he could see. They were pretending to be descending through the thickening layers of Jupiter's atmosphere, sinking lower and lower until the atmospheric gases were compressed by the planet's titanic gravity into the liquid state. Since they knew so little about the environment below the clouds, there was very little for them to simulate—unless Wo threw some malfunctions at them.

Instead, the hours passed by so uneventfully that Grant had to fight against boredom. Strangely, he felt no urge to yawn, as he normally would. Maybe breathing this gunk suppresses the yawn reflex, he thought.

At last Karlstad and O'Hara returned to the bridge.

"Muzorawa and Archer to your berths," Krebs ordered needlessly. Grant was already floating toward the hatch that led to the closet-size sleeping area. Karlstad referred to it as "the catacombs."

Then Krebs added, "When you two return, we will all link with the ship's systems."

Grant was too tired to care. All he wanted was his four hours of sleep. But then he caught the look on Lane's face: She was glowing with anticipation.

Sleep did not come easily. As soon as he closed his eyes, it hit Grant all over again that he was immersed in this cold thick fluid, breathing it into his lungs, wallowing in a completely unnatural world, as out of place as a fish on a mountaintop. The fear that had been submerged while he was on the bridge among the others rose to the surface of his mind now, his chest heaved, his aching legs twitched with the barely suppressed urge to run, to get away, to find someplace safe, some refuge where he could hide and breathe real air and feel the warmth of the sun on his face.

He opened his eyes and even in the darkness of his screened-off berth he saw that he was in a metal womb, a man-made cave that was pressing in on him, closing down on all sides. And outside this crypt, beyond its metal shell, unbearable pressures were squeezing, pressing, inexorably working to crush the ship, to crush *him* into a bloody pulp.

Grant could feel his heart pounding frantically in his chest, sense every nerve in his body telling him to get away, to escape, to get out of this deathtrap.

He tried to pray. He tried to conjure up a mental picture of Marjorie, of their times together, of those brief moments when they shared the warmth of their bodies pressing close on a world where the sky was blue and there were trees and grass and birds singing.

Nothing worked. He was imprisoned inside this metal tomb, breathing a horrible alien slime, a billion kilometers from home, from Marjorie, from his parents, from safety. Even God had forgotten him. He was alone and forsaken.

Yet he must have drifted into sleep, because he found himself surrounded by monsters, vague dark shapes that growled and snarled and shambled after him in a world of shadows and menace. One of the shapes looked like a gorilla, only much bigger, looming over him like a mountain. Another pursued him in a powerchair, growling at him.

Grant's eyes popped open. The growling sound was the clock, its normal alarm buzzer sounding strange, alien in the liquid. Sleep shift was over. Time to return to the bridge.

Grant slid out of the bunk; there was no room to stand except outside in the narrow common area. He bobbed gently off the deck, decided there was no point to changing the tights he'd been wearing. No point to trying to go to the toilet; the predigested pond scum they pumped into his veins produced almost no waste matter at all.

Feeling like one of the damned souls in Dante's Hell, Grant swam through the hatch back onto the bridge.

Krebs was still there, hovering over Karlstad and O'Hara, who were at their consoles, their backs turned to him. The captain glared at Grant as if he'd somehow done something wrong. Then he realized she was looking past him. Turning slightly, he saw Zeb coming through the hatch.

Krebs stared at the two of them as if she didn't recognize them. Her eyes flicked back and forth from Muzorawa's face to his own.

"Returning for duty," Muzorawa said gently.

"Ah. Dr. Muzorawa," Krebs replied, as if seeing him for the first time. "And Mr. Archer."

"Yes, ma'am," Grant said.

Krebs drifted back away from them as Grant took his station between Lane and Zeb. Then she said in a commanding tone, "Now we will all connect with the ship's systems."

O'Hara turned from her console and nodded, smiling. Karlstad looked—Grant couldn't decipher the expression on Egon's face. He seemed to be trying to keep his features frozen, impassive, like a little boy pretending that he doesn't know he's about to be showered with Christmas presents.

Muzorawa said, "Ready to link, Captain."

"Proceed," she said.

Grant did what he saw the other three do: He flicked open the slim panel set into his console's front. A set of hair-thin fiber-optic wires snaked out of the narrow compartment, floating lazily in the perfluorocarbon liquid like the coiling hair of a murderous Medusa. The end of each fiber was color-coded to match the anodized color spots on the electrodes in Grant's legs.

Grant watched the others out of the corner of his eye as he fumbled with the devilishly thin fibers. His fingers seemed too fat and clumsy to handle them. The others were finished before he had done even one of his legs. Thankfully, the fiber ends were electrically charged to mate with specific electrodes; they would not connect with the wrong electrode; instead Grant felt a slight but very real repulsive force, like trying to put two north poles of a magnet together.

"We are waiting, Mr. Archer," Krebs said as he finished one leg at last and started on the other.

Finally he got it done. He straightened up, feeling a little like a puppet with his legs connected to the wires. He saw that the fibers on Krebs's stubby legs connected to a panel set into the overhead. If she's not careful, Grant thought, she'll get herself tangled in those wires. The thought of the captain wrapping herself in her own set of wires, struggling to get herself loose like some fat fly in a spider's web, almost made him laugh out loud.

"You are amused, Mr. Archer?"

Grant realized he was smiling. Startled, he didn't know what to do, how to respond to the captain's accusative glare.

"We are all pleased that we are about to link with the ship, Captain," said Muzorawa, beside him.

"We're looking forward to the experience," O'Hara chimed in.

"Indeed." Krebs's angry glare shifted back and forth. "And what have you to say?" she demanded, pointing at Karlstad.

"Not a word, ma'am," Egon replied. "I'm waiting for your next order."

Krebs mumbled something too low for Grant to make out, then said grudgingly, "Very well. Activate the linkage."

Each of them reached to the console, lifted the plastic cover plate from the switch that triggered the linkage, then clicked the switch on.

Grant expected some surge of power, a jolt of electrical energy, perhaps a thrill of euphoria or at least pleasure. Better than sex, they had told him. Instead, he felt nothing. A slight tingling in his legs, as if they were going asleep. But that passed almost before he recognized the sensation and he was left with . . . almost nothing.

Almost.

Grant stood there, ignoring his crewmates alongside him, and felt an odd tremor begin to pulse through his legs. Unlike anything he'd ever sensed before. No, not just along his legs. His entire body seemed to be vibrating, humming inside like a plucked string of a bass viol. He stared down at his hands. They looked steady, not shaking at all, yet inside he felt as if he were quivering like a man hit by a seizure.

He closed his eyes and realized that it wasn't he who was vibrating, it was the fusion generator, deep in the core of the ship, reverberating with the power of transforming matter into energy, fusing atomic nuclei together to extract their hidden might, converting the blinding radiation into electrical power that raced along the ship's wiring like blood pulsing through arteries and veins. Grant could *feel* the throbbing, relentless force of this man-made star buried behind layers of dense shielding as it powered the universe that was their ship. He wanted to reach out his hand and let his fingers touch that glowing hot plasma; he could virtually hear the thunder of its endless blaze.

It was like music, like a symphonic orchestra playing in his mind, in his body, along every nerve, every blood vessel. The electrical currents racing through the ship tingled like a thrillingly beautiful cadenza, endless, eternal, glorious.

The propulsion system was shut down, more's the pity. Grant wanted to sense it, to connect with it, to feel the drive and force of raw energy hurtling out of the ship's thruster vents, pushing them forward, onward.

Dimly he heard a voice. He ignored it. This was too much pleasure to allow anything to distract him from it. The whole ship's electrical systems were part of him. I am the ship! Grant thought. We are one. It's pure delight. Ecstasy! It's like being a god.

"Are you all right?"

He forced himself to open his eyes, saw Zeb peering at him worriedly.

"I'm fine," Grant said. And he meant it. He'd never felt so . . . so *alive* in all his life.

"It can be a powerful feeling," O'Hara said. Grant turned his head and saw that she too looked concerned. "Don't let it sweep you away now."

He nodded. Yes, I've got to be careful. It *is* powerful. Overwhelming. Better than sex. Better than drugs. They were right. It's enough to sell your soul for.

"Are we ready to return to work?" Krebs's sour voice cut through Grant's excitement.

"Yes, Captain," he said sharply.

"Very well. Now we will go through the separation and ignition simulation once again."

But this time, Grant realized, this time we'll be connected to the ship. I'll feel the electrical currents. I'll power up the thrusters. I'll move the ship with my own will.

DEPARTURE

I am the ship.

Grant had never felt so powerful and excited in his entire life. When Krebs called a halt to their simulations exercise he didn't want to stop, didn't want to disconnect from the ship. Let's go on, he urged silently. Let's power it up for real and get going. Let me feel what it's like to dive through those clouds and into the Jovian sea.

"I said disconnect, Mr. Archer! Now!"

Krebs's hard, demanding voice cut into him like a whip. With enormous reluctance, Grant did what the others had already done: reached to the console and clicked off his linkage to the ship's electrical and propulsion systems.

It felt like a lobotomy. One moment he had all the power of a miniature star pulsing through him, part of him, as intimately interwoven into his consciousness as his awareness of his own identity. Then with the click of a switch it was all gone; he was a solitary weak hairless ape again, alone, isolated from the rest of the universe.

He had to blink several times before he realized that the others were unplugging the fiber-optic leads from the electrodes in their legs. Feeling a sullen resentment rising within him, Grant yanked the fibers from his legs one by one. The loose ends floated lightly, bobbing gently in the perfluorocarbon as if beckoning to him. When he was finished he activated the spring that pulled the fibers back into their slim storage rack and snapped shut the door that covered them.

"The simulation is completed," Krebs said. "Now we all sleep. When we return to duty, no more simulations. The mission begins in five hours and fourteen minutes."

The four crew members drifted back toward the catacombs and their coffin-sized berths. Krebs remained on the bridge, floating up near the overhead, fitting a communications headset over her bald skull.

"Doesn't she ever sleep?" Karlstad whispered.

Muzorawa whispered back, "She must."

"But when?"

The captain was already deep in discussion, presumably with Dr. Wo.

"Well, now," O'Hara said to Grant, with a smile that looked a bit forced, "how did you like being linked?"

Grant realized he was breathless. It took him several tries to make his voice work. "Overpowering," he said at last.

"Yes, 'tis that, isn't it?"

Karlstad butted in, "When do we link with each other like that?" He leered at O'Hara. "That's what I'm looking forward to."

She frowned at him. Muzorawa said, serious as usual, "You must be wary of being overwhelmed by the experience. It *is* extremely powerful, but you must not allow it to overcome your judgment."

"That's right," O'Hara said. "We're here to run the ship, not to invent some new form of depravity."

Karlstad smirked. "All work and no play isn't good for you."

Muzorawa floated between him and O'Hara. "Egon, the first mission was wrecked, possibly because one of its crew allowed the sensations of linking with the ship to overwhelm his judgment."

"Or her judgment," Karlstad said, nodding toward Krebs, still floating in the bridge, deep in discussion with Dr. Wo.

There was absolutely no privacy in the catacombs: nothing but a bare, confined common area so small and tight that the four of them could hardly fit into it together. Their shelflike berths took up one side of it, the hatch to the bridge the other.

"I've got to get into a fresh outfit," O'Hara announced, and she began to strip off her tights.

Grant couldn't help staring. Karlstad grinned wolfishly and asked, "Do you need any help, Lane?"

"Grow up, won't you!"

He shrugged and began taking off his own tights.

"Yes, we should put on clean clothes," Muzorawa agreed.

Grant was surprised that he felt no physical arousal at the sight of O'Hara's naked body. Yet his breath quickened, his mind raced. She was slim, with small breasts and slender hips, totally hairless, but still this was a naked woman with smooth creamy skin and beautiful green eyes less than an arm's length from him. He felt embarrassed more than anything else, especially when Zeb and Egon peeled off their tights. Neither of them was aroused, either, Grant saw.

Without a word he ducked into his bunk, pulled the privacy screen shut, and started wriggling out of his own tights. The fresh clothes were in a locker out in the common area, he knew. So was the recycler for the old tights. He decided to wait until the others were in their berths and asleep before venturing out again.

You're being silly, he told himself. Silly and prudish. There's nothing sinful about any of this. Your sex drive has been practically eliminated by the surgery. It's like looking at a painting of a nude.

Yes, said another voice in his mind. But you enjoyed looking at her. The most important sex organ in the human body is the brain, and you took pleasure in seeing her naked body. That's sinful.

He heard O'Hara slither into the berth next to his; nothing between them but a thin plastic partition. He sensed her stretching out on the bunk, still naked, absolutely hairless. He squeezed his eyes shut and tried to drive the image out of his mind.

"What do you think of her?" It was Karlstad's voice, whispering outside his berth.

"The captain?" Muzorawa's deeper voice replied.

"Right."

"What about her?"

"Do you think she's ever going to sleep?"

"Yes, of course. She takes her responsibilities very seriously."

Grant remembered his earlier conversation with Zeb, when he'd brought up the possibility that Krebs might be a suicidal Zealot.

Karlstad asked, "Have you noticed the way she gives you the fish-eye? As if she doesn't recognize you."

"Yes, it is strange," Muzorawa agreed.

"Gives me the creeps."

"As long as she does her job properly we have nothing to complain about."

"Maybe you don't," Karlstad replied, still whispering, "but I don't like it, not one microbit. She's weird. I think she's crazy."

For several heartbeats Muzorawa said nothing. At last he replied, "Get some sleep. We're going to need all our energy in about five hours."

• • •

"Engage the linkage," commanded Krebs.

Grant clicked the switch that energized the fiber-optic links to the chips implanted in his legs. He closed his eyes as he felt the thrumming power of the ship's fusion generator vibrating within him, warming him, filling him with sensations he had never felt before linkage. He had a blazing man-made star within him. The electricity it generated was pulsing through him, the ship's wiring was his own nervous system, the ship's conduits were his own arteries and veins.

He could sense the vibrations of the life-support fans circulating the perfluorocarbon liquid through the ship's living space; each light and display screen on the bridge's consoles was like an extension of his fingers. He felt the ship's sensors powering up, peering into the space outside the hull like searchlights from an ancient lighthouse sweeping a stormy seacoast.

It took a concentrated effort of will to open his eyes and recognize that he was standing in front of his console on the bridge, feet anchored in the floor loops, flanked by Muzorawa and O'Hara, Karlstad on O'Hara's other side, Krebs floating behind him.

O'Hara was at the communications console, with its multiple touchscreens staring at her like the eyes of a spider. Wo's chunky, intense face filled the central display screen.

". . . automated separation sequence begins in fifteen seconds," the director was saying.

"Fifteen seconds," Krebs repeated, her voice flat, unemotional. If separating from the station and launching *Zheng He* into Jupiter's clouds excited her, she hid it completely.

Grant licked his lips. The computer's synthesized voice began the final minute of countdown.

"Power and propulsion?" Krebs asked needlessly. She could see Grant's screens as easily as he could himself.

"Power and propulsion all green," he said.

"Life support?"

"In the green," said Karlstad.

"Communications?"

"Communications normal," O'Hara replied.

"Sensors?"

"All sensors on and functioning," reported Muzorawa.

"We are ready for separation and launch," Krebs said to Wo's image.

Precisely at that moment the computer's voice announced, "Automated separation sequence initiated. Separation in thirty seconds . . . twenty-nine . . ."

The seconds stretched endlessly. Grant stood there, aware that he was breathing a cold, slimy, oxygenated liquid but no longer caring about that. The ship was coming alive, electrical currents racing through all its systems now, the propulsion units starting up, pumps beginning to stir, the electrons in the powerful superconducting coils singing their eternal hymn of perpetual motion, ceaseless devotion to their task.

"Full internal power," Krebs said.

"Ten seconds," announced the computer.

Grant could feel the magnetohydrodynamic channels stirring into life, preparing to take the star-hot plasma exhaust from the fusion generator and accelerate it through the ship's thruster tubes. Along his nerves Grant felt the trembling thrill of anticipation.

The clamps and bolts that held *Zheng He* to the station opened like a dozen faces breaking into smiles. Grant broke into a smile himself. We're free, he knew. We're on our own now.

"Ignition."

The plasma thrusters started softly, gently. Grant felt their strength as if it were his own arms reaching out and lifting a heavy burden. As the thrust built up, his strength multiplied, tripled, quadrupled. He was stronger than any mere human could ever be, stronger than Sheena, stronger than a whole tribe of gorillas, he was lifting the entire ship, hurling it with fine purposeful power and precision, flinging it away from the station and down into the waiting clouds of Jupiter.

Better than sex? This was better than life! I can rev up the thrusters to full power and blast this ship past Jupiter in an eyeblink. I can push us out to the stars! To the farthest edge of the universe! Grant knew he had all the power of the universe throbbing inside him, superhuman energy, the strength and power of a god.

That surge of arrogance snapped him back to reality. *Pride goeth before a fall*, he heard his father's voice in his mind. All this power, all this sensation of godlike strength, is a trap, a snare, a temptation to the kind of hubris that has hurled many a good man into eternal damnation. *Vanity, vanity, all is vanity . . .*

He stood trembling before his console, trying to regain control of himself, battling to keep the enormously seductive power of this illusion from deceiving him. It's an electronic mirage, he told himself. You are nothing more than a man who is linked electronically to the machinery of this ship. Control yourself.

Still, he trembled.

Is this what wrecked the first mission? Grant asked himself. Is this linkage so overwhelming that someone ran amok with the ship's systems? He had touched a place in his own mind where he had wanted to run wild with the plasma thrusters, tear away all restraints, push full throttle just for the sheer joy of power. Yes, he realized now. And if I'd done that, I would have killed us all.

Still he trembled, but now it was with the understanding of the enormous dangers that dwelled within his own mind, his own soul. It's the age-old war, he realized, the never-ending struggle between responsibility and pleasure, between good and evil. This ship is simply a new battlefield in that eternal war. As long as we're human, the war goes on.

But for an instant, Grant knew, he had been more than human. He still was. He still felt the pulsing power of the ship's generator and plasma thrusters, they were still a part of him.

I am the ship.

Power requires responsibility, he told himself. Extreme power requires extreme care.

BOOK IV

Why dost Thou stand afar off, O Lord?
Why dost Thou hide Thyself in times of trouble?

—Psalm 10

INTO THE CLOUDS

"Disconnect," Krebs ordered.

Grant hovered uncertainly in the viscous perfluorocarbon atmosphere of the bridge, his feet anchored in the floor straps, his arms floating chest high, his mind battling against the seductions of power.

"Disconnect!" Krebs insisted. "Now!"

The flight plan was for them to orbit Jupiter at least twice, long enough to make certain that all the ship's systems were indeed functioning properly. Only then would Krebs give the order to descend into the clouds.

Grant turned off the linkage with all the reluctance of an addict withdrawing from his drugs. He was alone again, separate, nothing more than a blob of protoplasm inside a shell of flesh.

"How do you feel?" Muzorawa asked as he slipped his feet free of the floor loops and bobbed gently in the viscous liquid.

"A little shaky," Grant admitted.

Karlstad floated up to them. "I don't see why we have to orbit around the damned planet like this. Why don't we stay linked and get on with the job?"

"You must rest," Krebs answered from over their shoulders. "Eat. Take a nap. Staying linked with the ship for too long is not good."

O'Hara, still at her comm console, said, "Captain, Dr. Wo wants to speak to you on the private channel."

Krebs nodded and slipped a headset over her bald pate.

"When does she sleep?" Karlstad whispered.

Muzorawa nodded. "I don't think she's disconnected herself since we first linked up."

Grant shrugged and headed for the food dispensers. He felt jumpy inside, weary yet keyed up. Maybe a nap is what I need.

It still made him squeamish to plug the feeding tube into the socket in his neck, but Grant did it. When the counter on the dispenser's metal face clunked and the flow of liquid shut off, he pulled the tube free with a shuddering grimace.

"What's the matter, doesn't it taste delicious?" Karlstad jibed.

Grant headed for his berth without answering, leaving the three others huddled at the dispenser.

Knowing that he'd have to be awake and alert in a few hours, Grant could not sleep. He kept thinking about the thrill of power he'd felt when linked to the ship. Will it get easier as we go on, he wondered, or will it become more seductive, more corrupting? God, help us! he prayed. Give us the strength to resist temptation.

He thought about composing a message for Marjorie, even though he wouldn't be able to send it until they returned from this mission. *If* we return, he found himself thinking. Then he heard the other three come into the catacombs, talking quietly, grumbling really, and finally slipping into their own berths.

Grant gave them enough time to fall asleep, then crawled out of his bunk as quietly as he could and swiftly stripped off his tights and pulled a fresh pair from the storage bin in the common area. Wide awake, knowing that he wouldn't be able to sleep, he slid the screen open and floated into the bridge.

Krebs was sleeping, bobbing gently up near the overhead, eyes closed, a soft burbling noise that might have been a snore in normal air emanating from her half-open mouth. And she was still connected to the ship. Grant saw that the wires from the overhead compartment were still firmly linked to the electrodes in her chunky, hairless legs.

She sleeps connected, Grant said to himself, wondering what that must be like. Then he wondered if that was a good thing. Is she addicted to it? He asked himself. Is that the joy she gets out of life?

One by one Muzorawa, Karlstad, and O'Hara returned to the bridge, almost like sleepwalkers, and took their stations at their consoles. Krebs still snored gently, bobbing up near the overhead. Grant slipped his feet into the floor loops and saw that his console was showing all systems normal. Nothing but green lights. He ran a finger across the console's central touchscreen to check the subsystems. He frowned, slightly nettled at the cumbersomeness of the manual procedure. If we were linked I could *feel* all the systems, I'd know how they're doing with my eyes closed.

But they would not engage the linkage unless Krebs gave the command, and she was still asleep, floating behind the four of them.

"Well, at least we knows she sleeps," Karlstad stage-whispered.

"That's good," O'Hara whispered back. "Everyone needs to sleep sometime."

"You are eager to work." Krebs's cold, hard voice slashed at them. "Good."

Karlstad rolled his eyes toward heaven.

"Connect your linkages," Krebs commanded.

Grant linked up smoothly this time, actually finishing before Karlstad. He felt a glow of anticipation warming him, saw that O'Hara looked the same way.

"Engage linkage," said Krebs.

Again Grant felt the power of the fusion generator surging through him, felt the music of electrical currents racing through every section of the ship. The thrusters, he begged silently. Ignite the thrusters.

Instead, Krebs patiently checked through the navigation system, waiting to reach the precise point in their orbit around Jupiter's massive bulk where they were to insert the ship into its deorbit burn and plunge toward the hurtling, multihued Jovian clouds.

"Approaching the keyhole," Muzorawa called out.

Without asking permission, Grant closed his eyes and linked momentarily to Zeb's sensors and saw what they were showing: the racing multihued clouds of Jupiter, streaming madly as the planet's tremendous spin whirled them into long ribbons of ocher, pale blue, and russet brown. Lightning flickered through the clouds, crackles of vast electrical energy. He felt the heat radiating up from those clouds, he heard the eternal wailing of winds that dwarfed the wildest hurricanes of Earth.

And he realized that there was a storm, a vast swirling whirlpool of dazzling white clouds, screaming its fury in the area where they had expected to make their entry into the cloud deck.

"The entry area's covered with a cyclonic system," Muzorawa said tightly.

Grant opened his eyes. Zeb's face was set in an expressionless mask. Turning, he saw that O'Hara and Karlstad both looked concerned.

Krebs made a sound that might have been a grunt. Or a suppressed growl. "Very well. We'll go on to the alternate injection point."

Grant glanced up at the main wallscreen display. It showed their orbital path against the swirling clouds. The alternate entry position was a quarter-orbit away. Closer to the Red Spot, Grant saw. Not close enough to be dangerous, he knew. Still, getting closer to that titanic storm was unsettling.

No one spoke for the forty-nine minutes it took to reach the alternate insertion point. Grant occupied himself by concentrating on the fusion generator; it was like standing by a warming, crackling fireplace on a cold winter's day. Soon we'll be in the clouds, he told himself. And then the ocean. That's when we'll see how accurate my mapping of the currents has been.

"Automated countdown," Krebs called out at last.

Grant unconsciously licked his lips as the countdown timer began clicking off the seconds. For the first time since their immersion, Grant consciously thought about the taste in his mouth. It was odd, not unpleasant, but the perfluorocarbon liquid was unlike anything his taste buds had encountered in the past. He had no memory references for it, down at the cellular level where instinct lived.

"Retro burn in ten seconds," the computer's synthesized voice called out. Despite himself, Grant trembled inwardly with the anticipation of the thrusters' power.

The thrusters blazed to life. Grant felt their strength surging through him like a tidal wave smashing down seawalls, trees, buildings, leveling hills, tearing away everything in its path. He gritted his teeth, fighting with every atom of his willpower against giving way to it. He was strong! So powerful that he could tear the ship apart with his bare hands. Eyes squeezed shut, he could *see* the blazing plasma hurtling from the thrusters, feel the energy streaming from the fusion generator as if it were his own arms, his own muscles driving the ship deep into the clouds of Jupiter, down into the unknown, beyond the reach of help or the understanding of the pitiful frail two-legged apes clinging to their cockleshell station in orbit around Jupiter.

Outside, wind began to howl and shriek, as if protesting their entry into the atmosphere. Grant laughed inwardly. Come on, do your damnedest! he challenged Jupiter. The power of the ship's thrusters was his own might, his own body standing against the fury of this alien world's resistance. The ship staggered and bucked but it kept on its course, driving steadily deeper into the wild tangle of clouds. Grant felt like a pitiless conqueror forcing himself into a violently struggling woman. He was raping Jupiter, and no matter how the planet resisted he was too powerful, too ruthless, too driven to show mercy or restraint.

Abruptly the thrusters shut off. Grant felt it like a blow to his groin. He gasped, almost retched. For an endless moment he stood swaying in his foot straps, arms floating before him, hands clenched into fists. He was aghast at his own thoughts, his own emotions. Guilt, shame, terror at the primitive savagery buried within him racked his soul. He could hear the wind shrieking louder as the ship's furious, howling plunge through the deep Jovian atmosphere continued. He could feel the ship's outer skin glowing with the white heat of friction.

They were falling through the deep atmosphere now, dragged down by Jupiter's powerful gravity, no longer conquerors but humble servants obedient to the planet's massive pull.

Forcing his eyes open, Grant looked across at the screens of Muzorawa's sensor console and saw that they were plunging through a maelstrom of swirling clouds. Zeb himself stood transfixed before the screens, eyes staring, fists clenched at his sides, body rigid.

Tentatively, furtively, without orders, he again linked with Zeb's sensors and suddenly *felt* the blazing heat of their hypersonic entry into those thick, turbulent clouds. The ship was shuddering now, bucking like a pumpkinseed in a hurricane as it plunged deeper into the Jovian atmosphere, turning the tortured clouds around it into white-hot plasma, a howling, shrieking sheath of burning gases surrounding them, trailing back in their wake like the long glowing tail of a falling star.

Grant wanted to shout defiance at the burning gases that sheathed the ship. You can't hurt us! he snarled silently. You can't do anything except what we *want* you to do, he told the giant planet. We're using you, using your thick blanket of atmosphere to slow us down enough to enter your sea and learn your secrets.

Jupiter thought otherwise. The ship lurched, plunged, slewed sidewise as a tremendous jet stream buffeted it. Grant swayed, tottered, his stomach going hollow within him. He would have sailed across the bridge if he hadn't been anchored by the floor loops. As it was, he had to brace his hands against the console to prevent himself from being slammed into it.

The ship slowed. Grant recovered his balance, glanced around, and saw that no one had noticed his near frenzy. Or if they had, they paid no attention to it. Zeb, Lane, Egon—all locked in their own private universes, all feeling, hearing, seeing, even tasting the sensations from the ship's sensors and systems. Grant had tasted raw, primal power, and now he felt empty in its absence, deprived, sullenly angry. And afraid.

"Approaching the bottom of the cloud deck." Krebs's voice sounded alien, distant, a disturbance in Grant's universe of power and strength, like an alarm clock's buzzing interference in a warm, exciting dream.

The thrill of the thrusters' surge was gone, but the fusion generator still sang its beguiling song of power, whispering to Grant of universes beyond the beyond, worlds to discover and conquer.

"Look at that!"

Grant could not tell who said it, but the words stirred him out of his nearly hypnotic trance.

"Put it on the main screen." That was Krebs's voice, definitely. Even in the eerie distortions of this liquid gunk in which they lived, her thick harsh tone was unmistakable.

The wallscreen above their consoles showed a wild cloudscape, as far as the scanners could see, a vast panorama of billowing clouds scudding along on powerful streams of wind that tattered and shredded them even as the alien invaders from Earth watched, wide-eyed. Clouds boiled up from far below, only to have their tops sheared off by the furious wind. High above it all, the sky was covered with its eternal cloak of colorful clouds, stretched across the world like a blanket, the colors of its underside strangely muted, pastel.

The hydrogen-helium atmosphere was as transparent as . . . Grant almost giggled as he realized it was as transparent as air. It was thickly dotted with those fat billowing clouds scudding madly along, almost like fluffy cumulus of a tropical sky on Earth.

Far below was nothing but haze. Grant remembered that Jupiter's atmosphere gradually thickened until it became liquid, with no clear demarkation between air and sea. Somewhere down there the inexorable pressure thickened the atmosphere until it liquefied into a world-girdling ocean, its water corrosively acidic, heavily laced with ammonia and exotic compounds.

Not like Earth, Grant said to himself. Not at all like Earth, where the oceans fill basins in the rocky crust and the gravity's too light to squeeze the air into liquid. Not like Mars or Venus or even the Galilean moons, not like any of those balls of rock or ice. This is an alien world, different, totally different from anything we've ever seen before.

Zheng He was shuddering now, bucking in the jet-stream winds. Grant pictured the ship as a tiny sliver of a discus being tossed and tumbled by the ferocious currents of wind streaking across the face of Jupiter's all-encompassing ocean.

"Long-range sensors," Krebs ordered.

The wallscreen view abruptly shifted. Far off on the distant horizon Grant saw a dark, ominous tower of clouds flickering with lightning bolts, climbing like a wrathful giant out of the ocean and rising to the cloud deck high above.

"That's the Great Red Spot," said Karlstad, his voice hollow with awe.

Krebs ordered, "Thrusters on. Minimum cruise power."

The ship had been coasting since they had entered the clouds, using Jupiter's thick atmosphere to slow them from orbital speed, turning velocity into heat as they rode through the thick cloud deck and down into the clear hydrogen-helium atmosphere, gliding across the skies of Jupiter.

"Thrusters on, I said!" Krebs growled.

Grant blinked and activated the thrusters with a thought. For good measure he pressed a fingertip against the touchpad on his console.

This is dangerous, he realized, an awful lot of temptation to put into the hands of mortals. Feeling the surge of power building within his own senses, Grant told himself, I can control the engines with a thought. I can destroy us all with a foolish impulse.

DEFIANCE

Deeper and deeper into the Jovian atmosphere they plunged, farther into the all-encompassing haze that gradually thickened into the global sea.

Still feeling the thrumming power of the ship's generator, the muted thunder of the thrusters, Grant strained his eyes to pierce through the darkening haze that the wallscreen showed. There was nothing to see; not even the infrared sensors detected anything in the fog, yet still Grant stared hard at the screen. Partly he focused his attention there because it helped to keep him from falling completely under the hypnotic spell of the enhanced sensory systems in his implanted biochips. Like his father's advice about impure thoughts, when he'd been a preteen first awakening to the seductions of the body: "Think about something else, son. Don't dwell on the temptation."

Grant stared into the emptiness and tried to ignore the deep, unbidden, relentless urge to power up the thrusters and dive the ship straight down into the ocean that waited for them deep below.

Where are the Jovian life-forms? he asked himself. Where are the medusas and those soarbirds that the probes found? And the algal colonies that float in the clouds? The sky here looks empty, barren.

He realized that none of the others had spoken more than a few words since they'd linked with the ship's systems. It's working on them, too, Grant told himself. They're just as absorbed by this electronic seduction as I am. Just because they've had more experience with it doesn't mean it's any easier for them to handle it.

"I thought we'd see airborne organisms," he said aloud.

Karlstad seemed to twitch, as if suddenly awakened from a trance. "They're out there," he said.

Muzorawa countered, "The sensors haven't detected any."

"Not even on the microscopic scale?"

"Ah, well . . . microorganisms are present everywhere," Muzorawa agreed.

"But what about the big life-forms?" Grant asked.

"They're pretty thinly scattered," Karlstad replied. "They need a lot of territory to support themselves."

"Maybe they're afraid of us," O'Hara suggested in a subdued voice.

"Afraid?"

"After all, we did come crashing down here like a great blazing meteor, didn't we?"

Karlstad hesitated a moment, then conceded, "Yes, there is that."

O'Hara started to add something, but bit the thought off and said instead, "Message from the director coming in, Captain."

The wallscreen view of the unbroken haze was instantly replaced by a grainy, static-streaked image of Dr. Wo. He looked grimly angry.

"The IAA inspection team is making their final burn to rendezvous with the station," he said without preamble. "I have been ordered to recall your mission. You are supposed to return to Station *Gold* immediately."

Everyone on the bridge froze. Grant turned slightly and saw Krebs floating up near the overhead, one thick-fingered hand pressed against the metal paneling to hold herself in place. She was staring at the screen, the stony expression on her face unreadable.

"You are to acknowledge receipt of this message," Wo said, drawing out each word as if to emphasize them.

The silence on the bridge was palpable. Grant felt shocked, bitter disappointment that the mission was being aborted, anger at the IAA for cutting it short. He wanted to go on, to stay linked with the ship, to probe deeper into that alien sea.

O'Hara reached for the keyboard of her console.

"What are you doing?" Krebs snapped.

"The director said we should acknowledge receiving his message."

"*I* will decide when to acknowledge it," said Krebs.

"But—"

Krebs hovered up by the overhead for several more silent moments. Then she pointed toward Grant and commanded, "Increase thrust twenty percent."

Grant reacted automatically, and instantly felt the surge in power, like flexing a well-lubricated muscle. It felt good, strong, right. From beyond where O'Hara stood with a frown of uncertainty on her face, Karlstad glanced toward Grant with a puzzled, troubled look.

The bridge seemed to tilt noticeably. Muzorawa called out, "Flight angle steepening past twenty degrees . . . twenty-five . . ."

"No need to call out the flight angle," Krebs snapped. "We are going into the ocean at maximum rate of descent."

Muzorawa hesitated a heartbeat, then said slowly, "Captain, the director has ordered us to abort the mission."

"I am aware of that," Krebs answered sharply. "I have decided to enter the ocean sooner than planned."

"Shouldn't we answer Dr. Wo?" O'Hara asked.

"How can we?" Krebs said. "We are beyond direct communications contact."

"But we're not—"

"We are beyond direct communications contact," Krebs repeated with iron in her voice. "We never received the abort command, so we cannot acknowledge it."

She's going in! Grant marveled. Despite the IAA's order, she's going ahead with the mission. Zeb looked concerned but kept silent. No use arguing with a decision she's already made, Grant told himself.

Krebs said to O'Hara, "Your communications duties are finished. Maintain an open comm channel for monitoring incoming messages only. We will not respond to any messages from the station."

Lane looked as conflicted as Grant felt: worried about disobeying Dr. Wo, yet eager to go on with the mission.

"You will pilot the ship from now on, O'Hara. Under my direct command, of course."

"Yes, Captain," Lane said, almost in a whisper.

"Maintain dive angle of thirty degrees."

"Yes, Captain," Lane repeated as her hands busily rearranged the controls on her console touchscreens.

Grant looked to Muzorawa; Zeb seemed concerned, worried. Turning to look past O'Hara, Grant saw Karlstad looked positively shocked. Worse, he looked frightened.

But no one said a further word. Grant found that he was glad for Krebs's decision to defy orders. Joyous. It was obvious that Dr. Wo had been forced to send the recall command. But we're here, below the clouds, heading into the ocean. We're going to do what we came here to do, and not Wo or the IAA or the New Morality can stop us. Grant grinned inwardly as he felt the ship's thrusters purring smoothly, propelling them through the thickening Jovian atmosphere, down toward the world ocean.

O'Hara finished resetting her console. "Ready to take the conn, Captain," she reported softly.

Krebs pushed down from her usual spot to stand beside O'Hara, hooking one foot into a floor loop.

Pointing to the small screen in the upper left corner of O'Hara's console, Krebs said, "Keep that one open for incoming communications. There is to be no outgoing message unless I specifically order it. Understood?"

"Understood."

Turning to Muzorawa, she said, "Prepare a data capsule for launch."

"Yes, Captain," Zeb replied.

Krebs leaned past O'Hara and touched the communications screen, then said in a flat, calm voice, "Data capsule number one. We have penetrated the clouds and are descending into the ocean. All systems functioning normally except communications, which are totally blocked by unexpected electrical interference in the Jovian atmosphere. Since we are unable to receive or transmit messages, we will continue on our mission plan and report through data capsules as necessary."

Then she turned to O'Hara and asked, "Did you get that recorded?"

"Recorded," Lane answered.

"The capsule is ready to be launched," Muzorawa announced.

"Good. Launch it."

Nothing happened. Grant suddenly realized it was his job to launch the capsule. Too late. Krebs pulled her foot free of the floor loop and whirled halfway about, staring wildly.

"Archer!" she bellowed. "Archer, where are you?"

Blinking with surprise, Grant said, "I'm right here, Captain."

Krebs advanced on him like a barbarian army. "Why are you just standing there! Launch the capsule! Launch it!"

"Y-yessir," Grant stuttered, desperately trying to remember the launch command sequence. The capsules had to be launched manually, he recalled that much; they were not included in the biochip linkage.

With fumbling hands, he tapped his central touch-screen and called up the launching program. It was simple enough, he saw, but with Krebs hovering over him like a smoldering volcano, it took Grant two tries before he got the commands in the right order.

He felt the capsule's launch like a tingle of excitement shimmering through him. It reminded Grant of the thrill he'd felt the first time he'd skied down an expert slope in the snowy Wasach Mountains. Breathless. Exhilarating.

Until Krebs growled, "Wipe that stupid smile off your face, Archer, and get back to reality."

It took an effort of will, but Grant did it.

Hours passed. The ship still dove toward the sea. Krebs put different camera views from the sensors onto the big wallscreen, but they showed nothing but blank, featureless mist, all gray, colorless. To Grant it looked empty and dead.

Until Muzorawa shouted, "Look at that!"

"What?"

"Let me increase the magnification," Zeb mumbled, his fingers working the console. "There. See?"

"Snow!" Grant said. Soft white flakes were sifting through the haze. It looked beautiful. Something like Earth, like home, on this distant alien world.

"Not snow," Karlstad said. "Organics. They form in the clouds and precipitate out."

"Manna from heaven," said O'Hara.

"Food," Karlstad corrected.

Muzorawa chuckled. "It is only food, my friend, if there are creatures in the sea to eat it. Otherwise it is merely organic snow."

Grant thought of the distant, shadowy shapes that Dr. Wo had shown him from the record of the first mission. Life-forms? As big as whole cities? Dozens of kilometers across? It seemed impossible.

"Karlstad and Archer, rest period," said Krebs. "Disconnect, take a meal, and sleep for four hours."

Grant had to consciously force his hand to switch off the linkage. Suddenly he was no longer connected to the ship, he was alone again inside his own flesh. Feeling naked, vulnerable, he pulled the optical fibers from the chips in his legs and stowed them away, then floated off toward the nutrient dispenser.

Egon was already plugging the dispenser tube into the port in his neck. "The soup line," he said as he turned on the dispenser's pump.

Grant hooked up, too. There was no satisfaction in eating this way. He never seemed to feel hungry, probably because the perfluorocarbon liquid kept his stomach filled. But there was no pleasure in eating, either. No taste, no aroma.

Karlstad broke into his thoughts. Leaning his head so close it almost touched Grant's, he whispered, "Did you notice the way she couldn't find you?"

"What?"

"When you were supposed to launch the data capsule. You were right in front of her, no more than three meters away, and she couldn't see you."

Remembering, Grant said, "Yeah, that was spooky."

"She damned near panicked."

Glancing over his shoulder to make certain Krebs wasn't watching them, Grant whispered, "She has a funny way of looking at me."

"At all of us."

"What do you think it is?"

"Temporary spells of blindness, maybe."

"She's blind?"

"Maybe. In flashes. Her vision blanks out for a moment or two."

"Is that possible?"

Karlstad made a barely discernible shrug. "I don't know. I'll see if I can find anything in the ship's medical library."

"Could the implants be affecting her vision?"

"Could be. What's worse, though, is her defying Old Woeful's abort order."

The dispenser bell clunked. Karlstad yanked the feeding tube from his neck like a man pulling a leech off him.

Grant said, "I'm with her on that. We shouldn't scrap this mission just because some IAA committee says so."

Karlstad's brows rose. "You? The True Believer? Now you're ready to commit heresy?"

"It's got nothing to do with religion!"

"The hell it doesn't. Those IAA inspectors are probably all your New Morality people, or the equivalent."

"No matter what they want, I want to go on with the mission," Grant insisted. "Don't you?"

"Certainly. But what happens when we get back to the station? How do you think those inspectors are going to treat us? Refusal to obey orders is called mutiny, you know."

Grant's jaw dropped open. Mutiny?

The timer bell went off.

"Stop your muttering," Krebs called to them. "Get to sleep, both of you."

Grant disconnected the feeder tube, his mind churning. Mutiny? Are we going to be treated as mutineers when we get back?

STORM TOSSED

Grant slept fitfully, dreaming that some giant hand was shaking him, pummeling him mercilessly. He snapped awake and found that it was no dream. The ship was shuddering, lurching, as if caught in the jaws of some vicious terrier and being shaken to death.

He banged his shoulder as he slid out of the berth, barked his shin when he got to his feet. There shouldn't be this much turbulence so deep in the atmosphere, he told himself. Maybe we're in the ocean now! This could be turbulent currents of liquid water. He wished that he'd been allowed to carry out his fluid dynamic mapping more completely. The truth was that neither he nor anyone else in the solar system had any except the vaguest of ideas of how Jupiter behaved at this depth, where the atmosphere imperceptibly merged into the ocean.

Grant staggered through the hatch that connected to the bridge. He knew that *Zheng He* was constructed of a series of shells, the innermost module being the one that the crew inhabited. Between each oblate shell was a buffering pressurized liquid that helped to cushion the rigid metal walls from the Jovian pressure outside the hull, and also damped down any vibrations caused by turbulence.

If we're banging around this hard here inside the core of the ship, Grant thought as he staggered to his console, we must be caught in the mother of all storms outside.

The Great Red Spot! Lord have mercy, Grant thought, are we tangling the Great Red Spot? He got a vision of the ship being sucked into the maw of the overpowering superstorm, pulled in and crushed like a tiny fragile leaf.

"What are you doing?" Krebs snapped at him as Grant started to connect with the ship.

"Linking up, Captain," he replied.

"Mr. Archer, did I order you to cut your rest period short?"

"No, ma'am, but with the storm—"

"You are supposed to be resting."

"But I thought—"

"Follow orders, Mr. Archer. I am quite capable of handling the ship without your help."

Grant hovered before his console, three optical fibers connected to his implants, the other threads bobbing in the liquid. Muzorawa and O'Hara were at their stations, fully linked. Zeb glanced down at him and smiled gently. Lane was concentrating on her console, fingers playing rapidly, smoothly across the keyboard.

"Return to your berth, Archer," Krebs commanded. "When I need your help I will call you."

Shamefaced, Grant disconnected and swam the few meters to the hatch. The ship lurched violently again and he had to grab the hatch to keep from rolling into Krebs, who was floating in the middle of the bridge. He looked over his shoulder at the captain and saw that she was smiling. Smiling! She was enjoying the turbulence. Fully linked to all the ship's systems, she was riding out this storm with something approaching joy.

He recalled how he had felt when they'd entered the cloud deck, the thrill of power, the sexual excitement of feeling the ship's generator and thrusters overcoming the turbulent winds and storms of Jupiter. How must it feel, Grant wondered, to be connected to the *whole ship* while it's fighting its way through a storm? The surges of thruster power, the flashes of electrical energy, the superhuman views through the sensors. She must feel each tremor of the ship as a shudder of her own body. It must feel like she's being stroked, caressed. He studied her face: eyes half closed, that strange little smile on her doughy face. My God, she looks as if she's engaged in foreplay.

Grant dived through the hatch and slid into his bunk. He squeezed his eyes tight and tried to force the image of Krebs out of his mind. The ship lurched and staggered, tossing him from one side of his narrow berth to the other. Sleep was impossible.

"Grant . . . are you awake?" It was Karlstad's whispering voice.

Sliding feet-first out of the coffin-shaped cubicle, Grant saw that Karlstad was sitting on the end of his bunk, feet hooked on its stumpy metal legs, hunched over a palmcomp he held in one hand. Its screen threw a ghostly greenish light on his face that wavered in the ripples of their liquid milieu.

"Are we near the Red Spot?" Grant asked.

Karlstad looked up at him. "Huh? The Spot? No, nowhere close. We're on the other side of the planet."

"Oh. Good."

The ship lurched heavily, almost throwing Grant off his bunk.

"This is bad enough, don't you think?" Karlstad asked, looking up toward the overhead with wide, frightened eyes. "Don't even *mention* the Spot."

"I just thought . . ."

"She's deliberately pushing us through this storm," Karlstad said grimly.

"Why would she do that?" Grant questioned.

"She's taking us back to our primary entry position," Karlstad said. "She's following the mission plan as blindly as a lemming marching off a cliff."

"Right back into the storm we avoided? That's crazy!"

Karlstad held his palmcomp to his mouth and began speaking commands to it. Grant moved across and sat beside him on the end of his bunk. The ship plunged briefly, then surged upward. Grant's stomach heaved.

"Here, take a look." Karlstad held the computer so Grant could see its glowing screen. His hands were shaking so much that Grant put his own hands over Egon's to steady them.

"Wind speed's dying down, at least. It's just a tad under fifty-five hundred centimeters per second," Karlstad muttered, tapping the screen with his forefinger. "That's less than two hundred kilometers per hour. We're coming out of it."

"I imagine she didn't expect the storm to be whipping up so much turbulence down at this low altitude," Grant muttered.

"I wouldn't bet on that," Karlstad grumbled. Then he said to the computer, "Display exterior pressure gradients."

The screen went blank for a moment.

"You're linked to the ship's computer?" Grant asked.

"What else?"

The screen showed a wildly undulating curve with a huge dip at its center.

"See?" Karlstad pointed at the graph. "It's a small, compact storm. There's the eye. We're skirting through this region, here."

"Why didn't Krebs avoid the storm altogether?" Grant wondered. "We didn't have to go through any part of it."

With a bitter smile, Karlstad answered, "Like I told you, she's following the mission plan. We're supposed to be at this location, so we go to this location, no matter what the conditions outside."

Grant shook his head. "That doesn't make sense."

"It does if you're a pathological anal retentive, the way she is."

"Maybe she just wants to get data on the storm," Grant suggested. "She's a scientist, after all. Nobody's gotten data from inside a Jovian cyclonic system. This is an opportunity."

"The true scooter," Karlstad sneered. "Out to get the data even if it gets us all killed."

"The ship's not in trouble," Grant said. "Not really. We can ride through a storm like this." But in his mind's eye he still saw Krebs's enraptured expression as the ship shuddered through the storm's fury. And remembered his own passion.

Karlstad's expression soured. "I've gone through the ship's medical files."

"Is there anything about her?"

"The personal files are all locked," Karlstad said. "Nothing in the open files much more than first-aid instructions and directions for cryogenic freezing in case of a major accident."

"It was no help, then?"

"I think I can set a broken bone now, but no, there's nothing here that helps us determine what's ailing our squint-eyed captain."

"It's just as well, I suppose," said Grant. "What would we do with the information if we had it?"

Karlstad pursed his lips briefly, then said, "I'm not finished. The next time she takes a nap I'm going to access the station's medical files."

"But she's cut off all communications with the station!"

With a careless shrug, Karlstad said, "All I need is a quick squirt of data. A few picoseconds should be enough. She'll never know."

"But they'll know on the station," Grant said. "They'll know that we're not out of communication contact. They'll know that the message she sent in the data capsule is a bare-faced lie!"

Karlstad actually laughed. "So what? Don't be such a straight-arrow, Grant. Besides, nobody's going to notice a picosecond burst from the ship. No human being will even be involved. They don't have people monitoring the medical files twenty-four hours a day. It's just a medical query from our ship's computer to the station's medical computer, zap! That's all. They'll never even notice it."

"You hope," Grant said.

"Listen to me. Would you rather risk bending the captain's order against communicating with the station or risk riding down into that ocean with a crazy woman running the ship?"

The ship shuddered again. Grant thought he heard a hollow booming noise, like distant thunder.

"You can't say that she's crazy."

"Can't I? You think a sane person would deliberately drive us through a storm like this?"

By the time Grant reported for duty on the bridge, the storm was mostly behind them. The ship still trembled from occasional gusts, but the big heart-stopping plunges and yaws had stopped.

Grant hooked up and linked with the generator and thrusters once more. Remembering what it was like to be connected while driving through the clouds, his cheeks reddened with shame. He glanced at Krebs, floating stern-face behind him. She knows what it's like. She's connected with every system in the ship, not an electron vibrates in this vessel without her knowing it, feeling it. No wonder she doesn't want to disconnect. No wonder she avoids sleep.

Muzorawa and O'Hara unlinked and went to the food dispenser. Grant looked across at Karlstad, weaving slightly as he stood before his console, feet anchored in the floor loops.

"Dr. Karlstad?" Krebs called. Grant felt an eerie tingle along his spine. Egon's right, he thought. It's as if she can't see us.

"Captain?" Egon replied.

Krebs focused her eyes on him. "You will pilot the ship during this watch, in addition to monitoring the life-support systems."

"I'm honored, Captain."

If Krebs caught the sarcasm in Karlstad's voice, she gave no sign of it. "Mr. Archer?"

"Yes, ma'am!"

"You will monitor the sensors, in addition to the power and propulsion systems."

"Yes, Captain."

Grant began adjusting his console, using the touchscreens to tap into the sensor network. The data flowed through his implanted biochips, through his nervous system, and directly into his brain. His heart fluttered beneath his ribs. Once again he could *see* the world outside the ship, hear the sighing wind whistling past, feel its fluttering flow along the ship's metal hull, touch the ocean waves as they undulated past far below, taste the flavor of an alien breeze, rich with salts and compounds no human tongue had ever sampled. Lightning flared off on the horizon; Grant felt it as a tingle along his nerves. He did not need display screens or graphs or dials; Grant was not examining data, he was experiencing it, directly in the sense receptors in his brain, completely enveloped in the richness of this vast, unexplored world.

From deep inside his subconscious a voice spoke out: Be careful. Don't let all this overwhelm you. You've got to maintain control, stay in charge of yourself. Don't get lost in the sensations.

How does Zeb handle all this? Grant wondered. How can he stand at his console hour after hour and not completely immerse himself in this experience? How can he stay rational and calm when he can be a Jovian, breathing their air, seeing through their eyes?

Teach my Thy ways, O Lord, Grant prayed, and I will walk in Your truth.

"She's asleep."

Karlstad's whisper cut through Grant's inner turmoil. He blinked, turned to look at Egon, two consoles away.

It took a few heartbeats for Grant to remember where he was, who he was. With a shudder that was part lost joy, part desperate resolution, he forced the ship's sensations to a back corner of his mind.

"She's sleeping," Karlstad repeated, hiking a thumb past his shoulder.

Grant saw that Krebs's eyes were closed. She was bobbing gently up by the overhead, still linked but apparently sound asleep. What dreams must she have, connected to the complete ship the way she is? Grant asked himself.

"Now's the time," Karlstad whispered, tapping at his console screens.

"Don't do it!" Grant hissed.

Karlstad shot him a pitying look, his fingers still playing on the touchscreens.

LEVIATHAN

Starving, dying, Leviathan drifted in the cold empty abyss high above its usual level in the ocean. It took an effort of will to hold its parts together, to prevent them from spontaneously disintegrating.

We must stay together, Leviathan kept repeating. If we break apart each component of us will die, whether we bud or not. We will become food for the scavengers who wait below in the hot darkness of the depths. Together we might survive. If we can stay together long enough we might find food.

But the ocean was cold and barren at this level. Legends pictured monsters up in this frigid emptiness, slithering beasts that preyed on each other and any of Leviathan's kind foolish enough to drift this high.

Leviathan thought that the legends were mere tales, stories flashed by elders to frighten young ones away from climbing too far from the safe levels of the sea.

It is time for us to return to the warmer region, Leviathan knew. But it could not force its flotation members to contract. They no longer had the strength to expel the gas that filled them. It took energy to make their muscles contract, and starving members had no energy to work with.

Cold. Cold and empty. Leviathan could sense its control of its outer members begin to fade. A unit of armored hide peeled away spontaneously. Instead of the promised joy of budding, Leviathan felt a wave of uncontrollable grief wash through its mind. We are disintegrating. We will all die here, alone, never to bud, never to generate new life.

Unbidden, three of the flagella members broke loose, fluttering mindlessly in the frigid current. Leviathan realized that the end was near. Once the vital organ members dissociated, Leviathan's existence would be finished, without even the knowledge that its parts would generate new buds, create new members that would associate into offspring.

The Symmetry would be disrupted. The eternal cycle of life budding new life would end. It was not meant to be so, Leviathan knew. It had failed to maintain the Symmetry.

A sense organ shuddered, then began to quiver violently, the first step in its dissociation. There was nothing Leviathan could do to prevent it. Not now.

And yet . . .

The sense organ suddenly stopped fluttering and became still. It flashed a picture to Leviathan's brain. A monster. A long, flat, many-armed creature was quietly slithering toward Leviathan, grasping its dissociated members in its wriggling tentacles and pushing them into a circular, snapping mouth ringed with sharp teeth.

For a flash of a second Leviathan thought its sensor-member was hallucinating, hysterical on the edge of starvation and dissociation. But no, other sensors-members flashed the same picture. The creature was huge, almost as large as Leviathan itself, and it was nearly transparent, difficult to see until it was very close. It glided through the sea with hardly a ripple, making it impossible to detect at long range.

It was one of the mindless beasts that the old legends warned of. It was trailing Leviathan, gobbling up its members as they dissociated and drifted helplessly in the cold abyss.

It was heading for Leviathan itself, tentacles weaving, round tooth-ringed mouth snapping open and shut, open and shut.

Leviathan's first instinct was to flee. But in its weakened condition, could it outrun this scavenger? The monster slowed as it approached Leviathan, stretched out two of its longest tentacles and barely touched Leviathan's hide.

Pain! Leviathan had never felt an electric shock before, but the jangling, burning pain of the monster's touch made Leviathan recoil instinctively. The monster pursued leisurely, in no hurry to do battle with Leviathan. It seemed content to wait until more of Leviathan's members dissociated. It was more of a scavenger than a predator, Leviathan thought.

Weak, almost helpless, Leviathan studied the monster. Its main body was a broad flat sheet, undulating like jelly. That gaping mouth was on the underside; its top was studded with domelike projections that must be sensory organs. Dozens of tentacles weaved and snaked all around the central body's periphery. Two of them were much longer than the others, and ended in rounded knobs.

Can all the tentacles cause pain when they touch? Leviathan wondered. Cautiously it backed away from the creature. The monster followed at the same pace, keeping its distance, waiting patiently.

A new thought arose in Leviathan's mind. This monster could be *food.* The old legends pictured these beasts eating one another when they had no other food available. It wants to eat my members. Perhaps we could eat it.

But first, Leviathan knew, it would have to kill the monster. And to do that, it would have to avoid those painful tentacles.

If Leviathan had not been weakened and starving, there would be no contest. Its speed and strength would have made short work of this gossamer creature. Except for those pain-dealing tentacles. We must avoid them.

Leviathan conceived a plan. It was part desperation, part cunning. It called for a sacrifice.

Deliberately, Leviathan willed three more of its flagella members to dissociate. Faithful, mindless, they peeled away from Leviathan's body and began propelling themselves down toward the warmer depths.

The monster immediately dived after them, so fast that Leviathan realized its plan could not possibly work. But there was nothing else to do. It dived after the beast.

The monster's two longer tentacles touched the first of the flagella, instantly paralyzing it. They passed the immobilized member to the shorter tentacles so quickly that their motions seemed a blur to Leviathan. The tentacles, in turn, relayed the inert flagellum to that snapping, hideous mouth.

The two other flagella were instinctively fleeing, diving blindly toward the warmth of the lower levels of the sea. The monster pursued them single-mindedly. Which gave Leviathan its opportunity.

With its last reserves of strength, Leviathan dove after the beast and rammed into it. Waves of concussion rippled through the jellylike body of the monster; its tentacles writhed in pain.

Quickly Leviathan fastened as many of its mouth parts as possible onto that broad, flat body. The monster's longer tentacles snaked back and stung Leviathan again and again, searching blindly for the parts where the armored hide members had dissociated and the more vulnerable inner organs were exposed.

Despite the pain that flared through it, Leviathan tore through the monster's body, its mouth parts crushing the flimsy beast. The monster's tentacles went limp at last and Leviathan fed on its dead body. It tasted awful, but it was food.

Feeling stronger despite the strangely acid sensation simmering through its digestive organs, Leviathan resumed its course around the great storm, heading for the deeper waters where—it hoped—it would find plentiful food and others of its own kind.

Leviathan had a tale to portray to them.

INTO THE SEA

Karlstad nodded as if satisfied, then cast a quick glance over his shoulder. Krebs still appeared to be sleeping, floating in an almost fetal position up by the overhead.

Grant dared not ask the question, but Karlstad grinned at him and made a circle of his thumb and forefinger. He's gotten into the station's medical files, Grant understood. Despite his better judgment, he wondered what Krebs's file said about her.

With a blink of his eyes, Grant returned his attention to the sensors and concentrated his attention on them. The generator and thrusters were performing so close to their design optima that Grant could almost forget about them, relegate them to a corner of his mind, a background hum of power buzzing along his nervous system. The sensors were something else, though: He could see through the murky alien atmosphere as if it were a cloudy, hazy day on Earth

Off in the distance Grant saw a swirling snowstorm, a blizzard of white particles falling thickly into the sea. They're not really white, he reminded himself. You're seeing them in false color. Actually they're dark, sooty with carbon compounds; the manna that makes Dr. Wo think there must be living creatures in the sea feeding off this bountiful abundance of organic particles. Wo's reasoning is more wishful thinking than logic, Grant told himself. Just because there are organic particles raining—or, rather, snowing—into the ocean doesn't mean there have to be creatures in the sea to eat them. That's a classic fallacy.

They were getting closer to the blizzard. Hardly thinking consciously about it, Grant imaged the ship's planned course as a slim bright yellow line against the view of the blizzard. We'll pass by it, miss it by more than four hundred kilometers. He felt glad of that; he had no desire to ride through another storm. Yet, at a deeper level, he felt disappointment.

And curiosity. Why are the particles concentrated so thickly there, and not any of them falling anywhere else in sight? If the organics form in the clouds, why isn't there a steady drizzle of them everywhere? It must be that they form only in special places up in the clouds, the processes that create the organics aren't spread evenly throughout the entire cloud deck. I'll have to ask Egon about that. If there are creatures in the ocean that eat those organics, we're most likely to find them under the storms that produce their food.

The pressure outside was rising steadily as the atmosphere thickened into liquid. Grant could feel long, billowing surges of waves now, ripples and cross currents racing through the ammonia-laced water. Riding through this ocean won't be easy, he realized. There's a tremendous amount of power in these waves.

By the time Lane and Zeb returned to the bridge, Krebs was fully awake and snapping commands. Sonar *pings* were bouncing back to the receivers, reflecting off layers of true liquid now. Grant handed over the sensors to Muzorawa reluctantly. Zeb's going to be connected to them when we actually get into the ocean, he told himself, feeling jealous.

O'Hara started to call out altitude numbers. "Ten thousand meters to the reflecting layer. Sink rate nominal."

"Be quiet!" Krebs said. "I can see the data perfectly well."

She sounded testier than usual to Grant. She's just as clanked up about entering the ocean as I am, Grant thought.

"Thrusters to one-third power," Krebs ordered.

Grant cut back thruster power. He had to look up at the main screen to see outside now. There were waves out there, restless, ceaseless swells, almost close enough to touch. They were reaching for the ship, heaving angrily, surging higher and higher.

Grant wormed his feet deeper into the floor loops and grasped the hand grips on the front of his console. Glancing over his shoulder, he saw that Krebs was holding onto a handgrip set into the overhead with one hand, dangling like a thickset monkey.

Lower they sank, deeper into those long, powerful swells. Grant could hear his pulse thudding in his ears. Muzorawa looked tense, his hands squeezing on the console grips, making the muscles in his fore-arms ripple.

Grant turned toward O'Hara, but Krebs shouted, "Left five degrees!"

Looking up at the wallscreen, Grant saw a raging current surging straight for them, bloodred in the sonar system's false-color imagery, filling the screen.

"Full power on the thrusters!" Krebs snapped.

Impact! The ship slammed into the current as if hitting a mountainside. One of Grant's floor loops tore free and for a moment he lost contact with the thrusters. He stared down at his console, but the ship was shaking so badly the screens were little more than a blur. Then he felt the thrusters again, surging powerfully, singing their mighty song. Grant smiled inwardly as the thrusters drove the ship below the current's powerful stream, down deep beneath its shearing force.

The shaking eased. The shaking dwindled away. They were truly in the ocean now, safely beneath the turbulence, down where the currents flowed swiftly and smoothly—most of the time.

"Thrusters to half power," Krebs said, almost gently.

"We're in the ocean," said Karlstad, as if he couldn't believe it.

"Obvious but true," O'Hara replied.

"Stop the chatter," Krebs growled. "Check all systems."

Grant found that the generator was performing perfectly well, and so were the thrusters. The only damage he could find was the foot restraint that had torn loose.

"The forward infrared camera is not functioning," Muzorawa reported. "It must have been damaged on impact."

"Repair or replace," Krebs said flatly.

Muzorawa nodded. "I'm running a diagnostic now, Captain. If the damage is too severe to be repaired, I'll go to the backup."

O'Hara reported no major problems with the ship's maneuvering systems, although one of the steering vanes had unfolded only partway. The ship had six steering vanes and two backups. Krebs ordered O'Hara to deploy one of the backups and fold the stubborn vane back into the hull.

"Life support?" Krebs asked.

Karlstad said loftily, "All my systems are functioning nominally, Captain. No problems."

Before Krebs could comment on that, Lane said worriedly, "Captain, I can't get the vane back. It's stuck in the half-open position."

Krebs scowled at her. "Fold the vane on the opposite side of the ship to the same angle and freeze it there. Deploy both backups for maneuvering."

O'Hara nodded.

"Anything else?" the captain asked.

None of the crew had any other problems to report.

"Very well," Krebs said. "Take a half-hour break. But no sleeping! I want you awake and alert in case I need you."

They all disconnected and drifted back toward the food dispenser. Karlstad got there first and grabbed one of the feeding tubes. Grant let O'Hara go ahead of him.

"Going to be a gentleman, are you?" she teased.

Grant muttered, "Uh, yes, I guess so."

"Thank you, then," Lane said, taking the other tube.

It still bothered Grant to see her plug the tube into the socket in her neck. He felt a slight ache in his shoulders. Tension, he guessed.

Turning to Muzorawa, bobbing gently beside him, Grant said, "So we're in the ocean." It was idle chatter and he knew it.

"The captain handled the entry very well," Zeb said, his voice low. "When we hit the jet stream on the first mission, half the ship's power went out."

"How could that be?" Grant blurted. "It's all solid state."

"The generator isn't solid state," Muzorawa countered. "One of the deuterium feed lines was knocked loose. We had a devil of a time repairing it."

Grant was suddenly aghast. "The radiation . . ."

Muzorawa smiled gently. "The best thing about fusion generators, my friend, is that the radiation is all contained inside the reaction chamber. The deuterium and helium-three that feed into the chamber are not radioactive."

"Oh," Grant said, stretching his arms as far as he could in the cramped corner by the dispenser.

"Are you hurt?" O'Hara asked.

"No, just a pain across my shoulders. It'll go away."

"I've got a headache," she said, "if that makes you feel any better."

"Me, too," said Karlstad. Turning to Muzorawa: "What about you, Zeb? Any complaints?"

The Sudanese said nothing for a moment. Then: "We will all have aches and pains, and they will grow worse as the mission continues."

"That's comforting." Karlstad huffed.

"I believe part of it comes from being linked. We feel the ship's systems as our own bodily sensations."

Grant nodded.

"And as the systems wear down," Muzorawa went on, "we will feel their pain."

"Yes, I remember," O'Hara said, nodding.

"So we've got more and more pain to look forward to," Karlstad grumbled.

"Yes."

"It's not that bad," said O'Hara. "It can be handled, really."

Muzorawa smiled knowingly. "The ship's machinery may break down, but we will not. Machines have no spirit, no courage, no drive to succeed no matter what the cost."

"Maybe you feel that way," said Karlstad. "I certainly don't."

"Yes you do, Egon," O'Hara contradicted. "You just don't want to admit it. Not even to yourself."

Karlstad looked uncomfortable for a few seconds. Then he turned to Grant. "Which reminds me," he whispered. "After this delicious repast, we should take a peek at the medical report."

Grant couldn't help turning to look at Krebs, floating in the middle of the bridge, linked to the entire ship. He couldn't see her face, but her limbs looked relaxed, as if she were floating in the sun-warmed waters off some tranquil tropical beach.

Muzorawa looked puzzled. Grant explained, "Egon queried the station's medical computer about the captain."

Muzorawa's expression flashed to disapproval, almost anger. "That was not wise, my friend."

Pulling the tube from his neck, Karlstad replied, "Let's see what we've got."

He ducked through the hatch to their sleeping quarters, with Muzorawa close behind him.

"Wait for me," O'Hara hissed.

Grant said, "Finish your meal, Lane. You won't miss anything."

Zeb and Egon were sitting together on the end of Karlstad's berth, hunched over his palmcomp. Grant floated up to the overhead and held himself there with a hand against the metal ceiling.

"You actually hacked into Dr. Krebs's personal medical file?" Muzorawa whispered.

Karlstad nodded. "I'm the life-support specialist on this mission, remember. Rank hath its privileges."

They dared not put the file on the wallscreen of their common area; Krebs could tap into that through the ship's main computer. So Grant squinted at the tiny, green-glowing display of Karlstad's palmcomp, hardly aware that O'Hara floated in and joined him up by the ceiling without saying a word.

"I don't see anything unusual here," Muzorawa muttered.

O'Hara whispered, "This is prying into her personal affairs. It's an invasion of her privacy, Egon."

His head still bent over the palmcomp, Karlstad answered, "She could get us all killed, Lainie. That supersedes her right to privacy, as far as I'm concerned."

"But her medical report is fine," Muzorawa said. "She's fully recovered from her injuries from the first mission. 'Fit for duty.' It says so right there." He pointed to the glowing green screen.

"Wait," Karlstad whispered impatiently. "Here's the psychology material."

"It's normal."

"Boringly normal," Karlstad agreed, sounding disappointed. "It's almost as if—hold it! What's this?"

Grant saw the words buried in a paragraph so filled with jargon it was barely understandable: *as a result of these physical trauma, the subject is afflicted with moderate visual agnosia.*

"Visual agnosia?" Grant asked aloud. "What's that?"

"Keep your voice down!" Karlstad snapped.

"But what is it?" O'Hara echoed.

"I think I know. I'll have to look it up to be certain."

Muzorawa said, "You can't access the ship's references without the risk of the captain finding out what you're doing."

"And you can't query the station's computer again," Grant added.

"Why not?" Karlstad demanded.

"Because you'll get caught!"

Karlstad shut down his palmcomp. Grant pushed down from the overhead and settled on the deck, followed by O'Hara.

"Listen to me," Karlstad whispered urgently. "We may have a crazy woman running this ship. We ought to know what this condition of hers is all about. We have that right!"

Muzorawa said, "It doesn't matter. Now that we are in the ocean we are truly out of contact with the station."

"Unless we trail out the antenna," said O'Hara. "It's five kilometers long. At our present cruising depth we could use it to contact the station."

"Krebs would find out," Grant warned.

"Not if we do it when she's asleep," countered Karlstad.

"If she goes to sleep before we start descending deeper," O'Hara said.

"Lane, do you agree with Egon?" Muzorawa asked.

She frowned, trying to put her emotions into words. "I'm not certain. She does behave peculiarly, don't you think?"

Grant wanted to argue against it, but instead he asked Muzorawa, "Zeb, what do you think? Should we take the chance and query the station's medical computer again?"

For a long moment Muzorawa remained silent, obviously weighing the pros and cons of the matter. At last he said gravely, "Yes, I'm afraid we must take the risk. The psychologists may have reported her fit for duty, but the stresses of the mission might aggravate her condition—whatever it is."

"We have a right to know," Karlstad repeated.

"Yes," Muzorawa agreed. "Probably it's nothing and we are being foolish. But we should know, even if for no other reason than our own peace of mind."

Grant suddenly got a different idea. "We could ask her," he blurted.

"What?"

"Ask her about her condition," Grant said.

Karlstad groaned at the thought. Muzorawa shook his head. O'Hara said, "I don't think that would be the thing to do, not at all."

COMMUNICATIONS

Back on duty, Grant kept one eye on O'Hara's navigation plot. *Zheng He* was cruising fifteen hundred meters beneath the point where the atmospheric density equaled the density of water on Earth's surface. The communications antenna was more than three times longer. As long as Krebs didn't order them to go deeper, they could unspool the fiber-optic cable and contact the station.

When Krebs slept. She showed no indication of doing so. They cruised through the ocean, checking all the ship's systems, Muzorawa standing glassy-eyed at his console while the sensors poured an unending stream of data into the computers—and sights, sounds, all sorts of sensory impressions directly into his nervous system.

The power and propulsion systems were working so smoothly that Grant almost felt bored, standing at his console. His legs ached now, and a vague, dull pain nagged at him, behind his eyes, barely on the threshold of consciousness, just enough to be bothersome. He tapped into Zeb's sensor data, intending to peek at the incoming data for only a few moments.

Instantly he was awed by the flow of sensations that enveloped him. He could see through the water clearly, see the swirl of manna trickling from above, and—far in the distance—thicker streams of the organic particles sifting downward into the darker depths. The water flowed past him smoothly, as if he were gliding through the ocean like a fish. And the ocean was warm; Grant felt a steady glow of heat rising from the bottomless depths.

There were no creatures in this sea, he realized. No fish, no fronds of plants. We've got to go deeper for that. Dr. Wo said they detected the moving objects more than ten kilometers below the surface, and even then they were so far away—

"She's asleep."

Grant snapped his attention back to the bridge. He had to blink several times, get his perspective adjusted. I'm in this ship, he told himself, consciously disconnecting from the sensors' data stream.

Turning, Grant saw that Krebs had actually left the bridge. The optic fibers that linked her to the ship's systems were tucked back in their storage locker in the overhead.

"She finally left the bridge," Karlstad said softly, furtively, "after almost fifty hours straight on duty."

"She took a couple of naps," O'Hara said.

"Run out the antenna," Karlstad told her. "Quick, while we've got the chance."

Muzorawa said, "Grant, it might be wise if you go to the hatch and keep an eye on her. Warn us if she gets out of her bunk."

"I'll have to disconnect," Grant complained.

"I'll monitor your systems," Muzorawa said.

With even more reluctance than usual, Grant disconnected while O'Hara spooled out the antenna and powered up the microwave transceiver.

"Oooh, there's a great lot of incoming messages waiting for us," she said. Then, her expression turning puzzled: "No, wait. It's only one message, but they've been repeating it over and over again."

"Never mind the incoming crap," Karlstad snapped. "Link me to the medical computer."

Grant hovered by the hatch, one eye on Krebs's berth, the other on the wallscreen that began showing blocks of medical jargon. Krebs's bunk was shuttered off by its privacy screen. The captain was resting, alone, disconnected from the ship for the first time since they'd left the station.

He wondered about Krebs, what drove her. Nearly killed in the first deep mission, here she was back in the Jovian ocean, staying linked to the ship far longer than she had to, longer than she ought to. Is she surrendering to the emotional power of the linkage? Grant asked himself. But if she did, how could she disconnect herself voluntarily after so many hours of being linked? She must be tough, he thought; a lot stronger than I am.

"So that's it!"

Karlstad's exclamation made Grant turn to the bridge. The three of them were still at their consoles, and the wallscreen was covered with medical terms.

"Visual agnosia," said Karlstad, "means she doesn't recognize things visually. Her visual sense is impaired."

"You mean she can't recognize faces?" O'Hara asked.

Nodding vigorously, Karlstad said, "That's why she looks so funny at you. She can't tell who she's looking at until you say something to her. Then she recognizes your voice."

"That's strange," Muzorawa said.

Scrolling through the medical dictionary display, Karlstad said, "It's rare, but there's a considerable history on it."

"What causes it?"

"Often it's physical trauma to the brain, the visual cortex. A cerebral hemorrhage, for instance."

"A stroke?"

"Or a physical blow to the head," Karlstad added.

"But she's had neither," Muzorawa pointed out.

Karlstad said, "True, but she was badly injured in the first mission."

"No head injuries, if I recall rightly," said O'Hara.

"Yeah, that's right." Karlstad sounded disappointed.

Grant spoke up. "What about living in this high-pressure environment? Could that cause injury to the brain?"

"The earliest experiments did cause some nerve damage," Karlstad said. "That's why we raise the pressure slowly, give the body time to adjust."

"Do you think that's what's happened to Dr. Krebs?" O'Hara asked.

"Obviously," said Karlstad.

"Then what do we do about it, do you think?" she wondered aloud.

"Nothing," Muzorawa said,

"Nothing at all?"

"Krebs has adjusted to her problem. It hasn't interfered with her work, has it?"

"No," O'Hara said slowly, "I suppose it hasn't."

"Not yet," Karlstad said.

"The medical board approved her for this mission," Muzorawa pointed out. "The psychologists did not object."

Karlstad looked unconvinced. "She's a walking time bomb," he muttered.

"I disagree," Muzorawa said.

"She could get us all killed."

Muzorawa's expression was utterly serious. "Egon—all of you—I think our best course of action is to watch Dr. Krebs carefully. If she shows signs of disability, if she begins to behave erratically, then we will have to decide what should be done. At present, she's performing quite normally."

"Staying linked to the ship for nearly fifty hours is normal?" Karlstad challenged.

"Did she perform her duties well?" Muzorawa shot back. "Have we accomplished our mission goals so far?"

The two men were glaring at each other, Grant saw: Karlstad with his usual haughty, almost sneering expression; Muzorawa stolid and determined.

O'Hara broke the deadlock. "I'd better take a peek at this message the station's been beaming to us all this time."

Muzorawa said, "Good idea." Karlstad nodded.

The medical dictionary's text vanished from the wallscreen. In its place the blue-and-white symbol of the International Astronautical Authority appeared, quickly replaced by the scowling face of a man in a gray tunic, sitting at what appeared to be a workstation aboard a spacecraft.

Grant twitched with surprise. He knew that face. It was Ellis Beech, the New Morality official who had recruited him to spy on Dr. Wo.

Beech's dark eyes were steady and calm, his long narrow face looked composed, almost indifferent. Yet to Grant there seemed to be something seething beneath that impassive cool exterior, something unrelenting, implacable.

"Dr. Krebs, I am the chairman of the IAA inspection team approaching the station. You have previously been ordered by Dr. Wo to abort your mission and return to Station *Gold*. He gave that order at my insistence. Now I personally order you to return to the station. In the name of the IAA, I order you to abort your mission and return at once! We know that the message you sent with the data capsule is a deliberate falsehood. You are still able to maintain communications contact with the station. Return at once or you will be stripped of your position at Station *Gold* and your professorship in Heidelberg will be forfeited. Abort your mission and return immediately!"

Grant stared at Beech's icy image on the wallscreen. How could he be chairman of the IAA team? he wondered, his mind spinning. The New Morality must have taken control of the inspection team. Maybe they've taken over the entire IAA!

Karlstad also stared at the wallscreen, mouth hanging open in shock.

"They found out about your tapping the medical computer," Muzorawa said softly. It wasn't an accusation, merely a statement of lamentable fact.

"That they did," O'Hara agreed sadly.

Karlstad closed his mouth, shrugged, then said, "Okay, so they found out. What do we do about it?"

"I don't know," said Muzorawa. "This is an awful situation."

"For Krebs," Karlstad said.

"For all of us," Muzorawa corrected.

"Maybe not," Karlstad said. "She's in command, after all. We're just following her orders. She's the one who told us not to acknowledge Wo's order to return to the station."

"Dr. Wo gave that order under duress," Grant said heatedly. "It's obvious they were forcing him to make that call."

"That still doesn't help us to decide what we should do about this," O'Hara said. "Should we—" She stopped, her eyes going wide.

From behind him, Grant heard Krebs's harsh voice. "So you've put me into the meatgrinder, eh?"

Grant whirled around. How long had she been standing there at the hatch? How much had she heard?

"Let me assure you, all of you," Krebs snarled, "that if I go down, the four of you go down with me."

DETERMINATION

We are here to explore the ocean," Krebs said firmly. "We are not turning back because some bureaucrat in the IAA has allowed the politicians to overrule his own sense of responsibility."

"But, Captain—" Karlstad began.

"Silence! Men and women have died in this effort. Do you think that I'm going to spit on their graves by turning back? Not before we've done our damnedest to find out if there's life down here."

"Yes, Captain," Karlstad said, as if he'd never considered any other course of action.

"I agree completely," said Muzorawa.

"It doesn't matter whether you agree or not," Krebs spat. "We are going deeper. Now." She leveled a finger at O'Hara. "And no communication with the station! Nothing! For no reason. Even if we are dying in this coffin we make no attempt to contact the station *unless I tell you to*. Is that clear?"

"Perfectly clear," Lane answered.

"Good. Now take your stations. We are going down to ten kilometers."

Wordlessly the four of them began to link up to the ship's systems. Krebs did also. Grant felt almost relieved. At least she knows it all now. We're not sneaking around her back anymore. The visual amnesia or whatever her condition is doesn't affect her ability to run this ship.

"Ready for linkage," he reported. Before the others, he noticed.

"Very good, Mr. Archer. You may link."

As Grant reached for the console switch that would unite him again with the power and propulsion systems, he realized that Krebs couldn't possibly be a Zealot terrorist. She doesn't want to destroy this mission, she wants to carry it through, no matter what the consequences afterward.

He felt better about her. And about the mission. He tried not to think about what would happen to them after the mission, when they returned to the station and the waiting Ellis Beech.

Once the others were linked, Krebs gave the order to dive to ten kilometers. After several hours, the headache behind his eyes was throbbing through Grant's skull. The pressure's building up, he realized. As we dive deeper the pressure outside the hull goes higher, which means the pressure here on the bridge goes up to compensate.

How deep can we go? he asked himself. He knew the submersible's specifications, but those were merely numbers. How much pressure can we stand? Zeb was wrong: This vessel can take a lot more pressure than we can. We'll crack long before the hull does.

He glanced at Karlstad, tending the life-support console. Egon looked tense, his lips a thin tight line, his face even paler than usual. If we weren't immersed in this fluid he'd be sweating, Grant thought. Egon can *feel* the pressure squeezing on the hull; it must seem like a giant vise trying to crush his body.

"Ten kilometers," Lane sang out.

"Maintain descent angle," said Krebs. "We're going deeper."

Grant heard a groan. It didn't come from anyone on the bridge. It was a metallic, grinding complaint.

"Pay no attention to that noise," Krebs told them. "It's not important."

As if in obedience to her, the grinding noise stopped.

"Support cylinder nine needs lubrication," Krebs said, trying to reassure them. "Nothing to worry about."

The nested shells that comprised the *Zheng He* were connected by buttressing cylinders that contained hydraulic pistons within them. They compressed slightly as the pressure outside the hull squeezed on the ship. Grant began to wonder how well the cylinders would support the shells if one of them was already showing signs of strain.

Maybe I'm the one who's wrong, he realized. Maybe the ship will fail before our pain becomes unbearable.

After a tense four hours of steady descent, Krebs told Muzorawa and Karlstad to take a rest period.

"One hour, then report back here to relieve O'Hara and Grant," she commanded.

Grant took over Karlstad's life-support systems. True to his expectations, he could feel the pressure inside each level of the ship building, mounting, pressing in on him, slowly crushing him to death like a giant boa constrictor wrapping its coils around him. It was getting difficult to breathe; it took a conscious effort to lift his chest to inhale.

Stop it! he chided himself. It's 90 percent imagination. Ninety-nine percent! Look at the pressure graph; it's only gone up a couple of percentage points since we entered the ocean. You're letting your emotions overpower your brain.

Still he felt as if he were being smothered. His headache pounded. He glanced at O'Hara. She seemed normal enough, intently piloting the ship deeper into the sea, watching with glowing eyes the sensors that Zeb normally monitored. Grant fought an urge to tap into the sensor net and see what she was looking at. No, he told himself, you've got enough to do. Don't allow yourself to be distracted.

Then he wondered what the increasing pressure was doing to Krebs. Her condition was due to pressure-induced trauma to her brain. It would be worse as they descended deeper. Did she feel pain? Confusion? He shot a glance over his shoulder at her. Krebs seemed perfectly normal, floating in her usual spot up by the overhead, scowling at him.

"She's following the currents of organic particles," O'Hara said to Grant once they were back to the sleeping area.

"You can see them that clearly?"

With a smile Lane said, "In the sonar they show up like a whirlwind, except that they appear white as snow."

Gesturing to the wallscreen of their common area, Grant asked, "Can you show me?"

O'Hara nodded and spoke into the screen's microphone. "Display sonar imagery."

The screen brightened to life, showing a stream of bright white swirling through the dark ocean. It's just as Lane described it, Grant thought: a whirlwind of snow. He knew the white color of the imagery was an artifact created by the computer program. It made the organic particles easier to discern against the ocean background, easier to track. Lord, Grant thought, if I'd known about this I could've used the particles to map out the ocean currents.

With sudden enthusiasm, he stepped to the microphone and said, "Correlate sonar returns with mapping imagery."

"Please provide more specific input," the computer's synthesized voice replied.

Grant ducked into his cubicle and stretched the length of his bunk to pull his palmcomp from its resting place on the shelf above his pillow.

"I'll be at this awhile," he said to O'Hara as he sat on the end of his bunk.

She shrugged and crawled into her own cubicle.

After a few minutes, Krebs appeared at the hatch, trailing her optical fibers from her legs. "You are supposed to be resting, Mr. Archer, not writing your thesis."

"This isn't my thesis, ma'am," he said, totally missing her irony. "I'm setting up my fluid dynamics program to use the particle streams as tracers—you know, the way aerodynamicists use smoke particles in their wind tunnel tests."

"You need your rest."

"Yes'm. In a few minutes, please."

Krebs watched him in silence for several seconds, then turned and floated back into the bridge. Grant was still working on the palmcomp when Muzorawa and Karlstad came in for their rest period.

"She wants you on duty," Muzorawa said.

"In a minute," Grant said. "I'm almost finished here."

"Can I help?" Zeb asked, settling on the end of the bunk beside Grant.

"It would take longer to bring you up to speed than it will for me to finish this."

Muzorawa laughed softly. "The cruel honesty of youth."

Grant didn't reply. He barely heard the older man. He hardly noticed when Muzorawa got up and went back to the bridge.

When at last he was finished and the program was running properly, Grant pushed himself up from the bunk and swam through the hatch. Muzorawa was at his console, fully linked up, with O'Hara beside him.

"Are you finished, Mr. Archer?" Krebs asked, dripping acid.

"Yes, ma'am. The program's working fine now. Thank you for being so patient."

"Thank Dr. Muzorawa; he is doing your work instead of enjoying his rest period."

Grant fumbled with his optical fibers in his hurry to get linked. Zeb shot him an understanding smile.

"You have thoroughly messed up the work schedule, Archer,"

growled Krebs. "I hope your inspiration improves the fluid dynamics program enough to compensate."

Grant nodded, thinking, It does. It certainly does. But he knew enough to keep his mouth shut.

They passed seventy kilometers' depth, following the spiraling flow of the organic particles, still diving deeper. Karlstad complained of a constant headache, O'Hara said she was starting to feel nagging pains in her arms and back, even Muzorawa said he was having some difficulty breathing. Grant's own headache was still there, not much worse than earlier but certainly no better. Krebs said nothing, neither complaining about her own condition nor making the slightest comment on their gripes. She seemed utterly disdainful of their frailties; whenever she barked a command at him, Grant thought she was looking through him, not at him.

The ship creaked and groaned constantly now, making Grant wonder how deep they could safely go. He recalled that the ship's design limit was ninety kilometers.

Ninety? Grant marveled. We've all got physical problems now, at seventy; how will we be when we're twenty klicks deeper?

Still Krebs kept the ship descending.

"Do you realize where we're heading?" O'Hara asked Grant during one of their reliefs.

He felt bone-tired; his throbbing headache was sapping his energy. Lane looked weary, too. She floated a few centimeters from the deck of their common area, arms half bent before her.

"What do you mean?" he asked. What he really wanted was to crawl back into his berth and sleep for the four hours that were due him.

"The Spot," Lane said.

That made Grant's eyes snap wide. "The Great Red Spot?" His voice squeaked, even in the tone-deepening perfluorocarbon.

She nodded as she hooked a heel against the end of her bunk and forced herself down to a sitting position.

"We can't be going into the Great Red Spot," Grant said.

"That's where the currents lead," O'Hara said, "and we're following the currents."

"But she'll turn off sooner or later."

"She's convinced that if there are creatures that eat those organics, they must follow the thickest streams of them. So we're following the thickest stream and it flows into the Spot."

"But she'll veer off," Grant repeated. "Before we get too close."

O'Hara closed her eyes. "I suppose so. At the moment I don't really care. All I want is a good sleep—and to wake up without this backache."

Grant slid into his berth and fastened the mesh webbing that kept him from floating off the mattress while he was sleeping. It was like nestling into a cocoon, one of the few comforts on this mission. He fell asleep almost instantly.

And dreamed of being dragged into a never-ending whirlpool, crushed and drowned, his screams unheard, his pain unending.

TENACITY

"Approaching ninety kilometers," said O'Hara, her voice edgy, tinged with strain.

Maximum design depth, Grant knew. He and Lane were on duty, Karlstad and Muzorawa in their berths. O'Hara looked tense, tired. She's in pain, just like me, Grant thought. Like all of us. We're all suffering. The pressure's getting to us, physically and mentally.

"Level off at ninety," said Krebs, "and maintain course."

Continue following the stream of organics, Grant interpreted the order. Continue heading toward the Great Red Spot. At least we won't go any deeper, he thought. We can't. The ship can't take it; neither can we.

There was still no sign of any Jovian creatures, great or small. The organic particles swirled and flowed through the great surging ocean, but there was no sign of creatures that fed on them. They had even driven all the way across the turbulent stream, the ship bucking and heaving as their instruments sucked in some of the particles for analysis.

"Jovian carbohydrates," Karlstad announced, after testing the samples. "Good enough to eat—almost."

But if the first mission had actually detected giant beasts deep down in the ocean, they certainly had not shown up here. Dr. Wo's hypothesis that where there was food there must be eaters was proving to be nothing more than wishful thinking. Grant said to himself, Propter hoc ergo post hoc is just as fallacious as the other way around.

Although the fusion generator was performing well, as reliable as a tiny little star, the thrusters were showing signs of wear. Grant felt the erosion of their metal chambers as fatigue, a painful weariness in his bones atop the real pain and weariness of his true body. There was nothing he could do about it. All the diagnostics showed the metal was well within tolerable limits, it just felt so *tiring* to be linked with it, like being chained to an oar in an ancient galley. Grant thought about disconnecting from the thrusters and relying on the ordinary display screens of his console, but he hadn't worked up the nerve to ask Krebs for permission to do so.

He was also monitoring the sensors on this shift, striving consciously to avoid being hypnotized by the constant swirling stream of the organics flowing through the ocean. It was fascinating, soothing, lulling him into forgetting about the thrusters and the headache that throbbed behind his eyes and—

What was that?

A flashing glint of something. At first Grant thought he had imagined it, but then he saw it again through the sensors' multispectral cameras. Something glittering in the stream of organic particles, smaller than the organics, reflecting the light from the ship's forward spotlights.

Without saying a word, Grant opened the ports for the samplers to suck in some of the particles. Most of them were the organics that they'd been following all this time, but these new things . . . he wondered what they could be.

The samplers scooped in a batch of particles and automatically fed them to the gas chromatograph/mass spectrometer for analysis. The data flashed into his mind almost instantly. He saw graphs, diagrams, photomicrographs.

Carbon. Nothing but plain old carbon. Crystallized by the pressure, he saw. Then it hit him.

"Diamonds!" he blurted aloud.

O'Hara, standing beside him, turned toward him. "What did you say?"

"Those smaller particles . . . they're tiny diamonds!"

"No!"

"Yes, really," Grant said. "Tap into the analysis. They're pure crystallized carbon. Diamonds."

"Glory be," said O'Hara.

Krebs, monitoring the analysis equipment along with everything else, said, "Congratulations, Mr. Archer, you have discovered a diamond mine."

"We can bring some back with us," Grant said, grinning for the first time in days.

"Ah, but they're too small for jewelry," said O'Hara sadly. "Microscopic, don't you see."

Krebs grunted behind them. "Considering the cost of this mission, they will be the most expensive diamonds ever found."

That dampened Grant's mood almost completely. He returned to monitoring the sensors. Still, he thought, rivers of diamonds flowing in the Jovian ocean. A snowfall of diamonds. I wonder if the Jovians appreciate what God's giving them?

For nearly thirty-six hours they cruised at the ninety-kilometer level, the ship groaning and creaking, the crew in greater and greater discomfort. Karlstad grumbled constantly; even Muzorawa was clearly having a difficult time of it, despite his stoic refusal to complain. No sign of Jovians, nothing seemed to be moving in the ocean except the streams of particles constantly flowing past.

All that time Krebs remained on the bridge, fully linked to every one of the ship's systems. Grant and the others took their rest periods, tried to get a couple of hours of sleep, injected analgesics into their neck ports to ease the constant pain and pressure. Yet Krebs remained awake and on duty.

"Captain," said Karlstad at last, "as life-support specialist and the closest thing we have to a medical doctor, I must remind you that you've been on duty without relief for more than two days straight now."

"Thank you, Dr. Karlstad," Krebs replied, her voice heavy with irony. "You have reminded me. Now take your station and do *your* duty."

"It's my duty to remind you that you must rest," Karlstad said, looking worried.

"I am not ready for a rest period," Krebs said firmly. "I do not need it."

Grant and O'Hara were still linked to their consoles, ready to come off duty. Muzorawa was hovering by the hatch that led back to the berths.

Swimming over to the life support console, Karlstad pointed at one of its display screens. "Captain, it's not me. It's the mission regulations. The medical monitors show a dangerous level of fatigue poisons in your blood. Your reflexes have slowed. Your pulse and respiration rates are approaching the redline."

Krebs said nothing. She merely floated in the middle of the cramped bridge, glowering at Karlstad.

Muzorawa said reasonably, "Captain, if you don't rest, your performance will deteriorate even more. The mission regulations *require* you to relinquish command when your physical parameters—"

"I know the regulations!" Krebs snapped.

"You must rest, Captain," Muzorawa said, even more gently. "Even if it's only for an hour."

Grant thought, She doesn't want to disconnect from the ship. She's hooked on being connected, like an addict.

To Grant's surprise, though, Krebs's baleful frown dissolved into a dejected mask of defeat. "Very well, if you insist."

"It's for the better, Captain," said Muzorawa.

"Yes, I understand." Krebs began disconnecting, slowly, begrudging every move, as far as Grant could see.

The bridge fell absolutely silent as she disconnected.

When at last she was free of the fiber-optic lines, she said sourly, "Very well. Dr. Muzorawa, I place you in charge. Dr. Karlstad, wake me in one hour."

"In one hour," said Karlstad. "Right."

She pushed off the overhead with one hand and swam toward the hatch. Muzorawa was still hovering there, looking surprised as Krebs headed straight for him.

She banged into Muzorawa and bounced off, with a gasp of surprise, her eyes going wide.

"Pardon me, Captain," Muzorawa said, also looking shocked.

"I-I didn't notice you there," Krebs stuttered. She reached gropingly for the edge of the hatch, gripped it in one chunky hand, pulled herself through and slid the hatch shut behind her with a bang.

For a long moment no one on the bridge said a word.

Then Karlstad whispered, "Jesus Christ, she's blind!"

"No," said O'Hara. "That can't be."

"You saw her," Karlstad insisted. "She ran smack into Zeb. She didn't see him! She said so herself."

"That's why she wants to remain linked with the ship," Muzorawa said slowly. "She can see through the ship's systems."

Karlstad nodded grimly. "But when she disconnects she's blind as a bat."

CONFUSION

"Well, what are we going to do about it?" O'Hara asked.

"We can't have a blind woman running the mission," said Karlstad.

Muzorawa, connecting the optical fibers from his console, pointed out, "But she's not blind when she's connected."

Karlstad began to link up, too. "Whatever damage was done to her visual cortex, it's gotten worse."

"'Tis the pressure we're under," said O'Hara.

"Right. It's damaging her brain even more," Karlstad agreed.

"It only seems to affect her visual cortex," Muzorawa said.

"So far," said Karlstad. "How long will it be before other parts of her brain start to cave in?"

His eyes riveted on the closed hatch, Grant heard himself say, "She's sailing us toward the Red Spot."

"She'll turn off long before we're in any danger," Muzorawa said.

"Will she?" Karlstad asked.

"Of course she will."

"I think she's going crazy," Karlstad said. "She was always a tyrant Now she's getting fanatical, ignoring a direct order from the IAA."

"We all agreed that we want to continue the mission," Muzorawa said.

"Did we?" Karlstad shot back. "Nobody asked me."

"Are you afraid, 'Gon?" O'Hara challenged him.

"Afraid? Me? Ninety kilometers down with a crazy blind woman in command who's telling the IAA to stick it in their lower intestine? What's there to be afraid of?"

Muzorawa finished connecting his optical fiber links. "I think a certain amount of fear is a healthy sign. But we mustn't let it overwhelm us. We must not panic or take rash actions."

"What do you mean by rash?" O'Hara asked.

"Relieving Krebs of command," Karlstad replied instantly.

"We can't do that," Grant said.

"Not even if she's going to get us all killed?"

"There is no evidence of that," said Muzorawa. Then he added, "As yet."

O'Hara looked toward the closed hatch. "She must be in terrible pain."

"She doesn't act it," said Karlstad.

"Not physical pain, perhaps, but . . . imagine being blind. Unable to see."

"Unless she's connected to the ship."

"Yes," said O'Hara, in a whisper. "There is that."

"So what are we going to do?" Karlstad demanded.

No one had an answer.

Krebs returned to the bridge exactly one hour after she left, without the need for Karlstad to rouse her.

Watching her link up, it now seemed obvious to Grant that she couldn't see. She fingered each of the optical fibers, her eyes unfocused, and ran its end across the electrodes in her legs until its minuscule electrical field clicked into place with the proper implant. She can't see the color codes on the fibers, Grant realized. She can't see anything at all.

Until she was completely wired and activated her linkage. Then she straightened up and took command.

"Mr. Grant, what are you gawking at?" she demanded.

Grant snapped his head around and stared at his console. "Nothing, Captain."

"You tend to your duties, Mr. Grant, and I will tend to mine."

"Yes'm."

"Dr. Krebs," said Muzorawa. "We must discuss your condition."

"There is nothing to discuss."

"I'm afraid there is."

"I am fully capable of executing my responsibilities," Krebs said. Grant thought he heard the slightest of tremors in her voice.

"Dr. Krebs, the trauma to your visual cortex is worsening."

Krebs glared at him but said nothing.

"It is possible that it will continue to worsen," Muzorawa went on calmly, reasonably. "It could lead to a cerebral hemorrhage."

"I know that," said Krebs, her voice several notches lower than usual. "I accept that risk."

"We should abort the mission and return to the station," Muzorawa said. Grant marveled at how impersonally he managed to put it. No blame. No shame.

Krebs hovered in the middle of the bridge, breathing hard enough for Grant to see her chest rising and falling. The ship was running smoothly enough; he still felt the steady thrum of the generator and the energy of the thrusters, but that was all background now, like the constant aching pressure behind his eyes, like the growing dull pain in his back, pushed to one side as he focused consciously on the interplay between Muzorawa and Krebs.

At last she said, "If we return to the station with nothing to show for our efforts, they will never permit another mission. They have already ordered us to abandon our work. I will not do that. Not under any circumstances. Is that clear?"

"But your health is in danger. Your life—"

"What good is my life if I can't pursue the search to which I've devoted it?" Krebs's voice rose powerfully. "What use would my life be if I am not permitted to do the work which I love? I have already sacrificed everything else in my life—family, friends, even lovers—to be *here,* in this damned ocean, seeking the answer to the greatest question of them all: Is there intelligent life here? Will we find a companion species, another life-form with which we can converse? Will the human race's loneliness end here, in the hot sea of Jupiter?"

None of the crew could say a word. They all stared at her.

Krebs broke into a bitter smile. "I see the disbelief on your face, Dr. Karlstad. You find it difficult to believe that I had lovers?"

"Uh, n-no, not at all," Karlstad stammered.

"We go on," Krebs said. "I don't care if I die here. Better here than in some dusty classroom where I wouldn't even be allowed to teach about extraterrestrial life."

Muzorawa replied meekly, "Yes, Captain."

Krebs nodded as if satisfied, then turned her baleful look toward O'Hara. "Dr. O'Hara, dive angle of five degrees. Now."

Lane glanced at the others, then asked, "We're going deeper?"

"Deeper," said Krebs.

Grant's head throbbed with pain. Each beat of his pulse was like a hammer banging inside his sinuses. His back hurt as if it were slowly petrifying. They had passed the hundred-kilometer depth and were still pushing deeper, in a shallow dive that ran parallel to a bright swirling stream of organic particles.

Somewhere out in that dark sea waited the Great Red Spot, Grant knew. He could not see it, not even when tapping into the ship's long-range sensors. But it was there, that enormous vortex, that eternal storm that was bigger than the entire Earth, sucking currents into its voracious maw. It was waiting for them, drawing them to it like a magnet pulls on a tiny filing of iron.

They were riding one of those inflowing currents now, buffeting noticeably whenever they drifted toward its turbulent outer edge. As long as they remained well within the current, though, the ship rode easily, smoothly. Grant was able to cut down on the thrusters' power. The Red Spot was doing their work for them, but Grant feared that the work would lead to their destruction.

On a rest break with Muzorawa, Grant pleaded, "Zeb, you can't let her drag us into the Red Spot."

"She'll turn off long before we get into danger," Muzorawa said. But his red-rimmed eyes would not maintain contact with Grant's.

Pulling himself down wearily to sit on the end of his bunk, Grant pointed out, "The current's getting stronger. I don't know how far we can go before it'll be too strong for the thrusters to break us free."

Muzorawa considered that for a long, silent moment, then looked directly at Grant. "What does your fluid dynamics program tell you?"

"I'd have to make a calculation . . ."

"Do that," Muzorawa said wearily. "Then show it to me. It might be the point that forces a decision."

"A decision?"

"About her," said Muzorawa, gesturing toward the bridge.

Still they descended. A hundred kilometers, a hundred ten, a hundred fifteen. The ship creaked and groaned, metal screeching with strain. She sounds as if she's in agony, Grant thought. Just like the rest of us.

O'Hara came back onto the bridge after a rest period with a smile on her lips. It surprised Grant; he hadn't seen any of them smile in days.

"You must have had a good dream," he said as she hooked up.

"No dream," O'Hara replied. "I didn't sleep at all."

Grant closed his eyes. The headache seemed to abate a little when his eyes were closed, and he saw the glowing star at the heart of the fusion generator, felt its warmth, thrilled at the harmonies of electricity coursing through the ship's wiring.

"Look at this." O'Hara nudged him. "I took them from the sampling system."

She held a dozen or so tiny pebbles in the palm of her hand. No, not pebbles, Grant thought. They were so minute they looked almost like dust motes, except that they were a glassy light gray rather than sooty black.

"Your diamonds," O'Hara said, her voice lilting with delight.

"Is that what they are?"

"They're truly diamonds, they are. Not gemstone quality, I'm afraid, and very small. But how many women can say they've held a fistful of diamonds in the palm of their hand?"

"Hey, let me see," Karlstad said, from his console.

Krebs's sour voice broke in, "You are supposed to be on duty, Dr. O'Hara."

"I was showing Mr. Archer the diamonds that the sampler's scooped in," Lane replied somewhat defensively.

"You should have spent your rest period *resting*," Krebs growled. "You know that—"

"Something's moving down there," Muzorawa said.

"What?" Krebs shot over toward him like a stumpy torpedo.

"Very long range," said Muzorawa. "Sonar return. But definitely a moving object."

"Distance? Speed?" Krebs demanded. "We need numbers!"

"There's more than one!" Muzorawa's voice was shaking now.

Grant tapped into the sensor net and saw three, no four, fuzzy things moving slowly in the same direction as the ship. Another slid into view, then two more.

"They're seventy-eight point six kilometers, slant range," Muzorawa called out.

"How deep are they?"

"Fourteen kilometers deeper than we are."

"O'Hara, give me a two-degree angle of descent."

"We can't go deeper!" Karlstad cried out. "We're far beyond our design limit now!"

"Silence!" Krebs roared. "Deeper!"

LEVIATHAN

Leviathan cruised slowly through the stream of food, eating constantly to regain its strength. The flagella were already in bud, to replace the members that had been lost, and that took even more energy. Leviathan ate greedily but swam steadily around the great storm, heading back for the haunts of its Kin.

Several of the skin members were budding, too, but it would be a long time before their offspring could be thickened and hardened to replace the armor Leviathan had lost when it was up along the edges of the cold abyss.

Leviathan was impatient to find its Kin, eager to replay to them the tale of its battles with the Darters and the eerie, tentacled monster up in the cold distance. Yet it knew that the Elders would display their displeasure. Many times they had warned Leviathan against moving away from the Kin. Youngsters often wanted to strike out on their own, they had pictured to Leviathan time and again, their imagery flashing deep red to show their seriousness. But youngsters usually disregarded the wisdom of their elders. Many never returned to the Kin.

Leviathan would return, it told itself, and return in triumph. It had gone to regions of the all-encompassing sea that no one of its kind had ever seen before. It had traveled up toward the cold abyss and survived. The Elders treasured knowledge, or so they imaged. Yet how could new knowledge be gained if no one moved off into the unexplored parts of the world?

Leviathan envisioned itself swimming with the Picturers, drawing the scenes of its epic journey so that they could add the depiction of its tale to the Kin's history of images. No matter how many times its members dissociated and recombined, this adventure would remain in the minds of all who could see. It would never be forgotten.

But first Leviathan had to get back to the Kin. It followed the food stream, heading toward home. It would be good to return, even if the Elders flashed pictures of discontent over its adventure. They will be jealous, Leviathan thought. While they remained in the same old feeding grounds, I explored new regions. I will add to the store of knowledge, and that is a positive thing.

Leviathan realized that some time in the future it would become an Elder. The thought startled Leviathan. But it resolved never to cease exploring, even when it was an elder. And it would never discourage a youngster from exploring, either. Leviathan was certain of that.

Then a cluster of its sensor members felt a distant tremor in the darkness of the ocean.

Darters! they warned. Following us and coming up fast.

CONTACT

"Number-four cylinder's failed!" Karlstad yelped.

"I see it," said Krebs, her voice tight. "The piston has jammed. Structural integrity is not threatened."

"It can't take any more pressure," Karlstad insisted.

"We are deep enough," Krebs said. "Almost."

Grant had tapped into Zeb's sensor returns. He saw a herd of enormous things out there in the ocean, objects the size of mountains, of islands, so huge that size began to lose all meaning.

"Distance?" Krebs demanded.

"Fifty-two point four kilometers," answered Muzorawa.

It made no sense to narrow the distance to them, Grant thought. They were so immense that getting closer would mean the sensors could focus only on one of them. On just a part of one of them, at that.

"Hold here," Krebs commanded. "Conform to their course and speed."

Grant felt the thrusters straining to match the speed of the Jovians. They were Jovians, he was certain. No doubt about that at all. Mind-boggling in size, they were gliding through the ocean, propelled by rows of flippers five times bigger than *Zheng He*. They seemed to be cruising leisurely through the stream of organics, sucking the particles up into many openings that lined their undersides.

They're alive, Grant told himself. But could they be intelligent? They're grazing like cows.

A light flashed on one of them, a sudden yellow glow that flared for a moment and then winked out.

"Did you see that?"

"A light of some kind."

"Natural bioluminescence, do you think?"

"Look! They're flickering back and forth!"

"Like signals!"

"Be quiet!" Krebs snapped. "Attend to your duties. Make certain that everything is being recorded."

Grant's heart was racing with excitement. He could see the giant creatures flicking lights along their massive flanks, red, yellow, a piercingly intense green. What does it mean? Are they intelligent signals? Can we make any sense of them?

"Maintain this distance from them," Krebs repeated. "Conform to their course and speed."

Grant had never felt so small, so dwarfed. From a distance of fifty-some kilometers the Jovians reminded him of a stately herd of elephants, but they were so blessedly *big*. Bigger than any creature that had ever lived on Earth. Bigger than a city. We're just puny little insects compared to them. Ants. Microbes.

"They're following the flow of organics," O'Hara said.

"Cruising in the current," Karlstad agreed.

"I can see that," snapped Krebs. "Stop this chattering! Check all systems. Now."

Grant felt resentful as he disengaged from the sensor data. Why can't we all watch them? he grumbled to himself. We don't need to check the damned systems. If there's something wrong we'll know it right away.

He realized that his headache was still pulsing away; he had ignored it during the excitement of seeing the Jovians. But the pain in his back was nagging at him, too, no longer merely stiffness but an ache that he couldn't quite pin down, like an itch that moved when you tried to scratch it.

Then he saw it in razor-sharp clarity. The number-two thruster was sputtering, its plasma flow no longer smoothly laminar. The hot ionized gas was crinkling, twisting in the thruster tube. The magnetic fields that should be guiding and accelerating the plasma were pulsating fitfully.

Grant felt the thruster's imminent failure as an increasingly sharp pain. His first instinct was to shut down the thruster and allow the automated repair program time to reline the tube with heat-shielding ceramic spray and replenish the liquid nitrogen coolant for the magnets.

To do that, though, he needed the captain's approval. The thruster could not be shut down unless Krebs physically relinquished her control of the propulsion system.

"Captain, thruster number two—"

"I see it," Krebs said.

"We should take it off-line for repair," Grant told her.

"Not now."

"But it's headed for catastrophic failure."

"Not for another twenty hours."

Grant saw the diagnostic and double-checked it with a glance at his console screens. "But, Captain, that's only an estimate. It could fail much sooner."

Her voice heavy with disdain, Krebs said, "If we shut down the thruster we will slow down. The beasts out there will move away from us. We must keep pace with them."

"Even if we lose the thruster altogether and can't get ourselves out of the ocean?" Grant demanded.

"We are here to get data. We can always fire off a data capsule."

"But we'll die!"

"The data comes first. That is what is important."

She doesn't care if we live or die, Grant said to himself. Our lives, even her own life, isn't as important to her as observing these creatures.

"The thruster can be repaired without taking it off-line," Krebs said calmly.

Grant checked into the maintenance program and found that she was right, up to a point. "It would only be a temporary patch," he said. "The program recommends complete shutdown for necessary repairs."

"Do what you can, Mr. Archer," Krebs said. "The rest of us have observations to make."

Fuming at the idea that he was forced to do a grease monkey's work while the others were acting as scientists, Grant rechecked the maintenance program, then activated the automated sequence that started the repair work without shutting down the thruster.

The problem was a vicious circle, a closed negative feedback loop. The ceramic lining that shielded the thruster tube from the star-hot plasma flowing through it had eroded away in spots, allowing too much heat to soak through the metal walls of the tube and boil away some of the liquid nitrogen that kept the thruster's superconducting magnet properly cooled. The magnetic field was wavering, kinking in spots, which became hotter than normal, thereby eroding away more of the ceramic heat-shield material.

Grant saw the problem as a visual image against his closed eyelids, felt it as a twitching pain that was spreading across his back. I've got to get the magnetic coil cooled down properly, he knew. If it heats up past its critical temperature, the whole magnetic field will collapse and release enough energy to explode like a bomb.

But pumping more liquid nitrogen to the magnetic coils was like sticking a finger in a dike that was crumbling. Nothing more than a stopgap. I've got to resurface the tube with ceramic. But how can I do that while the plasma's still flowing through the goddamned tube?

The maintenance program showed him how. He saw the recommended emergency procedure: Pump the liquefied ceramic into the plasma stream while alternating the magnetic field so that it made the electrically conducting plasma swirl in a helical motion as it moved down the tube. The ceramic will be forced to the outer edge of the swirling helix, plastered against the wall of the tube. Some of the ceramic will stick to the wall and begin to solidify.

Fine, Grant thought as the images flashed through his brain. But most of the ceramic will flow right down the tube and out the thruster nozzle.

It's a brute-force fix, he realized, but the only one that could be done as long as Krebs refused to shut down the thruster for proper repairs.

Swallowing hard, Grant spoke the sequence of alphanumerics that triggered the repair system. He watched the ceramic being injected into the plasma as the magnets began pulsing according to the preset program. His back throbbed and twitched, his head felt slightly giddy. This isn't going to work, he told himself. All I'm doing is pumping the ceramic out of the ship.

But slowly the temperature along the thruster tube wall began to creep down. A single sharp *ping* rang in his ears and the program automatically increased the flow of liquid nitrogen to the superconducting coils. Grant saw the magnetic field stabilize, the plasma's swirling smoothed to a clean laminar flow.

It's done, he saw. The heat transfer across the tube wall is back to within tolerable levels. The pain in his back had eased away.

But it was only temporary, Grant realized. A stopgap repair, a thin patch on a gushing wound. The problem would recur. Checking the system reserves, Grant saw that he had used more than half of the available ceramic. If—no, *when* the thruster got into trouble again, it would take all the ceramic that was left to fix it. If that would be enough.

• • •

"Karlstad, prepare a data capsule," Krebs ordered. "I want everything we have recorded to go into it. Every bit of data."

"Captain, that's the communications specialist's job," Karlstad replied.

"You do it," Krebs snapped. "Dr. O'Hara must devote her full attention to piloting."

Zheng He was still cruising some fifty kilometers from the herd of Jovians. The creatures were still grazing placidly along the stream of organic particles. Grant was still worried about the plasma thruster. It was performing well enough, but the thrusters were running at almost full capacity as the ship struggled to keep pace with the Jovians.

They're gliding along easily, Grant thought, almost lolling in the water. Even so they're going so fast that we're barely able to stay with them. What do we do if they get frightened and run away?

But the idea of anything frightening such massive beasts almost made Grant laugh. What could possibly bother them? They are the lords of this creation, stately and immense, unperturbed in their power.

He had lost track of time. They had all been on the bridge continuously since they'd first detected the Jovians, taking only quick breaks to plug in a squirt of food when the life-support program called out their scheduled mealtimes.

The lights that the Jovians flashed back and forth among themselves fascinated Grant. What can it mean? Are they signaling to one another? Could it be a language of some sort, a visual language? Or is it just some kind of display, like a peacock showing off his feathers?

"They don't seem to be using sound for communications," Muzorawa reported aloud. "Our audiophones are not picking up anything except the slight turbulence caused by their rowing motions."

"They swim stealthily," Krebs observed.

"Yes," Muzorawa agreed, nodding. "They hardly make a sound."

"That could be to keep them from being noticed by predators," Karlstad said.

"Who would even think of preying on some great huge creature like them?" O'Hara asked.

Karlstad snickered. "You've got predators in your bloodstream right now, Lane. We're thousands of times bigger than bacteria."

"Less talk, Dr. Karlstad," Krebs grumbled. "Get that data capsule prepared."

"It's almost ready, Captain," said Karlstad, tapping at his console's touchscreens.

Grant asked, "Could they be talking to each other at sound frequencies that the phones don't pick up?"

"They go down to ultralow frequency," Muzorawa answered, "less than ten cycles per second."

"What's the upper limit?" asked Karlstad.

"Nearly a hundred kilohertz, far beyond the range of human hearing."

"We should have brought a dog aboard," Karlstad muttered.

"Or a few of the dolphins," said O'Hara.

"Sound waves of that intensity," said Krebs, "can destroy living tissue."

"Or crack this submersible like an eggshell, if they have enough power behind them," Muzorawa said.

"Happy thought," Karlstad groused.

"My point is," Krebs said, "that those creatures would not use such a high frequency to communicate. It would hurt them."

"But they might use it as a weapon," Karlstad said.

"If they're communicating with each other," Muzorawa said slowly, "I would think it would be visually."

"They light up like signboards, don't they?" O'Hara said.

"Like those airships that hovered over football matches when I was a child," Karlstad agreed.

The lights flickered on and off so quickly that Grant couldn't tell if they were forming patterns of any sort. They were almost as fast as strobe lights.

"Where is my data capsule?" Krebs demanded.

"I was just about to tell you, Captain. The capsule is ready for your input."

Scowling, Krebs pushed off the overhead and settled next to Karlstad like a bulky log sinking down beside a willowy undersea reed. Karlstad tapped one of his touch-screens and the yellow communications light winked on.

"Data capsule number two," she said, her harsh voice flat, emotionless. "We have encountered a group of very large organisms. They appear to be ingesting the organic particles that drift through the sea. We are following them and will continue to do so until our life-support supplies go critical."

Krebs touched the screen and the light went off.

"Is that all you'll be saying?" O'Hara blurted. "Won't you tell them about their signaling lights?"

"They'll be able to see the lights as well as we do," Krebs said. "They can draw their own conclusions as to whether they are signals or not."

"But they've got to be!" O'Hara said. "What else could they be?"

"Launch the capsule," Krebs said to Karlstad. Giving O'Hara a sour look, she retorted, "They could be almost anything, anything at all. Don't leap to conclusions."

Karlstad launched the capsule with the touch of a fingertip against a screen. Grant felt it as a slight shudder.

"The lights flicker on and off so fast," Muzorawa said, "that it's impossible to tell what they are."

"Can't we slow them down?" Grant asked. "I mean, run our imagery of them at a reduced speed."

"Slow motion?"

"Yes."

Muzorawa thought it over for a moment, then said, "Yes, that's a good idea. Captain?"

"Do it," Krebs snapped.

It took several minutes for Muzorawa to program the imagery stored in the sensors' computer memory. Finally he told them he was ready.

"Put it on the main screen," Krebs ordered.

The ache in Grant's back was returning. He could not see anything wrong in the display screens of his console, but the ache warned him that the thruster was starting to decay again.

Looking up, he saw on the wallscreen what appeared to be a still picture of one of the Jovians. No, its flippers were moving, but so slowly that Grant could see little silvery particles in the water tumbling in the wake of those powerful paddles of flesh. Diamonds, he realized anew. They're swimming through a cloud of diamonds—and food.

Though the beasts were still some fifty kilometers distant, the cameras' magnification showed them in some detail: Their skins looked gray, rubbery, but mottled with rough lumps and knobs and—eyes. Those things had to be eyes; rows of them, hundreds of them staring out into the hot, dark sea. Grant shuddered. For a moment he felt as if those eyes were looking at him, watching him, appraising the intruding aliens from another world.

They're so huge, Grant thought. How could any creature grow to such enormous size? How does its nervous system control those flippers? Where is the brain located? Lord, one of those flippers could crush us with just a flick.

He saw patches of different colors here and there on the skin of the beasts. Parasites? There's a whole biosphere in this ocean, with plenty of ecological niches for all sorts of creatures. The organics from the clouds are at the bottom of the food chain and these gigantic superwhales must be at the top. What else are we going to find?

Red and orange lights glowed along the huge flanks of the massive creatures, strange puzzling designs that lit the ocean with their eerie glow. They made no sense to Grant, they gave no hint of meaning.

"Well, at least they're not saying 'Earthlings go home,'" Karlstad wisecracked.

"But look," Muzorawa pointed toward the wallscreen, "they are all repeating the same set of symbols."

"Is it writing?" O'Hara asked.

"Impossible," spat Krebs.

"And yet . . ."

"It must mean *something*," Karlstad said.

"It means something to them, I should think," Muzorawa murmured.

Krebs started to say, "Do not leap to—"

She stopped, open-mouthed. Grant saw it, too. So did all the others.

One of the Jovians displayed an image of a round, saucer-shaped object with a single row of lights dotting its forward side. The saucer was in deep red, the lights a bright orange. Almost immediately, the others began to show the same picture.

"That's us!" Karlstad yelped.

The same picture flashed back and forth among each of the Jovians in the screen's display.

"They've seen us," O'Hara said in an awed whisper.

"They know we're here," Krebs agreed, her own voice hushed with astonishment.

"My God," said Grant, "they *are* intelligent."

LEVIATHAN

Gulping down the streaming food greedily, Leviathan realized it had been congratulating itself too soon. A lone member of the Kin was always prey to the Darters, and it was too far from the giant storm to use the same tactics that had saved it from the earlier pack.

Speed. Speed was Leviathan's only hope. If it could get back to its own Kin, rejoin the others, then the Darters would not dare to attack. Even if they were foolish or desperate enough to try, an entire gathering of Kin could crush the Darters with ease. Darters almost always broke off their attacks when they saw a whole gathering swinging into a defensive sphere. They preferred to attack lone members, waiting until one of the Kin moved off by itself to dissociate and begin budding.

But the Kin were still far, far off. And the Darters were moving in fast. It was going to be a race, Leviathan knew, urging its flagella members to their utmost speed. A race against time. A race against death.

PURSUIT

"Nonsense!" Krebs snarled. "Just because they can mimic what they see doesn't make them intelligent."

"It doesn't make them stupid," Karlstad quipped.

"Parrots can mimic human speech," Krebs said. "Dogs, horses, many animals can respond to human commands. Does that make them intelligent?"

"Dolphins speak with us," O'Hara said.

Krebs shook her head stubbornly. "Intelligence requires culture, technology. Dolphins have none."

How could they, Grant wondered, living underwater, without hands to manipulate their environment, without the ability to make fire? They're stuck with their own muscle power, and that's a dead end.

"Ants have culture and technology," Karlstad said.

Before Krebs could respond, O'Hara countered, "The mark of intelligence is the ability to communicate abstract ideas among others of your species. The dolphins do that."

"Abstract ideas?" Muzorawa asked.

"Yes," O'Hara replied firmly. "They can understand friendship and loyalty. They have family ties."

Krebs, still looking utterly unconvinced, said, "We are not here for philosophical debates. Maintain the same course and speed as the whales. The more data we get on them, the better."

The pain in his back was getting worse. Grant closed his eyes and visualized the faulty thruster. The pain told him that it was sputtering again.

Before he could call out the problem, Krebs complained, "I need full power from all the thrusters, Mr. Archer."

"Number two is failing again," he said.

"I can see that. Fix it!"

"If I could shut it down . . . just for half an hour . . ."

Krebs seemed to consider the possibility. Then she shook her head. "No. We will lose the whales."

Muzorawa spoke up. "Captain, we know the herd's course and speed. We could catch up with them once the thruster is repaired."

"We are barely keeping pace with them now," Krebs growled. "Once they move away from us we'll never catch them."

"The stream of organics that they are grazing on follows a curving path," Muzorawa said, calmly reasonable, displaying Grant's map of the ocean currents with the organics' course highlighted. "We could cut across the current, once the thruster is repaired, and intercept the herd."

Krebs closed her eyes. She's visualizing Zeb's map, Grant thought, using the implants to give her a picture that her eyes can't see. The pressure must be affecting her optic nerves, not her visual cortex.

Krebs opened her eyes, but they stared blankly. "Very well," she said reluctantly. "O'Hara, reduce speed to minimum cruise. Archer, shut down number-two thruster for repair."

As Grant began to bubble out a sigh of relief, Krebs added, "And get the repair finished in thirty minutes! Not one second more!"

"Yes, Captain!"

Twenty-eight minutes later Grant surveyed the relined plasma tube. Through his implanted chips he felt the ceramic lining as if he were caressing it, running his hands along its smooth length, still warm from the star-hot stream of ionized gas that had been flowing through it. Yes, he told himself, it's the proper thickness and surface smoothness. All within the specifications. The liquid nitrogen coolant was refrigerating the superconducting coils on the other side of the tube. The coils were well below their critical temperature.

"Well?" Krebs demanded. "Are you finished?"

With a single small nod, Grant said, "Yes, Dr. Krebs. Thruster number two is ready to go back on-line."

"Good," she said, and Grant realized that this would be as close to a pat on the back as he would ever get from this dour, hard-driven woman.

As the thrusters roared up to full power, Grant fought to pull his attention away from the impulses his chips were sending through his nervous system. It took an effort, but through clenched teeth he asked Muzorawa, standing next to him: "Have we lost them?"

The wallscreen showed nothing but empty darkness.

It took a moment for Zeb to reply. "They've moved off beyond our sensor range," he answered, rubbing his eyes, "but if they are still following the organics, we should intercept them in about one hour."

And if they've changed course we've probably lost them forever, Grant thought. And it will be my fault. At least Krebs will blame me for it.

Then he asked himself, Are there other herds in the ocean? There must be. There couldn't be just one group of a few dozen of these creatures. There must be others of their kind . . . and other kinds of creatures in the sea, as well. We have a whole world to explore, a whole ecology, an ocean thousands of times bigger than Earth.

If the thrusters hold out, he reminded himself. They're working fine now, but you've used up all the reserve ceramic. If anything goes wrong again, we either head back for the station or die here. There's nothing left to repair them with. And we're running them full-out. If one of them fails, we're gone.

Grant glanced at Muzorawa, then at O'Hara and Karlstad, all at their consoles, all straining their senses to find the herd of Jovian whales. They're not whales, Grant chided himself. They're nothing like whales. They made whales look like minnows, for God's sake.

None of the others seemed to know that the thrusters were in critical condition. Looking over his shoulder at Krebs, though, Grant felt that she knew. Those blind eyes notwithstanding, she knows that the thrusters are on the knife-edge of breakdown. And she doesn't care. She'd rather die than give up this quest.

"I see one!" Muzorawa sang out. It reminded Grant of old stories about whalers, iron men in wooden ships, and their cry of "Thar she blows!"

Everyone tried to tap into the sensor data at once. Grant got a sensation of a faint, trembling touch along his arms, as if someone were stroking his skin, gently, very gently.

"Give me visual imagery," Krebs snapped.

"It's too far off for anything but sonar right now," Zeb replied.

"Let me *see* it!" Krebs demanded.

"In a few minutes," Muzorawa said. "Ah! It's lighting up the water! Can you see the glow?"

Grant saw a faint deep red shimmering in the otherwise black visual imagery.

"It seems to be alone," Muzorawa said, sounding puzzled. "I can't detect any other creatures near it."

O'Hara chimed in, "It's not on the same course that the herd should be following. And it's moving at much greater speed."

"It's an intercept course," Krebs said. "But it's coming from a different direction than we are."

"I'm starting to get visual imagery," Muzorawa said.

"Yes, I see," said Krebs.

"It's alone," Karlstad said.

"Yes," Muzorawa agreed. Then: "No, I don't think it is—there are others coming with it. Two . . . six . . . ten and more! They're smaller, though. Different in shape."

Grant saw them, faint and fuzzy at this distance. But the scene made a dreadful kind of sense to him.

"They're chasing him!" Grant yelped. "The smaller ones are chasing the big one."

"The *smaller* ones are five times the size of this ship," Karlstad pointed out.

"Predators," said Krebs. "Archer is right. They are chasing the whale. We're seeing a hunt in progress."

"What can we do?" O'Hara asked.

"Get closer," Krebs snapped.

"Closer?"

"Yes! Before it runs away from us."

The thrusters were running at full power, straining to cut across the Jovian's path and close the gap between them. Grant felt as if he were running a marathon; every muscle in his body ached.

"It's going too fast," O'Hara shouted. "We'll never catch up with it."

Tapping into the sensor net, Grant saw the mammoth Jovian streaking through the depths, pursued by the ten smaller beasts.

"Get closer!" Krebs demanded. "Muzorawa, are the sensors getting all this?"

Zeb did not reply immediately.

"Muzorawa!"

"Yes, Captain," Zeb said, his voice shaking. "The sensors . . . I . . ."

Grant pulled out of the sensor imagery and turned toward Zeb. Muzorawa just stood blankly at his console, his legs bent slightly at the knees, his feet held down by the floor loops, his arms floating chest-high, his head lolling to one side.

"I . . . can't . . . breathe . . ." he gasped. "Pressure . . ."

"We're too deep!" Karlstad yelled.

"What's wrong with him?" Krebs demanded.

Karlstad stared frantically at his console. Grant could see a string of baleful red lights glowering along its screens. "His breathing rate's gone sky-high. Something wrong with his lungs. Capacity is down, still sinking—"

"Archer," Krebs ordered, "disengage Dr. Muzorawa and get him back to his berth."

Grant quickly began to yank the optic fibers loose from Zeb's legs.

"I'm sorry . . ." Muzorawa panted. "Too much . . . can't . . ."

"Don't talk," Grant said, trying to sound soothing. "Save your strength."

Muzorawa's eyes closed. His head rolled slightly, then slumped down, chin on chest. He's unconscious, Grant realized. Or dead.

"You're the life-support specialist," Krebs was snarling at Karlstad. "What should we do?"

"Get the hell out of this pressure!" Egon snapped.

"No!" she shot back. "Not yet. Not now, with those animals so close."

"You'll kill him!" Karlstad insisted. "You'll kill us all!"

Turning back toward Grant, Krebs said, "Take him back to his berth. Lower the pressure in the chamber there."

Feeling helpless, confused, Grant began to ask, "How do I lower—"

Krebs said, "Seal the hatch once you get him into his berth. I'll take care of depressurizing."

"You can't depressurize it enough to help him," Karlstad wailed. "Not unless we go back up toward the surface."

Krebs turned toward him, looking as if she were ready to commit murder.

"I make the decisions here," she said to Karlstad, her voice venomously low. Turning back to Grant: "Get him back to his berth! Now!"

"Yes'm." Grant began pulling his own optical fibers free.

Suddenly the ship lurched as if it had been hit by a torpedo. Grant was torn loose from his foot restraints and went sailing across the bridge, optic fibers popping loose. He banged painfully against the far bulkhead as all the lights went out.

ATTACK

The emergency lamps came on, dim, scary. Grant blinked in the shadowy lighting. Everything looked tilted, askew. Then he realized that he was floating sideways next to the food dispenser, his right shoulder and side afire with pain. Red lights blinked demandingly on all the consoles.

". . . back on-line!" Krebs was shouting. "The auxiliaries can't power the thrusters for more than a few minutes."

Muzorawa was floating in the middle of the bridge, a haze of blood leaking from his open mouth. Krebs bumped into him and pushed him aside, in the general direction of the sleeping quarters. O'Hara was at her console, but doubled over as if in overwhelming pain. Only Karlstad seemed to be unhurt, but he looked bewildered as Krebs rattled off commands rapid-fire.

"Get back to your console," she said to Grant, grabbing him by the scruff of his neck and shoving him toward the console. Grant's shoulder and ribs were thundering with pain. I must have hit the bulkhead there, he realized.

"What happened?" he asked dazedly as he fumbled with his optical fibers.

"No time for linking," Krebs snapped. "Go to manual control. Get the generator back on-line."

"But Zeb—"

"There's nothing you can do for him now. Get the generator back on-line!"

Grant saw that the same floor loop that had torn loose earlier was flapping again, held only by one remaining bolt. He slid his foot into the other and scanned the glowering red lights of his console.

"O'Hara!" Krebs barked. "Disengage and take care of Dr. Muzorawa."

Lane looked sick, positively green in the eerie light of the emergency lamps. She nodded and began pulling off her optical fibers.

"I'll handle the ship," Krebs went on. "Karlstad, take over the sensors. Archer, why isn't the generator back on-line?"

"I'm working on it," Grant said, fingers racing across the console touchscreens.

The bridge seemed to be rising and sinking, twisting as if on a roller-coaster ride. Glancing to his right, Grant saw Krebs at O'Hara's console, moving her fingers along the touchscreens, her mouth a thin, grim, bloodless line.

The ship lurched again, and this time Grant heard a definite thump, as if they had banged into an undersea mountain.

"Those sharks are attacking us," Krebs said, her voice strangely low, controlled. "They think we are food."

Karlstad screeched, "The hull can't take this kind of pounding! It'll crack!"

"I am trying to get away from them," Krebs agreed. Turning to Grant she bellowed, "For that, we need power!"

"It's not the generator," Grant reported. "The generator's working fine. It's the power bus; it shorted out from the first concussion."

Another thump. The bridge tilted crazily. Even the emergency lamps blinked.

Hanging onto one of the console's handgrips, Grant worked madly to reboot the power bus. One by one the circuit breakers clicked on. One by one the red lights on his console flicked to amber or green. The thrusters came back on-line, although Grant saw that their telltale lights were amber. There must be a lot of damage, he thought. Maybe the tubes have been dented by the sharks. He wished he had time to link with the ship, then he'd know immediately what was wrong.

"Here comes another one!" Karlstad yelped.

"Thrusters to max!" Krebs said. She didn't need Grant to turn them on, she did it herself from O'Hara's console.

Even immersed in the thick liquid that filled the bridge Grant felt the surge of thrust. Another thump, but this time it was a glancing blow. Still, it set the ship spinning.

"I don't know how long the thrusters can maintain full power," Grant yelled.

"We have to get away from them," Karlstad shouted back.

Krebs shook her head. "They're faster than we are. They're racing ahead of us."

"If only we had a weapon," Karlstad muttered, "something to defend ourselves with."

Grant heard himself say, "What about the plasma exhaust?"

"What?"

"The exhaust from the thrusters. It's over ten thousand degrees when it leaves the nozzles. It boils the water behind us. They mustn't like that."

Krebs seemed to think it over for a moment. "If they stayed behind us . . ."

"They're not," Karlstad said, his closed eyes seeing what the ship's sensors showed. "They're forming up in front of us again."

"We're moving at top speed and they race past us," said Krebs, sounding defeated.

"They're too fucking stupid to realize we're not food," Karlstad grumbled.

"By the time they discover that fact, we will be dead."

Grant said, "Can't we spin the ship? Or turn in a tight circle? Spray our exhaust in all directions?"

"What good would that do?"

"It might discourage them."

Karlstad laughed bitterly. "Brilliant! You want to circle the wagons when we only have one wagon. Absolutely brilliant."

"It's worth a try," Grant urged.

"We have nothing else," said Krebs. "We have nothing to lose."

With the power back on, Grant grabbed for the loose optical fibers and slapped them onto the chips in his legs. Pain! Sharp, hard needles of pain jabbed at him. The thrusters were running full-out but they were damaged, their tubes dented from the battering by the sharks.

At least the sharks were not attacking now. Krebs was turning the sub in tight circles, spinning a helix of superheated steam around them, keeping the predators at bay.

For how long? Grant asked himself. He knew the answer: Until the thrusters give out. Then it won't matter if they renew their attacks or not; it won't matter if they think we're food or not. We'll be dead, drifting in this alien ocean, without the power to climb back to the surface and leave. We'll sink until this eggshell is crushed by the pressure. We'll die here.

LEVIATHAN

Leviathan could scarcely believe what its sensing members were telling it. The Darters had broken off their pursuit to chase—Leviathan did not know what to call the tiny round, flat thing that had caught the Darters' hungry attention. It was unlike anything the Kin had seen before, except for the tale that had been flashed among them about a strange cold alien that had appeared briefly and then vanished into the abyss above.

Leviathan remembered sensing something like this stranger, when it had been in the barren cold region on the other side of the eternal storm. It was not one of the Kin, not even a member unit that had broken away to bud.

Whatever it was, the Darters were swarming around it and the stranger—whatever it was—was spinning madly, squirting hot jets of steam that boiled the sea into wild bubbling froth.

Where are the Kin? Leviathan wondered. How far from here could they be? Leviathan considered calling to them but feared that its distress signal would rekindle the Darters' attention.

The Darters had forgotten about Leviathan in their blind hunger for this small, almost defenseless creature. The stranger was giving Leviathan a chance to race away, unnoticed by the instinct-driven Darters.

That would mean leaving the stranger to the predators. It did not seem able to get away from them. Every time it tried to climb higher, to head back toward the cold abyss above, the Darters drove it back down again. One of them came close to the hot steam and twisted away in agony, howling so loudly that Leviathan's sound sensors shut down for several moments. Two of the Darters immediately attacked their wounded companion, silencing it forever with a few voracious bites.

But the others kept circling the stranger, holding it at bay, waiting for it to exhaust itself.

TRAPPED

You've got to get higher!" Karlstad demanded, his voice almost a hysterical shriek. "We've got to get away from them!"

Krebs shot him a venomous glance. "Every time I try to lift, they swarm above me and batter us down again."

"We can't take much more pounding," Karlstad said. "Hull integrity . . ."

Grant was awash with pain. His console lights were flickering from amber to red. The thrusters were close to failure and there was nothing he could do about it.

Krebs seemed to be fully aware of the situation. Grimly she muttered, "Full thruster power. We break loose from them or we die here and now."

Vision blurring, his whole body spasming with agony, Grant felt the thrusters strain as he diverted all available power to them. The lights went out again as the bridge tilted dizzily, the emergency lamps glowed feebly. Grant reached for the handgrips on his console.

"Look out!" Karlstad screamed.

Something hit the ship with the power of an avalanche. If Grant hadn't been hanging on he would have been flung across the bridge again. Krebs went sailing, banged against the food dispenser with a solid, sickening thud of flesh against metal. Karlstad was holding on to both his console's handgrips, his feet torn free of the floor loops and flailing wildly.

"We're sinking!" Karlstad yelled. "Hull's been breached!"

Grant saw that Krebs was unconscious. Or dead. An ugly gash across her forehead was streaming a fog of blood into the fluid they were breathing. The optical fibers had been torn loose from her legs.

"What can we do?" Karlstad screeched. "What can we do?"

Grant tried to ignore his pain as he tapped at his console's touchscreens, calling up all the ship's systems. The sudden rush of information boggled his mind and body. *Everything*—every chip, every wire, every square centimeter of structure, all the sensors, the ship's steering controls, the thrusters, the power generator, the auxiliaries, all the life-support systems, the medical monitors, the lights, the wiring, the welds along the hull—every molecule of the ship, every bit of data flowing through all its systems, all flooded in on Grant like a huge overpowering tidal wave. He was flung into a maelstrom, mind spinning madly as he desperately tried to cling to some vestige of himself, some trace of his own soul in this deluge of sensations, some thread of control.

He could no longer feel his own body. That reality had been flung aside, left far behind in this new reality of—power. That's what it is, Grant told himself. Power. *I am the ship*. I have all its power, all its pain, all its destiny within me.

Godlike, he expanded his senses. He saw, sensed, felt every part of the ship. The crack in the outermost hull was like the sharp slash of a knife wound; the labored straining of the thrusters like the excruciating knotting of cramped, overworked muscles.

Zheng He was losing buoyancy, maintaining its position only by dint of the thrusters' full-throated push against the ever-present power of Jupiter's pervasive gravity

And he saw the sharklike creatures, more than a dozen of them, swarming above and on both sides of the slowly sinking submersible.

Karlstad was babbling, but it was a faint jabbering noise far in the background of Grant's consciousness. I am the ship, he told himself. I'm wounded, badly hurt. How can I get out of this? How can I get away? When Krebs tried to climb out of this they battered us so hard the hull cracked. What should I do? What *can* I do?

Go inert, he heard a voice in his mind say. Shut down the thrusters. Let the sharks think you're dead. Let them find out that you're metal, not flesh; an alien, not food.

You'll sink. You'll sink deeper, the outside pressure will increase, the crack in the hull will get worse, you'll be torn apart, crushed, before you can get the thrusters started again.

Maybe. All this flashed through Grant's mind in less than a second. Through it all, the one—only—hope he had was the fusion generator. It purred along as if nothing outside its alloy shell mattered in the slightest. That little artificial star kept on fusing atomic nuclei, transforming matter into energy, oblivious to the wants or needs of the humans who had built it, those whose lives depended on it. Grant felt its warmth like the fire in a hearth, comforting, protecting against the raging storms outside.

He shut down the thrusters. He turned off the outside lights. The ocean out there went black, sunless, a blind oblivion. Except that Grant could see; through the ship's infrared sensors and sonar he could see the imagery of the huge sharks gliding around and above him.

"We're sinking!" Karlstad repeated, his voice high and shaking, even in their fluid environment.

"Take care of Krebs," Grant said evenly. "See how Lane and Zeb are doing."

"But we're sinking!"

"We'll be all right," Grant said, hoping it was true. "I've got her under control," he lied.

The sharks were coming closer, nosing around the slowly settling *Zheng He*. Can't you sense that we're metal? Grant asked them silently. Are you too stupid to see that we're not food?

One of the huge creatures brushed against the sub, knocking it sideways. Grant saw it coming, held on to his console.

"Jesus!" Karlstad yelped. "Jesus. Jesus."

Grant almost smiled. We could use His help, he thought. Does God see us this far down in this alien sea?

A low rumbling sound, so low-pitched that Grant felt it along his aching bones rather than heard it. Long, like the rumble of distant thunder, but so powerful that it made the bridge vibrate. An earthquake sound, here where there was no ground to shake, not a solid clump of soil or a rock for tens of thousands of kilometers.

The sonar was tingling along Grant's nerves. He closed his eyes and saw the imagery: Something was heading their way, something superhuman, a huge power streaking through the water toward him, and it was emitting this low, thunderous profundo note as steadily as an avalanche roars down a mountainside.

The sharks pulled away, turning in unison so fast that Grant felt the sharp waves they made as a single unified pulse in the water. The infrared sensors kicked in and showed what was approaching: that immense solitary whale. It was rushing toward the sharks like a huge cannonball fired at supersonic velocity.

The sharks seemed to be gathering themselves into a battle formation, facing the onrushing whale. They've forgotten about me, Grant saw. They're ready to confront the whale. Maybe I can slip away . . .

Cautiously he lit the thrusters again. Minimum thrust. Don't call attention to yourself. Balance your sink rate. Maintain buoyancy by using thrust to balance the leak.

Zheng He rose a little. Grant watched through the ship's sensors as the gigantic beast raced straight toward the waiting delta-shaped sharks. He edged the thrusters slightly higher and maneuvered the battered submersible away from the predators. All the while the ocean reverberated with that lone, sustained, low-pitched note, like the melancholy howl of a solitary wolf in a snowy wilderness, but many, many octaves lower and enormously more powerful and sustained far longer than Earthly lungs could ever achieve.

The gigantic creature barreled into the sharks. Instead of fleeing from it, as Grant had expected, the sharks spread their formation into a wide-space net and surrounded the whale. They're not running away from it, Grant saw. They're attacking it!

LEVIATHAN

Leviathan knew it was a foolish gesture, most likely a fatal one. The alien creature seemed to be dead, gone dark, sinking slowly toward the hot abyss below.

Still, the stranger had diverted the Darters and saved Leviathan from them. It was too late now to turn back. Once Leviathan had sounded its distress call to the Kin, the Darters left the stranger and rediscovered it, alone and near enough to attack.

Leviathan did not wait for the predators to strike. It roared in toward them, urging all its members to their utmost effort, desperately hoping to confuse the Darters and scatter them before they could form their attack pattern.

But they were too fast, too agile for that forlorn hope. Even as Leviathan rushed toward them, the Darters spread themselves into a screen, above, below, and on both sides of Leviathan's charge.

Bellowing its distress call, Leviathan barely had time to notice that the stranger was not yet dead. Even though it had gone dark and a trail of bubbles showed that its shell had been cracked, it began to emit a jet of heated water—not as vigorously as before, but still it was a sign of life.

And then the Darters were upon Leviathan, nipping at its flanks, tearing at its flagella members. Cripple the flagella and Leviathan was helpless. But the mindless flagella were weapons as well as propulsion members. Leviathan clubbed at the Darters, felt bone snap and flesh rupture, madly hoping that if it killed a few of them, the rest would begin feeding on their own and leave Leviathan alone.

But the Darters would never leave a lone and wounded prey. In a growing frenzy they would attack and feed, ripping through Leviathan's protective armor to get at the vital organ-members, while the vibrations of their furious struggle would signal others from far away to join the battle and the inevitable feasting.

Still Leviathan fought. There was nothing else to do.

The sharks on one side suddenly scattered away from Leviathan, swooping off in rapid retreat. Leviathan wondered why, even as it fought with all its waning strength against the others. The stranger! That alien creature from the cold abyss had charged in alongside Leviathan, spraying painfully hot steam into the midst of the attacking Darters.

But it was not enough. There were too many of the Darters, and more were coming. All the stranger had accomplished was to make certain it would be killed alongside Leviathan.

Then the water quivered with a new vibration: a chorus of undulating notes that rose and fell in perfect unison.

The Kin.

RESCUE

Grant watched, awed, fascinated, rapt so completely that he forgot the pain that racked his body, forgot even the pains that the ship suffered. That enormous, magnificent creature was battling the sharks, fighting them in a struggle that shook tiny little *Zheng He* like a dead leaf in a hurricane.

The sub rattled and tossed in the wild waves thrashing through the ocean. Grant saw that the sharks were tearing at the big whale, ripping away acres of flesh with teeth the size of buzz saws. The whale was fighting back, but it seemed a hopeless, one-sided battle. Here and there a shark drifted aimlessly, broken, oozing its internal fluids. But the others kept on attacking, their frenzy growing by the minute.

Get away! Grant told himself. While they're busy killing each other, get the hell away from here!

But he couldn't. No matter how his rational mind insisted that these creatures fought each other all the time, that this was *their* world and he had no place in it, that there was nothing he could do to help—still Grant lingered off to one side of the titanic struggle.

Maybe there *is* something I can do, Grant said as he powered up the thrusters and moved toward the flank of the enormous creature. It was like driving along a mountain range, or coming toward a big city whose towers loomed before you tall and powerful. Feeling like an insect approaching an elephant, Grant drove *Zheng He* into the battle, hoping that the thrusters' exhaust would boil some of the sharks or at least frighten them away.

It worked—but it wasn't enough. The sharks didn't like the superheated steam; they raced away from the sub's exhaust plume. But Grant saw that they merely jetted farther up along the great whale's flank and resumed their attack there.

The whale's oarlike flippers were just about the size of *Zheng He* itself. Rows and rows of them, by the hundreds. And eyes just above them.

It was eerie, uncanny, to see hundreds of eyes, all turned toward him, watching him, staring at him.

Grant was accomplishing almost nothing. The sharks simply avoided the sub. The whale was so big that there were plenty of other places for them to attack. It would have taken a fleet of submersibles to protect this one creature. An armada.

Get away, Grant told himself again. There's nothing you can do to help here. Get away while you can.

The sub suddenly began to reverberate with an eerie, undulating sound. Up and down, it rose and fell like a police siren, only deeper, lower, so profound that it sounded almost like the bottom bass note on the most tremendous church organ in the universe. God's own chorus, a call to arms that might have been trumpeted by Gabriel himself. It grew swiftly louder, painfully louder, rattling the bridge, thundering in Grant's ears, cracking his eardrums with its tremendous, frightening, awesome overpowering resonance.

The sharks stopped their attack. Every one of them pulled away from the whale and seemed to freeze in place, some of them with gobbets of the whale's flesh clenched in their teeth.

The sound was painful. Grant felt as if hot needles were being jabbed in his ears. Louder and louder it rose, until he could hear nothing at all. The excruciating pain lanced through him as if a drill were driving through his skull. Touchscreens on the consoles began to shatter, bursting into showers of plastic shards and electrical sparks. The bridge vibrated as if some immense beast was shaking it in its jaws the way a terrier shakes a rat to death.

Grant hung on, vision clouding as one by one the ship's sensors went out. The main wallscreen shattered, blowing sparks and broken pieces across the bridge. Grant ducked and cringed as plastic shards sliced through the fluid past him, tumbling slowly in the thick perfluorocarbon liquid. He could feel the sub's multiple hulls quivering, reverberating like bells struck by a giant iron fist.

Like a school of minnows suddenly darting in unison, the sharks turned as one and fled away. One instant they were hovering everywhere, all pointed toward the source of the sound, the next they were gone, leaving nothing but bubbles in their wake.

The sudden turbulence of their swift departure tossed *Zheng He* fitfully, flipped the submersible upside down. Grant held on to his console with one hand, teeth gritting in pain. He couldn't tell whether the agonies were his own body's or the ship's. What does it matter? What does anything matter now?

The sub was beyond his control. The turbulence left by the sharks had overpowered Grant's ability to keep the vessel on an even keel. The thrusters were actually powering the ship downward now, spinning in a lazy uncontrollable spiral like a plane heading for a crash in slow motion. The thought flashed through Grant's mind that the nearest solid ground must be tens of thousands of kilometers down, deep in Jupiter's hot, dense core. We'll be crushed and boiled long before we hit anything solid, he told himself.

With growing terror he tried to work the controls, running his hands madly across the touchscreens. Not even the thrusters responded to his commands. Everything must be so badly damaged, Grant said to himself. We're going to die. We're going to die. If only Krebs were conscious, he thought, she might be able to handle the controls and get us out of this. Or even Zeb.

I don't know what to do! I can't get her straightened out.

Zheng He plunged deeper.

Grant was totally deaf now, as if his ears were wrapped in thick towels or layers of insulation. Dimly, through the few sensors still working, he saw a sight that shook him to his soul. Dozens of the immense Jovians, scores of them, maybe a hundred or more were speeding through the water toward their wounded, exhausted comrade.

My God, Grant thought as the gigantic creatures neared, we had only glimpsed a small portion of the herd. There's so many of them! And they're so huge!

Many of them dwarfed the one that had fought the sharks. All of them were flashing lights, signaling each other in hues of brilliant red, flashing yellow, and that bright piercing green. The water was alight with their signals.

But *Zheng He* was sinking away from them, spinning slowly, revolving over and over again despite Grant's frantic efforts to regain control.

A tap on his shoulder made Grant jump. Whirling, he saw it was Karlstad, wide-eyed, frightened. The man's mouth moved, but Grant could hear nothing. When Grant tried to speak, he couldn't hear his own voice.

Karlstad frantically jabbed both forefingers toward his ears. He's been deafened, too, Grant understood.

The bridge was a mess. Most of the screens had blown out. Splinters of plastic and optical fibers from the unoccupied consoles floated uselessly in the dim emergency lighting.

His eyes showing sheer terror, Karlstad pushed himself over to the console on Grant's left and tapped on its keyboard. Its one intact screen wrote in glowing orange letters:

GOT TO GET OUT OF HERE.

Grant shrugged helplessly.

GET US UP!!! Karlstad typed.

Grant ran his fingers along the touchscreens. The thrusters were running at a fraction of their full power, but with the sub out of control he was afraid to run them up higher, afraid that they would simply drive the vessel deeper into the dark hot sea. What should I do? What can I do? In desperation, he shut down the thrusters completely.

TOO MCH PRESSURE! Karlstad typed.

Suddenly Grant understood what he must do. Get all this information back to the station. We're not going to make it, he thought, but this information has got to get to Dr. Wo and the others.

Reaching for the keyboard on his console, Grant wrote, DATA CAPSULE.

Karlstad's fingers flew across his keyboard. NOT NOW. GET US CLOSER TO SURFACE.

NOW, Grant insisted. SEND TWO.

Karlstad stared at Grant, finally understanding what he was trying to say. We're as good as dead; there's nothing left for us to do except this gesture of sending data back to the station.

Grant grabbed his shoulder and shook him hard, banging on his keyboard with his other hand. DO IT. TWO.

Karlstad blinked, then nodded his agreement. Bending over his console, he replied, TWO NOT NECESSARY. DATA COMPRESSION.

Grant tapped him on the arm. SEND TWO, he repeated. REDUNDANCY.

Even though one capsule could hold all the data they had recorded, Grant wanted to take no chances of that lone capsule failing. Briefly he thought about sending all four of the remaining capsules, but he decided two would be sufficient. Keep recording data with the few sensors still working. Send the final two when the last moment comes.

Turning his attention back to the sensors, Grant saw that the whales were some distance above them now. The Jovians were hovering around their wounded comrade, flashing lights back and forth with blinding speed. Grant got the impression they were jabbering to each other.

Two of them glided downward, lights flashing along their mountainous flanks.

Are they trying to communicate with us? The thought startled Grant.

Zheng He was still sinking slowly into the depths, despite Grant's feeble efforts to get the submersible under control once again. The ship's systems were not responding to his commands. No matter how he worked the touchscreens, the submersible continued to spiral slowly deeper. Backups, Grant thought. There are supposed to be backups for each of the main systems. But most of them were out of action, too, he saw.

Several more Jovians coasted down toward the sub, Grant saw, swimming in gigantic circles around the wounded little submersible, flashing their lights in endless complex patterns.

Are they trying to communicate with us? Grant asked himself again. Almost without thinking consciously about it, he turned on the sub's outside lights. Only two of them still worked, and one of them flickered dimly.

And the whales matched its flicker rate exactly, in less than a heartbeat. Grant gasped with awe. The pictures running along the whales' immense flanks were far too complex for him to understand, but they were flashing on and off at the same rate as the damaged lamp's flicker.

Mimicry or intelligence? Grant asked himself.

Karlstad's nudge against his shoulder startled Grant.

GET US UP!!! Egon had typed on his console screen.

I can't, Grant confessed silently. I can't. But his fingers typed, TRYING.

Grant ran a quick diagnostic. His heart sank as the results flashed across his closed eyelids. The thrusters were close to catastrophic failure. The crack in the outer hull was spreading, branching like a crack in an ice-covered pond. The inner hulls were still intact, but the pressure was building. It was only a matter of minutes before they started to break up. Worst of all, the sub was still spiraling downward, its steering vanes useless, its control jets too weak to stop its sinking spin.

"We're finished," Grant said. He couldn't hear the words. Neither could Karlstad, a meter away, who launched both the data capsules at that precise moment.

LEVIATHAN

The stranger was trying to talk to them, Leviathan saw. Its language was odd: one steady light and one flashing on and off in an irregular rhythm. What could it mean?

Leviathan nosed deeper, watching as the stranger slowly spiraled down toward the hot abyss. Several of the Kin circled near it, watching, calling to it, trying to imitate its enigmatic signals.

It is hurt, Leviathan flashed to the Kin.

Yes, it seems so, one of the Elders agreed. It no longer boils the water.

Still they did nothing but watch. Sinking into the hot abyss will kill it, Leviathan thought. It came from the cold above; it must be so hurt that it cannot control itself.

It will die, he said to the Elders.

Swimming patiently around the wounded Leviathan, the Elders replied in unison, Perhaps it will begin to bud.

It is too small to bud, Leviathan said.

How can you know that? This strange creature has its own ways undoubtedly.

We cannot allow it to die without trying to help it, Leviathan insisted.

Help it? How?

Help it to go up toward the abyss above, where it came from.

What good would that do?

That is its home. Even if it must die, we can help it to die in the realm of its origin.

The Elders turned dark, thinking. New ideas were difficult for them to accept.

Leviathan decided not to wait for them to make up their minds.

SALVATION

Grant felt as if his entire body were in a vise that was slowly crushing him. Dimly he remembered that the Puritans in Massachusetts had crushed a man with heavy stones during the Salem witchcraft hysteria.

He started to pray, but the thought that flooded his mind was I don't want to die. O God, God, don't make me die. Don't kill me here, in this dark and distant sea. Help me. Help me.

Karlstad hovered beside him, eyes blank and staring at whatever inner universe filled his soul, his body curled into a weightless fetal posture. He's given up, Grant thought. He knows we're going to die.

Still Grant's fingers raced across the touchscreens, seeking some measure of control over the sinking submersible, picking out links to the backup systems, trying to bring the auxiliaries on-line.

Help me, God, he pleaded. Don't tell me this ocean is beyond Your realm. God of the universe, *help me*!

The ship shuddered.

Instinctively Grant looked up, then turned toward Karlstad. Egon blinked, stirred.

The bridge seemed to tilt, then righted itself. Grant floated free of his one intact floor loop, then his feet touched the deck once more.

Closing his eyes, he tried to see outside through the few sensors still working. Nothing. Only a mottled gray—the ship quivered again, swayed. One of the glowering red lights on Grant's console suddenly turned amber and then green.

Peering through the ship's sensors, Grant realized that what he was seeing was the immense stretch of a Jovian, so close that it was actually touching the sub, nudging it gently, like an elephant delicately balancing a baby carriage on its back.

Grant could hardly breathe. Glancing at his battered console, he saw that the green light was the attitude indicator. *Zheng He* was no longer spiraling downward.

He reached across and shook Karlstad by the shoulder, then typed, SENSORS.

Egon licked his lips, purely a reflex in their liquid surroundings, then tapped into the sensors.

Grant squeezed his eyes shut and saw that the sub was resting on the gigantic back of one of the whales. No, not just any of them; it was the Jovian who'd been attacked by the sharks. Grant could see wide swaths of raw flesh where the sharks had ripped away its skin.

WE RISING? Karlstad asked.

YES!!!! Grant's heart was hammering beneath his ribs. A guardian angel! A million-ton, ten-kilometer-long Jovian guardian angel is carrying us up and out—

His elation snapped off. The Jovian can't carry us out of the ocean. It can't fly us home.

The thrusters. Grant checked the entire power and propulsion systems. The fusion generator was undamaged, working normally. The thrusters—could they last long enough to push them out of the ocean, through the atmosphere and clouds, out into orbit?

DATA CAPSULES, Grant typed. Even if we don't make it, we have to give them all our information. He banged away on his keyboard as Karlstad prepared the last pair of the data capsules.

They were rising swiftly now. Through the ship's sensors Grant could see the entire community of Jovians swimming around them, sleek and smooth, making hardly a ripple as they propelled themselves through the sea far faster than *Zheng He* could have gone on its own. The Jovians flashed signals back and forth among themselves; pictures, Grant was certain, hoping that the ship's cameras were still working well enough to record it all.

The thrusters were still shut down. Can I power them up without causing them to fail? Then a new thought struck him: I can't power them up while we're riding on the Jovian's back. The superheated steam would hurt him.

Would it? Yes, of course it would, Grant told himself. The Jovian's made of flesh, its skin isn't a heat shield. You killed a couple of the sharks with the thrusters' exhaust, of course it'll hurt the Jovian.

But if I don't light them up we won't get out of here. The whale can carry us only so far. The rest of the way we'll need the thrusters.

Grant turned toward Karlstad, but he would be no help, he saw. Egon was standing rigidly now, fists clenched at his sides, eyes squeezed shut, watching the scene outside through the ship's sensors.

Decide, decide! Grant raged at himself.

He called up the flight program, then instructed the computer to plug in their current velocity. The screen went blank for a heartstopping instant, then displayed a graph with a green curve showing the thrust vector needed to achieve orbit. The computer can hear my voice, Grant marveled, even though I can't.

The numbers showed that he had a very small window of opportunity to ignite the thrusters. It would open in twelve seconds and close half a minute later.

Without further debate, Grant started the thrusters. Low, just minimum power, he told himself. Give the Jovian a warning of what's to come. In the back of his mind he realized that the giant creature was performing as a first-stage booster, giving *Zheng He* an initial burst of energy in the long battle to break free of Jupiter's massive gravity and achieve orbit.

Not a nice way to treat someone who's saved your life, Grant said to himself. Sorry, my Jovian friend.

He edged the thrusters to one-quarter power.

Even through its thickly armored hide, Leviathan felt the heat. Its sensor-members shrilled an alarm. The others of the Kin, swimming with Leviathan, flashed their warnings, also.

Leviathan hesitated only for a moment, then plunged down, leaving the stranger to itself.

The Elders flashed superior wisdom: The alien rewards you with pain.

Its ways are different from ours, Leviathan answered.

It is just as well, the Elders pictured as one. We could not have climbed much farther into the cold. Come, let us return to our home region and resume the Symmetry.

Leviathan agreed reluctantly. But it took one last look at the tiny, frail stranger. It was shooting up through the water now, driven by the hot steam emerging from its vents, heading upward into the cold abyss.

The steam pushes it through the water! Leviathan marveled. Like the Darters, it uses jets instead of flagella!

And it is racing up into the cold abyss. It must want to be there. That must be its home region.

How could anything live up there? Leviathan wondered. There is so much that we don't know, so much to be learned.

One moment they were riding the Jovian's back, climbing smoothly through the ocean. Then, when Grant edged the thrusters' power higher, the Jovian flicked them off its massive back and dove downward, returning to the warmer layers of the ocean. Grant pushed full power and *Zheng He* climbed, rattling, its cracked and battered hull shaking like an ancient fragile airplane caught in a storm.

Even in the viscous liquid Grant could feel the growing acceleration as he watched the one working screen on his console. A red blip showed the ship's position along the green curve of the orbital injection trajectory. They were close to the curve, not exactly on it, but close.

Close enough?

Maybe, he decided. If the ship holds together long enough. Then he remembered the rest of the crew. He reached for Karlstad's shoulder again, shook him out of his concentration on the sensors' view.

He typed on his keyboard: ZEB? LANE? KREBS?

Karlstad shrugged helplessly.

TAKE A LOOK, Grant commanded.

Slowly Karlstad disconnected his optical fibers and swam back to the hatch. It was sealed shut; Egon had to punch in the emergency code to get it to slide open. It must have closed automatically when we were in all that turbulence, Grant thought.

He stood alone on the wrecked bridge, feeling the ship straining against the jealous pull of Jupiter's gravity, struggling to climb through the thick heavy ocean, through the deep turbulent atmosphere with its swirling, slashing deck of clouds, and out into the calm emptiness of orbital space.

Karlstad swam back beside him. Without bothering to link his biochips he typed, I STRAPPED THM IN.

HOW ARE THEY? Grant asked.

ALL UNCONSCIOUS. ZEB BLEEDING INTERNALLY. KREBS CONCUSSION, MAYBE WORSE. LAINIE IN COMA, NO PHYSICAL SYMPTOMS I CAN DETECT. GET US OUT OF HERE!!!

TRYING, Grant wrote.

WHAT ABOUT CAPSULES?

Grant thought it over swiftly, then typed, WAIT.

The seconds ticked by slowly as the ship rose, shuddering, buffeted by swift currents. Through the sensors Grant peered into unending darkness, broken only by an occasional glimmer of light so faint that it was gone when he turned his full attention to it. Luminescent creatures out there? he asked himself. Optical illusions? Or maybe just flickers of nerve impulses; maybe my brain cells are starting to break down in this pressure.

He felt the power of the thrusters as an animal roar in his mind, a mighty beast screaming in mingled strength and pain. Keep going, Grant pleaded silently to the thrusters. Only a few more minutes, not even half an hour. You can do it. Just keep on going. Yet the pain was growing worse. The thrusters were heading for catastrophic failure; the only question was how soon.

The view outside seemed to brighten somewhat. The utter darkness gave way grudgingly to a slightly lighter tone. Yes, it was definitely getting gray out there, Grant saw, like the sullen dawn of a midwinter morning.

He felt a pressure on his arm, turned to see Karlstad squeezing his shoulder.

GETTING OUT OF IT, Karlstad had typed on his screen.

Yes, Grant thought. If the thrusters hold up.

Definitely lighter outside. They were climbing through the murky haze of the region between Jupiter's planet-wide sea and its hydrogen-helium atmosphere.

CAPSULES READY? Grant asked.

YES!!!

Grant touched his communications screen. Nothing. It remained dark, inert.

YOUR COMM SCREEN WORKING? he asked Karlstad.

Egon tapped his screen and it lit up.

"This is Research Vessel *Zheng He,*" Grant said, even though he could not hear his own voice. He hoped the comm system could. "We are lifting up, out of Jupiter's ocean, hoping to reach orbit and return to Research Station *Gold.*"

On and on Grant talked, unable to hear a syllable of his own recitation, as the badly damaged submersible climbed into the clear air above the ocean, shaking and shrieking, rising on its plume of star-hot plasma toward the racing jet streams of Jupiter's cloud deck. Karlstad stood silently by his console, fully linked to what remained of the ship's systems now, unable to hear any of Grant's long speech.

At last Grant finished. *Zheng He* was climbing through clear atmosphere now. Far off in the vast distance Grant could see a cluster of colorful balloonlike medusas floating placidly through the air.

He typed, SET CAPSULE TRANSMITTERS FOR WIDEST POSSIBLE FREQUENCIES—FULL SPECTRUM.

Karlstad looked puzzled. NOT NECE—

Grant slapped his hand away from his keyboard. DO IT, he insisted.

With a shrug, Karlstad did as Grant commanded.

READY TO GO, he typed.

RELEASE BOTH CAPSULES.

DONE.

The thrusters were close to failure now. Grant felt their pain flaming across his shoulders and down his back. The underside of the cloud deck was inching nearer, nearer. The graph on his one working screen showed that they had almost achieved orbital velocity, but if the thrusters failed while they were below the clouds or even in them, atmospheric drag would pull them down to a final, fiery plunge back into the ocean.

Lightning flashed across the underside of the clouds. Grant could hear through the ship's microphones the rumble of thunder. The audio centers in my brain still function, he realized. It's my ears that are damaged.

Winds began to buffet the ship. Doggedly Grant watched the tiny red blip on his screen crawling along the green curve. Almost there. Almost. Almost.

They plunged into the clouds, shaking and rattling. The thrusters' pain was making Grant's eyes blur.

Everything went dark. For a moment Grant thought the lights had gone down again, but then he realized he was giddy with pain, awash in agony. The view outside was black; they were in the clouds. Hold on! he commanded himself. Just a few more minutes. Hold on!

He couldn't hear it, but he knew he was screaming. The thrusters were breaking down, whole chunks of their jet tubes ripping apart. The superconducting coils exploded, dumping all their pent-up energy into a blast that shredded the rear half of the ship's outermost hull. Grant felt as if he were being flayed alive, his skin and the flesh beneath it torn away by the claws of a giant, vicious beast.

He squeezed his eyes shut. The pain disappeared, yet its memory echoed brutally. Every muscle in Grant's body was sore, stiff, aching horribly.

He floated into near oblivion. Eyes still closed, he saw tiny bright unblinking points of stars scattered across the darkness.

Something, someone was shaking him. Opening his eyes, he saw it was Karlstad, floating beside him. Egon was laughing hysterically, although Grant could not hear anything at all.

Karlstad gesticulated, pointing to one of the screens on the unoccupied console on Grant's right. It showed the same view Grant had seen when his eyes were shut: the view that the ship's sensors were seeing.

The stars.

The serene black infinity of space. Off to one side, the curve of a mottled red-orange moon. Io, Grant realized. And then the massive flank of mighty Jupiter slid into view, wildly tinted clouds hurtling by far below them.

"We made it!" Karlstad mouthed.

Grant closed his eyes and saw the same view that the screen showed, only clearer, in sharper detail. We've made it, he realized. We're in orbit.

BOOK V

For they exchanged the truth of God for a lie, and worshiped and served the creature rather than the Creator . . .

—Romans 1:25

RETRIBUTION

The thin whine of a medical monitor woke Grant from a deep, dreamless sleep.

His first thought was, I can hear!

Opening his eyes, he saw he was in the infirmary, his bed screened off by thin plastic partitions. He ached from head to foot, but the pain that had throbbed behind his eyes for so long was gone now. His head felt clear, not even dizzy.

The memories came tumbling back, all in a rush. Climbing out of the ocean in the battered, barely functioning *Zheng He*. Achieving orbit. The frantic messages from the station, all displayed on his one working console screen because his hearing was still gone. Too hurt and exhausted to do more than float numbly in the bridge, Grant had engaged the ship's automated rendezvous system to get them back to the station. It worked well enough for the controllers aboard the station to bring the ship in and dock it successfully.

They had rushed the whole crew to the infirmary. Grant remembered fuzzily Dr. Wo wheeling along beside him as a medical team hurried him through the station corridor, the director's mouth moving in what must have been a thousand questions, but Grant unable to hear a word.

How long have I been here? he wondered. Lane, Zeb—Krebs. How are they? Did they make it? Did they survive?

Gingerly he pushed himself up to a sitting position. The bed adjusted automatically, rising to support his back. The tone of the medical monitors changed subtly.

"I can hear," Grant said aloud. There was a faint ringing echo to his words, as if he were speaking them from inside an echoing metal pipe. "I'm alive," he marveled, "and I can hear."

"Me, too."

It was Karlstad's voice, from the other side of the partition on his left.

"Egon!" Grant shouted. "We made it!"

"Yeah. You saved our butts, Grant."

"Me?"

"Nobody else, kid. You got us out of there all by yourself."

"But I only—"

The crack of hard heels on the floor tiles sounded like rifles firing. Several people were approaching, walking fast, impatiently.

The screen at the foot of Grant's bed screeched back. Ellis Beech stood there, sullen anger clear on his dark face. A younger man stood slightly behind him, sallow-faced, thin pale blond hair. Like Beech, he wore a somber gray business suit.

But Grant stared at the other person standing with Beech: Tamiko Hideshi, dressed in a midnight-black silk floor-length robe with a high mandarin collar, her round face expressionless except for the smoldering resentment radiating from her almond eyes.

"I suppose you think you're a hero," said Beech.

Grant blinked at him, pulling his attention away from Tamiko. Then he remembered. The final two data capsules. The pair they had fired off *Zheng He* while the ship was straining to break free of Jupiter's pull and establish itself in orbit.

"No," Grant replied, shaking his head. "I just did the job that needed to be done."

"You betrayed us!" Hideshi snapped.

"I shared new knowledge with the rest of the human race. How can that be a betrayal?"

In those frenzied moments when he didn't know if the ship would make it or plunge back into Jupiter in a fiery death ride, Grant had programmed the capsules to broadcast their data on the widest bandwidth possible. He had remembered Dr. Wo's words: *Then we beam the information back to Earth. To the headquarters of the International Astronautical Authority, to the scientific offices of the United Nations, to all the news networks, to every university. Simultaneously. We make our announcement so loud, so wide, that it cannot possibly be overlooked or suppressed.*

That's what Grant had done: beamed every bit of data they had collected to every available antenna on Earth.

"There are three shiploads of news media people on their way to this station," Beech said, almost snarling his words. "Every scientist in the solar system wants to come here, to study your godless whales, to make a mockery of the truth faith, to—"

"What makes you think the Jovians are godless?" Grant interrupted.

He spoke quietly, but his words stopped Beech in midsentence.

"Don't you think that God created them, just as He created us?" Grant asked.

Beech glowered at him, speechless.

"When we were down in that ocean, crippled and sinking, I prayed to God for help. One of those creatures lifted us on its back and carried us upward. It answered my prayer."

"That's blasphemy," hissed the young man behind Beech, his voice hollow, his eyes staring at Grant.

"No," Grant replied. "God worked through that giant Jovian creature. That's all I'm trying to say."

Beech pointed at Grant with a long, accusing finger. "You will say nothing about this to anyone. You will not speak to any of the news reporters. You will be held incommunicado until we decide what to do with you."

He turned on his heel and stamped away, followed by Hideshi and the slim young man, all of them walking in military lockstep.

Grant swung his legs off the bed and pulled back the partition separating him from Karlstad. Egon was sitting up in his bed, a palmcomp and headset resting on the sheets. He looked normal, no obvious signs of injury.

"Incommunicado," Grant said. "I guess they're pretty upset about what I did."

Karlstad grinned at him. "If he thinks he can keep the reporters away from you, he's living in dreamland."

"You think so?"

Chuckling, Karlstad nodded. "You're going to be the news media's darling, kid. The brilliant young scientist who saved his fellow crew members deep in the boiling sea of Jupiter. It'll be great!"

"Fellow crew members," Grant repeated. "What happened to them? Zeb? Lane?"

"Lainie's okay."

"But she collapsed."

"They haven't found any permanent physical trauma. They're keeping her in the women's ward for observation." He tapped a knuckle against the wall behind the head of his bed.

"And Zeb?"

Karlstad's face turned more serious. "Bleeding in his lungs. Tissue must've been ruptured by the pressure."

"Is he all right?"

"They stabilized him and shipped him to Selene. He should pull through, they think."

"And what about Krebs?"

Egon laughed again. "That old bird's too tough to keep down. She got a concussion from slamming into the bulkhead. She's in the women's ward, too, but she's already busy helping Old Woeful to write reports back to the IAA."

"How long have we been here?" Grant wondered.

"Three days. Like Christ rising from the sepulcher, you've come back to consciousness three days after going under."

Grant frowned at Karlstad's derisive impiety.

"For what it's worth," Egon continued, "neither of us suffered any major trauma, aside from having our hearing temporarily blotted out."

Grant still heard that annoying metallic ringing echo to each word Karlstad spoke. Maybe my hearing is permanently damaged, he thought. That's not so bad, considering what might have happened.

"If we're okay, then why are they keeping us here?"

"Two reasons. The medics want to make sure we get a complete rest. And your friend Beech wants us kept away from the rest of the station personnel."

"But that's ridiculous," Grant said.

"Tell that to your Mr. Beech. None of us is allowed to speak to the news media. By the time the reporters get here, Beech will probably have us shipped off the station. He wants us under wraps. Permanently."

"But you said—"

"The reporters will find you, Grant. No matter where Beech puts you, they'll ferret you out. Trust me, I know how they work."

Grant sank back onto his upraised bed, thinking hard. They can't keep the news secret. I blared it out to the whole world. But Beech and his team can punish us, all of us. He was furious with me, and he's going to do his damnedest to prevent us from seeing the media in person. I hope Egon's right. It's not going to be easy for any of us, though.

He spent the rest of the day catching up on the messages that had accumulated. There were half a dozen from Marjorie and almost as many from his parents.

He stared at Marjorie's face in the tiny screen of the palmcomp one of the nurses had lent him. She was smiling radiantly at him.

"I'm so proud of you, Grant," Marjorie said in the headset's earphone. "You've made an enormous discovery and you saved the lives of your crew . . ."

She's acting as if I did it all by myself, Grant thought. He found that he didn't mind that at all. In fact, he basked in the warmth of her smiling admiration.

"I love you, Grant darling," his wife said. "And I miss you terribly. I hope you can come home soon. Sooner. Soonest."

Grant adjusted the microphone of the palmcomp's headset so close to his lips that they almost touched it, then whispered a long, rambling, heartfelt message to Marjorie, telling her how he yearned to be with her, how he would take the first vessel heading Earthward as soon as the authorities gave him permission to leave the station.

But when he tried to transmit the message, the screen glared: **ACCESS TO UPLINK DENIED. NO OUTGOING MESSAGES PERMITTED.**

Incommunicado. Maybe the news media would be able to get to him, once they arrived at the station, Grant thought, but probably Beech and his people will have moved us by then. It's not going to be as easy as Egon thinks.

There were more messages, Grant found, hundreds of messages from total strangers that radiated hatred and fury at his "godless humanist blasphemy." None of them were from people he actually knew; all strangers, most of them did not even speak their names. More than one contained a death threat. "It is the duty of God's disciples to strike you dead," said one particularly chilling ascetic-looking young man.

There was also a long list of incoming messages from the news media—but the messages themselves were all blanked out, censored, except for the name and affiliation of the sender.

Startled by the hate mail, smoldering at the censorship, Grant composed a long and upbeat message for his parents, keeping it totally personal, assuring them that he was fine, carefully avoiding any hint of scientific information. Still, when he commanded the palmcomp to transmit, the screen again answered: **ACCESS TO UPLINK DENIED.**

If I ever get back to Earth, he began to realize, it will probably be Siberia—if some Zealot fanatic doesn't kill me first.

Karlstad seemed unworried, though, confident that the news media would find a way past the New Morality's stone walls. Grant was not so certain. He tried to put in a call to Dr. Wo, but even that access was denied him.

I'm a prisoner here, he told himself. Egon and I are being held prisoners. But what about Zeb? Once he's up and around at Selene he can tell everyone about what we did. Unless he dies there. Unless some Zealot gets to him in the lunar hospital.

The hours dragged by. Grant felt strong enough to get up and go back to his own quarters, but the nurse on duty told him that he was to remain in the infirmary. Grant at least got to walk the length of the ward, noticing that his and Karlstad's were the only beds occupied. Through the window in the infirmary door he could see two hefty security guards outside in the corridor.

We're in prison.

Sleep would not come that night. Grant lay in his bed, wide awake, wondering what would happen to him. The New Morality was deciding his fate. Ellis Beech was determining the course of his life.

He had to get away, had to break out of this trap. But how?

It was almost 6 A.M. when someone entered the still-darkened infirmary. More than one person, Grant realized, listening to their footsteps approaching his bed.

Assassins? Grant's heart clutched in his chest. He was completely defenseless. There was no place to hide in the infirmary; he couldn't even run away, there was only the one entrance to the ward.

It was two men, walking quietly past the empty beds, guided by the pencil-beam of a small flashlight.

"Which one?" he heard a man whisper.

A hesitation. Grant slipped out of bed, fists balled at his sides, legs trembling. Despite his fear he felt slightly ridiculous, ready to fight for his life in a flimsy knee-length, open-back hospital gown.

"Archer . . . here's his bed."

They were two security guards, in uniform. They played the beam of light along Grant's bed, then swung it to catch him standing there.

"You're awake. Good. Come with us."

"Where?" Grant asked.

"Dr. Wo wants to see you."

"Now? At this hour?"

"Now. At this hour. Come on, he doesn't like to be kept waiting."

FAREWELL

Grant threw a robe over his hospital gown and followed the two guards out into the dimly lit corridor. It was still nighttime throughout the station. "Dawn" was at seven, when the lights in all the public spaces turned up to their daytime brightness. The corridor was empty; no one else was in sight.

"This way," said one of the guards. They were both bigger than Grant, hard with muscle, unsmiling.

"Dr. Wo's office is down the other way," Grant said.

"He's not in his office. Come on."

With growing trepidation, Grant went along with them. He couldn't think of anything else to do. His legs felt rubbery, not entirely under his control. The biochips, he told himself. I can't even walk well; if I tried to run I'd probably fall on my face. Besides, where could I run to? If these two are Zealot assassins, he reasoned, they would've killed me in my bed. And Egon, too.

Still, he didn't feel reassured by his attempt at logic. Killers aren't always rational, he knew.

With growing desperation he tried to think of some way out of this, some tactic to save his life. Nothing. He followed meekly, frightened but uncertain of what lay ahead, unsure of what he could do, what he should do, to save his life. This must be how the Jews felt during the Holocaust, he thought. Who can help me? Where can I run to?

At last they reached the heavy metal hatch that sealed off the aquarium. As one of the guards opened it, Grant asked the other, "Are you going to drown me?"

The guard's granite face broke into a sardonic smile. "I thought you could breathe underwater."

They gestured him through the hatch, then led Grant down the long row of thick windows, the lights from the fish tanks playing fitfully along the narrow passageway. The hard metal floor felt cold to Grant's bare feet. The fish seemed to be watching, big-eyed, their mouths working silently. The dolphins glided along in their tanks, smiling as ever.

Sheena! Grant realized. They're taking me to Sheena's pen. She'll tear me apart and it will look like an accident.

His mind was racing. Maybe I can get Sheena to help me. If only I could show her that I'm her friend . . . if only she could overlook that one time I hurt her.

Something was blocking the passageway near the gorilla's pen. Grant saw that it was Dr. Wo in his powered chair. The guards stopped a respectful twenty meters from the station director. Grant walked the final steps alone, shakily.

Dr. Wo looked up at Grant from his chair, a strange little half smile on his lips. "Mr. Archer, the medical doctors tell me that you are fully recovered from your injuries."

Grant nodded, awash with relief that he wasn't about to be murdered.

"I am leaving the station tomorrow. I have been replaced as director here."

"Leaving?" Grant blurted. "They've kicked you out?"

Wo actually grinned at him. "They have kicked me upstairs. It is a compromise worked out between the New Morality and the IAA. I will go to the IAA center in Zurich and assume the directorship of the entire astrobiology program."

"But the work here . . . the Jovians . . ."

"That is for you to continue. And Dr. Muzorawa, when he returns."

"He'll be returning?"

"Once he has recovered, yes. I have nominated him to be my successor. Both the IAA and the various religious factions have agreed. But he will not participate in any future missions into the ocean."

Grant thought that over for a few seconds. Zeb's coming back. He'll be the station director. And I'm expected to continue the studies of the Jovians.

He said slowly, "Then the New Morality hasn't totally gutted our work."

"How could they? The entire world is watching us now, thanks to you. Some are fearful, many are curious. You have opened a new chapter in human history, Mr. Archer."

"Not me. I didn't—"

"You had the presence of mind to broadcast *Zheng He*'s findings to the entire world. No one could keep our discoveries secret once those data capsules began singing their song."

Grant's legs felt too weak to hold him up. He leaned his back against the cold metal wall and slid down to a sitting position.

"The religious fanatics are very angry with you, Mr. Archer," said Wo. "The Zealots want to kill you."

"What good would that do them?"

"Not much, but they are furious and frustrated. An evil combination."

Grant suddenly remembered, "They killed Irene Pascal, didn't they?"

Wo's expression hardened. "Dr. Pascal's death was an accident. An inadvertent suicide."

"No," said Grant.

"Yes," Wo insisted. "She took an overly large dose of amphetamines, which led to her death in the high-pressure environment aboard *Zheng He*."

"Irene didn't take the drugs knowingly," Grant said.

"A board of inquiry has examined the incident. They have made their decision. The case is closed."

"It wasn't an incident," Grant snapped. "It was a murder!"

Wo's voice took on a steely edge. "No, Mr. Archer. Let it rest."

"But I know—"

"The case is closed!"

For a long moment the two men stared at each other, eyes locked. Grant could not fathom what was going on in Wo's mind. But he knew his own thoughts: It may be over for you and your board of inquiry, he said silently, but it's not over for me. I know Irene was murdered and I know who did it.

"The IAA has appointed Dr. Indra Chandrasekhar as interim director here."

Grant stirred out of his inner turmoil. "Chandrasekhar? I don't know her."

"Your recognition is not a prerequisite for the position," said Wo, smiling thinly.

Grant made no reply.

"She has been heading the studies of the Galilean moons. A very good leader. She comes from a long line of excellent scientists."

"She'll be in charge until Zeb returns?"

"Yes, and you will direct the studies of the Jovian creatures that you found in the ocean," Wo said, his smile widening. Then he added, "Whether they are intelligent or not."

"They're intelligent. I'm convinced of that."

"Good! Now all you have to do is prove it so completely that the rest of the world will believe it."

"Including the New Morality?"

Wo laughed. "The New Morality, the Holy Disciples, the Light of Allah . . . even the Zealots."

Grant nodded, accepting the challenge. The first thing I'll have to do is go over the data we recorded. We can slow down the visual imagery so we can see the pictures the whales are flashing to each other. We've got to repair *Zheng He* or maybe build a new vessel . . .

Dr. Wo broke into his train of thoughts. "It will be necessary for you to remain here."

"Yes, I understand."

"You have earned a release from your Public Service obligation, of course. You could go back to Earth if you wish."

"But the work is being done here."

"Exactly. And—frankly—you are much safer here than on Earth, where some Zealot fanatic can murder you."

There's a Zealot fanatic here on this station, Grant thought. At least one. And I know who it is.

"Beech is keeping me incommunicado," Grant said. "Egon and the women, too. I can't even get a message out to my wife."

Dr. Wo nodded knowingly. "I have seen to it that you can have the freedom of the station. You needn't be confined to the infirmary. As for messages home . . ." He shrugged his heavy shoulders. "I'm afraid Mr. Beech has the upper hand in the communications department."

Grant stared at the older man. It's a struggle, he realized. A battle between Wo and Beech. Neither side has a completely free hand. And I'm caught in the middle of their power struggle.

Dr. Wo intruded on his thoughts. "Very well, then, Mr. Archer. There is one last farewell for you to make."

"Farewell?" Grant asked.

Wo gestured toward Sheena's darkened pen.

"Sheena's leaving?"

"We have no further need of her. Perhaps the dolphins can be of help in your attempts to establish meaningful contact with the Jovians, but Sheena is too much like us to be of any aid in your work."

"What's going to happen to her?"

Wo sighed heavily. "The simplest thing to do would be to sacrifice her. Then we could dissect her brain and—"

"No!" Grant shouted.

Raising both his hands placatingly, Dr. Wo said, "I agree. It would be a criminal act. I am taking Sheena back to Earth with me, to a primate research center in Kinshasa. They are quite eager to have her, in fact."

"She'll be all right there?"

"She will be welcomed. They have augmented several other apes. Sheena will not be an anomaly there. If all goes well, she will be the mother of a new breed of creatures, the founder of dynasties. And another challenge to the fundamentalists."

"She'll be protected there?"

"By force of arms, if necessary. She is an extremely valuable entity."

Grant felt a glow of satisfaction. "She'll be among her own."

"I believe so," said Wo.

"I wish . . ." Grant could not finish the sentence. He swallowed hard and fought back tears, feeling embarrassed to be emotional about a gorilla.

Wo touched the keypad built into his chair's armrest, and the overhead lights brightened to their daytime level.

"I can make the sun rise," he said wryly. "One of the privileges of being station director."

And Sheena wakes up with the sun, Grant remembered. He turned expectantly toward the entryway to her pen. Will she still be angry at me? he wondered.

Very gently, Wo said, "She asked to see you."

"She did?"

"When I told her you had been injured, she became rather upset."

Grand didn't know what to say.

He heard her shambling out of her pen, huffing and snuffling like anyone who'd just awakened from a good night's sleep. As he scrambled to his feet he caught a trace of the thick animal scent of her. Then Sheena appeared in the entryway, massive hairy shoulders brushing both edges of the open hatch.

"Grant," the gorilla rasped.

"Hello, Sheena."

She turned her eyes briefly to Dr. Wo but immediately looked back at Grant. "Grant hurt."

"I'm all right now, Sheena. I'm fine."

"No hurt?"

"Not anymore," said Grant. "It's good to see you, Sheena."

"Sheena no hurt."

She remembers the neural net, all right, Grant realized. But maybe she's forgiven me for it.

The gorilla glanced at Dr. Wo again, then took a knuckle-walking step toward Grant. Grant extended his hand to her, palm up. Sheena reached out her enormous hand and touched Grant's palm lightly.

"Grant friend," she said.

"And Sheena is my friend," he replied.

"Yes. Friends."

Dr. Wo broke in, "Sheena and I are going to a new place where Sheena will make many new friends."

The gorilla seemed to consider this for a moment, then said, "New friends. Grant, too?"

"I'm afraid not, Sheena. I've got to stay here for a while. Maybe later I'll come and see you."

"You come. See new friends. See Sheena."

"I will," Grant promised, hoping that he would one day be able to keep his word.

THE BEAUTY OF THY HOUSE

Surprised at how difficult it was for him to bid farewell to Sheena, Grant returned to the infirmary where he and Karlstad stood patiently for a final checkup by the little martinet who headed the medical staff. Once officially released, they dressed quickly and headed for their quarters, both of them walking awkwardly, their electrode-studded legs still feeling alien, barely under their own control.

Grant went past his own door.

Karlstad, tottering along beside him, said, "Have you forgotten where you live?"

"I have something to do," Grant said. "A lot of things, come to think of it."

"The only thing I want to do is get a decent meal and get the medics to shut down these damned biochips, so I can feel like a whole human being again."

Grant nodded absently and kept on going as Karlstad stopped in front of his own door.

"And then I'm going to look up Lainie," Karlstad called after him. "For real."

Grant paid him no attention. Tamiko. All this time, Tamiko has been working for Beech. *Really* working for him, not just going through the motions the way I did. She's a Zealot. She's dangerous.

He went to Hideshi's quarters and rapped on the door. It rattled slightly. Funny, Grant thought, I never noticed how flimsy these doors are.

"Who is it?" Hideshi's voice called.

"Grant Archer."

She slid the door back and ushered Grant into her compartment with a silent gesture. As he stepped in he saw a garment bag lying open on the bed, clothes scattered around it. The drawers of her desk hung open and empty.

"You're leaving?" he asked.

"With Beech, yes."

"You're one of his agents, aren't you?"

"That's obvious," Hideshi said, walking back to the bed and sitting on it, among the clothes.

"And you're a Zealot."

Hideshi did not answer.

"You'd kill me if Beech told you to, wouldn't you?"

She made a sour face. "He won't. It'd be pointless now. You've done your damage. No sense making a martyr out of you."

"How could you kill a human being?" Grant asked, incredulous despite himself.

"'To prepare the way for His kingdom," she said, as if reciting from rote. "To do His work. I'm willing to give my own life, if needed."

"But that's not what God wants."

"How would you know?" she sneered. "You're on *their* side. You'll all burn in hell."

Grant went to her desk and sank into its chair. "Tami, this isn't about religion."

"Oh, no?"

"No," said Grant, feeling weary, drained. "It's politics. Don't you see? The New Morality is using religion as a cover for its political agenda. It was never about religion. It was always politics."

"You're dead wrong, Grant. We're doing God's work. You secularists are on the side of the devil."

"By their fruits—"

"Don't quote Scripture at me!" Hideshi snapped. "Don't try to convert me to your atheist ways!"

"But I'm a Believer!"

"So you say."

It was like talking to a statue, Grant thought. Then he recalled his real reason for coming to her.

"You killed Irene Pascal, didn't you?"

Hideshi looked surprised, almost shocked. "Me? Why would I do that?"

"To wreck the deep mission."

She laughed at him. "Brightboy, are you ever wrong! I didn't kill anybody."

"Then who did?"

"Kayla."

"Kayla! She's one of you?"

With a satisfied smirk, Hideshi said, "Go ask her."

Grant prowled through the station, searching. Kayla, he was telling himself. She's one of the Zealots. The whole station must be infested with them. I've got to find her before she does any more damage. Before she kills someone else or tries to blow up the whole station.

The more Grant thought about it, the more he was convinced that Tamiko had told him the truth. The Panther, with her perpetual angry scowl, had been alone with Irene that last night. Kayla fed her the amphetamines that killed her.

At first he had thought it must have been Devlin. The Red Devil has access to all kinds of drugs, and he'd sold some to Irene, Grant knew. But Irene was too intelligent to take a harmful dose. She would never do that to herself. No, the overdose had to be slipped to her unknowingly, by someone she knew and trusted. Someone she loved.

Kayla Ukara. A Zealot. A fanatic. A murderer.

He searched the station for her, starting with her usual workstation in the sensor lab and combing labs and maintenance shops until at last he pushed through the doors of the mission control center.

The center was silent, dimly lit, the big wallscreens blank, the consoles dead. Except for the one at which Ukara sat, staring into one small screen, hunched over, elbows on the console keyboard, head resting in her hands, eyes locked on the single glowing screen.

Grant padded softly down the ramp that had been built to accommodate Dr. Wo's wheelchair. He stopped when he could see, over Ukara's shoulder, that the screen she was watching displayed a video of Irene Pascal.

"You killed her," Grant said.

She wheeled around, shock showing clearly on her face.

"You murdered Irene."

For an instant Grant thought she was going to leap at him, fingers curled into claws. Then she relaxed, the anger and surprise in her face faded away, and she slumped back in the little wheeled chair.

"I killed Irene," Ukara admitted. "It wasn't murder, but I killed her, yes."

"You tried to wreck the deep mission," said Grant.

Ukara shook her head. "All I wanted to do was to save Irene. I didn't want her to go on the mission. She herself was frightened of it, terrified almost, but she was too loyal to refuse the assignment."

"Save her?" Grant snapped. "By feeding her enough amphetamines to kill her?"

"It wasn't a fatal dose," Ukara replied, looking miserable now. "I didn't know it would kill her. I just wanted her to get sick enough to be taken off the mission."

Grant pulled up one of the other chairs and sat down next to her. "I wish I could believe that."

"I didn't know it would affect her so strongly in that soup they were living in. I didn't want to kill her. I loved her."

Grant studied her face. Ukara didn't look like a panther now. She looked desperately unhappy, close to tears.

"But you're a Zealot, aren't you?" he asked.

Ukara's eyes flashed wide. "A Zealot? One of those fanatics?" She broke into a bitter, angry laugh. "Oh, yes, certainly. A black lesbian. They have troops of us in their ranks. Whole battalions full!"

She jumped to her feet. "I killed the person I loved! Isn't that punishment enough, without an idiot like you asking stupid questions? Dr. Wo understands what happened. Who appointed you to be the prosecutor-general around here?"

Again Grant thought she was going to strike him, but instead Ukara strode angrily out of the control center, leaving him sitting alone, stunned, with Irene Pascal's face still framed on the single working console screen.

He sat there for a long time, thinking, remembering, replaying the hours and days and weeks. So much has happened, Grant said to himself. Everything's changed so much. The whole world has changed.

He turned to the console and powered up its communications systems.

"Security office," Grant said firmly.

The screen showed one of the young men who had accompanied Beech in the infirmary. He was still dressed in a somber dark suit, clean shaven, hair neatly combed.

"I want to make a call to my wife," he said.

The young man shook his head. "You are being held incommunicado. That means no outgoing calls. Be grateful that we allowed you out of the infirmary."

Grant nodded curtly and cut the connection.

"Red Devlin," he told the communications computer.

The screen remained blank for a few moments, but at last Devlin's youthful, mustachioed face grinned back at him.

"Hey, there, Grant, what can I do for you?"

Devlin appeared to be in the kitchen area. Grant could see tall stainless-steel freezer doors behind him and the corner of what looked like an electric stove.

"I need to make an outgoing call," Grant said, "and the powers-that-be want to keep me incommunicado."

Devlin arched a brick-red eyebrow. "You want me to skirt around the New Morality blokes, is that it?"

"Yes. Can you do it?"

"For you, chum, damned right I'll do it. You're a bloody hero and those silly bastards are a major pain in the backside."

Grant hesitated. "Uh, it'll be a personal message. To my wife."

Devlin nodded. "I understand. Compress it and squirt it to me on the regular phone system. I'll send it to a pal of mine Earthside along with my usual purchasing list. He'll shoot it off to the proper party for you."

"Thanks, Red," said Grant. "I owe you one."

Laughing, Devlin replied, "Hey, you're gonna be a big mucky-muck around here one o' these days. I've gotta be on your good side, don't I now?"

Grant kept his message to Marjorie brief. He told her he was fine, but there were some problems with the official red tape that kept him from calling her directly.

"We'll get it all straightened out pretty quickly, I'm sure," Grant said, thinking of the shiploads of journalists heading for the station.

"But . . ." He hesitated, licked his lips, then made the decision. "But I'm going to be staying here at Jupiter, at the station here, for a long time, Marjorie. I want you with me. I need you with me. Will you come out here? I know it means dropping your work with the Peacekeepers, but your two years of Public Service are almost finished anyway. Come here, please. I love you, Marjorie. I miss you terribly. Come work with me, live with me. This is where I've got to be, and I've got to have you here, too."

Not daring to review his message, Grant data-compressed it and fired it off to Devlin.

Red will get it through to Marjorie, he told himself. It might take a day or two, but she'll get my message.

He got up from the console and walked slowly up the ramp and out into the corridor. Then we'll see, he thought. Will she come out here to be with me?

Grant felt confident that she would. Despite the time and distance between them, he still loved his wife. Does she still love me? Enough to come all the way out here?

Yes, he answered silently. I think she does. But even if she doesn't, I've got to stay here. I've *got* to.

He walked aimlessly along the station's main corridor. People greeted him with smiles and hellos and even pats on the back. Grant smiled and helloed and waved at them all.

And found himself at last in the station's observation lounge. Alone, he stepped inside and softly closed the door behind him. The lounge was dark, with only tiny lights on the floor to mark where a couch and a pair of padded chairs stood. Its long windows were shuttered. Almost like a blind man, Grant went to the faintly glowing switch that activated the shutters.

They peeled back smoothly, without a sound except the muted hum of an electric motor.

Light from Jupiter's massive globe flooded into the lounge. Grant felt the breath catch in his throat as he saw the colorful roiled clouds rushing across the face of the giant planet. There are living creatures beneath those clouds, he reminded himself. And in the ocean there are *intelligent* creatures.

Of that he was certain. He also realized that he was ready to spend the rest of his life trying to prove it.

So much work to do. So much to learn, to discover.

The view of Jupiter slid by as the station turned slowly and Grant saw the curve of the glowing planet give way to the blackness of infinite space. It took a few moments for his eyes to adjust, and then he saw the stars, thousands of stars, staring back at him.

"O Lord," said Grant, remembering the ancient psalm, "I love the beauty of Thy house and the place where Thy glory dwelleth."

Then he smiled. They can try to keep us incommunicado. They can try to silence us. But knowledge is more powerful than ignorance. Curiosity is more powerful than fear.

Grant laughed aloud, then turned and left the observation lounge, heading for his new tasks, his new responsibilities, ready to do God's work.